Dear Reader,

This month I am delighted to bring you the second longer novel by best-selling author Patricia Wilson, who is, we know, very popular with romance readers. And we're sure that Julie Garratt's second book for *Scarlet* will greatly please her existing fans, and capture the interest of many new readers. In addition, we are glad to offer you the chance to enjoy the talents of two authors new to the *Scarlet* list: Jean Walton, who lives in the USA, and Michelle Reynolds from the UK.

One of the many joys for me when I select each month's books for you, is that I am able to look forward to hearing *your* reaction to my selection. Of course, as *Scarlet* grows, the task of choosing new stories to offer you is becoming ever more interesting as so many talented authors are keen to join our list. Naturally, this means that it is also more of a challenge for me to get the balance of the four books right for you. As always, I invite comments from readers, as such feedback is vital in helping me do my job properly – so I look forward to hearing from *you*.

Till next month,
Best wishes,

Sally Cooper

SALLY COOPER,
Editor-in-Chief – *Scarlet*

About the Author

At sixteen years of age, like a lot of teenagers, **Michelle Reynolds** claims that she 'thought she knew it all', so instead of furthering her education, she donned her rucksack and began to travel, sometimes in England and sometimes abroad.

Michelle took various jobs, but she always worked with children and animals, though at one stage she was also a croupier in a casino.

Her late teens and early twenties were an absolute riot, and she thoroughly enjoyed herself. Michelle says she has no regrets, and, if she had her time over, she would make the same decisions.

Michelle met many people on her travels and her books are based on her personal experiences. The author's writing style is very fresh and often lighthearted and we hope that readers enjoy *Carousel*, Michelle's first published novel.

Other *Scarlet* titles available this month:
BLACK VELVET – Patricia Wilson
CHANGE OF HEART – Julie Garratt
A CIRCLE IN TIME – Jean Walton

MICHELLE REYNOLDS

CAROUSEL

SCARLET

Enquiries to:
Robinson Publishing Ltd
7 Kensington Church Court
London W8 4SP

First published in the UK by Scarlet, 1997

A copy of the British Library Cataloguing in
Publication data is available from the British Library

ISBN 1-85487-934-0

Printed and bound in the EC

10 9 8 7 6 5 4 3 2 1

ACKNOWLEDGEMENTS

The author wishes to acknowledge: Anthea Kenyon, Roger Fox, MRCVS, Sue Shires and Pat Hughes.

Special thanks must go to David Reynolds, Carol Dawson, Terry and Michael Lowe.

Reference for veterinary guidance: *Landers Veterinary Toxicology*, published by J.A. Nicholson/London, Bailliere, Tindall & Cox.

And lastly, to my long-suffering editor, Sue Curran.

CHAPTER 1

The first hint of trouble I had was when Adam, one of the stable lads, came running over to us looking worried.

'Ben, I think you ought to look at one of the horses.'

Ben Carmichael's eyes narrowed slightly. 'Why, what's the problem?'

'It's Mistral. He seems to have colic. Thrashing about something awful. I think we'd better get the vet.' The boy's voice rose anxiously.

'OK, calm down. I'll take a look at him. When did he start showing the signs?'

'Well, we only fetched him in from the field a few minutes ago,' said Adam as we made our way over to Mistral's box.

Reaching the horse, we found a sweating, groaning creature, kicking at his distended belly with front and back feet. 'Lord!' said Ben faintly. 'I'll get hold of Dick Fox!' And he shot off into the tack room to phone the local vet. Dick Fox arrived within twenty minutes, by which time Mistral was dead.

Five minutes later, he came over to us, frowning.

'Ben, I'm afraid it looks as if this horse has been poisoned.'

'Are you sure?' Ben looked dazed.

'Positive,' said Dick firmly.

'But what with?'

Dick sucked his teeth thoughtfully and turned to face Adam. 'Did you see the horse die?'

'Yes,' he replied shakily. 'It was odd. He just went down like a bag of manure, sudden-like!'

Dick nodded and turned back to Ben. 'I've seen this once before, many years ago. I think it's *Taxus baccata*, yew poisoning, but I can't be sure unless I open him up and do a post-mortem.'

'Yew?' Ben, looking blank, pursed his lips. 'We don't have any yew growing anywhere on the property, because of the horses. How did he get hold of it?'

'My guess is somebody fed it to him, mixed in with some sugar beet or molasses, something nice and sweet so he'd take it easily. Nobody would have a problem getting hold of it. You'll find yew in every town and village, even Loxton. It grows in abundance in graveyards, you see.'

'There are several of those near here,' said Ben, and Dick nodded solemnly.

'Can't you do a blood test or something to confirm it?' I asked.

Dick shook his head. 'I could do a blood test, a saliva test, urine test, the whole damned works; it wouldn't show up. As I said, it'll only be known for sure by doing a post-mortem. I'm pretty sure, though, the way Adam described how he died; it's a typical reaction. They go down as if they'd been shot.'

Oh, heavens, what have I let myself in for? I thought. I was already beginning to wonder if taking this job was such a good idea. It had all seemed so harmless when I'd studied the 'Situations Vacant' page in *Horse and Hound* . . .

★ ★ ★

As my eyes slid down the advertisements, one had seemed to leap out at me. It wasn't a display, just a couple of lines. It read, 'Chaotic household requires live-in help. Three boys, horses and pets need ferrying, walking, feeding and loving', then a telephone number. Reaching for the telephone, I dialled the number.

'Yes?' rasped a male voice.

'Oh, er – hello. I'm calling about the advertisement in *Horse and Hound*,' I said, putting on my best telephone voice.

'Yes?' the voice repeated, unhelpfully.

'Well, er – would it be possible to come and see you for an interview?'

'Any experience with horses and children?' barked the voice.

'Er – yes, yes, I have. I've been around horses all my life. Raised with them, in fact. A bit like Tarzan and the chimps.'

'Apes.'

'What? Oh, yes, of course, apes.'

'Well, be here at ten-thirty tomorrow morning. Ask for Ben Carmichael and someone will show you up to the house.'

After taking the address and several directions, I hung up, pondering. He didn't sound very friendly, I thought, and was just considering answering another advertisement when John, my brother, came bounding into the room.

'Any luck?' he asked.

'I've got an interview tomorrow. Didn't sound terribly friendly, though.'

'Probably just not very good on the telephone,' he said, unconvincingly. I shot him an old-fashioned look and nibbled the end of my pen.

5

'Don't worry.' John smiled encouragingly. 'I'm sure you'll be OK.' Raising an eyebrow, I just grunted. 'Fancy something to eat?' he asked.

'OK.'

'Will scrambled eggs do?'

We ate in silence, John reading *Woman's Own*, and me idly wondering what to wear tomorrow for the interview. Seeking respite from this mildly irritating problem, I studied John, his eyes skimming over the pages of the magazine.

My brother had very short, very dark hair, huge dark eyes heavily fringed with thick, long lashes, a slightly broken nose and a wide, sleepy mouth. His face had an overall tapering appearance down to a determined chin. He was of average height and build, and I thought him utterly ravishing.

Bias, I reflected, like love, was totally blind to any flaws or faults. I dearly loved my brother. He had always been there for me, putting me up in his flat, or rather putting up with me in his flat, when I returned from various jobs I'd taken, both in England and abroad, always with horses and children.

John was twenty-nine, two years older than me, and people always said I was the spitting image of him – apart from the broken nose!

Suddenly aware of being watched, he looked up from his magazine and smiled, showing very white, very even teeth.

'Are you really OK?' he asked.

'Fine.'

'Right!' he sighed, chucking down his magazine. 'If you wear a skirt and high heels tomorrow he'll think you're a useless female who'll be bothered about

6

breaking a fingernail switching on the washing machine! So, as you'll be helping with horses as well as children, it might be wise to wear casual clothes. Trousers and a jumper. Don't pick your nose, don't sit with your legs apart, even in trousers, and don't dribble coffee down your chin!' He sat back with a satisfied smile.

I grinned and asked him what he was reading.

'An article about how to satisfy your man, so if I ever decide to swing both ways I'll know exactly what needs tickling!' He beamed at me.

I snorted. John adored all women, even the ugly ones!

Suddenly feeling tired, I bade my brother goodnight and retreated to my room. Casually flipping through my wardrobe, I chose a pair of trousers, a big fluffy jumper with a moose on the front and my jodhpur boots. No doubt Mr Carmichael would want me to test-drive a Thelwell double to check I could be trusted to supervise his precious little darlings when they chose to ride.

To counteract my sudden feeling of nervousness, I took myself off and had a bath and washed my hair. This done, I went to bed and slept fitfully.

Next morning I rose early, washed and dressed, and was now burrowing through several large folders in the kitchen, trying to find my CV. Organization was definitely not one of my strong points.

John wandered into the kitchen, yawning and running a hand through his hair, and, catching sight of my frantic scrabblings, he sighed and gently steered me into the living room, where my CV was laid out on the coffee table. Smiling sheepishly, I kissed him lightly on the cheek. Perhaps bias wasn't quite as blind as love, I reflected.

7

Gathering up my CV, I then had a frustrating five minutes trying to find my car keys. I finally tracked them down in the vegetable rack, nestling under some carrots I'd dropped in there yesterday.

Grinning apologetically at John, I muttered that I'd see him later and headed for the door. He called to me, 'Good luck!'

'Thanks.' Tripping over the back doorstep, I scuttled off to my car, an old battered red Fiesta, nicknamed 'Bloody Mary'. John had given her the name because she often refused to start and could reduce me to screaming bloody murder!

Starting up with a scrunch of gears – only out of sheer nervousness, I might add – I set off for my interview.

The mild weather did nothing to still my churning stomach as I bucketed along narrow lanes lined with oaks, beeches and elm, sunlight blinding me through their outstretched arms, their leaves making a gentle sighing sound as though relieved that spring had finally sprung.

When I reached The Yard riding stable, I chugged into the yard and parked. 'Bloody Mary' decided to be extremely bloody and let off the most enormous bang. Two horses in a nearby paddock leapt into life and charged off towards the far end of it. A woman screeched.

'My word!' she gasped, appearing from behind a rose bush. She patted her chest. 'I'll have you know a blast like that to the ticker could have finished me off!'

Apologizing profusely, and going very pink, I explained that I was here for the interview.

'Oh, I see,' said the woman, who turned out to be a Mrs Travis, Ben Carmichael's housekeeper. She was a woman of mature years with grey hair, a doughy face,

and kind, twinkling blue eyes that belied a rather disapproving little mouth.

Mrs Travis took me up to the house, whereupon I was
shown into a small, untidy study. Ben Carmichael was
perched on the edge of his desk with his back to me,
bellowing down a telephone.

'I don't care! I want him over here now!' And he
slammed down the receiver.

I swallowed hard and glanced nervously about me.
The study was dominated by a large, heavy oak desk
awash with paperwork, a green swivel chair, a bookcase
containing numerous books on various equestrian activities (including piles of *Horse and Hound*), and biogra-
phies. Several horsey prints hung on the wall, along with
a couple of landscape watercolours. An occasional table
in the corner held a lamp, a paperweight and a pair of
binoculars, made from the innards of two toilet rolls and
several tons of glue and painted a luminous pink. *I hope
they belong to the children!* I thought.

At the end of the study was an old armchair. Swivel-
ling my eyes back to the desk, I discovered that Ben
Carmichael was staring at me, his eyes studying my face.
Slowly, he looked me up and down. I squirmed in
embarrassment

'Mr Carmichael,' announced Mrs Travis in a hoity-
toity voice. 'This is the lady who's here for the interview.'

'Oh, well, sit down, Miss . . .?'

'Farthing,' I replied. 'Penny Farthing.' And I waited.

His face creased into an incredibly sweet grin that
threatened to become a helpless titter at any moment.

'I know, I know!' I mumbled. 'No jokes, please, about
riding an old bike!'

'Well, I could have mentioned coins or the spending of them!' He peered at the moose on my jumper with mild distaste. I tried to look through him, but knew I'd only managed to look bored and sulky.

I was also slightly irritated with myself. I'd only given him my surname on the phone, because trying to get directions from someone while they are convulsed with mirth is not easy. But this is not a great start to my interview, I thought sourly now, regretting that I hadn't got it over with before.

'OK,' said Ben, more businesslike. 'Take a seat and tell me all about yourself.'

'I think this might cut a long story short.' Handing him my CV, I parked myself in the armchair.

Absorbing the information extremely quickly, he then asked several questions in quick succession. Why had I moved around so much, spending six months here, a year there, sometimes in England, sometimes abroad?

'Because that's how long they needed me for,' I replied.

'But you have ten O levels and three A levels. Why didn't you go to university?'

'Because I don't like books, except as doorstops!' I snapped, slightly irritated. God, I hope he's not going to lecture me, I thought petulantly.

'I see.' He surveyed me coldly. Oh, dear, back to 'Situations Vacant'. I suppose I've given the impression I'm basically a bum, I thought.

'What makes you think this is the job for you?' Folding his arms, he looked at me expectantly.

'I presume this is a permanent position?' He nodded. 'That's why I want it. Time to settle down.'

'Good. My wife died in an accident and I have three sons to look after: Rory, Alexander and Harry. They

10

need a woman's influence, a woman who is going to stay and not mess them about. I do have a business to run, mainly hunters and liveries in the yard. We also do a bit of teaching and driving "tours" in the summer. To keep going, we literally do a bit of everything.

'The boys,' he continued, 'have ponies of their own, which you will be required to supervise them with. As for yourself, there are plenty of horses to choose from in order to accompany them.

'Mrs Travis is my housekeeper. She does most of the housework, cooking, etc., but a little help would be appreciated. You'd also be expected to help out in the Yard when we have one of the lads off – sickness, etc.'

Phew! What he wanted was a dogsbody! He obviously read my thoughts, as he said, 'What I need in general is a dogsbody, willing to muck in and out! Well, what do you think so far? Are you up to it?'

'I think so,' I replied.

'Good! Perhaps you'd like a tour of the place?'

'Yes, please.' Rising to my feet, I realized I only came up to his chest.

'OK, let's go.'

As we were already in the house, it seemed a good place to start. It was a very large, rambling old house, which only he and the boys occupied; Mrs Travis lived in the small market town about a mile down the road. I followed him out of the study, into the spacious hall and up the wide staircase which wound its way on to the upper floor.

A door on my left, Ben informed me, with a flap of his hand, led to his domain. He'd gone completely self-contained, he said, because he was fed up with rubber ducks and toy soldiers getting lodged in awkward places, so the boys now had a bathroom of their own. I had to resist an urge to take a peek inside his room. Silently padding along on his immaculate shagpile, I wondered if I ought to take my less than spotless shoes off.

Doors led off to the left and right. The landing seemed to go on forever, and had a tall window at one end. A wilting plant, perched precariously on the window-sill, looked as if it needed a big dose of TLC. A large bronze statue sat on a table underneath it wearing a scarf and a pom-pom hat.

I laughed, and then hastily shut up as Ben snatched them off the benign-looking figure and shot me an impatient look.

Starting from the window end, he opened a door on the right and led me into a bright, airy room which he informed me was to be mine. Carpets, curtains, the striped wallpaper, all were a fresh-looking lemon colour. I hoped it didn't make me look jaundiced. A pine chest of drawers stood under the large window facing me.

Another door in the corner of the room led into a small bathroom with a white suite, and a broken wooden toilet seat. I made a mental note to be very careful of it.

Going back into the bedroom, one wall, it seemed, was a mass of fitted wardrobes. Enough there to hold the skeletons of the entire British Cabinet.

The bed was large, and had a duvet on it covered in daisies. I suppose it gave one the impression of making whoopee in a field. Put on a tape cassette of a bird warbling and the fan on cool, and one could actually imagine one was outside.

I turned to face the door and found Ben watching me, his face an inscrutable mask. He jerked his head towards his runway of a landing.

'C'mon, I'll show you the boys' rooms.'

A door opposite my room led into Harry's room, so Ben told me. More fitted wardrobes and another large window straight in front of me, which again gave the room a light, airy feel.

The beige carpet was littered with little plastic animals and pieces of a jigsaw puzzle. A straight-backed chair beside the bed had a teddy bear seated on it wearing flying goggles and Wellington boots.

Harry was obviously a cartoon junkie. The wallpaper and duvet cover were awash with Donald Duck, Goofy and Bugs Bunny, in various poses.

Following Ben out of the room, I frightened myself to death: as I stepped forward, a muffled parp rent the air as I squashed a battered-looking clown underfoot.

Ben very nearly laughed but didn't. Shame, I thought, I nearly had him going there. We entered the room adjacent to mine, which Ben remarked belonged to Alex. Again, the same sort of set-up, and Alex also had a teddy bear, which was sitting askew on the deep blue duvet cover with his legs crossed and an eye missing.

Alex had chosen wallpaper with various equestrian activities ranging from showjumping to dressage on a white background. Carpet and curtains were a deep blue, and, something which surprised me, he had a small bookcase standing at a jaunty angle in the corner of the room.

Obviously a studious little fellow, our Alex. I also noticed his room was incredibly tidy.

As we came out of Alex's room, Ben pointed to a door opposite us.

'That one's just a spare room.'

13

He opened the door and I had a quick peek inside. The peach decor gave the whole place a warm glow. The furniture was heavier, darker, and a door in the corner, I guessed, led into its own little bathroom. A vast double bed dominated the room. Ben was standing very close to me, and I became aware that I was staring at the bed. Hastily, I averted my eyes.

'And this one belongs to Rory,' said Ben, amused, as he opened the door next to Alex's room.

Rory's room had basically the same furniture as the others. His choice of decor was a cool peppermint colour, with the walls covered in posters of various macho male movie stars. I see, I thought.

He'd decided he hadn't wanted boring old curtains · and had blinds instead. Several comics and science fiction books were dumped on the Batman duvet cover.

Opposite Rory's room was the boys' bathroom. (Honestly, they could use this place as a hotel with the amount of washing facilities, I reflected). Ben hadn't been wrong. The bath contained so many ducks, soldiers and aliens, I doubted whether there was room for the boys as well. Toothpaste, squeezed from the middle, sat on top of the toilet cistern with the top missing, while a one-legged soldier bobbed gently in the bowl. The mirror was smeared where little paws had rubbed a peephole through the steam. Something resembling a shower cubicle occupied a corner and seemed to be buried under a pile of large towels. Obviously it doubled up as a drying rail.

After this I saw two more spare bedrooms which were both done out in cream and were apparently hardly ever used. Then Ben stopped briefly at a door opposite the staircase. 'This just leads up to the attic,' he observed.

So we returned to the lower floor. I found I couldn't take my eyes off his long legs as he bounded down the stairs two at a time.

At the bottom of the stairs there were three doors on the right and three on the left, with a huge oak front door straight in front of me, which according to Ben nobody used because everyone used the kitchen door which led outside via the side of the house.

Clomp-clomping my way I followed Ben across the polished wooden floor of the hall, and Ben opened the first door on the left, which led into the sitting room.

It was like stepping into another century. The upper floor had been exceptionally modern, which to be honest in such an old house really didn't do it justice. It gave one the impression of a big German shepherd wearing a tartan coat and pearl collar.

The sitting room, on the other hand, though it looked old and tatty, was still beautiful in a timeless way, the remnants of past glories still visible.

The room had only one window on the wall opposite the door. Large heavy curtains with faded cabbage roses clung for dear life on to the brass rail.

The Regency striped wallpaper was so faded that it was difficult to say what colour it had once been. It was now a yellowy brown where generations of Carmichaels had sat, smoking contentedly. The green patterned carpet was so threadbare in places that a few strands of hessian backing were clearly visible.

My eyes skimmed over the sofa and the two armchairs, which were upholstered in the same pattern and colour as the carpet, and equally threadbare.

Occasional tables were dotted about all over the place, bravely supporting potted plants and piles of old magazines. On a coffee table, bowls of withered fruit grew their own brand of penicillin. To the left of the door, an enormous sideboard held willow-patterned plates and half a ton of Royal Doulton.

A large fireplace with cracked ceramic tiles dominated the far wall, a bronze companion set stood on the hearth.

My eyes were drawn to the far corner of the room, where a conglomeration of space-age equipment looked rather out of place. A huge TV and a wafer-thin video recorder stood next to a hi-fi with a manual the size of a phone book.

An impatient sigh coming from the direction of the door alerted me to the fact that Ben was waiting to get on with the tour.

The second door opened into the drawing room. Again, it looked old and tatty but still held a timeless charm. Here, red and cream Regency stripe wallpaper had faded to a dull pink, the claret-coloured carpet giving the green patterned a run for its money. Perhaps this one was not quite so threadbare, I considered.

The grey sofa and chairs no longer displayed a pattern of any recognizable sort. Heavy velvet claret-coloured curtains were going pale around the edges, faded by the sunlight filtering in through the window.

A grand piano hogged the corner of the room on my right, a Union Jack draped over it. My eyes scanned the walls, taking in the obligatory equestrian prints and several seascapes in oils, and came to rest on a beautiful stone fireplace with a long brass fender running around the red-stained hearth. A log basket stood at the ready for the long, cold winter evenings.

A small drinks cabinet behind me contained every tipple known to man, clearly visible through the glass doors, the whole thing made of beautiful rosewood. Again, occasional tables were everywhere, groaning under more potted plants, a chessboard, huge lamps and playing cards in a small wooden box.

I was about to remark to Ben how lovely the room was when I realized he'd gone. Hastily, I bolted out of the room, catching sight of a dartboard hanging on the back of the door, and suppressing an urge to collapse in hysterics.

Ben was waiting in the hall, moodily surveying the wall. I slithered to a halt beside him. He pointed to the third door. 'You've already seen that room.'

I nodded, remembering that was where we had started from: his study.

We then began on the three doors on the right, and the first one opposite the study was the kitchen. It had masses of space, with a large scrubbed wooden table in the middle of it on flagstone tiles. An Aga on my right had a rack above it drying bunches of herbs. The rest of the kitchen was full of heavy wooden cupboards hiding all the food, and modern appliances. Several gleaming copper pans hung from the ceiling, hovering dangerously close to head-height above the table.

Mrs Travis appeared to be pummelling a great slab of dough, obviously about to concoct some edible work of art.

Smiling at her, I turned around and realized Ben had, yet again, moved on without me. I caught up with him in the next room along, which was the dining room, boasting a long table that would easily seat a dozen people. Silver candlesticks were intermittently placed all the way along it. A white tablecloth covered the table like an enormous dust-sheet.

A few Carmichael portraits along the walls gazed haughtily down at us. A vast dresser where the exquisite dinner service lived also held many decorative plates, most with fruit painstakingly hand-painted on them. I blinked and wondered if I ought to be touching my separated forelock and curtseying on my dicky knee.

Huge potted plants were parked in the corners of the room. A window straight in front of me gave a marvellous view of the garden. Ben seemed to have a thing about roses. They were dotted all around the garden with apple trees running alongside the neat rows of home-grown vegetables.

I brushed past one of the curtains and wished I hadn't: at once a little cloud of dust sprinkled me and set off a sneezing fit. The heavy velvet curtains looked slightly opaque with the film of dust coating them, as did the pelmet.

The whole room had a musty smell about it, as though it was hardly used. I supposed the family ate at the kitchen table; at least there you wouldn't need a megaphone to converse with each other.

'What a beautiful room,' I murmured, noticing that the plain carpet looked relatively new.

Ben grimaced. 'A bit on the large side just for us.'

'Well, we could always stretch a fishnet stocking across the table and have a game of ping-pong.'

I grinned, then felt it fading like the curtains at the stony look on his face.

Without a word, he turned on his heel and stomped off to show me the delights behind the third door. It was a downstairs toilet. Well, more of a cloakroom really. A loo and a tiny washbasin were along one wall with a row of hooks along the other.

Someone had cut a newspaper into squares and hung it off the loo-paper holder. Hiding a smile, I stepped back into the hall, and, bumping into the wall, apologized to the hat stand.

'I'm sorry, I thought it was . . .'

Ben raised an eyebrow. For something to do, I suddenly took a great deal of interest in the copper warming pan hanging on the wall, and tried desperately hard not to look at my discomfited reflection in the gilt-edged mirror.

A grandfather clock just inside the front door began chiming the hour. Ben inclined his head and gestured towards the kitchen, intending for me to follow him to take a look around the Yard.

'OK so far?' Ben enquired.

'Fine. You have a beautiful house.'

Ben merely shrugged, 'Well, it's home. I'll show you the stables.'

We tramped out of the house down a fairly long gravelled drive, at the bottom of which, bearing right, were the stables. These, I had to say, were exceptional. All the boxes were large and airy and ran in three blocks, eight stables to each block, with one of them acting up as a store room for hay and straw. The block facing us had a tack room on the end. All were painted a glossy black and white, and were kept immaculately, as were the horses in them.

I also noticed that all the stable hands were male. I asked Ben if he had an aversion to female grooms.

'I've always found men more reliable than women,' he snapped. I raised my eyebrows, slightly taken aback.

I was swiftly introduced to the lads, and then taken to meet the Thelwell doubles.

They were the spitting image, just as I'd imagined: short, fat, hairy and incurably greedy.

Trundling over to us, they immediately began nuzzling my pockets for mints. They looked a bit tatty, for there were huge great holes in their fur as they shed their winter coats.

'Aren't they sweet?' I cooed, patting a furry neck while at the same time dodging a snotty nose.

'Hardly!' muttered Ben. 'This one is Merrylegs.' He prodded a fat grey pony, which was trying to eat my jumper. 'The roan is Flicka and the black one is Badger.'

'Do the boys ride often?' I asked.

'As often as they can.'

Setting off up to the house again, I heard muffled giggles and, turning around, I saw three dark-haired, dark-eyed children peering at me from behind a willow tree.

Ben remarked, 'Oh, that'll be see no, hear no and speak no!'

The three rather grubby boys shuffled towards us and stopped just in front of me, gazing quite openly at me with three pairs of innocent, inquisitive eyes.

'Hello,' I said, thinking that was a good place to start.

'Hello,' they chorused.

'So, who's who?' I enquired.

The tallest boy said, 'I'm Rory, and I'm ten years old. This is Alexander.' And he pointed to a boy who was absent-mindedly sucking his thumb. 'He's eight,' he added, eyeing his brother in mild disgust.

'Get your thumb out of your mouth!' barked Ben. 'You'll have to excuse Alex, he's the one who never managed to stop sucking his thumb. Little baby!'

Alex removed the offending digit and lamely introduced his brother. 'Harry – he's five.'

'I think a cup of coffee is in order,' said Ben. 'Come on, you lot, let's go and get a drink.'

He marched us all into the kitchen, where Mrs Travis made the coffee and tactfully retreated upstairs to give the bathrooms 'a lick and a promise'. I had a feeling that, like Captain Oates, she might be gone for some time.

'Well,' smiled Ben, 'I'll give your references a check over and, if all is well, you can start immediately.'

'Fine,' I replied faintly, somewhat surprised that he was offering me the job on the spot, especially when I thought I'd blown it.

'I'll call you tomorrow and arrange for you to move in on Monday, OK?'

'No problem.' I watched Ben watching me, and felt my cheeks burning. Hastily I finished my coffee, said my goodbyes and left.

Driving back to John's flat, it suddenly occurred to me that I hadn't been asked to ride the Thelwells, or any of the horses for that matter. Perhaps he'd forgotten. Maybe I'd reacted well to the dribbly, hairy creatures, or perhaps it was because I'd been so complimentary about his house, I thought.

Letting myself back into the flat, I found John in the bath playing Battleships with a rubber duck, a green sponge, a lot of foam and a bottle of anti-dandruff shampoo.

'You're back early,' he said, his hair standing up in a peak. 'Well, how did it go?'

'OK. Mr Carmichael's checking my references and then he's going to phone me tomorrow with a view to me moving in on Monday.'

John's face fell. 'So soon? I thought I might have the pleasure of your company for at least another week! Still,' he said, brightening, 'it's not as though you're going miles and miles away this time. I can always descend on you! What's the place like?'

'A bit like Grandfather,' I replied. 'Old and rambling, and once very beautiful. Except for the stables. They were immaculate.'

I told John all about my interview, in great detail, until I noticed he was shivering, so I took myself off to the kitchen to make a coffee. I wonder if Ben Carmichael is always that grumpy, I thought.

That night, John and I had a Chinese take-away, eating off trays on our knees. In fact, we had a very cosy evening playing poker and laying bets on how long it would take me to get Ben to crack a smile that went as far as his eyes. I said it would be the day I handed my notice in!

The best part of Sunday was spent with me packing and John getting in the way. Cleaning out my room was a pretty horrific experience. I found two odd socks (unwashed), a rotten apple core and a half-eaten cheese sandwich under my bed.

Ben Carmichael phoned as he said he would, confirmed that my references were fine and told me he'd see me in the morning.

On Sunday night I went to bed early and fell into an uneasy sleep. Starting a new job always gave me the jitters. I hated being new somewhere. I always felt slow and wondered if people thought I was a bit of a drip.

Rising early, I got washed and dressed and loaded 'Bloody Mary' with my luggage.

John came out to the car to see me off.

'Well,' he said, 'you make sure you come and see me. I want to know if I win my bet!' His voice sounded thick and unsteady, and I smiled.

'John, I'm like eating pickled onions. I keep coming back on you!'

Giving him a huge cuddle, I got into my car and drove off, feeling the usual mixture of excitement and nerves.

What I didn't know at that time was that I would be walking right into the middle of something quite sinister.

CHAPTER 2

Having driven to the Yard without incident, which for me was pretty rare, I was met by Ben, who grunted at me, showed me to my room and left me to unpack.

I spent the day getting acquainted with the household: Mrs Travis (who was bossy in a motherly sort of way), Mr Travis, who did the garden and any odd jobs around the place, and the stable lads.

As I wandered around the yard, I decided to get to know the lads. I had nothing better to do and by the looks of 'em it wouldn't be any hardship!

'How long have you worked here?' I asked a beautiful dark-haired boy, who had huge dark eyes in an elfin-like face. I remembered his name: Will Armstrong.

'Oh, about a year.' He had a soft voice

'And do you like it here?' I enquired, forcing my wayward thoughts into order.

He nodded. 'Yes, Ben's a good boss, firm but fair, and he's kind to his horses.'

'Do you live in the town?' I asked, having mentally undressed him.

'Yes,' he replied, absent-mindedly scratching his ear.

'What about the other lads?' I enquired, trying to stop myself from grinning stupidly.

'Well, Adam shares with me. It's a cottage just on the edge of the town. Mark, Finn and Dominic all share the same house, not far from our cottage, actually. It's easier to pay the rent when you share.'

I remarked that it must get rather tiresome, having to share, for privacy reasons. Will merely shrugged, didn't quite meet my eyes, and said he'd better get back to work. I watched him walk away, and couldn't help feeling a nagging suspicion about young Will.

Suddenly, knowing I was being watched, I turned and saw Dominic staring at me. His expression was one I couldn't read. Turning abruptly, he stalked off towards a large chestnut horse and began to groom it. Intrigued, I wandered over to have a closer look.

Dominic Arden, or hard-on, the other lads called him, was extremely good-looking. Dark, lean, sensual, he appeared to be in a bad mood.

'Hello,' I said, peering into the gloom of the box. 'You're . . . Dominic! I've got it right, haven't I?'

'You have. Well done!' He eyed me rather as you would a cat in its litter tray.

'Do I win five pounds?'

Dominic stopped in mid-stroke and surveyed me with raised eyebrows. A ghost of a smile played about his mouth. I shot him a sweet smile in return. 'I bet you're as hard as nails on the outside, and as soft as butter on the inside!' I mused, tilting my head on one side. 'Do you mind if I call you mollusc?' I added, and, seeing the look on his face, scarpered.

Charging round the corner of the stable block, I literally ran into Adam, carrying a hay net which he very nearly throttled me with.

'Sorry!' he said, catching hold of me. 'Are you OK?'

'I'm fine,' I replied, picking hay off every bit of me. 'It's my fault, I shouldn't run around corners. Didn't they teach us that at school?' I grinned.

Adam grinned back. He had a very handsome, very kind face, his eyes permanently looking as if they found something amusing. Yes, I thought, Adam Bridger is definitely competition for Will on who's the fairest an' all that!

Adam and I hit it off immediately, and as time went on we became quite good friends. He introduced me to Mark Styles, whose name, I thought, sounded like something an incontinent territorial dog might do. He was rather ordinary-looking, with eyes that were set wide apart, mousy hair, a skinny frame and a charming personality. He was so laid-back, I wondered how he kept upright.

Looking past Mark and Adam, I noticed Finn, whom I remembered because of his unusual name, waving to a man he'd just been speaking to outside the Yard. He sauntered over to us, beaming, and said, 'Hello. It's Penny, isn't it?' I nodded.

'I've remembered yours. It's nice. I like it,' I commented, thinking how friendly he was.

Finn Buchanan had very light brown eyes and fair hair cut very short. He had a sexy, sleepy smile, appeared to be an easygoing sort of chap and was the tallest of all the lads. His lovely eyes wandered over my face and started to make their way downwards until Adam slapped him reproachfully and said, 'Pack it in!'

'I'm in love!' sighed Finn, with a comical expression on his face.

I burst out laughing, while he wandered off, patting his chest as though his heart were jumping out of it! Raising his eyes to heaven, Adam got back to work, and, after a few more minutes of gossiping to me, so did Mark.

I made my way back up to the house, got side-tracked, and ended up spending an hour talking to Mr Travis. We sat on his wheelbarrow and gazed out across the fields, watching a few of the horses grazing and playfully chasing each other, while he reminisced about the war, Mrs Travis and when she was eighteen, and the time when men took their hat off when a lady walked into the room.

Finally, reminding him that Mrs Travis and her legs were not eighteen any more, I suggested that she'd probably appreciate a hand around the house.

When I asked her, she grinned at me mischievously, produced two glasses and a bottle of cider, and, sitting down at the kitchen table, we gossiped and drank the whole afternoon away.

At about four o'clock the boys came home from school. I sucked a mint to disguise the cider. I didn't want them to think I was a roaring drunk.

'Hello, Penny,' they chorused.

'Hello, boys,' I said, giving them, I hoped, my most engaging smile. 'How was school?'

'Oh, pretty much as normal,' replied Rory, depositing his school bag on top of a snoring red setter. 'Bracken, shift!'

Bracken opened an eye, rolled it, and pretended he hadn't heard him.

'Go on, move!' Rory commanded. 'He's like a great set of bagpipes,' he added, grinning at me. Bracken finally moved, after shooting him the filthiest look, and collapsed on a pile of old shoes.

Alex said he was hungry, and Harry said he needed to go upstairs.

'OK,' I replied, helping Harry off with his jacket. 'Let's get you all out of your school clobber and changed, and then I'll get you some tea.'

They requested fish fingers and beans for tea, and as they ate, I idly began to study them.

Alex, I decided, was a shy, quiet boy. Not a chappie of many words, but when he did say something it was well observed and sensitive. He was also very nervy and incredibly gentle.

Harry was cheeky, happy, achingly cute and inclined to ask questions that should not be asked, like, 'How did I get here?'

Rory was a good-looking boy, very easy-going, but given to punch-ups with anyone who gave his brothers a hard time! It was quite clear to me that he doted on his younger brothers. Perhaps he felt so protective towards them because they had no mother.

After tea they all usually went out to play, but my newly arrived presence seemed to warrant an evening in.

We played several hands of rummy (because Harry knew how to play that one), and after an hour or so I decided it was homework – and bath-time.

Groans of mild anguish met this suggestion, which I couldn't blame them for. I'd always detested homework as a child, and hadn't been too keen on the washing bit either! But after a lot of face-pulling the boys eventually complied.

Later that night I read a bedtime story, first of all to Harry, and then to Alex. Harry fiddled with the teddy bear's ear and anything else within reach.

Alex was totally different. He listened attentively, held my hand and gazed at me with the trust only small boys and stray dogs displayed. Sighing, he drifted off to sleep, thumb firmly in mouth. His reaction told me all I needed to know. The boy desperately missed his mother.

Downstairs, I found Ben in the kitchen, a large scotch in his hand.

'Do you want one?' he asked, holding up the amber liquid.

'Oh, no, thanks.' I wrinkled my nose. 'Not really my tipple. I'd prefer a gin and tonic.' That should go down well with the cider, I thought. Nodding, Ben fixed me a drink and asked how I was faring on my first day.

'Not bad, actually. They're nice kids. Harry wants to know how old I am, Rory thinks I've got nice eyes and Alex thinks I'm just nice all over!'

Ben snorted, and shook his head.

I sat down at the kitchen table and sipped my drink. Ben sat opposite me and clearly noticed I was thinking about something which appeared to bother me.

'Come on!' he barked. 'Out with it!'

'What?' I blinked.

'Well, something is obviously bothering you, so tell me. Is it one of the boys?'

'Er – yes, it is. I know I've only been here a day, but I've noticed Alex . . .' My voice trailed off to a miserable dribble, as I saw Ben's face grow hard.

'Go on.'

'Well, he – er – he obviously misses his mother desperately,' I finally blurted out.

Ben looked at me meditatively. I suddenly took a great deal of interest in my drink, and wondered if I'd find my way home around the country lanes in the dark!

Much to my surprise, after a long silence, Ben merely said, 'I know.' Looking up, I saw that his face had softened slightly, but it quickly recovered its usual hard appearance.

'My wife died in a car accident about three months ago. Mrs Travis has been looking after the boys, but she's getting on in years and they tire her. They need a younger woman to do things with them, go places. Far too many men about the place. They'll all end up frightened of women at this rate!'

I laughed, partly with relief, and even Ben joined in. Shame he didn't do it more often. All the creases in the right places, bringing his dark eyes alive. Good grief, I thought, he really is quite good-looking. Dark hair in wings over the ears, not receding on top, and curling ever so slightly into the neck. Kissable mouth, neat, straight nose, high cheekbones and a strong jawline. Those lovely long, lean legs were stretched out just inches from mine. You ought to be on the cover of a romance novel, and that brother of mine just won the bet, I noted.

'Well, I hope I can be of some use. Rory and Harry, I notice, seem to be coping fairly well about losing their mum. Rory's quite protective towards his brothers, which he seems to enjoy, and Harry, if he gets upset, can be easily pacified with a cream horn and a wagon wheel.'

Ben gave a bark of laughter, and said, 'You're very observant. You seem to have got 'em all sussed in a few hours!'

'Well,' I shrugged, taking a sip of my gin, 'I suppose it's because I've been doing this kind of job for a few years now, since I left school. You get to know that kids only vary slightly. They're either very good or bloody awful! Yours are just typical boys, except Alex. And that's not a problem. I'll get round him eventually.'

'I don't think you'll have any problems with the boys in general. If you do, give us a shout and I'll have a word.'

Ben took a hefty belt of his scotch.

'I've noticed,' I commented, throwing caution to the wind, 'that there aren't any photos of your wife about the house. Perhaps a photograph would be a nice idea, to give to Alex. It might help him come to terms with his mother's death.'

'I think not!' said Ben, so vehemently that I jumped, spilling gin all over my jeans.

'Sorry,' I murmured through stiff lips. 'It was just an idea.'

'Well, it was a very silly idea!' said Ben crossly, and got up with such force that he cracked his knee on the table, which really didn't help matters. Without another word he stalked off to his study.

Raising my eyebrows, I wondered what had brought on that little tantrum. Strange way to behave over a photograph. It was as if he was trying to erase every little detail of his wife's existence. Not the usual way of dealing with grief, I noted. Still, his grief, I supposed, was his to deal with as he wished.

Half an hour later, Ben came into the drawing room, where I was reading the local newspaper, and apologized for biting my head off.

'It's OK.' I smiled.

'Perhaps it's wisest not to talk about my wife for a while. Still a bit raw, you understand?'

I nodded, feeling enormously relieved that the storm was over. 'Fancy a brew?' I asked.

'Go on, then,' he said, collapsing into an armchair. He looked tired.

As we drank our tea, I found he stared at me a lot, so I read some adverts in the local paper. I couldn't stop laughing at one in particular, which read, 'Kiss Those Haemorrhoids Goodbye!'

Ben continued to stare. I wiped my eyes and sniffed. Feeling one of those awful silences coming on, I asked, 'Have you – um – got much business for the summer?'

Ben gave a slightly lop-sided grin. 'Not really. Hopefully it'll pick up in another week or two.'

'Mark told me you loan horses out for the day. That way, people don't have to put up with nose-to-tail riding lessons; they can enjoy themselves on their own and at their own speed.'

'That's right,' he replied, suddenly looking uncomfortable.

'What's wrong?' I asked, frowning.

Ben heaved a great sigh and rubbed his hands over his face. 'We had a woman – a Mrs Murphy. She took one of the horses out a few weeks back. She had an accident. The horse freaked out at something in the road, according to a local farmer, and then it reared up and fell on top of her.'

'Heavens! Is she OK?' I asked.

'She's dead.' He said it bluntly but I could imagine the horror of it at the time. I was stunned. I didn't know what to say.

Eventually, I mumbled, 'I'm sorry. It must have been awful for you. I mean, her family and everything.'

Ben nodded. 'Yes. It was. Her husband wanted to sue me, but she'd signed the form saying she was both fit enough and experienced enough to go out on her own. That's why we have the forms, to protect ourselves.

'At the inquest, the coroner gave a verdict of accidental death. Her husband just sat there, gazing into space. Apparently, he doted on her; he was really broken up over it. I felt so bad about it, I had the horse destroyed. I wouldn't ever trust it again, and you can't sell on a horse like that. At least now it won't hurt anyone else.' Ben took a swig of his tea.

'Anyway,' he continued, 'enough of that. Do you think you'll like it here?'

I nodded, and smiled. 'Yes, I do. Everyone's been very nice to me so far, except one person.'

'Who wasn't nice to you?' he asked, looking cross.

'You,' I retorted, and shot him a comical glower.

Ben laughed and apologized again.

'Forgiven!' I said, and yawned. 'I think I'll go up now, if you don't mind. I'm quite tired. I'll see you in the morning.' I got to my feet and sidled off towards the door.

'Goodnight, Pen,' he said gloomily.

I went up to my room. God, he's a miserable sap, I thought in irritation, then cursed myself. The poor chap hadn't long lost his wife. Feeling slightly guilty, I had a bath.

When I'd finished, I padded into my bedroom and, hearing sobbing coming from Alex's room, shot in to see him.

Ben was already in there. Heaven knew how he'd heard the boy from the drawing room, I thought. Unless he'd been up here already.

Alex was sitting on his knee, clutching his teddy bear.

I sat on the bed, and, seeing me arrive, Alex got off Ben's knee and clambered on to mine.

'You're damp!' he said accusingly, and wiped his nose on his teddy bear.

'I know. I've just had a bath,' I replied, and, looking down, suddenly realized I was still only wearing a towel. Going pink, I gave it a tug at about the cleavage point. Ben grinned unashamedly at me, and continued to gawp. I put Alex around me rather like a back-to-front coat, with his arms and legs around my waist, and gently rocked him.

'So what's the matter?' I softly asked him.

'I had an 'orrible dream!' he said, burying his face in my neck.

'What about?' I asked, kissing the top of his head.

'Daddy got eaten by a monster, and there was blood everywhere!' he wailed.

'Daddy's fine. Look, you can see for yourself.'

'I know that now!' A large tear trickled off the end of his nose. 'But at the time I didn't!'

He pressed himself into me, desperately wanting some comfort. I looked at Ben, who, getting to his feet, came around the back of me and playfully poked and nipped Alex, who began to giggle, despite the fact that he didn't really want to. Ben took him from me, and put him back in bed.

Ben and I sat with him until he fell fast asleep. Shutting his door, Ben thanked me for helping him with Alex.

'Well, it is my job,' I replied, clamping my elbows into my sides to try to stop my towel falling off me.

'He has these nightmares now and again. I suppose, having lost one parent, he's terrified he'll lose the other.' He sighed.

'I'm sure,' I murmured. 'Well, I'll leave my door open, in case he wakes again. See you in the morning.' I padded off to my room, well aware of the fact that Ben was watching me.

There was no doubt about it: Ben and I had been instantly attracted to each other. I could fall for that one, I thought.

The rest of the week slid by uneventfully. The boys grew to know me a little better. Ben, spending an hour or two talking to me in the evenings, seemed to lose some of his brusque manner, much to my relief, and took to staring at me when he thought I wasn't looking!

The weather seemed, at last, to be in keeping with June, and grew milder by the day. It had been one of the longest, hardest winters I'd ever known, with even a smattering of snow in early May.

I decided I'd take the boys into town at the weekend. I hadn't seen Loxton yet. In fact, I hadn't even been off the property.

Time to get out, I thought.

CHAPTER 3

When Saturday arrived, having got up early and had breakfast, we all set off for Loxton in 'Bloody Mary'. The boys found my ageing vehicle a hoot, especially when she 'blew up', as Harry so appropriately put it!

We parked at the back of a supermarket. Walking around to the front of the store, we found ourselves in the high street. The *only* street by the looks of it!

It was indeed a very small market town. The market itself was under cover at the far end of the road. In between there was a butcher's, a baker's (no candlestick makers!), a chemist, several boutiques, a dry-cleaners, a newsagent and off-licence and a pub called the Cock of Hope. There was also a fair smattering of banks, and a Chinese take-away.

Dragging the boys off into one of the shops, I leafed through several racks of cheap and cheerful T-shirts, thinking of the approaching summer.

Harry was trying on ladies' hats. Rory was surreptitiously looking at ladies' underwear. Alex was staring hard at the shop assistant, who had a nasty cast in her eye.

'Alex!' I whispered hoarsely, flapping a hand at him. 'Come here and stop staring at that woman! It's rude!'

'Sorry,' he said, looking at me under his lashes. 'She's got a funny eye. I was trying to work out if she was looking at me or not.' I ushered the boys out of the shop, just managing to stop Rory pinching a pair of crotchless knickers he was thinking of bringing with him.

As we wandered up the high street, we came upon a little side road. At the end of it stood a small church. The boys suggested I see it, and, thinking perhaps this was where their mother was buried, I agreed.

The church was incredibly dainty, and very beautiful. Weak shafts of sunlight flickered on the stained glass windows. I didn't go inside. Not one for churches, me!

The boys began to wander around the headstones, stopping to read one or two.

I went and stood next to Alex, who was reading a relatively new one. It wasn't his mother's. Alex automatically slipped his hand into mine.

I read every headstone. None of them had the name 'Carmichael'. Curiouser and curiouser, I thought.

We made our way to the market. This was a busy, colourful affair, with a dozen or so stalls, ranging from saddlery to books to clothing to greetings cards. A couple of stalls were selling rabbits and ducklings. Alex was enchanted. Rory, on the other hand, was not.

'Disgusting!' he said, wrinkling his nose. 'Look at all that mess they've done! I shall never touch raisins again!'

Rory took me to a little side street at the rear of the market, where there was café, a garage and a hairdressers. Tramping into the café, I bought chicken sandwiches, tea for myself and milk for the boys.

Sitting at the table next to us was a girl about my age with short blonde hair, friendly green eyes, a snub nose, a wide mouth and dumpy little body. She smiled at me. I smiled back. The little boy next to her began happily lobbing cake at Harry. Shooting him a look of intense dislike, Harry picked a piece of chicken out of his sandwich and lobbed it back, where it struck the boy with a smack in the middle of the forehead, and there it stayed.

'Archie, you deserved that, you naughty little devil!' scolded the girl. 'I'm so sorry.' She flashed me an apologetic grin. 'My name's Sam, Sam West. I work for the Harrises. They live in that big house on the hill. Are you the new helper at Ben Carmichael's place?'

'Yes,' I replied, picking cake-crumbs out of Harry's hair.

'You lucky thing, you.' Her face adopted a far-away, wistful look. 'I think Ben Carmichael is just so lovely. Mind you, so are those stable lads of his.'

I found myself rather liking her, and we spent a pleasant half-hour chit-chatting, until Harry got bored and started a punch-up with Archie. Separating them, we exchanged telephone numbers and made a date to go out to the local pub one night.

As we walked back to the car, Archie was the main topic of conversation. Apparently the boys had always hated him. I could see why, he was a spoilt brat with a pug face. Enough to put anyone off.

We stopped at the newsagent's, where I bought sweets and comics for the boys.

While we were driving back to the Yard along the quiet lanes, a red car suddenly shot out in front of me, causing me to brake sharply. It veered off down a turning on the right.

'Oh, that's right!' I snarled. 'Don't bother to indicate! I'm a bloody clairvoyant!' I was so cross, I had to put the radio on to calm me down.

When we got back to the Yard, I toyed with the idea of telling Ben what had happened, simply because I was irritated, but he was busy doing something or other in the stables so it was left unsaid.

That afternoon, the boys and I rode the ponies. We took them off into the fields at the back of the stables, among which was an orchard, a wood and a canal.

About a mile along the canal, we came to a set of locks and stopped to watch a barge squeeze through them. The barge resembled a gypsy caravan with its array of colours, bright red, blue, green and yellow, flowers painted everywhere, brass shining on its nose and along its sides. A yapping dog was mildly threatened with a sound dunking if it didn't shut up, by its portly owner who sported a goatee beard.

On the ride back to the yard, Harry suggested a race. I have to say, there is nothing more exhilarating than galloping flat-out in an open field. I had been given one of the riding school horses, a great lumbering, steady, friendly horse who went by the name of Lord Lucan. He was a genius for getting out of his box and going AWOL. You had the devil's own job finding him again! Personally, I thought his name far too grand for him. Muffin would have suited him better.

Thundering along at a furious rate, we finally decided to slow down, or rather Lord Lucan did, which was fortunate, for suddenly a great rook shot out from the depths of a bush, startling Merrylegs. The pony shied violently, depositing Harry on the ground. Pulling up, I cantered back to Harry, flung myself off Lord Lucan and knelt down beside him. Harry sat up.

'I think I've broken my bottom!' he wailed.

Laughing, I helped him to his feet and quickly checked him over. Nothing broken, thank goodness.

'It's not funny!' said Harry indignantly, and sniffed.

'I know, I know,' I said, trying to keep a straight face. 'Eight out of ten for artistic merit!'

Harry shot me a wounded look, but his sense of humour finally restored itself, and we walked gently back to the Yard.

When I told Ben what had happened, and the remark Harry had made, he grinned, and mildly enquired, 'How's the pony?'

Harry shot him a disgusted look and, nose in the air, walked into a stable door!

The resounding clatter of a metal bucket being savagely kicked across the Yard brought me back to the present with an almighty jolt.

Dick Fox was still in full flow, warming to his subject: the yew poisoning.

'It's the alkaloid. It's rapidly absorbed from the alimentary tract. The chief effect is on the heart, a sort of heart attack. From eating to dying it's a matter of, say, half an hour.'

'What do you expect to find, when you do a post-mortem?' Ben asked, looking at Dick intently.

'Well, I'll more than likely find dark green gesta and yew sprigs and berries still in the stomach. The liver, spleen and lungs will be engorged with dark blood. His right heart will be empty and the left will contain dark, tarry-looking blood, with noticeable signs of inflammation around his stomach. I'll have to operate at a low temperature, to lower the risk of decomposition.'

'And if there are no leaves, or whatever, how will you know for sure?' Ben asked, looking completely lost.

'Taxine,' said Dick. 'If I extract a sample from the stomach, and put it in sulphuric acid, it should turn a shocking pink. There's your answer, although the state of him internally would confirm it really.'

I stood and gazed at Dick. Something was going on, and I was damned if I knew what it was. All I could work out was that a lot of odd things appeared to happen here. I had an awful feeling this was only the beginning.

In my eyes, Dick was bound to be right; after all, he was a man of fifty-odd years, who'd been a vet for most of his adult life. His heavily lined, weatherbeaten face took on a musing expression. 'If you'll pardon me for saying so,' he said, inclining his head, 'it's a most ingenious way of poisoning a horse. Well, killing one, in fact. They're not easy to kill. Even if I shot him, the sheer size of him, with all that muscle and thick tissue surrounding him, would mean I'd probably have to use a good few bullets to do the job. Someone's used their noggin. Yew grows everywhere, so no expense. A horse will eat it readily enough, without dressing it up. It's fast-acting, and virtually untraceable. It's only because I've seen one of these deaths before that I could hazard a guess, otherwise I'd have been stumped.'

Ben nodded, obviously impressed. Scratching his head, he looked pointedly at me.

'Er – I'll just take the boys up to the house, and, er – get them a drink,' I said, trying to sound jovial. 'OK, boys, get a wiggle on.'

Three pairs of eyes looked at me sorrowfully. How much of that conversation had they understood? I wondered.

Rory was quiet, but in control. Alex clung to me, shaking and whimpering. Harry just bawled. I did my

41

best to comfort all three of them. With Rory and Harry I seemed to be making some headway. Not so easy with Alex.

Ben came up to the house a few minutes later and helped himself to a can of beer out of the fridge. If I was expecting sadness at the loss of a much loved, tireless old friend, I couldn't have been more wrong. He was absolutely livid.

I settled the boys in the drawing room with a few jigsaw puzzles and books, and returned to the kitchen.

'You know what's happened here, don't you?' Ben snapped, savagely chucking a tea-towel in my direction.

'No. What?' I replied, diving for cover.

'Someone has poisoned one of my best horses!' he stormed.

'I know.' Feeling nervous, I enquired, 'Any idea who?'

Curiously, Ben said nothing, and fixed the Aga with a stony gaze.

'I don't think any of the stable lads could do something like that,' I went on nervously. 'Perhaps it's someone you sacked some time ago. Are there any enemies you can think of who would wish you harm, or see your business go down the pan?'

After a tense pause, Ben said quietly, 'No. No one.' Perhaps he would talk to me when he felt he could, I thought, unconvinced.

About half an hour later, Dick came back with his tractor and trailer, and took Mistral away. Adam, who'd looked after him, watched the tractor slowly trundle away with its pitiful load, his eyes swimming with unshed tears.

Rory and Harry perked up quite considerably when I gave them burgers and chips for tea. They'd been asking for them all day, which request I'd refused, but I'd relented.

Alex remained my constant shadow. As for Ben, he prowled around the house, scowling and banging doors.

Later that evening, Dick phoned and confirmed that it had been yew poisoning that had killed Mistral. Ben, it seemed, had an enemy.

Putting the boys to bed that night, I found Alex crying uncontrollably. He was such a quiet, reserved child that it took me several minutes to realize his tears were not for Mistral but for his mother.

'You won't leave me, Penny, will you? Promise you won't, promise!'

'I promise,' I said, truthfully.

Clutching my hand, he snuggled up against me, desperately wanting a cuddle. I obliged him and stroked his hair, until finally he fell asleep. Sleep would hopefully release him, for a short time at least, from his anguish.

Downstairs, I tidied away the toys and books, loaded the dishwasher and made a drink. Ben had shut himself away in his study, and, deciding it might be best to keep out of the way, I went to my room.

CHAPTER 4

Sunday turned out to be a warm, sunny day, with only a slight wind. I had decided on a picnic. The boys thought this a marvellous idea, and helped me to prepare the food. After practically demolishing the kitchen, we set off, loaded down with cheese and pickle sandwiches, fruit cake and a particularly cumbersome bottle of lemonade.

We walked along the canal and made our way into the woods. The boys thoroughly enjoyed themselves, chasing each other, playfully cuffing each other, yelping with excitement. Even Alex timidly joined in. Rory, to his credit, took great pains in paying Alex a lot of attention. I noticed wryly that his appetite didn't seem to be affected! And as the day progressed, Alex became brighter. I had been considering asking Ben if he might have the day off school, but with his speedy recovery back to his normal shy self, I had dismissed the idea. It would not be long now before the boys broke up for the summer holidays. By the evening Alex had relaxed enough to let go of my hand, though he insisted on hanging onto my jumper.

I slept badly, constantly listening out for Alex, thinking the whole awful incident might bring on another nightmare. It didn't.

During the week, while the boys were at school, I filled the days until their return in the late afternoon by exercising a few of the horses. As summer was fast approaching, so were the tourists. Every day I heard one of the stable lads on the telephone in the tack room taking bookings for the carriage tours. In the yard, we had five horses that were 'Ride and Drive', which meant not only could these particular horses be ridden, they could also pull a carriage, which required special training. That side of the business proved to be a viable breadwinner.

As each day passed, I got to know all the stable lads fairly well. Will, the shy, quiet beauty. Adam, his flatmate, more forceful with a wicked sense of humour. Basically, I thought, a good all-rounder. Finn was very easygoing, always laughing and joking, with Mark often playing his straight man. Dominic, on the other hand, was moody and sarcastic, often abrupt. He seemed to be always cross about something. Towards me he was acidly polite but distant, whereas the others always tended to be ready to have a laugh and a joke with me. Around Ben he was watchful and respectful. Ben kept him on, in spite of his moody demeanour, because he proved himself to be very hardworking. It had also been his idea to do the driving tours, which had been very successful. He had personally broken each one of the five horses that were now doing the tours. One had to admit, they were of a very high standard.

As for Ben and myself, we seemed to get a little closer as each day passed, often discussing the boys, the weather, and something that intrigued him – my past.

'Most women your age are married by now,' he commented one day, shooting me a suspicious look.

'Not these days!' I retorted, thinking that if he started on about spinsters and mouldy old cats in a smelly, flea-infested attic, I'd batter him to death with a bottle of disinfectant!

'You must have had offers, I mean, looking like you do,' he said, totally unabashed.

I went slightly pink and mumbled that I had been asked, but marriage was something older people did, that I wasn't sure about it at all and I didn't like the fact that you didn't get parole!

'My last job was in the Channel Islands, as you know from my CV. I lived with a chap out there. In fact, I've had a few men in my life. Admittedly though, not *that* many, and I've never really loved anyone. Not properly. I mean, I love my brother, but that's a different sort of love. I suppose I'm one of those infuriating people who sails through life, having a good time, never taking anything seriously, and frankly, I'm glad that I'm me! People are far too sensible for me, like knowing the rate of inflation. I'd always thought it was an expression for when a man got excited! John and I lost our parents when we were quite young, and an aunt raised us. She was lovely, always laughing, and she never said an unkind word to us. Aunt Agatha died some years back and on her death we came into some money our parents had left us. Put it this way: financially we've never had to worry. I suppose that's why I can afford to have the attitude I've got. John's a lot like me. We don't tend to dwell on problems. What we can't fix, we don't bother trying to!' I shrugged and smiled.

Ben couldn't hear enough about me, but seemed a little uncomfortable and shifty almost, when asked about *his* past. I decided to withhold further 'thrilling instalments' about myself until he opened up to me a little.

While having our breakfast on Saturday morning, I asked the boys if they felt like going to the local fête. This was greeted with enthusiasm, as apparently one of their teachers, a Mr Taylor, had volunteered to be the target in a pie-throwing contest. I thought Mr Taylor ought to be certified!

The fête was to be held in a field, just a few hundred yards from the stables. We chose to walk, taking Bracken with us. When we got there it was to find the fête already in full progress. Several people I'd seen about the town came over and spoke to me, now aware who I was and where I was working. A tradition in keeping with any small community, a new face was asked about, it seemed. The vicar, the Reverend Reg Harvey, heartily beamed at me.

'Good morning, Penny,' he boomed. 'Good turn-out, don't you think?'

'Yes,' I replied, 'there seems to be no shortage of helpers.'

'No, indeed. Just the sort of community spirit I like to see,' he enthused.

The vicar was a giant of a man with a bald pate, except for a few little tufts of hair hovering above his ears. He wore half-moon spectacles on the end of his rather large nose, which gave his face an overall benevolent look. His thick, bushy eyebrows looked as if they were due to pupate and fly off. Because of his great height he tended to stoop from constantly bending forward to catch what people were saying, as he was a little hard of hearing.

Turning around, he saw a large woman in a flowered frock and a floppy straw hat bearing down on him with a fierce expression, and visibly quailed.

'Ah, Mrs Harris!' He smiled warmly. 'How's it going on the cake stall?'

She nodded at me dismissively, and practically sneered at the boys. Disgusting old troll, I thought irritably.

'Vicar,' she said archly, clapping one hand over the other and shoving them under her enormous bosom, 'I'm afraid it's not going well at all. Someone's revolting hound has knocked my upside-down cake upside down, and what it has done to the Victoria, I refuse to comment on in the presence of children.'

'Oh, please do!' I said, grinning.

Compressing her lips, she shot me a filthy look.

'Now, now, calm yourself, my dear,' said the vicar in a soothing voice. 'Let's go and take a look at the damage. I'm sure we can sort something out,' and, taking her by the arm, he gently steered her off to her stall. Watching her go with some amusement, I suddenly felt a sharp nudge in my ribs.

'Look, Penny,' said Alex, plucking at my sleeve, 'Bracken's done a runner.'

Looking round, I saw that Alex was holding up Bracken's lead, with the collar hanging limply on the end.

'Oh, crumbs! He's slipped his collar again.' This was one of Bracken's party pieces. No prizes for guessing where he was. Galloping off to the cake stall, we found Bracken, cheeks bulging with Battenberg, looking sheepish. The stall had been completely demolished. One end of the table had collapsed, depositing cake all over the grass and the vicar. Grabbing Bracken, I slipped his collar on, tightening it slightly.

'Somebody shoot it!' screeched Mrs Harris, taking a swipe at Bracken with a cake-tin lid, to which Bracken gave the perfect retort by beginning to chew placidly on the strap of her handbag, which lay at the end of the table, on the grass.

'Well, really!' spluttered Mrs Harris, her three chins wobbling. 'I'm going to report you to your boss. Never have I been so humiliated. If Ben Carmichael has any sense, he'll sack you on the spot. Dogs and children running riot. You can't control them!' And she was off. There followed a five-minute blistering attack on my character, and my lack of respect in general. Finally, I got bored.

'Mrs Harris,' I said firmly, interrupting her tirade, 'you're very probably right. You are entitled to your opinions. In fact, as far as opinions go, you've probably never had one that wasn't heard!' And, turning on my heel, I stalked off, dragging a reluctant Bracken with me, muttering under my breath. I was so cross, I stepped in three cowpats, which did nothing to improve my temper.

Squelching across the field, we came upon a bric-a-brac stall and we stopped to browse. Chipped teapots, scratched records, a jigsaw puzzle with half the pieces missing. I couldn't help laughing at an old chest that had been inscribed with the message 'I like most girls' on one side. There didn't appear to be that many stalls, half a dozen or so selling jumble, old records and food, mainly.

The boys couldn't be contained any longer. Mr Taylor and his pies were beckoning. Making our way across to the other side of the field, we found the teacher in a badly constructed home-made set of stocks. Seizing a plateful of what looked like dyed shaving foam, Harry hurled it, bang on target, at Mr Taylor. Unfortunately, Mr Taylor was in the middle of saying something at that moment, and started to choke.

'Oh, dear,' I said faintly.

Mr Taylor, through streaming eyes, caught sight of Harry and was just about to start bellowing when Rory, Alex and several other children started lobbing pie after pie – all, I have to say, landing with precision on the desired area. I grabbed the boys and we slunk off behind a row of parked cars. I suddenly started to laugh, and found I couldn't stop. I must have been infectious, because the boys started to giggle, which quickly gathered momentum to raging hysterics. Really, I thought, this was exactly the sort of behaviour Mrs Harris would disapprove of.

'OK, boys,' I said, sniffing, 'let's have a go on the bouncy castle.'

The boys leapt joyfully into the yellow, billowing castle, and, kicking off my boots, I followed them. Bouncing around like a load of little crickets, we finally collapsed, exhausted, bobbing gently. Extracting ourselves, I slipped my boots back on and managed to entice Bracken to come out of the castle. I hoped he hadn't punctured it.

Peering across the field, I spotted a face I recognized and realized it was Mark giving pony rides, which Ben had very kindly provided. We made our way over to him, trying to merge into the background as we passed Mr Taylor.

'Hi, Pen, hi, kids,' Mark greeted us cheerfully. 'You're not allowed to ride the ponies today, I'm afraid. Ben said you can ride them any time, and this is especially for the kids who can't.'

'Oh, charming,' said Rory.

'But that's my pony!' Harry wailed.

'Yes, he is,' I agreed. 'But don't you think it would be a nice thing to do, to share him, just for one day? Imagine if you didn't have a pony and someone you knew did. Wouldn't you wish he would let you ride him?'

'I suppose so,' said Harry, albeit grudgingly.

Half of the people in the town, and their children, had had a go on the ponies. Several of the women were singing Ben's praises.

'Such a lovely man,' sighed a good-looking blonde girl called Sally who worked in the hairdresser's. Not first thing in the morning he isn't, I thought. In fact he was an obnoxious pig most of the time.

'Hello!' said a voice in my ear. I swung round and gave a yelp of surprise. It was my brother. Flinging my arms around his neck, I hugged him tightly.

'John, what are you doing here?'

'I've come to see you, of course. I went to the Yard first, and that Ben Carmichael told me where to find you. You were right, he's not very friendly.'

Grimacing, I introduced the boys. Harry and Rory were polite enough, but Alex just shot him a filthy look, which quickly softened when I explained that John was my brother. Realizing he wasn't a threat, Alex smiled. We all went to the tea tent and got ourselves a drink. I scrounged a bowl of water for Bracken.

Suddenly I noticed a man standing by the bric-a-brac stall. He was just staring at us. He looked quite like Ben, but it wasn't Ben. I stared back. The man, realizing he'd been spotted, turned abruptly and stalked off. Odd, I thought, frowning.

We spent another hour or so at the fête, rifling through boxes of old records and board games. John got quite upset at some of the records because he was old enough to remember when they were hits!

Making our way home, John accompanied us, as he'd left his car back at the Yard.

As we were walking along the lane, a red car shot past us at a furious rate, making us leap on to the verge; the driver, dark-haired, was hunched over the wheel. I'd seen that car before. Then it came to me. It was the same car that had cut me up the previous weekend, just as we were leaving the town. The time had come to talk to Ben.

Arriving back at the house, I said my 'goodbyes' to John outside, which was probably just as well, because Ben was in a filthy temper.

'I see your boyfriend found you, then,' he snapped, glowering out of the window at John as he pulled away. 'I hope I don't have to remind you that you're here to work, not to go off gallivanting with men friends!'

'Actually, John found me at the fête, where you'd sent him.'

'That's not the point. I wouldn't have had to send him anywhere if he hadn't been here in the first place!'

'Ben, since I've been here, have you ever known me not to do my job properly?' I asked. Ben stood in front of me, hands on hips, glaring. I sighed. 'For your information, John is my brother.'

Ben looked at me dumbly and blinked. All the tension seemed to die in him. 'Well why didn't you say so?' he said, shuffling his feet.

'You didn't give me much of a chance!' I retorted, 'And you didn't answer my question. Well?'

Ben shifted awkwardly, folded his arms, and said, 'I've never known the boys to be so well looked after. You give them a lot of time, especially taking them off to various events and so on. I'm very grateful. I made the right choice when I hired you,' he finished.

'It seemed to me,' I said, eyeing him with disdain, 'as if I was the only one who came for an interview.'

'You were,' he replied, and coughed. 'Your references were so glowing, I thought why waste time doing all that interviewing when here was the perfect girl?' He smiled at me. 'Can I stop grovelling now? I really am sorry for biting your head off.'

'As long as you promise me it won't happen again.'

I watched Ben's face with badly concealed amusement. He looked both terrified and flustered, because he knew he'd be snapping at me again before the day was out, never mind a long-term promise. Suddenly realizing he was being had, he scowled at me and said, 'To think I was going to ask if you'd like to come to the horse sale with me tomorrow.'

'I'd love to,' I said, grinning.

'Well, I'm not sure you deserve to now.'

I put my head on one side. 'Who started this?'

'OK, you can come with me. I have to find a replacement for Mistral.'

'And do you promise not to shout at me all day?'

'I promise,' he said, giving me a lopsided grin.

I nodded and parked myself at the kitchen table. Ben went over to the fridge and started rootling around in it for a can of beer.

Thinking about the fête, I remembered I was going to speak to him about the man I'd seen.

'Ben,' I faltered, 'I need to talk to you about something.'

'Oh?' he grunted from the depths of the fridge. 'Fire away.'

Taking a deep breath, I began, 'I get the feeling that something is going on here and I don't know what it is, but on two separate occasions I've seen a man, who looks quite like you actually. The first time he cut me up in his red car, coming out of the town, and the second time was today, at the fête. He was standing by a stall, just staring at us. When I spotted him, he left, rather abruptly. Then on the way home he shot past us in his car. He damn near flattened us! It's very odd, you have to admit. He makes me nervous.'

Ben had gone very still. Finally, he looked at me, and seemed to be on the point of telling me something, then for reasons known only to himself he changed his mind.

'Just stay close to the house for a while,' he ordered mysteriously. 'Don't take the boys anywhere they don't have to go. And tell me straight away if you have any more sightings of this man.' And with that he stalked off to his study, banging the kitchen door so hard that the calendar fell off the wall. Sighing, I hung it up again, and made a start on the boys' tea. He still wasn't going to open up to me, it seemed.

That evening, the boys and I played Scrabble; I helped Harry, and Rory helped Alex. We had to put the game away in the end, because Harry wouldn't have it that 'arf' was not how you spelt 'half', and had got extremely argumentative.

When I finally got into bed that night, I found it very difficult getting to sleep. All I kept seeing when I closed my eyes was Ben's worried face. Tossing and turning, thumping pillows, I eventually drifted off in the early hours.

CHAPTER 5

Ben and I set off early in the horse-box for the horse sale. As it turned out, it was to be held quite near to the Yard, only twenty-odd miles away in fact.

It was a beautiful, warm, sunny day, the sky a deep azure. I hoped it would improve Ben's temper. It didn't. I tried making polite conversation, but, seeing Ben's hard face stonily surveying the road ahead, I decided to shut up. If this was what he meant by his promise not to shout at me, I would have preferred screaming abuse. This morning he'd tried to wangle more information out of me about my past and, since I kept vaguely side-stepping the issue, he'd obviously got my meaning and been in a foul mood ever since.

Pulling up in a large car park where dozens of horse-boxes were already parked, we made our way over to several large pens. These had been divided into much smaller units by iron gates. I looked at the rows and rows of horses, some in their prime, some so old and broken down I felt it would have been merciful to shoot them. Ben took absolutely no notice of the poor wretched creatures. Heartless pig, I thought, in annoyance.

We made our way over to a makeshift ring with sawdust on the floor. This was where the bidding would take place. I gazed over the iron gates at the terrified creatures, getting prodded and poked quite brutally by their handlers, who mostly wore trousers held up with baling twine. The auctioneer gabbled on so fast and loud that I could barely understand what he was going on about.

Ben surveyed the frightened animals totally deadpan. Feeling a wave of intense irritation sweep over me, I swung round and stormed off back to the horse-box. Ben caught up with me and, seizing my arm, said acidly, 'And what is wrong with you?'

'I could ask you the same thing!' I snapped, shaking his hand off.

'What's that supposed to mean?'

'You've been in a rotten temper all morning!' I spat. 'You brought me here on purpose just to upset me, and frankly I'm sick and tired of your moods! I don't know what I'm supposed to have done wrong! Perhaps you'd like to enlighten me!' I glared at him, reminding myself that this was not how one addressed one's boss!

Ben stared at me coldly. 'We came here to buy a horse and we're not leaving until we do!' Grabbing my hand, he dragged me along behind him, back to the pens. He stopped to look at a pen full of what appeared to be fairly decent-looking animals. He ran an expert hand over several of them, giving each one a pat and a kind word – which was more than he did for any of us! He seemed to be taking a lot of interest in a large black gelding. Looking about him for the owner, he spotted a man coming towards him. There followed an intense discussion, a spitting on hands and finally a shake, then, turning to me, he said, 'Well, what do you think of the new addition to our stables?'

'He's very nice,' I said, not wanting to talk to someone so bad-tempered.

It suddenly occurred to me that the deal Ben had just done was not strictly kosher. He assured me, with an exasperated look, that it happened all the time.

Getting the horse, who happened to be called Pennine, into the horse-box proved to be very trying. Planting his feet firmly into the gravel, he refused to move. When Ben hauled on the end of the halter, he was literally whisked off his feet, as if he had been a child, by Pennine's merely lifting his head. There followed a stream of extremely bad language. Eventually, several people loading up their horses came over and, grabbing a leg each, virtually threw Pennine into the horsebox. Pennine snickered.

'And so say all of us!' I laughed.

Ben scowled at me and said, 'Fancy a quick look around?' knowing full well I didn't.

'No, thanks.'

Ben turned away, thanked the chaps for helping us load Pennine, and we set off for home.

I travelled in the back of the horse-box with Pennine. He was so frightened, stamping his feet, snorting, sweating and shaking his head. Ben had thought it a wise move to have me in with him to ensure we still had a horse-box when we got home.

Arriving back at the Yard, Ben unloaded Pennine, or rather Pennine unloaded himself. He shot out of the horse-box in reverse and charged off around the Yard at the speed of a thousand gazelles, tail thrust upwards, arching his neck, until finally he slithered to a halt, just in front of Adam, and sneezed all over him. Gently stroking him, Adam led him to his new box. Muttering, Ben went off to get a shovel and proceeded to muck out the horse-box.

I took myself off up to the house, where I was greeted warmly by the boys, especially Alex, which was a relief after the frosty morning I'd had with Ben.

'Did you get one?' asked Rory, following me into the kitchen.

'Yes,' I replied. 'He's called Pennine, he's black and he's big. He's also quite young, so I think Dominic's going to have his work cut out for him, breaking him to harness.'

'Why is he called Pennine?' asked Alex, plonking himself on to my knee.

'Well, because apparently he comes from near the Pennine Way,' I explained.

He was just about to ask where that was when the telephone rang. Tipping Alex gently off my knee, I answered it.

'Hello?' A brief pause, then the phone went dead. Ben's voice came on the line from the phone in the tack room.

'Penny, who was that?' he barked.

'I have no idea, they hung up.'

There followed an uneasy silence.

'All right, probably a wrong number.'

'Mmm,' I murmured, unconvinced. I went back into the kitchen and sat down at the table, where Alex resumed his seat on my knee. I was idly pondering, when the telephone interrupted my thoughts again. I moved so quickly to answer it, Alex barely had time to swing his legs off mine – but it stopped ringing. Ben had obviously taken the call on the tack room extension.

After about ten minutes, Ben came up to the house. He made himself a cup of coffee and then studied me with some amusement. Catching sight of him, I asked, 'What have I done now?'

Ben pursed his lips. 'I've just had Mrs Harris on the phone.'

'Oh, dear,' I replied bleakly.

Ben, scratching his nose, said, 'Apparently, according to you, she hasn't had an opinion that wasn't heard.'

I opened my mouth and shut it again. Oh, lord, this is where I get a rocket, I thought, and tried to hide behind Alex. Fortunately, rescue came in the form of Rory.

'She deserved it!' he said, an indignant expression on his face. 'She was horrible to Penny, and she hadn't done anything wrong.'

Ben raised his eyebrows and, smiling gently, watched his son defending me. Rory went an unbecoming shade of puce.

Patting his hand, I murmured my thanks. 'That woman dislikes me intensely for some reason. I hardly know her. Admittedly there was a slight blemish to her stall.'

'A slight blemish!' he snorted. 'According to her, it looked as if a nuclear bomb had been dropped! A wasteland, I think she said – not to mention the hand-bag!' His lips twitched with suppressed laughter.

I looked at him under my lashes. Ben could contain himself no longer and started to laugh, helplessly.

'Penny!' he finally gulped out, 'you are so endearing!'

'I am?'

Gaining control of himself, he continued, 'Mrs Harris grumbled about your behaviour and general lack of respect. By the way,' he added innocently, 'did you enjoy yourself on the bouncy castle?'

'Yes, thank you!' I lapsed into a sullen silence.

'Penny!' he roared, 'I'm not telling you off! Now pull in your bottom lip and stop sulking! I haven't found anything so funny in years!'

'Really?' I eyed him suspiciously. 'So you're not going to sack me, then, as Mrs Harris no doubt suggested?'

'No. I have absolutely no intention of letting you go.'

Blushing slightly, I squeezed Alex, which he responded to by pressing himself against me. Ben stood watching us with an expression I couldn't read. Finally he said, 'Have you had a drink in our local pub yet?'

'No,' I replied, still crotchety.

'Well, would you like to go tonight? I'll get Mrs Travis to babysit. About time you had a night off.'

'Thank you, I'd – I'd love to,' I stammered, touched that he'd noticed I hadn't had a night off since I'd arrived here.

'Be ready at about eight o'clock, OK?'

'Suits me.'

I was so absurdly pleased to be going out, I decided to catch up on all those boring little beauty routines one tended to neglect when one was busy. I shaved my legs, did my nails and plucked my eyebrows, to the accompaniment of my own pained howls. Then I had a long hot soak in the bath and washed my hair.

Feeling relaxed and happy, I surveyed myself in the mirror. High-cheekboned face, large dark eyes, which looked bigger and darker than ever because I'd used mascara and eyeliner. Short dark hair, following the shape of my head at the back, a few tendrils down my neck and on the sides of my head, feathered in towards my eyes and across my cheekbones, a feathery fringe which made the whole of my face look, as my father had always said, 'cheeky, elfin-like, impish'. My eyes

61

travelled down to my slightly too wide mouth, the slender neck, the almost gamine body in jeans, shirt and a jacket. Sighing and thinking I'd have to do, I added a squirt of perfume and made my way downstairs. Ben was waiting for me, impatiently rattling his car keys.

'Seeing as it's only the local pub, I thought jeans would do. Is that OK?' I asked.

'Fine,' said Ben, staring at my face and clearly taking absolutely no notice of what I was wearing. I cast around for something to say. How can he just stand there and stare without feeling the slightest bit embarrassed? I thought in annoyance.

'Er – shall we go?' I muttered, feeling awkward.

'Yes, yes, of course.' he said, visibly shaking himself, and strode off to open the door for me.

We made the short journey in the Land Rover and parked on the road. The Cock of Hope didn't appear to have a car park. As we went in, we spotted a table in the far corner of the pub and made our way over to it. Several heads turned and stared. Perhaps they thought it was too soon after the accident for Ben to be out with another woman – bad taste and all that, I thought, slightly perturbed.

'Gin and tonic?' he asked, slipping his jacket off.

'Yes, please,' I replied, taking my own coat off. As I parked myself in a chair, my eyes wandered around the pub, taking in the horse brasses nailed to the heavy black beams, the pictures on the walls, hunting scenes, landscapes, fishing boats, the old heavy furniture, the burgundy curtains and the green patterned carpet. Perhaps the landlord had bought the end of the roll from the Carmichaels; the carpet was similar to the one in the sitting room.

Ben returned with our drinks. Two men at the bar looked in my direction and smiled. I smiled back. What else can you do? I thought. I looked at Ben, but he didn't seem very pleased, and glared at me. 'Know them, do you?'

'No,' I said, grinding my teeth, thinking, this is going to be a jovial evening out.

He stared at the two men coldly and they looked away. I took a sip of my drink, not knowing what to say. Lord, he was moody.

'Do you come here often?' I asked, wincing at the not very original line of patter.

'No!' he snapped. 'Penny, I have a confession to make. I brought you here because I want to talk to you. Away from flapping ears.'

'Go on.'

He took a hefty belt of his whisky.

'I think I'm falling in love with you,' he said, and stared at his peeling beer mat.

I stared at him, dumbfounded.

'What?' I finally managed to blurt out.

'You heard! I know you don't feel the same, but you might grow to in time, I hope.'

'I had no idea,' I replied, feeling the blood drain out of my face.

'Well, now you do.'

I eyed him speculatively. 'Are you doing this for the boys?' I asked, not unkindly.

Ben took a further sip of his whisky. 'No, I'm not. I want you for totally selfish reasons. The fact that the boys adore you too is a bonus. It was a fair question, though,' he added understandingly.

'Ben, has it occurred to you that you might be on the rebound? You only lost your wife four months ago. I mean, I've only been here a few weeks. How can you love someone you've known such a short time? A bit whirl-wind, isn't it?'

Ben shrugged. 'Not to me it isn't, and I can assure you I'm not on the rebound. My wife and I married because we had no choice. There was certainly never a great romance or earth-shattering passion between us. We'd been drifting apart for years. I'm sure she had outside "interests". We agreed to stay together for the boys. I felt terribly guilty when she died in that accident, because I should have been utterly broken up, but I wasn't.'

He looked at me steadily, tracing the rim of his glass with his finger. 'It was bound to fail from the start. I was only nineteen when I met Annabelle. We had a "fun" relationship, always in bed. We laughed a lot, had a lot of good times. Then, one day, she told me she was preg-nant. Well, you can imagine what her folks thought of that, and of me. So we married. It wasn't what I really wanted but, as her pompous father kept pointing out, it was my responsibility. So I did the "decent" thing. They were very old-fashioned people.

'Unfortunately, we weren't suited. As soon as we married, I realized I didn't really know her. She swiftly changed. She became a real shrew. I started to resent her, just as I'm sure she resented me. We hadn't wanted to marry each other in the first place. I'd hoped to work abroad; she'd planned to go to RADA. Anyway, we'd had two sons when my father died, and I inherited the Yard. She hated it. Hated the thought of moving here, away from all her friends, and so our marriage deterio-rated even further. Things got so bad in the end, we tried a trial separation, but the boys got so upset that we decided we'd try again. Apart from Harry, it wasn't exactly a success.'

'What did you do before you inherited the Yard?' I asked.

'I was a manager on a farm in Somerset.' He drained the last of his whisky. 'I went to agricultural college when I left school, and got a job as a general farmhand, working my way up to a manager. Once I'd got a couple of years under my belt, that's when I intended to go abroad.'

I looked at him sadly. He had had his life mapped out for him in a direction he hadn't wanted to go. Typical of a lot of men, he'd just got on with it.

He sighed and pressed on, 'As to your other question, I couldn't take my eyes off you the first time I met you at the interview. Then, when you accepted the job and moved in, well, the way you are has completely knocked me for six. I don't want you in my life as just an employee. I want you in my life in every other way *except* that. That's where the problem starts. If you don't want me, I can't have you working for me.'

'Why not?' I asked, suddenly feeling panicky.

'Oh, come off it. Relations would be a little strained, and I couldn't stand to see other men rolling up to take you out.'

Alex, and my promise to him, flitted across my scrambled brain. My heart-strings tugged. Before I could sort out my thoughts, I heard my voice saying, as if from far away, 'Well, in that case, then, I'll give it a go.'

Ben's gaze held mine. 'You could tell me you're at least fond of me.'

'I *am* fond of you, when you're not shouting,' I retorted. He dropped his eyes, a smile tugging at the corners of his mouth. An awkward pause followed.

'Now it's my turn to ask you if you're doing this for the boys, or just to keep your job in general.'

'Of course I'm not,' I lied.

Ben looked at me with an expression that clearly said rubbish!

'OK,' I sighed. 'I'm agreeing to this because I've grown to love the boys and I also made a rash promise to Alex that I'd never leave him. He was terribly upset at the time and made me promise, so I did. But I was telling the truth. I don't ever want to leave him. You mean quite a lot to me too. Actually, I've always been attracted to you, had feelings for you. I just didn't think you liked me, which is hardly surprising when you shout at me so often.'

Ben grinned and held one of my hands, gently stroking the palm. 'I'm sorry I shouted at you, in fact for being a "rotten pig" in general, as you put it, but I was so scared of betraying myself.'

'So what's made you tell me now?' I asked.

'Well, Mark and Finn are always discussing you, going on about how gorgeous you are, not to mention some of the local lads. You're the talk of the town. I just wanted to get you before someone else whisked you away from me.'

'Mark and Finn, you say?' I enquired thoughtfully, grinning at him.

'Watch it.' Pulling a face, he squeezed my fingers.

I laughed, then leaned across the table and kissed him full on the mouth; then, pulling away, I sat back with a sleepy smile. I'd been wanting to do that since I'd first clapped eyes on him.

'I think I need another drink,' he said, fanning himself. 'Same again?'

'Yes, please.' I grinned.

Ben set another gin and tonic in front of me, but he had to make do with an apple juice.

We didn't stay very much longer, as a few of the locals seemed to be taking a lot of interest in our progress. 'It's been a bad year for "ratting" in this neck of the woods,' said Ben in an undertone.

When we got home, Ben tentatively suggested I move into his room while he took Mrs Travis home. I remarked that he clearly didn't believe in hanging about! We stood in the kitchen, Ben with his arms around my waist. He kissed me lightly on the nose. I put my arms around his neck, curling my fingers into his hair, and kissed him hard. After a long time, he finally came up for air. It was such a nice change to have Ben looking at me tenderly, rather than with his usual hard expression.

Frowning slightly, he said, 'You don't feel I'm rushing you, do you?'

'No. I'd tell you if I did.'

Ben still looked doubtful

'Ben, we're not a couple of kids playing at this. I think we both know what we're doing.'

Gently stroking my face, he kissed me again. 'You're so beautiful,' he murmured.

'So are you,' I whispered, gazing into his huge dark eyes that were so like my own. Giving me a little peck on the cheek, he reluctantly went to fetch Mrs Travis from the drawing room.

I watched them drive away, and, feeling a wave of sudden desire for this brusque, oddly tempered man grip me, galloped off to my room. I stuffed clothes any old how into suitcases and bags and belted off down the landing.

Opening his door, I gazed about me. So often I had wondered what was behind this door, what his room was like. Secretly I'd wondered what he'd be like in his bed, too.

The decor was obviously Annabelle's choice. The whole room was very feminine, with pink rosebuds everywhere: curtains, duvet cover, even the wallpaper.

A kidney-shaped dressing table with a huge gilt-edged mirror stood under the window, cleared of all the cosmetics, jewellery boxes and expensive perfumes I could imagine Annabelle surrounding herself with. I couldn't resist taking a crafty peek into the drawers. Empty.

Feeling guilty, I crept over to the dark, heavy chest of drawers in the corner and, easing open the drawers, found serried ranks of rather loud knickers, socks and slightly more conservative T-shirts, all belonging to Ben.

I eyed the wardrobes along the wall on my left, and shot across to wrench the doors open and scan the contents. Two were heaving with chinos, jeans, trousers and immaculately cut suits. Ben had literally dozens of shirts in all colours. Moving along to the last two wardrobes, I saw that these were empty, the hangers rattling against each other.

Curling my toes into the dusky-pink carpet, I scuffed my way over to the door in the corner of the room leading into his bathroom, receiving several little crackles of electricity as I went.

The bathroom, predictably, was also pink, with a sunken bath and a bidet. I smiled, suddenly remembering a friend who had one and used it to keep her goldfish in.

A shower had been fitted over the bath, with one wall made up entirely of mirrored tiles. I spotted Ben's aftershave on top of the cistern, and took a deep sniff of it. The lemony tang filled my nostrils and immediately conjured up the image of Ben, to the point where I felt he was actually in the room with me. It suited him.

Returning to the bedroom, I hastily unpacked my gear, undressed and got into bed.

Ben came hurtling into the room about ten minutes later. I was half dozing. Coming over to the bed, he kissed my bare shoulder. Looking up at him, I smiled sleepily. It seemed completely natural to be there waiting for him.

Undressing himself as if he was on fire, he got in beside me and pulled me against him. I could feel the proof of his excitement pressing into my belly. As I gently stroked his back, my hands wandered down his body, exploring, and I kissed him lingeringly, working my way down his neck. Tipping him on to his back, I slowly kissed my way downwards, until, reaching his lap, I stroked him gently, making Ben moan in soft anticipation.

Sliding his fingers into my hair, he pulled me down beside him, and, rolling me over, he gently slid inside me. He moved slowly, always stroking, kissing and caressing. My legs wrapped themselves around his body, pressing him deeper into me. The penetrating strokes became more urgent, harder and faster, until finally, moaning loudly, Ben and I were both swept away by pleasure and collapsed, gasping for breath.

We lay for a long time, just gazing at each other, holding each other so close.

Ben was a good, gentle, considerate, generous, passionate lover – though not necessarily in that order! We talked into the wee small hours, a strong bond forming between us. If I'd have known he was this wonderful in bed, I'd have probably thrown him down and had my wicked way with him sooner! Finally, exhausted, we drifted off to sleep curled around each other.

CHAPTER 6

Next morning, for a fleeting second I wondered where I was. Then I remembered. Looking up, I found Ben resting his head on his hand, leaning on his elbow, looking down at me.

'Hello, you,' he said, softly.

Smiling up at him, I stretched, and said sleepily, 'What time is it?'

'Half past nine.'

Catching my breath, I sat bolt upright. 'The boys!'

'They're fine.' He pushed me down and wriggled on top of me. 'I heard them talking to Mrs Travis. I asked her when I took her home last night if she would see to them this morning.'

Bending his head, he kissed me tenderly, an action which led to a re-run of the previous night, if somewhat less urgent. Teasing, nibbling, caressing, Ben nudged me on to my belly and, separating my legs with his own, he slipped inside me, moving leisurely, unhurriedly, the lovemaking more of a gentle show of feelings rather than the fierce, passionate writhings of last night. We took our time and, finally, spent, I lay underneath Ben, dreamily stroking his long fingers, kissing the tips. Finally, deciding rather reluctantly to get up, we had a bath together, and went downstairs. By then it was lunchtime.

The boys studied us intently. Ben told them a simplified version of what he and I had in mind. They'd had an idea something was up (no pun intended) because Mrs Travis had given them their breakfast and I usually did that. As they caught the drift of what their father was telling them, we got a few sniggers. Alex climbed on to my knee.

'Does this mean we can call you Mummy now?'

'You can call me what you like, as long as it's not rude!' I replied. Alex grinned.

'Does this mean you love us?' he asked.

'Well, I do remember the advert said something like that!' Then, catching sight of the wounded expression on his face, I quickly added, 'Alex, I'm joking! I love you all very much.'

'Really?' he said hesitantly, still not quite sure.

'Really!'

Throwing his arms around my neck, he squeezed me as hard as he could. I caught Ben's eye and smiled. Happily, Rory and Harry seemed to be just as pleased as Alex, if somewhat more restrained. Mrs Travis just beamed at us. She, the saucy meddler, had known Ben's feelings for me all along, and it had been at her instigation that he'd finally got around to telling me. Personally, I think she was also fed up with his moods, and couldn't trust herself not to throttle him!

'Aye,' she said, clasping her hands in front of her and fixing me with a dewy-eyed expression. 'Penny's a smashing lass, fair of face and nature, kind and loving. You'll not go far wrong with her.' She grinned at me and wiped her nose on the back of her hand. I smiled at her

72

with a fondness I would, I was sure, have felt for my own mother.

News quickly spread to the Yard. Ben was subjected to a lot of back-slapping and several lewd comments.

The following Friday, Ben and I were invited to a barbecue that Will and Adam were having at their cottage. It appeared half the town were invited too. During the day, about lunchtime, I popped down to the Yard to ask Will if there was anything I could bring with me for that evening. Will suggested I make lots of little nibbles – sausage rolls, vol-au-vents and such like – as Adam was supposed to be doing the cooking, and Will wasn't entirely convinced he would produce anything even remotely edible.

I idly watched Dominic long-reining Pennine in the little paddock, where the Thelwells usually lived. Wandering over to the paddock, I leaned on the rails, listening to his firm, unhurried commands. His skilful handling of the young, strong horse was a pleasure to observe. I felt a pair of hands slip around my waist. Ben pressed himself against me. I let my head fall on to his chest. Kissing the top of my head, he said, 'He seems to be coming along nicely.'

He nodded in the direction of Pennine. At that moment, Dominic seemed to be having no problems in making the horse reverse.

Ben squeezed me tightly, making me groan. Since we'd got together, I had been constantly surprised – and pleased, I have to say – to find Ben exceptionally attentive and affectionate. All the moody surliness had gone.

Dominic watched us, the misery on his face quite apparent. Rather abruptly, he decided to call it a day with Pennine and his training. As he led the horse back to his box, I kissed Ben lightly and said I just needed a quick word with Dominic. Ben shrugged, said, 'OK,' and rather reluctantly let me go.

When I reached Pennine's box, Dominic was crouching down, busily checking his legs for any signs of heat or distress.

'Hello,' I said, over the stable door. Dominic glanced up, the usual fierce expression on his face.

Determined not to be put off by this, I said, with an air of indifference, 'Are you going to Will's barbecue tonight?'

'Not sure.'

'Oh, go on. You might actually enjoy yourself. It should be a good turnout at any rate.'

'And what do you know about what I like?' he hissed, and swung round to face me.

'Oh, I might just surprise you there. I think I have a good idea.'

He surveyed me suspiciously from the depths of the stable. Just then, Will came over and popped his head around the door. Dominic slunk behind Pennine's head.

'Dominic, would you mind giving me a hand with Bodmin's poultice?' asked Will, in his softly spoken voice.

'All right,' Dominic said, from behind Pennine's head. Will sauntered off to Bodmin's box. Removing Pennine's bridle, Dominic gave him a final pat and, coming out of his box, stopped briefly to study my face. I stared back at him steadily.

'We might see you later, then?' I wondered whether, if he smiled, his nose would drop off.

'Maybe,' he replied tersely. He looked over at Bodmin's box and his eyes flickered. Bolting Pennine's door, he loped across the Yard, and disappeared into the gloom of the stable.

Frowning slightly, I wished Dominic weren't so unapproachable. He could do with a sympathetic ear; he was patently full of explosive energy and misery. What bothered me was that, eventually, it would have to come out. In what way, only time would tell.

Deep in thought, I made my way back up to the house, and made a start on Will's 'nibbles' for that evening.

Ben and I left for the barbecue at about seven o'clock, leaving Mrs Travis to babysit. When we arrived, most of the guests were already there. Taking several large containers out of the back of the Land Rover, Ben and I made our way round to the back of the cottage and into the kitchen. I dumped my boxes on a table and asked Will where he'd like them put.

'Oh, we've put a table in the garden, next to the barbecue. Just stick it all on there, thanks, Pen.'

'OK,' I replied, gathering up most of the containers again, and, with Ben following with the remaining few, we tramped out to the garden.

I began to lay out large paper plates with napkins spread over them, Ben putting the food out as I went along.

Turning round, I spotted Dominic talking to the blonde, gorgeous Sally from the hairdresser's. I focused my attention back to the table, a ghost of a smile playing about my mouth. He was trying very hard to prove something to himself, or disprove. I know your secret, Dominic, I thought, and sighed.

'OK?' Ben asked, looking at me with mild concern.

'Fine.' I smiled up at him.

Adam came over to us, handing me a glass of wine and Ben a can of beer.

'How's it going being the chef?' I asked, grinning.

Adam gave me an old-fashioned look. 'It's not. Will's doing it now. I've already set fire to a packet of napkins, a bag of paper cups and very nearly my eyebrows!' He looked comically aggrieved. 'Thanks for doing all that food, Pen,' he said, looking at the groaning table.

'My pleasure.'

Adam's face took on a slightly irritated expression. 'So much for Will's faith in me.' He paused in reflection. 'Mind you, he has a point,' he said, suddenly grinning. He took a swig from his can. 'I just wish he wouldn't complain so much. He usually does the cooking, and he was looking forward to a night off. He hasn't stopped whining. It has to be said, Will has suffered in many ways lately, but never in silence.'

Laughing, I remarked on how nice it was that Dominic had shown his face.

'Yes,' said Adam, glaring across at Dominic, 'speaking of which, he's got a kind face.'

'A kind face?' Ben looked blank.

'The kind you never get tired of kicking!' Adam retorted, and taking another swig from his can of beer, he moodily surveyed Dominic, who was now talking to Finn.

'Adam!' yelled Will. 'Can you give us a hand a minute?'

'Just coming!' Adam yelled back. Sighing dramatically, he drawled, 'Let's see what I can set fire to now,' and sauntered over to Will.

As the evening wore on, people were really beginning to relax. Adam had parked a cassette player on a patio table and most people were now bopping energetically to several tapes of various artists. All credit to Will and Adam, there was a constant supply of beer, wine and lager. Pretty standard stuff, but nobody appeared to be complaining, or even noticing, judging by the rate it was going down. Everyone helped themselves to the food I'd brought, which I was pleased about. I didn't think Adam and Will would fancy eating sausage rolls, vol-au-vents and such-like for the next two months!

I'd spent a gruelling half-hour being subjected to the most boring, spotty youth banging on about motorbikes and the Isle of Wight. I knew I was beginning to get a glazed look. I looked around, desperately searching for Ben, but he was talking to Mark. He was laughing. I wondered, dolefully, if I'd ever laugh again. Surprisingly, rescue came in the form of Dominic.

'Excuse me, Nigel,' he said, taking my hand. 'If you don't mind, I'd like to dance with Penny.'

Nigel muttered, 'Of course,' and Dominic led me over to the other side of the garden, where we bopped briefly, before flopping into a couple of garden chairs.

'Thanks for rescuing me,' I said gratefully.

'No problem,' said Dominic. 'He has a nickname around these parts. He's well known for making the most ferocious passes at women's breasts through their clothing. We call him the "Muffled Titter". His idea of a challenge is a high neckline on a frock.'

I laughed so hard, even Dominic cracked a smile.

'Well, every village has to have its idiot, I suppose,' he said wryly. 'Where he comes from, all they do is grow spuds and interbreed.'

Used to seeing Dominic cross and reserved, I found it a pleasant surprise to discover that he was very witty, and intelligent, if somewhat slightly malicious.

'How do you like it at the Yard?' I asked, mildly curious.

Dominic shrugged non-committally. 'It's all right. Most of the lads are OK. Except Adam.'

'Why don't you like Adam?' I asked.

'Because he doesn't like me!' His unwavering gaze held mine.

'Well, have you ever done anything to upset him?'

'Not yet, I haven't.'

'Meaning you're going to?'

His face hardened. 'Not up to me,' he retorted, and, getting somewhat unsteadily to his feet, wandered away to find a drink.

I decided I could do with a break. Entering the cottage, I went hunting for the bathroom. I virtually walked into a couple, locked in each other's arms, kissing passionately in a doorway.

'Sorry,' I said, embarrassed.

The couple abruptly pulled apart. I looked steadily at Adam, my gaze transferring to the person he had been kissing. I nodded, smiling gently.

'It's all right, Will, don't look so scared.'

'You know?' Will, obviously shocked, didn't know what to do with himself.

'Yes, I know, or rather I had a good idea.'

Will swallowed and glanced nervously at Adam. 'Is it that obvious?'

'Only to me. In the past ten years or so, I've worked all over. Seen a lot of things, met a lot of people. Nothing shocks or offends me any more. I'm very broad-minded.

Had to be. I've met plenty of people on my travels. I just know the signs, that's all. Adam I wasn't so sure of.'

'Will you tell Ben?' asked Adam, putting an arm around Will.

I felt quite flattered that Adam obviously felt he could display such affection in front of me. It was obvious they hadn't told anyone else.

'No, it doesn't reflect on your work. You're discreet, and it's none of Ben's business, or mine for that matter.'

'Thank you,' Adam said, kissing me on the temple. 'I couldn't stand to lose him. I love him.'

'I'm sorry, I really have to use your bathroom.' Crossing my legs in mock discomfort, I hopped about the hall.

Will laughed, and pointed to a door on the right.

When I came out of the bathroom, Will and Adam had gone. I spotted them back among their friends, in the garden, chatting and laughing, contented and happy. I looked at them reflectively. This was rather like anything you wanted to keep hidden: it was certain to come out, one day. I just hoped they survived it.

Ben's voice interrupted my thoughts, angry and impatient.

'Where have you been?' he demanded.

'In the bathroom,' I replied, blinking at him.

'What was Dominic talking to you about?' he asked, a note of suspicion creeping into his tone.

'Mainly about that revolting chap I was cornered with,' I said, with a shudder. 'You could have rescued me. That's what Dominic was doing.' I looked at him reproachfully.

'I'm sorry. I was talking to Mark about one of the horses.'

'Why did you want to know what Dominic was talking to me about, anyway?'

'No reason,' said Ben, immediately making me think there was one! Never mind, it could wait.

Ben slipped his hands around my waist, and swept me off to dance. Several people were, rather indiscreetly, rolling around on top of each other, hands burrowing energetically in the most intimate places. We spotted Finn, draped in an ungainly posture over a beer crate, two garden gnomes and several plant pots; he was out cold. Apparently he couldn't get the hang of 'Cardinal Puff Puff' (a party game involving a lot of booze, especially if you did happen to get it wrong). Finn had passed out having still not got it right. Mark was making heroic efforts to appear as sober as possible to Sally the hairdresser. Fancying his chances, he then spoilt it by hiccuping violently and falling off his chair with a pained, 'Oof!' Will and Adam had disappeared again. It must be awful, I reflected, not being able to touch, kiss or hold hands when other people were around. I gazed up at Ben, dreamily, and yawned.

'Tired?' Gently he kissed the corner of my mouth.

'Mm,' I murmured.

'OK, come on, let's go home.'

Adam and Will reappeared, and smiled knowingly at me. I smiled back. Ben and I thanked them for a lovely evening, said our goodbyes and departed.

When we got home, I flopped down on to the bed. I was so tired, I had no energy to undress. Ben obliged me, quite happily, I might add. Having undressed and got into bed himself, he pulled me against him. I smiled in the darkness. Ben said he couldn't sleep unless he was curled around me. He reminded me of a dog we had when I was a child. The dog's name, incidentally, had also been Ben, and he had slept on top of my feet so I couldn't sneak off without him knowing about it! Thinking Ben had eyes rather like my spaniel, I drifted off in what seemed a matter of seconds.

CHAPTER 7

When I woke the next morning, my head felt as though I'd got up sharply from a chair and hit it rather hard on something. Groaning weakly, I reached out my hand, groping for Ben. The bed was empty. In his place was a note.

'Pen, I'm down the Yard. I love you. Ben.' Smiling and wincing all at the same time, I finally managed to get myself washed and dressed.

Making my way downstairs, somewhat unsteadily, I had three cups of strong black coffee and a piece of toast. I doubted if I could have kept anything else down. So much for my self-control, I thought.

I staggered through the kitchen door. The sunlight skewered me in the eyes. I groaned and felt dizzy. I made slow progress down the gravelled drive, and into the yard. Ben, disgustingly perky, deliberately dropped a metal bucket, making a loud clang, at which Finn and Mark scowled comically. Will and Adam, apart from the shakes, seemed not to be too bad, and as I approached, they smiled, after a fashion. Dominic's eyes flickered over me, and, giving a curt nod, he shut himself in a stable.

'Ah!' said Ben, briskly rubbing his hands together. 'You've surfaced, then. Oh, dear,' he added, giving a snort of laughter, 'you do look poorly!'

I surveyed him sourly, and said that if he didn't stop being a pig I would have to resort to the 'hair of the dog' and spend the whole day in the pub.

Ben sniffed. 'Don't expect sympathy from me. It's all self-inflicted!'

I pulled a face and called him a pompous old bore.

Around the corner of a stable block, the boys came towards us, and to my throbbing head it sounded as if there were at least fifteen of them.

'How's your head?' enquired Harry. 'Dad said it was hurting this morning because you drank some funny juice.'

'Oh, very droll,' I remarked, scowling at Ben.

Alex pulled on my arms for me to bend slightly so he could reach me, which action, incidentally, did nothing for my head. I obliged him, and he kissed me on my forehead, saying, 'There, it's all better now.' I smiled, thinking how nice it would be if it were that easy. Ben, finally relenting, came over to me and slipped an arm around my shoulders. I looked at him with a mutinous expression.

'If it's any consolation, Finn and Mark feel even worse than you do.' It wasn't!

'Finn's been sick in the water trough,' observed Harry cheerfully.

I told Ben grimly that I needed to pop into town to do a bit of shopping.

'OK,' he said, 'I'll see you later,' and, kissing me lightly on the cheek, took the boys off to check their ponies. He still wouldn't allow the boys out on 'unnecessary' excursions.

Nipping back up to the house to collect my purse and car keys, I set off for the town. I drove into Loxton, parked, and did my shopping in one of the supermarkets. I was just coming out of the store when the breath was literally knocked out of me by a man bumping against me. Gasping for breath, I looked up at the person who'd nearly flattened me, and felt faint. It was the man I'd seen before, once cutting me up coming out of the town, and then at the fête. Idiotically, I just stood and stared at him, my eyes drawn to the livid scar on his cheek. He stared back, totally deadpan. The silence was deafening. Finally, when I could almost feel the tension around me, I mumbled, 'Sorry, I didn't see you.'

'You're the girl who works for Ben,' he stated.

'Yes, I am. Well, I was,' I stammered, 'I mean, we're together now.' Irritated with myself, I silently cursed. What did I say that for? It was none of his business.

'Even more reason we should finally meet.' He smiled. 'I'm Ben's brother, Matt Carmichael.'

He held out his hand, which I shook, limply. To say I was shocked was an understatement. Finally, I managed to croak, 'I'm sorry, Ben's never mentioned he had a brother.'

'Really?' He raised his eyebrows. 'Well, I don't suppose the need to has arisen so far.' He looked at me, mildly amused about something. I had the feeling something wasn't quite right here.

'Look, I can see it's been a bit of a shock. Why don't you let me buy you a coffee?' His eyes scanned my face, silently daring me.

It has to be said, I am one of those people who are riddled with insatiable curiosity. He'd been the reason for a few nervous moments over the past few weeks. Now, facing him, it seemed, illogically, to reassure me.

84

Like confronting a childhood fear head-on, and squashing it. I looked at him reflectively. 'You can come back to the Yard with me if you prefer.' It was half a challenge, and he knew it but chose not to accept.

'The café will do. I have an appointment shortly.' He briefly consulted his watch.

'OK,' I shrugged. 'The café it is.'

We sat at a table near the window. I casually watched the townsfolk scuttling past, doing their shopping, going about their business, totally oblivious to a few surreptitious stares from across the café. Matt sat opposite me, placing a cup of steaming milky coffee in front of me.

'So, how long have you – er – been with Ben?' he asked, eyeing me steadily.

'Oh, only a week or so,' I replied, taking a sip of my coffee.

'Didn't take Ben long to hook you!' he retorted. 'Mind you, who can blame him? You really are absolutely gorgeous.'

He stared at my face. Choking on my coffee, I went pink, and the blush annoyingly spread down my neck.

'And you behaved very strangely,' I remarked. 'Why didn't you come over and introduce yourself at the fête?'

'I didn't want to intrude on you and your boyfriend.'

'That wasn't my boyfriend. He's my brother, John,' I replied.

'Well, I didn't know that at the time.'

Before I could stop myself, I asked, 'How did you get that scar?'

A long pause ensued, by which time even my toes were blushing. I shouldn't have asked.

'In an accident,' he replied, his face giving nothing away.

85

I studied him over the top of my coffee cup. 'You look very like Ben.'

'I know. I've been told many times before. He's two years older than I am. My big brother,' he said, rather bitterly.

Catching sight of my puzzled expression at his obviously unintentional slip-up, he composed his features into an impassive mask. 'And how are my nephews?' he enquired.

'Oh, adorable, funny, cheeky, and coping very well with the loss of their mother.' I damn well wasn't going to tell him about Alex.

'Good,' he said, lighting a cigarette. 'You obviously adore them.'

Smiling gently, I nodded.

'And Ben?' His eyes narrowed through his cigarette smoke.

'Yes.' I quickly took a sip of my coffee, thinking he had a nerve. Who did he think he was, Ben's mother?

Matt grinned mockingly. 'I see. Love's young dream, is it?'

Ignoring his sarcastic remark, I said, 'It strikes me that, for someone who doesn't volunteer much information about himself, you're rather nosy when it comes to other people's business.'

He leaned back in his chair with a smirk.

'I think I'd better be getting back,' I snapped, and, rising to my feet, gathered up my bags of groceries.

'Give my love to Ben,' he murmured, with a malicious gleam in his eyes. I looked at him stonily, deciding I really didn't like him.

'See you around,' he said, flicking cigarette ash on to the floor.

I stalked out of the café, feeling jolted and uneasy. The feeling stayed with me all the way home.

I was unpacking the groceries in the kitchen, when Ben came in, walked straight over to me and kissed me hard.

'I've missed you,' he whispered, nuzzling kisses around my ear.

I looked at him reproachfully. 'Ben, why didn't you tell me you had a brother?'

He drew away from me as though I'd hit him. 'What?'

'I've just had a cup of coffee with one Matt Carmichael,' I said.

Ben just stood and stared at me for what seemed an eternity. When he did speak, it left me reeling.

'Oh, a nice cosy cup of coffee with my brother. What else did he suggest you do – sleep with him?' he spat.

I was totally taken aback by his sudden rage. 'Ben,' I stammered, 'what are you talking about? I've never spoken to him before today, and I didn't particularly like what I saw.'

'Don't come the innocent with me!' he shouted. 'You damn women are all the same. Cheap and nasty and utterly disloyal.' And suddenly he was shouting abuse at me. Eventually he told me I disgusted him and, with that, stalked out of the house, slamming the door behind him.

I stood in the middle of the kitchen, shocked and bewildered. It was crazy and I didn't know what to make of it. I was terribly hurt at all the awful names he'd called me. Numbly I finished putting away the shopping.

I found Mrs Travis in the garden, hanging out the washing, and asked her if she would mind attending to the boys' tea, as I was going out. She assured me it would be a pleasure.

I took myself off for a long walk by the canal. I sat down under a large oak tree, watching the gentle ripples on the surface as some unknown creature underneath disturbed the smooth glass-like appearance of the water. I don't know how long I sat there, but I suddenly realized it was dark. I made my way back to the house, hoping Ben had calmed down.

When I stepped into the kitchen, one look at his murderous expression told me he hadn't. He was standing by the Aga.

'And just where the hell have you been?' he spat, and off he went again, convinced I'd been with his brother. Or 'my boyfriend', as he put it. His behaviour was so irrational, I didn't have a clue how to deal with it. In the end I screamed back. I told him, again, that I hadn't the faintest idea what he was going on about. I told him I was sick and tired of his irrational moods. I told him that if he stopped to think about it, I hadn't even known he'd got a brother, which he'd kept hidden from me for his own reasons. So how could I be having a relationship with Matt Carmichael?

My outburst only served to make Ben more irate. His departing retort was a complete shock. Eyes blazing angrily at me, he bellowed, 'And don't come sneaking into my bed again; you can sleep in your old room for tonight. I want you out of here, first thing tomorrow morning.' And with that, he stomped out of the house. Where he was going, I had no idea.

Licking my dry lips, I digested this outburst, and slowly went upstairs to my old room. I lay down on the bed, and, burying my face in the pillow, finally gave way to tears. Now I'd lost Ben, I realized, ironically, that I really, truly loved him. In all of my twenty-seven years,

I'd never really loved anyone before. There were times I'd thought I did, but it had never hurt like this. Acknowledging this revelation did nothing for me whatsoever.

When I'd reduced myself to something ghastly enough to appear in a horror movie, I got up and had a bath and washed my hair. My head throbbed. I took two aspirins.

Going back into my old room, I picked up my two suitcases and went into Ben's room to pack all of my belongings, trying not to look at the bed where we'd shared such tender moments. This done, I parked my suitcases back into my old room and got into bed. I lay there, dry-eyed, sleep eluding me. I lost all track of time.

Somewhere downstairs, a door banged. Barely hearing it, I lay still, nibbling the end of my finger in some sort of bizarre comfort gesture. Suddenly my door opened, and Ben padded quickly across the room. I lay on my side, not moving, hoping he hadn't changed his mind about the morning and was intending to throw me out right now.

Ben, grabbing me by the shoulders, pushed me on to my back and almost fell on top of me. Putting his arms around my waist, holding me tightly, he said in a choked voice, 'Penny, I'm sorry. I'm sorry. I'm so sorry.' On and on, he repeated the words into my neck.

I sighed, wearily. It had all been too much. Never one for dramatics, I felt completely drained. I felt something wet and warm splash on to my neck and trickle down my chest. Ben, I realized, was crying.

'Please forgive me,' he said hoarsely. 'Please don't leave me.'

Finding my voice, I said, 'Perhaps an explanation is in order.'

Ben shifted himself so he was half on me, half on the bed, which my ribs were truly grateful for, I have to say. Slipping a hand underneath my body, he laid his head on my chest.

'My wife had an affair with my brother. That's why she did it, because he was my brother. She enjoyed hurting me. Humiliating me. It wasn't she who hurt me, though. It was Matt. We'd always been close. I just couldn't believe it when I found out, which incidentally was long after everyone else knew. Isn't that the way it goes, though?

'Anyway, they'd been seen together at various times, but Matt is the boys' uncle, so nobody thought anything of it for a while. But then they started to be indiscreet. Passionate kisses in full view of everybody, but she didn't care. What was the point of having an affair with my brother if I didn't get to hear about it?

'One day, I was in the town and I saw them together, kissing. When she got home, I confronted her with it, and it all came out, in graphic detail. I remember her face as she told me, malicious and mocking. She was actually enjoying herself. I threw her out, forbidding her to take the boys. Obviously I've never told them this, but she didn't seem unduly concerned about them. Couldn't wait to get to Matt at some sleazy hotel. She even rang him from here.

'Matt came to see me the next day. We had a hell of a row. I told him she could go jump, I was glad to get shot of her, and that she would bring him misery, just as she had me. I told him I would never forgive him for betraying me. We threw our fists about, until the boys interrupted us, and then Matt slammed out of the house.

'They made several attempts at trying to snatch the boys. God knows where they would have taken them. Abroad, probably. Anything to hurt me. That's why they did it, because they know how much I love my sons. She never wanted me to see them ever again.' He sighed heavily.

'Matt and Annabelle had only been together a short time when they had a car accident. They ran into a tree, head-on. Knowing her, she was probably arguing with Matt, wrecking his concentration. She died instantly, from a broken neck. She never wore a seatbelt. Matt, who always does, survived but was badly injured. Broken legs, arms, ribs, head injuries – he was a bit of a mess.'

'That would explain the scar he has on his cheek,' I said, almost to myself.

'Does he? I wouldn't know. I haven't seen him since the day he came here and we had that fight.'

'Why didn't you go and visit him in hospital?' I asked. 'He is your brother.'

'I said I would never forgive him, and I meant it.' He lifted his head, the bitterness on his face quite stark.

'Where is Annabelle buried?' I asked, curiosity getting the better of me. 'I noticed she's not in the churchyard in the town.'

Ben rubbed his cheek gently down my shoulder.

'She's buried down south, near her parents' home, where she was born. They requested it, and I didn't argue. They could do what they liked with her. I'm not ashamed to say, I hated her at the end. It's only because she's dead that I don't hate her quite so much now. Although she's still hurting me. Look at what she's done to the relationship Matt and I had. We'll never be close again.'

91

I lay there thinking that, in all fairness, Annabelle had hardly raped Matt, yet she seemed to be the sole bearer of the blame. However, Annabelle did sound an absolute bitch. Ben certainly had more staying power than I had. I'd have got rid of her years before he did.

'Ben,' I said, turning my head towards him slightly, 'you knew it was Matt who cut me up coming out of the town, and that it was him at the fête, didn't you?'

He nodded.

'Why didn't you tell me all this when I mentioned the incidents?'

'I was going to, several times. To be honest, I was embarrassed. I felt humiliated. Stupid. I kept meaning to tell you before someone else did, but I just couldn't get the right words out.'

A pity, I thought. It would have avoided all this upset now. Ben pressed himself against me, holding on to me tightly.

'Your seeing Matt today has brought it all to a head. He hates me so much, mainly from guilt, I think. He knows what he's lost, how we were together. That kind of suppressed hatred is dangerous. That's why I didn't want the boys going anywhere they didn't have to. I'm scared he'll snatch them, or worse. He seems to be making a play for you. He wants to hurt me through you. He took you for that coffee, knowing you'd ask me exactly what you did, why I didn't tell you about him, knowing I'd go mad and we'd be at each other's throats.'

'As I was walking along the canal, thinking about it all, it suddenly hit me, this was exactly what he wanted to happen and I played right into his hands,' Ben said softly.

Ben groaned, raised himself up on to his elbow and began to stroke my face. 'Penny,' he said, almost pleading, 'don't leave me. Please don't go. I know I've behaved like a prize idiot. I said some awful things to you, none of which I meant. My only excuse is that I was so scared he'd take you away from me. I love you so much. I couldn't stand to lose you.'

I looked at him. His eyes were loving and concerned. In mine he must have seen hurt and disappointment. He rolled on top of me.

'Say something.' He put his hands beside my head, touching my hair with his fingertips. His eyes jerked to the pillow. 'Penny, your pillow's wet through. You've been crying,' he said, almost accusingly.

I looked at him, as, totally beyond my control, a single large tear rolled down my cheek. Then another. Then another, until I was sobbing, helplessly. Gathering me up in a tight embrace, Ben buried his face in my neck, and murmured words of comfort, appalled at how much he'd hurt me. How long we were like that, I couldn't say. We were both trembling, violently. Finally, when I got to the sniffing stage, Ben pleaded with me again not to leave him.

'All right,' I said, feebly, 'I won't.'

The relief on Ben's face was quite blatant. He kissed me gently, and we made love so tenderly that during the course of it I told Ben I loved him. To say he was pleased was the understatement of the year.

'Tell me again,' he begged, over and over. But then Ben kept up his own running commentary the whole way through my declaration, telling me over and over how much he loved me. The thought that he'd very nearly lost me had frightened him badly. Finally, Ben suggested whimsically we have an operation that joined us at the hips, nips and lips!

When we'd finished kissing, Ben carried me to his bed, where as we lay holding each other tightly, talking softly to each other, I felt for all the upset caused by mischievous Matt. This was the closest we'd ever been.

When I awoke the following morning, Ben was already awake, gazing at me. I told him I loved him again, and kissed him. Something seemed to be bothering him. Getting out of bed, he pulled his jeans on and shot out of the room. A few seconds later he returned with my two suitcases, and, opening them, tipped them up all over the bedroom floor. Then scowling, he kicked my suitcases out of the door. I sat up, raising my eyebrows. He looked at me and grinned.

'Just in case you were thinking of doing a runner!'

I got out of bed and put on one of his shirts. Together, we put all my gear back into drawers and cupboards. During the course of our unpacking Ben found a pair of black stockings and a suspender belt, at which point he eyed me hopefully and I blushed to the roots of my hair!

We took a bath together, where, to be quite frank, not much washing got done. We used four towels, purely to mop up the water from the bathroom floor. Good job it was covered in lino. We've probably fused the light-fitting in the room below, I thought, and there'd already been quite enough explosions going on up here!

CHAPTER 8

We made our way downstairs, holding hands, and went into the kitchen. The boys were quiet and subdued. Then they caught sight of us and, glancing hopefully at each other, gave tentative grins.

Ben, in all fairness to him, apologized to his sons for shouting and being 'difficult', as he put it. Attila the Hun would have been more apt, I thought, sourly! He explained that it had been a misunderstanding between himself and me, and now it had all been sorted out. Alex hurled himself at me, throwing his arms around my waist. Stroking his hair, I said, 'I'm sorry if we frightened you, but it's all over now.'

Alex looked up at me with huge, sombre eyes. 'We thought you were going to leave us.'

'I promised you I wouldn't, do you remember?'

Alex nodded vehemently. 'Yes. I'm glad you're staying. We would have come and fetched you home anyway.'

I smiled down at him lovingly. He was such a rewarding child. I looked at Ben, who was standing between his other two sons, with an arm around each of their shoulders. All three surveyed me with quiet contentment.

After a leisurely breakfast, I asked the boys what they fancied doing that day. As they had just broken up for the school holidays, I was steeling myself for a hectic two months.

'Ride the ponies,' they chorused, predictably.

'OK,' I said, clearing the breakfast things. 'I'll just get this lot into the dishwasher, and we'll go.'

The boys and I had a very pleasant morning, galloping in the fields, alongside the canal. We rode into the woods. We tied the ponies to a tree and collected various leaves, studying their outline. We played hide and seek, and chased each other playing Tag, which, by cheating, I won most of the time. Eventually, we rode home, Harry singing nursery rhymes, Rory interrupting him with new, rude versions of his own!

We walked into the Yard, dismounted, and unsaddled the ponies. Will suggested the boys give them a bath; they could really do with one. I offered to do the horse I had been riding, as they were two hands down in the Yard: Adam and Dominic were both giving a driving tour around the quaint old villages to several tourists who had booked back in April. Will reassured me that bathing my horse would not put him out unduly.

I walked up to the house, and, stepping into the kitchen, heard raised voices coming from the study. Facing each other, Matt and Ben were having a blazing row.

'Don't think I don't know just what your game is,' spat Ben. 'Quite frankly, I didn't care that you took that vicious bitch away from me – a pity you didn't do it sooner – but Penny! You knew I'd mind like hell about losing her. I love her and you know it. Well, your nasty little game didn't quite come off, did it? I've told her all about you and Annabelle. She loves me and wants me, and nothing you can do or say will ever change that!' Ben looked his brother up and down contemptuously.

'I have to hand it you, brother,' Matt said, his voice dripping with sarcasm. 'You really fell on your feet. I mean, you have everything going for you. A beautiful, decent woman, a lovely home, a successful business and three gorgeous sons. I would love to have just any one of those things.'

'You had your chance,' Ben snapped. 'When Dad died, we inherited this place between us, and got on very well. That is until you spoilt it all, with a little help from that bitch. I've offered to buy you out several times, but your price is always too high. Isn't that the plan, though?' Ben stared at his brother, his face a mask of hatred and disgust. He went on, 'You hate me so much, you want to take it all from me, or destroy what you can't take. I know it was you who poisoned my horse!'

'I don't know what you're talking about!' bellowed Matt, his fists clenched by his sides.

'I might not be able to prove anything, but I know it was you. You're the only person I know who's sick enough to pull a stunt like that!' Ben shouted.

Matt suddenly hurled himself at Ben, knocking him to the floor. He threw his fists into Ben's face, hitting him over and over again, then into the ribs. Ben, managing to get a knee in between Matt and himself, pushed him off, hard, as Matt lay sprawled on the carpet. Ben leapt on to him, and almost in a frenzy, began to smash his fists into Matt's face.

Shooting into the study, I shouted at them to stop. When they paid absolutely no attention to me whatsoever, I knelt down on the floor next to Ben and leaned across Matt, shouting at him to stop, to think about what he was doing. Ben looked at me in a cold fury, blinked a couple of times, and finally got off his brother. They got to their feet, both bleeding from their mouths. I stood between them, shaking.

Breathing heavily, Ben glared at Matt,

'I never want to see your evil face again. I don't want you on my property ever again. Do I make myself clear?'

'This is not your damned property! Half of it belongs to me!'

'You can talk to me through my solicitor. You have his name and address. Make a sensible offer and I'll agree. Then you can do what you want, go where you like. I don't care. Just get out of my life!'

'Oh, you'll be hearing from me all right, and not through any solicitor!'

'Don't you threaten me!' shouted Ben, and lunged at Matt again.

Grabbing Ben by the shoulders, I pushed him back with what little strength I had, and yelled at Matt, 'Just go, will you!'

'Don't worry, I'm going!' he bit out, and, glaring at Ben, he turned on his heel and stormed out of the house.

Taking Ben's hand, I sat him down at his desk, and went off to fetch the first-aid-kit. When I returned to the study Ben was slumped forward, his head in his hands. Setting the box on the desk, I tipped his head back and got to work cleaning up his face. All Ben's anger had evaporated. He looked at me sadly.

'I'm sorry about that,' he said. 'He just walked in here, out of the blue. Came to gloat, I should imagine. I suppose he thought you'd have packed me in and gone.' He shot me a lopsided grin.

I stroked his face, gently soothing the bump on his eyebrow. 'I love you,' I said.

Ben took hold of my hand and kissed it.

'Can't you report him to the police?' I suggested.

Ben shook his head, and splaying my fingers out on the desk, traced the veins on the back of my hand.

'I don't have any proof, and technically he does own half of this property. Other than a court order stopping him coming within a mile of this place, there's nothing I can do.' He sighed wearily.

'Well, that's something,' I replied. Again, Ben shook his head.

'He'd only bide his time until you or the boys stepped off the property, and when it comes down to it, this place means nothing to me compared to losing you and the boys.' He paused, taking in my present state. 'You're still shaking,' he observed, accusingly.

'He frightens me, Ben. He seems to be a bit unhinged, to say the least. He's so jealous and envious and bitter. I think he knows what a terrible mistake he made with Annabelle and doesn't care much for the price tag that comes with it. I think he minds very much that he's lost your love, your trust. That's why he's lashing out, poisoning Mistral, threatening you. I just wish I knew where he draws the line.'

'He hasn't got one,' said Ben, savagely, then caught sight of the look on my face, obviously mirroring the horror I was feeling, and pulled me against him.

'Don't worry, I'll protect you and the boys.'

Clinging to Ben, I was startled by Harry and Alex barging into the room. 'Was that Uncle Matt I just saw running down the drive?' Harry enquired.

'Yes, it was,' said Ben. 'And you're not to have anything to do with him. Don't go anywhere near him. Don't talk to him and tell me or Penny immediately if you see him anywhere, whether it's here at home, in the town, anywhere.'

Harry and Alex glanced nervously at each other and swallowed, audibly.

'Dad, you're scaring me,' said Alex, twisting his fingers round and round. They couldn't take their eyes off Ben's battered face.

I got off Ben's knee and he held out his arms to Alex and Harry. They trotted into them and, picking the boys up, he plonked them both on his knee. Holding them tightly, he said, 'I'm sorry, I didn't mean to scare you. I just want you to be aware that Uncle Matt isn't quite himself lately.'

'Is he ill?' Harry asked.

Ben shifted uncomfortably in his chair. 'Yes, you could say that, but not in the usual way.'

'Do you mean it's his brains that's ill?' enquired Alex, bang-on in his usual stilted, well-observed way.

'Yes, but don't be scared. Just stay close to home, and when we're out, don't wander away from myself or Pen.'

The boys nodded solemnly at their father.

'Where's Rory? He ought to hear this.' Ben tipped the boys gently off his knee.

'Talking to Will,' said Alex, scratching his bottom.

'Right, I'll go and have a word.' Kissing me lightly on the mouth, Ben strode off down to the Yard.

He came back ten minutes later. He'd told Rory exactly what he'd said to Harry and Alex, but added that Rory, being the eldest, must try to look out for his brothers. This, I reflected, he did anyway.

I had hoped this particular incident would be the only drama of the day. It wasn't!

Dominic returned from his driving tour looking even fiercer than usual. Jumping down from his carriage, he walked round to the other side of it and proceeded to help the occupants down. All except one, a balding man with a pot belly, a wig and a broken camera. Puffing his cheeks out, he rather clumsily managed to extract himself from the carriage and, facing Dominic, began to yell at him.

'You are a disgrace. You did it on purpose, I know you did. And you've broken my camera! Where is your boss? I demand to see him!'

Dominic surveyed the man balefully. 'Right behind you, and speak up, sir, why don't you? Everyone's only catching two-thirds of what you're saying!'

The man swung round and said angrily, 'Are you the boss?'

'Yes,' replied Ben, politely. 'Ben Carmichael. How can I help you?'

The man went extremely red, and looked not unlike a fat bullfrog. 'My name is Bickerstaff. Gerald Bickerstaff. I wish to complain about your driver. He's rude, insolent, and a perfect menace. He's broken my camera!'

Ben looked at Dominic, who was leaning nonchalantly against Bodmin's shoulder, arms folded, looking bored.

'Dominic.' Ben beckoned to him. 'Let's hear your version of what happened.'

Dominic scratched the side of his face, unfolded his arms, and sauntered over to Ben and Gerald Bickerstaff.

'Well, we were trotting along quite happily, when Mr Stuffsticker . . .'

'Bickerstaff,' corrected Ben, gravely.

'That's the one.' Dominic pointed at him. 'As I said, we were trotting along quite happily, when – er – he complained the motion of the carriage was making him

101

feel sick, so I slowed down to a walk. Then, although I'd told him not to, he stood up in the carriage and started taking photographs. Well, Bodmin shied at a plastic bag, and we had "man overboard".' Dominic smiled engagingly.

'You mean, he fell out of the back of the carriage?' Ben was trying desperately hard to keep a straight face.

'With all the grace of an elephant!' said Dominic, rudely.

Ben put his hand up to his mouth and coughed several times. From where the boys and I were standing, in Bodmin's box Ben looked suspiciously like he was laughing.

'How dare you?' spluttered Mr Bickerstaff at Dominic.

'Well, that's how it looked from where I was. Anyway, I warned you not to stand up in the carriage when it was moving, whether it was to take photographs or anything else. I told you a horse is not a machine. They do have minds of their own, as Bodmin here so eloquently demonstrated. I did not do anything on purpose, and it's not my fault you flattened your own camera!'

Dominic scowled at Mr Bickerstaff, who retorted hotly, 'You see, the boy is insolent!'

Ben glanced down at his feet, resting his hands on his arms, lips twitching. With a heroic effort, he looked Mr Bickerstaff squarely in the eyes and said, 'I'm sorry, Mr Bickerstaff, but it seems my driver acted responsibly. He did warn you of the dangers of standing up in a moving vehicle.'

'Well, when was I supposed to take my photographs?' Mr Bickerstaff spat.

Dominic said, rather tartly, 'If you'd have asked me, I would have stopped the carriage, got out and held the horse's head, then she wouldn't have been able to move unexpectedly.'

This logical, reasonable answer just seemed to infuriate Mr Bickerstaff even more.

'You are an obnoxious upstart!' he screamed, his eyes bulging.

Dominic, by this time, had had enough. He looked as though he was going to land him one, but he merely said, 'Mr Constant Bickering, I can assure you it was not "pilot error", and your wig's askew!' And, with that parting shot, he turned on his heel and strode back to Bodmin.

Ben couldn't take his eyes off Mr Bickerstaff's head. Gerald Bickerstaff, realizing Ben was staring at his hairpiece, gave it a tug just above the left ear.

A plump, merry old lady with a walking stick, who introduced herself as Mrs Hooper, shuffled towards Ben and explained that Dominic wasn't really at fault, nor was the horse. Mr Bickerstaff had been argumentative and difficult the whole time, and quite frankly, he was a pompous old fool!

'And another thing!' she barked, brandishing her walking stick at Gerald Bickerstaff. 'You had the hump before we'd even got into the carriage!' Mrs Hooper explained, to howls of mirth from most of the party in her carriage, that his wig had fallen off in a swift gust of wind, and Mrs Hooper, not realizing it was a hairpiece, had beaten it to death, thinking it was a large rodent.

The whole Yard, I included, just erupted into hysterical giggles. Fortunately, the arrival of Adam with his carriage full of people calmed the situation down somewhat. Mr Bickerstaff, obviously feeling terribly silly as it was, didn't want any more of an audience, so, assuring

Ben in a loud voice that he'd never set foot in the place again, he strutted off up the drive to fetch his car. Mrs Hooper summed it up beautifully.

'Silly ass!' she said scornfully. Then, shouting happily, 'Thank you, Mr Carmichael, I've had a most enjoyable afternoon. Haven't had so much fun in years! Come along, Florrie, time to hit the bookies. If we hurry, we'll catch the three-fifteen at Haydock,' Mrs Hooper shuffled off with amazing speed, stopping briefly to give Dominic a large tip.

In a thin trickle, the rest of the party wandered off to their respective vehicles, shortly followed by Adam's group. Will told Adam what had happened to Dominic. Laughing, Adam looked at Dominic, who grudgingly smiled, then actually laughed!

'I shouldn't do that!' said Adam, sniffing. 'If you laugh, I might think you're happy!'

'Yeah, well,' said Dominic, 'it's working here that does it to me. You don't think I got this sense of humour by accident, do you?'

Adam looked at Dominic with a mixture of surprise and amusement. Dominic had shocked him, just as he had me.

'You really ought to be on the stage,' Adam remarked.

'Yeah, sweeping it!' snorted Dominic.

Adam raised his eyebrows, hardly believing what he was hearing. He and Dominic had barely exchanged this many words in all the time they'd worked together at the Yard. Adam eyed Dominic speculatively. Dominic stared steadily at Adam. Slowly their eyes wandered over each other's faces, as though actually seeing each other for the first time. Finally Adam said abruptly, 'Do you fancy a drink tonight at the Cottage?'

Dominic looked suspicious and wary. Adam hated him, he had thought.

'A drink? Er – yeah – why not?' he said, his guard dropping a millimetre.

'About seven-thirty?' Adam glanced at Will.

'Yes, fine,' replied Dominic, his gaze also transferring to Will, who smiled and nodded in agreement.

I watched them, intrigued. I was quite pleased that Adam and Dominic were speaking at last, but I also had an uneasy feeling that this would be the start of something. Good or bad, I wasn't sure.

It had been a hell of a day in one way or another, so as a little treat we had tea in the garden under one of the willow trees. It was so warm, all anybody wanted to eat were sandwiches, salad, crisps, chunks of cheese, fruit cake and glasses of lemonade. Picking at the food, Harry had found the past hour rather too lazy and, by way of bored mischief, criticized both Alex and his pony, Flicka.

'You're getting too big for him. You look like a monkey on a mangle. He's too fat as well. Wherever you stand you can still touch him.' Harry's cheeky little face creased into a toothy grin.

'Take that back!' howled Alex, and when Harry wouldn't he threw a cucumber sandwich at him, then a piece of tomato, then a spring onion, until eventually Harry retaliated and a full-scale food-fight ensued. Ben, jumping to his feet as an overripe tomato hit him, gave me a sidelong glance and chucked a piece of fruit cake at me. I seized the bottle of lemonade, shook it and squirted him with it, then ran for cover behind a rose bush. Ben sauntered over to one of the outside taps on the side of the house and, connecting the hosepipe, proceeded to water the lot of us. Finally, wet, breathless and giggling feebly, we cleared away the debris and squelched into the house.

An hour later we were all bathed and changed and sitting in the drawing room. I was listening to Harry who was reading to me. Alex, as usual, was sitting on my knee.

Rory was playing cards with his father, and sulked for the rest of the evening when Ben wouldn't let him win.

'But I'm a child!' he wailed. 'There should be allowances made.'

Ben remarked that if he didn't pipe down, he would be pocketing Rory's allowance for the next fortnight. So I had a few games with Rory, *and* made allowances, to which he responded that I hadn't even tried to win! I then played properly and he still trounced me, and then I sulked all night, instead of Rory!

Ben sighed, and told me to cheer up or I wouldn't get a chocolate bickie like the rest of the children!

CHAPTER 9

Ben suggested a day out at the Races. The day before had been so awful. In fact the past two days had been pretty traumatic; a little light relief was desperately needed. Ben was trying very hard to redeem himself with me after his 'difficult' behaviour.

The weather was absolutely glorious, warm and sunny with clear blue skies. It put us all in high spirits.

Ben drove us to the Races in his pride and joy, a Jaguar the colour of red wine. It was a beautiful car, with a grey interior, deep plush carpets, squashy leather upholstery which made the most ghastly noise when you sat on it, and a walnut-veneered dashboard. The whole car shone immaculately, inside and out. The boys occupied the vast back seat with a picnic hamper I'd prepared.

When we arrived at the Races (only a small local meeting), we parked the car in a roped-off area and made our way down a hill to the Parade Ring. As the first race was due to start in a few minutes, Ben charged off to place a bet.

The boys and I gazed at the horses walking around the parade ring. They were quite good-looking animals, all except one, which the boys couldn't stop laughing at. It was a large, dirty grey horse with huge floppy ears like a

107

lop-eared rabbit and about three hairs for a tail. His name was Merlin.

'Very apt,' remarked Ben, when he returned from placing his bet. 'It would take a magician to get him down to the start, never mind win the race!'

Within a couple of minutes the parade ring had been flooded with jockeys, a kaleidoscope of colours in their silks, talking to much bigger men mostly dressed in lightweight suits and trilby hats. The stable lads walking the horses around the parade ring brought them to a standstill and gave the jockeys a leg-up. All the horses filed out of the ring and cantered down to the start. Watching them go, I idly surveyed the sea of white bottoms, bobbing gently with each rhythmic stride. The boys, Ben and myself, made our way around the parade ring and walked further down to the bottom of the course so we had a good view of the race. The course seemed to be a huge oval in shape with several brush fences intermittently placed along the way.

The horses were now circling at the start, waiting for a man in a bowler hat, on a platform, to wave his flag. Finally, the horses lined up, and the man held his flag aloft for a few seconds then dropped it with a flourish.

The horses, eight of them, sprang forward. Ben stopped talking to Harry in the middle of a discussion about the time the boy was going to bed that night, his attention now focused on the horse he had chosen. He had backed a horse who went by the name of Friendly Henry.

The horses thundered down to the first fence, all sailed over safely, including Merlin. They cruised along at a moderate gallop, as they had to go twice round the course.

Jumping the fourth fence, one of the horses fell badly, thrashing about on the turf, badly winded. The jockey rolled away and got to his feet, unhurt. The horse struggled to *his* feet and set off in hot pursuit after the rest of the field.

The remaining seven horses completed the first circuit without incident. Merlin seemed to be thoroughly enjoying himself, clumsily throwing great dinner-plate feet out in his ungainly gait. Friendly Henry was lying in third place.

At the last fence, one of the runners fell. Ben groaned, thinking it was Friendly Henry, but it was a horse called Not Now, Dear – I suppose his trainer, and jockey for that matter, couldn't have put it better themselves! Friendly Henry seemed to be having a hard battle, neck and neck with the favourite, Southern Comfort, who had begun to flag. Great streaks of sweat appeared as white lather on his neck and along his flanks. Friendly Henry obviously had more stamina than the favourite, and belted past the winning post first.

Southern Comfort trailed in tiredly, in second place, his head bobbing with every stride. Surprisingly Merlin came in third, hardly sweating and looked like he would have gone round again if his jockey hadn't pulled him up! Ben gave a rapturous 'Yes, my son!' and hugged me tightly until I thought my ribs would crack.

'I've just won eighty-five pounds!' he said, joyously.

'Well done, Dad!' said Harry, jumping up and down excitedly.

'What are you having in the next race?' enquired Rory, thinking whatever his father had, he would too. As far as the racing game was concerned, Ben's credibility in Rory's eyes had shot up. And by the end of the next two races, it couldn't have gone much higher: his choices won both of the races. Rory nearly exploded in speechless excitement.

Collecting our winnings from the third race, we strolled back to the car. Spreading a blanket on the grass, I plonked the picnic hamper on it. The boys heartily tucked into the sandwiches I'd made for them, peanut butter and squashed banana. Ben and I had smoked salmon, which the boys hated. Fortunately I had also packed the compulsory bags of crisps, chocolate cake and lemonade. Ben, unbeknown to me, had sneaked in a bottle of champagne, hidden in a cool box in the boot.

We all sat on the grass, munching happily, gazing down the hill at the hundreds of people milling about, checking the boards of all the bookmakers for the best prices.

The loudspeaker crackled, hiccuped and announced that the fourth race would be starting shortly.

'OK, boys,' said Ben, standing up and stretching himself. 'Let's go and try to win some more money.' We packed away what was left of the food and stowed the hamper in the boot. Alex grabbed my hand, to make sure he got one of them, and, surprisingly, Rory held the other. Harry was having a ride on Ben's shoulders, peering ostentatiously down the front of ladies' dresses!

'Pack it in,' said Ben, giving Harry's leg a gentle tug.

'I was only trying to read what was on their betting slips,' lied Harry petulantly.

'A pity you're not so eager to read when it's your homework,' Ben remarked.

Harry put his hands over Ben's eyes and bit him gently on the ear. Ben very nearly cannoned off two old ladies wearing hearing aids and frosty expressions. Setting Harry down on the grass, he tickled him so much that the child's legs buckled under him; screaming with hysterical giggles, Harry shouted, 'Help! Help! Bully! Bully!'

I gave Rory a sidelong glance. Rory grinned and nodded. Charging up to Ben, we pushed him over, half on top of Harry, who was still giggling feebly, and jumped on him, squashing him. Groaning playfully, he moaned, 'Surrender! Surrender! I give in!' We gave one last nudge and then got off him.

Ben very slowly picked himself up and dusted himself down, looking at us from under his lashes. 'I shall not forget this and I will get all of you, some time, in some way, when the fancy takes me.' And with a sniff he set off down the hill. We followed him at arm's length.

Reaching the parade ring, we leaned on the rails, surveying the nine horses due to take part in the fourth race. After a brief inspection, Ben shot off to place a bet, with Rory close on his heels.

When Ben and Rory returned, the jockeys were on board and were now filing out on to the course.

'Who have you bet on?' I asked, taking Alex by the hand and steering him around a fat man with a cigar.

'Pavlova,' replied Ben, taking Harry by the hand and steering him around the man's even fatter wife.

Reaching the bottom of the course, we looked up towards the start, watching the circling horses. They all lined up. Bowler Hat was holding the flag in his outstretched hand. It held its position for a few seconds, then with a swish of his wrist they were off.

Just as the horses had done in the three previous races, they thundered down the course towards us. As they

111

drew level with us, there was a rushing, crackling sound as the turf was churned up and thrown into the brush fence. All the horses landed safely, and even though the runners were still on the first circuit they seemed to be going at a heck of a rate. Pavlova appeared to be comfortable enough in fifth place. Ben hadn't picked the favourite, who was called Holdmeup.

Nearing the end of the first circuit, things started to go badly wrong. Over on the far side of the course, one of the horses struck a fence hard and, staggering on landing, crashed headlong into the rails. The jockey found himself being flung over the horse's head and the rails, and landed on his head in a crumpled heap. The horse, on its knees, leapt to its feet and ran into the path of two horses, bringing up the rear. Both were brought down, again one of the jockeys not moving. The two horses seemed disorientated but basically unhurt, as was one of the jockeys, who, angrily flinging his whip down on the grass, stomped over to the unconscious jockey.

The horse who had been in collision with the rails went by the name of Calming Influence and, displaying everything but that, lurched into the rails on the other side of the course and rolled heavily on to his side, trembling violently.

An ambulance pulled up beside the motionless jockey who had been brought down, then crossed the course to inspect the jockey who had ridden Calming Influence. A limp lifeless body was put very gently on to a stretcher and loaded into the ambulance. It slowly made its way off the course.

Meanwhile, the rest of the field were still running the race. I realized the race would very probably be null and void, as Calming Influence was still stretched out on the course, impeding the remaining runners.

Two fences on from us a man was frantically waving a green flag, trying to get the runners to pull up, which mercifully they all did. The horses, quite tired now, slithered to a halt.

An estate car had now reached Calming Influence and two men got out and put a green screen around the horse. Presently, a loud bang rang out around the course and an uneasy silence ensued from the spectators. Calming Influence had hit his skull on the rails and had had to be destroyed.

Alex, as usual, got terribly upset. Wrapping my arms around him, I lifted him up and he placed his legs around my waist, my hands linking under his bottom. Burying his face into my neck, he wailed that he wanted to go home. I looked up at Ben, who nodded and stroked Alex's hair. Ben caught hold of Rory's and Harry's hands, and we walked back to the car.

When we reached the top of the hill, Ben asked a steward if the jockeys were OK. Apparently both had been taken to hospital, one with concussion, while for the other it was a mere formality. He had died from a broken neck.

We drove home, subdued. So much for light relief, I reflected. It had been, up until that point, a very pleasant day out. Alex was so upset, I sat with him in the back; Rory sat in the front, feeling grown-up and pleased to be next to his father.

When we got home, the answerphone's flashing red lights displayed there were two messages. The first was from my brother.

'Hi, Pen, it's John. Just calling to ask you and Ben to dinner next week. Get back to me when you can and we'll fix a date. Bye for now.' Smiling fondly, I pressed 'PLAY' again. The second message was from Sam West, the Harrises' nanny.

'Hi, Penny. I've been meaning to call you for a couple of weeks. About that date to go out to the pub? How d'you fancy the day after tomorrow? Call and let me know. Bye.'

I cleared the messages and padded into the kitchen.

'Who called?' enquired Ben, sloshing water into the kettle.

'Oh, John, and Sam West,' I replied, fishing a few chops out of the freezer.

'Sam West?' He wrinkled his brow, looking puzzled.

'The Harrises' nanny.'

'How d'you know her?' he asked, spooning coffee into two mugs.

'We met in the town a few weeks back. I think it was the first time I'd seen Loxton. I had the boys with me. I took them for lunch in the café. Sam West was there with Archie.'

'Yuk – him!' said Rory, taking his shoes off and chucking them in the corner, narrowly missing Bracken, who was having forty winks.

'I agree,' said Ben, with a disgusted look. 'I've only ever been to the Harrises' place once. Never again!' He shuddered.

'Why? What happened?' I asked, plonking myself at the table.

'It was about two years ago. Annabelle and I were invited to a barbecue there and we had a pretty good time, until Annabelle disgraced herself, then it all went horribly wrong. We ended up playing tennis on their court at one o'clock in the morning. I was so drunk, I couldn't have hit a cow's behind with a banjo. Anyway, all that running about made Annabelle ill so we got her into the house and Gwen – Mrs Harris – showed Annabelle to her bathroom. George Harris barged in on Annabelle and made a pass at her. Mrs Harris, unfortunately, didn't seem to mind. In fact, she thought this gave her the perfect opportunity to have a crack at me.'

Ben placed a mug of coffee in front of me and went on, 'She frightened the bloody life out of me. She lunged at me and knocked me flat on my back and threw herself on top of me. Then Archie appeared in Rabbit pyjamas, complete with ears, and emptied a whole bottle of wine all over me and his mother. I shall never forget his evil little cackle as long as I live. Trying to fight off Mrs Harris while her revolting son was repeatedly kicking me in the shins was seriously unfunny. Finally, I wriggled out of her clutches, ran into the bathroom, grabbed Annabelle and bolted. I won't bother mentioning how accommodating Annabelle had been to George.'

Ben looked rueful and continued, 'Pity I didn't leave her there. Anyway, for several weeks afterwards, whenever I saw Mrs Harris, she'd give me come-hither smirks and coy little waves. If I happened to wander within arm's reach, I was practically molested, so finally I had to put her straight, which she didn't like at all. She called me an idiot, said it was my loss and slapped me round the face. Annabelle in spite of the fact that she didn't want me herself, got extremely jealous, and didn't stop harping on at me about it. Things got pretty unpleasant, to say the least. As I didn't want to interrupt her in mid-flow; we didn't speak for weeks! Eventually, it all calmed down and now my relationship with Mrs Harris borders on chilly politeness.'

'You poor dear,' I said, smiling sweetly.

Ben glowered at me. 'Stop taking the mickey. That particular episode took years off me. It was like being ram-raided by a water buffalo.'

I laughed, got to my feet and parked myself on Ben's knee.

At that moment, the other two boys came wandering in and I felt a change of subject was in order, so I asked them what they fancied for tea.

'Lamb chops,' said Rory, fiddling with his toenails.

'You can't have them yet, they're not thawed out, and stop picking at your feet,' I said irritably.

'How about a take-away? It would give you a night off from cooking,' said Ben, watching Rory pruning his big toe.

'OK, you're on,' I replied, slipping off his knee. 'Let's get you lot bathed and then we can eat.'

Later in the evening, tucking into our Chinese meal, we watched a video, which bored Rory because it wasn't either violent or smutty. That boy was becoming a real worry! Were they all so terribly forward at ten years old?

Having put the boys to bed, Ben and I decided on an early night. Slipping between the cool sheets, Ben gently stroked my body. Lingering over my ribs and thighs, he mercilessly teased me, until in retaliation I teased him, licking everywhere, just ever so slightly missing the bits he wanted touched. Finally, impatiently, he pushed me on to my belly, and, lying on top of me, pinned my hands above my head. Urgent, passionate, he slipped inside me, both of us desperately needing the other. The teasing had been a little too intense. Ben reached his climax quickly, then, still inside me, he rolled me on to my side, his hand crept downwards, and with gentle but insistent pressure from his fingers, I, too, climbed the summit. Later, with my head resting on Ben's shoulder, he spoke softly against my neck, telling me how much he loved me, needed me, and that he wouldn't survive without me. Holding his hand, that was now stroking my belly, I repeated everything he'd just said to me, wanting him to know at once that I felt exactly the same. Contented and satisfied, in what seemed a matter of seconds we were asleep.

CHAPTER 10

The following morning I returned John's call, fixing a date to go to dinner. Ben was very keen to go. He wanted to get on with my brother and felt an apology was in order after John's visit the week of the fête. Ben had been extremely rude and unpleasant to him when he'd called in to see me. He admitted now that he had been lacerated with jealousy, thinking John was my boyfriend, though he felt very silly now. Looking at John and me, there was no mistaking that we were brother and sister. Ben just hadn't seen it at the time!

'Seven-thirty a week on Saturday,' I said to Ben, following him into the kitchen. 'Do you want to take the boys with us?'

'No, I think, for a change, just the two of us. Will John have anyone there?' he asked.

'More than likely!' I snorted.

I put the kettle on to boil and got two mugs out of the cupboard. Looking out of the kitchen window, I watched the boys playing with Bracken. Alex fell over his own feet. Smiling to myself, I made the coffee.

'Ben, do you mind if I go out with Sam West tomorrow night? It'll only be the local pub.'

Ben looked as if he minded very much. 'Yes, but I suppose I'll have to get used to sharing you.' His face took on a brooding expression.

Setting the drinks down on the table, I said, 'I promise I won't be late home.'

Ben nodded. 'Be careful. Matt may still be in the vicinity. I'm not saying he'll do anything, but just be aware.'

'If you'd rather I didn't go, I can put Sam off.'

Shaking his head, he said, 'No. You go. It's one thing to be aware, quite another to live your life around my brother.'

I looked at Ben steadily, smiled, and went off to phone Sam.

When I returned to the kitchen, Ben asked me to keep an eye on the boys, as he had to pop into town.

I took the boys off fishing in the canal. Three little nets dipped into the murky water. Alex was thrilled to bits with his tiddlers, as was Harry. Rory, by the look on his face, had had ideas of catching something along the lines of a Great White! Placing the tiddlers into three jam-jars we had brought with us, the boys dipped their nets again. More tiddlers, except for Harry, who had caught a beer can and a green sock.

After a while the boys decided they were bored, so we started to make tracks towards home. Passing the wood, something caught my eye and glancing round, I saw Matt watching us. My blood froze.

'Hello, Penny,' he said, and glanced at the tiddlers in the jam-jars. 'Ben and I used to catch those when we were small boys.'

'Did you?' I asked nervously.

'Yes. He seems to be getting quite a catch in other ways these days. Like you. Have I told you this before? You know, you really are very beautiful.' He smirked and put his head on one side.

'Once or twice,' I replied, embarrassed and scared, all at the same time. 'I know what you're trying to do, Matthew – '

'Matt,' he said quickly, interrupting me. 'Please call me Matt. I don't like the name Matthew. And just what am I trying to do?'

Taking a deep breath, I said, 'You're trying to get back at Ben. You're trying to hurt him through me. Why do you hate him so much? I mean, it's you who has done all the damage. You ran off with his wife. Ben didn't take anything from you, nor did he hurt you in any way.' I began to steer the boys behind me. Matt laughed scornfully.

'Afraid I might hurt them?' He looked past me at the boys.

'Frankly, yes!' I snapped. 'And you didn't answer my question!'

Matt's face grew hard. 'You stupid bitch! You don't understand anything. I didn't want Annabelle. I took her because I felt I had to. Trying to talk to Ben is like trying to talk to those tiddlers. He won't listen to me. Then I found out Ben was to have sole control over the whole property, and when Dad died, although we had joint ownership, Ben had the final say. What really finished me off is that Dad obviously thought I couldn't run the business. I wanted to borrow money and completely revamp the place, but because Ben wouldn't hear of it, nothing got done.'

'So, just because he wouldn't give the place a face-lift, you took offence. Has it occurred to you that there might be another reason for his decision? Suppose it had been

120

because Ben is the eldest and your father felt Ben should take responsibility for the property, the business, and you?' I said, trying to reason with Matt.

'And just what the hell would you know? You weren't even on the scene at the time!' he spat, moving towards me.

He stopped, just in front of me, his face inches from mine. I stared up at him, and said, almost disbelievingly, 'Are you telling me all this is about petty jealousy?'

Matt's face twisted in rage, and he grabbed me by the arms, roughly. 'No. Of course it isn't. Ben stopped me from doing anything I had in mind for that business, even down to the type of hay the horses ate. I got sick and tired of being treated like a pathetic stable boy. Ben didn't want me in the house, though God knows it's big enough! I wasn't allowed to feel like a joint owner. I wasn't allowed to help run a business or live in a house I half owned.'

I gazed at Matt, not sure what to say. Putting it like that, he had a point. Matt stared angrily back at me. I tried easing my arms free but he just put his arms around my waist, moving *my* hands behind my back. Turning my head slightly, I told the boys to go home and tell Ben where I was. The boys belted off, Rory holding his brothers' hands. Matt grinned evilly. 'Frightened, are you?' His voice was almost a caress.

It was pointless denying it. I was shaking, violently.

Matt, gripping both of my hands in one of his, entwined the fingers of his free hand into my hair, and twisted my head slightly to the side. I gazed into his eyes, which slowly wandered down to my mouth, and again, very slowly, he bent his head and kissed me.

121

Rooted to the spot, I remained as still as a statue, keeping my mouth clamped tightly shut. This annoyed him. He stopped kissing me and bit me, hard. I opened my mouth to yelp and he quickly kissed me again, pushing his tongue into my open mouth.

I prayed the boys had reached home and Ben was back from the town. It's amazing how things seem to happen in slow motion. After what seemed an awfully long time, Matt moved away from my mouth and started to kiss his way down my neck. Finally, he stopped kissing me and, looking into my eyes, said softly, 'I could quite easily fall in love with you.'

I swallowed. 'You only want me because I'm with Ben.'

Matt's face grew hard again. 'I don't blame you for thinking that, but you'd be wrong. How could any man resist you? Perhaps I should prove to you how I feel?' He glared at me, waiting for my response. I looked at my feet, then with an enormous effort I lifted my face up at him again. 'If you could love me, you couldn't possibly want to hurt me. That's all the proof I'd need.'

Matt gave me a slightly twisted smile.

'Did you honestly think I would hurt you in some way? Rape you or something?'

I quickly looked down at my feet again, not wanting him to see the blatant answer in my eyes. He yanked my head back. I know I must have looked at him with huge, frightened eyes, lips trembling.

'Hell and damnation!' he snapped. 'Just what the hell do you think I am? What's that bastard brother of mine been filling your head with?'

Violently pushing me away, he strode off into the wood.

I turned and ran. In fact, I didn't stop running until I got back to the Yard. When I got there the boys were talking to Ben in high, anxious voices. Alex caught sight of me first.

'Penny!' he cried, running towards me. Ben was across the yard in a flash.

'Penny!' Grabbing hold of me, he pushed my hair back off my face. 'Has he hurt you? Has that bastard done anything to you?' He couldn't stop touching me and stroking me, as though making sure I was real.

'I'm fine,' I muttered weakly.

Ben, seizing my hand, took me up to the house, with the boys trotting behind us.

Once in the kitchen, Ben packed the boys off to their rooms so he could talk to me without upsetting them. All three surveyed me with huge, troubled eyes. I kissed them, assuring them I was fine.

Now we were alone, Ben demanded to know what Matt had done and said. I told him. Ben walked around the kitchen three times, ranted and raved, and finally came to a halt in front of me. Looking absolutely furious, he went off into the drawing room and returned with a large glass of brandy.

'Drink this,' he ordered, kneeling down beside me.

'Ben, I'm fine, honestly,' I protested, feebly.

'Shut up and drink.' He held the glass to my lips.

Sighing, I swallowed some of the brandy, pulled a face, and said, 'Ben, I'm fine. Really. A little shaken up, perhaps, but that's all.' Putting my arms around his neck, I kissed him lightly on the mouth. Ben looked at me doubtfully.

'God help him if I ever see him again!' he spat.

'He feels hard-done-by,' I said, wondering why I was even bothering to put forward Matthew's case. Soft as butter, I thought. 'He made out to me that you ran this place as you wanted and virtually ignored him. He said he didn't feel like a joint owner, more like a stable boy.'

'Rubbish! All his ideas would have cost an absolute fortune. He wanted to give the horses the most expensive feeds, and they're hardly top-notch animals. He wanted to knock down the house and stables and rebuild. I know it could all do with a bit of attention, but that's all it needs. There is absolutely no need to gut the place and start again.'

'He mentioned that he wasn't allowed to live here, in this house.'

Ben sighed impatiently. 'Matt's living here was out of the question, with Annabelle being as man-hungry as she was. I didn't want her ruining the relationship Matt and I had. As it turned out, Matt didn't need to live here. They had an affair anyway, as you know. It appears I felt more for Matt than he did for me.'

I looked at Ben sadly and gently stroked his face.

'Poor Ben,' I murmured. 'What with Annabelle, this place, the boys, your father dying and now Matt the way he is. Got a lot on your shoulders, haven't you?'

Ben gazed at me and suddenly reminded me of Alex. Ben and Alex were the spitting image of each other, and Ben looked terribly vulnerable at that moment.

Ben called the boys to come down from their rooms. When they walked into the kitchen, Alex rushed straight over to me and parked himself on my knee. Matt had frightened him and I had a feeling Alex would be more clinging than ever. Rory and Harry were quiet, but not unduly bothered. As far as they were concerned, the incident was over.

Ben had several things to attend to in the Yard, which he did as quickly as he could. He joined the boys and myself in the garden when he'd finished, and we spent a quiet afternoon sunbathing.

Later that night, when the boys were in bed, I had a shower and went straight to bed myself. I felt completely exhausted. I'd only been in bed a couple of minutes when Ben came into the bedroom and said he was turning in as well. Getting in beside me, he said, 'Actually, I want to ask you something.'

'Well, ask away.' I snuggled up to him, nuzzling his tanned shoulder.

Ben stared at me in silence for a minute or two. Then, reaching over to his bedside cabinet, he rummaged in the drawer and handed me a small black velvet box. I looked first at the box, then at Ben.

'Open it.' Slipping an arm around my waist, he watched me closely.

Slowly, I opened the box. In it was a plain gold wedding band. I looked up at him, dumbstruck.

'Well,' he said softly, 'will you marry me?'

I blinked twice, said yes, laughed, sniffed and burst into tears. Holding me tightly, he told me he'd never been so happy.

'Ben, are you sure?' I asked doubtfully, wiping tears away on the back of my hand. 'I mean, you didn't want to be married the first time round, and you had such a rotten time.'

'You're not Annabelle, and you're right, I didn't want to get married. Not just to Annabelle, but to anyone. I love you so much, Pen, and I want you with me always. I've never been so sure about anyone or anything in my life.'

125

Gently he ran a shaking finger down my face, and smiled.

'How long have you had the ring?' I asked, pushing it around the palm of my hand.

'When I said I had to pop into town earlier today, that's what I went to buy. I've been wanting to propose since the first week you came here.'

I looked at Ben, wide-eyed in surprise. 'You were that sure, having only known me a matter of days?'

'Funnily enough, yes, I was. I'll say one thing for being married to Annabelle, I can spot a fake a mile off. I've become very adept at judging characters and yours is as beautiful as your face. I realize we've only known each other a few weeks now, but the thought of not having you near me scares the life out of me. You've completely bowled me over. If you'd *deliberately* set your cap at me, I'd have been a blithering wreck by now!' He grinned, and pushed me on to my back.

Taking the ring out of my hand, he slipped it on to my finger. It fitted extremely well. Ben was so pleased that I'd agreed to marry him. He'd clearly had his doubts that I would which I found very touching. He was all for waking the boys and telling them there and then, and it took all my powers of persuasion to get him to leave it until the morning.

'You make a date for the wedding,' he said, half lying on top of me. 'But don't make me wait too long, Mrs Carmichael.'

I sniffed. 'I may change my mind. Woman's prerogative and all that.'

Ben pinched me gently and said he'd feed me tranquillizers, take me to the church semi-comatose and work me with his foot! I laughed, then yawned. Seeing how tired I was, Ben pulled me against him, leaving the ring still on my finger. He wrapped his arms and legs around me until he thought we were sufficiently entangled, as usual, then we drifted off to sleep.

We were abruptly woken around midnight. Someone was hammering on the kitchen door. Ben and I, having woken up with a start, fumbled for our clothes, groggily trying to get our limbs to function. We tore downstairs to the kitchen to find Dominic frantically trying to beat the door down. Ben wrenched it open and Dominic practically fell in.

'What's the matter?' Ben asked, grabbing his arm.

Dominic, desperately trying to speak even though he was out of breath, finally gasped, 'The Yard. It's on fire!'

Ben shot off with Dominic down the drive to the Yard. I bolted to the telephone and rang the fire brigade, then pulled on a pair of boots and ran down the drive after them.

When I got there, Dominic and Ben were desperately trying to get several horses out of their boxes. Realizing they weren't going to get anywhere at this rate, Ben ran into the tack room, which he had to unlock first, all the while aware that the fire was spreading rapidly, and grabbed several cleaning rags. Bolting out of the tack room, Ben plunged the rags into the water trough and, handing a couple to Dominic, shouted above the roar of the fire, 'Tie these over their eyes. If they can't see the fire they might come out.'

Ben and Dominic shot back into the stables, Ben tying the rags over Bodmin's eyes and Dominic doing the same to Lurch. They finally coaxed them out and handed the reins of the two terrified, trembling horses to me. Whipping the rags off their eyes, Ben and Dominic disappeared into the smoky depths of the boxes again. After what seemed like forever to me, Ben emerged leading Pennine. Dominic still hadn't come out. He was trying to coax a horse called Winston to safety. A terrible crashing of timbers filled the air and, stumbling, coughing and spluttering, eyes streaming, Dominic mercifully appeared through the smoke, bringing Winston with him. Pennine and Winston, rearing in terror, were sweating profusely, their hind quarters thrashing about as they barged into each other. Bodmin and Lurch, being somewhat older, just stood and shook. A fire engine sped into the Yard, sirens blaring, lights flashing, which did absolutely nothing to calm the terrified horses. Pennine, being so young, lashed out at a fireman, making him dive for cover.

Turning the hose on to the blazing stable block, the firemen got to work, but sadly, not before the building collapsed completely, burying the two horses that Ben and Dominic had not been able to save. Their screams were something I shall never forget, nor the awful smell of burning flesh. Ben, stumbling over to Dominic, put his hand on the lad's back. Dominic was bent double, coughing and trying to get fresh air into his lungs. Finally, he straightened up and, looking not unlike a chimney sweep, surveyed the burning rubble. Turning to face Ben, he croaked, 'I'm sorry. There just wasn't enough time.'

Ben put a hand on Dominic's head and rubbed it affectionately. 'Dominic, we did our best. We got four of the six out. Don't feel too badly.'

Breathing heavily, Dominic started another coughing fit.

A car sped into the Yard and braked, sharply. Adam and Will virtually fell out of it. Will shot over to Dominic, gibbering at him about smoke inhalation, asking him if he was hurt anywhere.

'Stop fussing, will you?' snapped Dominic. 'I've had stronger cigars!'

Adam and Will just stood and stared at the burnt out mess that was once a hay store and stable block.

Ben thanked Dominic for his help, saying that without him he wouldn't have been able to save as many horses as they had.

'But what were you doing here at this time of night?' asked Ben, rubbing a hand over his face and streaking it further with soot, so that he looked as if he was wearing warpaint.

Dominic looked evasive and shifty and didn't quite meet Ben's eyes.

'I was on my way home. I'd been to see someone. As I rode past, I could see an orange glow coming from the Yard, so I stopped, and that's when I saw the fire.'

Dominic ran a hand through his hair, which stuck up like a punk rocker's, stiff with soot. Adam wandered over to join Will, who was gazing openly at Dominic. Ben was talking to a fireman. I was standing nearby, still holding the horses.

'How come you're here anyway?' asked Dominic, looking at Adam.

'You can see the fire from the cottage. The sky was glowing red. We couldn't make it out to start with. Then we saw the fire engine, and realized what it was.' Adam wrinkled his nose at the drifting smoke.

The fire had now been put out, and, walking the horses over to the little paddock, Ben checked them all for any

129

signs of injuries. Pennine had a slight cut on his hock, nothing serious. The rest, apart from being shocked and shaken, were fine. Ben tethered the horses in the little paddock with the Thelwells. At least by tethering them they couldn't gorge themselves on the rich grass. All four of the horses were hard at work this time of the year, and bloated bellies were not a good idea. One of the driving horses off with colic was all we needed.

Adam and Will went home, and Ben, Dominic and I plodded wearily up to the house. We all had a stiff drink. Ben sat slumped at the kitchen table. Nobody, it seemed, knew what to say. Looking at Ben's face, which was set in rigid lines, I glanced at Dominic. He must have seen something in my face because he looked as if he was going to say something, then wisely decided against it. Finishing his drink, he said he'd be off.

Ben looked up sharply, 'No, you don't have to. You can stay here if you like.'

Dominic shifted uncomfortably and said he hadn't got any clean clothes here, so perhaps he'd best go home. Ben shrugged and said it was up to him. Dominic looked at me steadily, trying to read what was in my face.

'Well, er – I'll be off, then. Thanks for the drink,' he said, heading for the door.

'Dominic,' said Ben abruptly.

Dominic turned to face Ben.

'Thanks, you were great. Take the day off tomorrow. You've done quite enough for one day.'

Dominic nodded and walked off into the night.

The door that led off the kitchen into the hall was slowly pushed open, and Harry, Alex and Rory wandered in, rubbing their eyes.

'What's going on?' asked Rory sleepily, giving his pyjama bottoms a tug.

Ben glanced at me, hesitating, wondering what to say.

'There's been an accident,' I said, far more calmly than I felt. 'The hay store caught fire. It's quite badly damaged, but - er - nobody was hurt.' I took a hefty belt of my drink, thinking to myself that badly damaged was slightly economical with the truth. There wasn't anything of it left standing.

Alex and Harry crossed the room and both of them got on my knee, complete with teddy bears. Harry couldn't take his eyes off Ben's sooty face and general grimy appearance. Rory helped himself, and his two brothers, to a glass of milk. Once they'd drunk them, I took them off to bed.

Rory and Alex drifted off to sleep almost immediately. Harry, surprisingly, seemed restless and uneasy, so I told him a story, the first one that came into my head, about the princess and the pea under her mattress. This didn't work. All Harry said was he'd had a pee in his mattress once and Dad had told him off!

Sighing, I picked him up, and his teddy bear, and took them off to our room. Plonking him in the middle of the bed, I went into the bathroom where Ben had just finished his shower. I explained about Harry. Ben was not very pleased. He didn't want the boys encouraged into thinking they could come in with us when they couldn't sleep.

'We'll probably have three raging insomniacs in with us every night from now on!'

He was right, of course, but I was just too tired to care at that point.

I showered, washing off the sooty smoke and put on one of Ben's shirts. I didn't usually wear anything, but with Harry in the bed I felt I should. Ben always slept in the raw also, and having Harry in our bed made not the slightest difference to him.

Ben hadn't mentioned Matt at all. I found this more disturbing than if he'd ranted and raved all night.

Slipping into bed, Ben put his arm around my waist, with Harry lying between us. Harry snuggled up to me. Ben inherited the teddy bear. Lying quietly in the darkness, Harry fell asleep virtually straight away. I lay awake for a long, long time. And, although I couldn't see him, I knew that Ben did too.

CHAPTER 11

Over breakfast the next morning – though it was more like brunch by the time we all got up – bickering broke out, as Alex became aware that Harry had spent the night in our bed. Harry took great pleasure in rubbing Alex's nose in it.

'If you all don't stop whingeing,' Ben yelled, throwing his paper down, 'you'll all sleep in the blasted garden tonight!'

Alex sulked all morning, as did I, when Ben ticked me off for bringing Harry into our bed in the first place.

'By the way, you'd better keep this,' I said tartly, and slipped the wedding ring off my finger and put it into his hand.

Ben glowered at me. 'I hope this doesn't mean you've changed your mind? Your prerogative and all that.'

'Actually, no, I haven't, but it's supposed to be bad luck. I'm not married yet, and anyway, how could I possibly change my mind about marrying such a patient, kind, understanding man?' I smiled sweetly. Ben shot me a filthy look.

Ignoring it, I said ruefully, 'I suppose I'd better phone Sam West and cancel that drink tonight.'

'You don't have to do that.' His face softened slightly. 'You go out and enjoy yourself; just keep your eyes open.

You should be be safe enough in the pub – too many people about for Matt to do anything silly. He doesn't want any witnesses. Don't take your car, though. I'm not risking you breaking down on the way home. Get a taxi there and back.'

It won't be the car breaking down at this rate, I thought. I looked at Ben miserably.

'You don't want to go?' he asked.

'Yes, I do,' I replied. 'I'm just fed up, scared, annoyed and irritated. I've just about had enough of our Matt. We're all having to look over our shoulders all the time, and be careful where we go. He's getting on my nerves.'

I looked out of the window, brooding. Ben came over to me and put his arm around my shoulders. Kissing me on my cheek, he said, 'I know, he's seriously getting me down as well, but rest assured, I will sort it out.'

I looked up at him, slightly disturbed. I didn't like his tone.

'Right, I've got a couple of calls to make.' Letting me go, he crossed the kitchen and went into the drawing room to telephone the vet about the horses, and then a local firm of builders.

When he had finished on the phone, he came back into the kitchen and informed me that they'd both be here by the afternoon. Standing in the doorway, he eyed me reflectively, then crossed the kitchen, knelt down in front of me and took one of my hands.

'Pen, I know I've been snapping at you. I'm sorry. As I said, all this business is getting me down. Still, that's no excuse to take it out on you. I just feel so helpless. Matt knows it's no use my calling the police in, as there's no evidence that it's him. He'll have made sure of that. If I could just have five minutes alone with him . . .'

His face was a mask of hatred and revenge. Sighing heavily, he smiled at me briefly. 'We still have some news to give to the boys.'

I frowned. 'Ben, are you sure we can afford to get married? I mean, we can wait. It doesn't have to be right now.'

'Having second thoughts, are we?' he said, a tad sourly.

'No, I'm not. I've already told you that. I'm trying to help. It'll cost a fortune to rebuild that stable block. I just don't want to add to the burden.' Sometimes, I couldn't do right for doing wrong, I thought crossly.

'Penny, you are never a burden. There is the insurance, though whether they'll pay out or not is another matter. I suppose we'll have the fire investigators here if I do put in a claim. Not that they'll find anything connected to Matt, I can assure you. Anyway, I know a guy in town where I can buy cheap materials to rebuild the stable block. So, let's go and tell the boys the good news. I'm not postponing marrying you – you really might change your mind, and I want you in a position where you can't.' He grinned.

I laughed, and, holding hands, we walked outside into the garden where the boys were playing football, and told them we were getting married.

Three huge grins met this piece of news, and Alex was beside himself.

'This means you'll have to stay forever now,' he said triumphantly.

'Yes, I suppose it does,' I replied, giving Ben a sidelong glance and thinking to myself, like father, like son. Ben grinned unashamedly back at me.

The boys said they wanted to see the damage to the stable block. Why did little boys have such a macabre interest in death and destruction? I wondered.

'All right,' Ben agreed. 'But don't go in, it's unsafe.'

We all tramped down to the Yard. Will, Adam and Mark were having a coffee break, having mucked out and fed the horses. Finn seemed to have disappeared. Much to our surprise, Dominic walked out of the tack room, carrying the grooming kit.

'I thought I told you to take the day off,' said Ben, as Dominic disappeared into a box to start on one of the horses.

'I didn't want to,' said Dominic, peering over the stable door at him.

'Well, suit yourself.' He shrugged. 'How do you feel?'

'Fine,' said Dominic, uncomfortable at all the attention he was getting.

'What's that smell?' asked Harry, clapping a hand over his nose and mouth.

Ben's eyes flickered towards me, then back to his son.

'It's all that water on the hot ashes,' he said, lamely.

This explanation seemed to pacify the boys. Ben instructed Will and Adam to swap over some of the riding school horses.

'Put these in the paddock, and those already in the paddock in their boxes. I don't want the driving lot stuffing themselves with extra food.'

I noticed that Ben had been very careful not to say how many horses there were. Still, it wouldn't be long before the boys realized we were two horses down.

In the afternoon, I took the boys into town. I had some shopping to do anyway. I felt it was a good idea to have the boys out of the way when the two horses' charred bodies were taken away. Ben agreed with me, there was no need to upset the boys unnecessarily.

Once in the town, I felt horribly uneasy. It was like having a rogue elephant out there and not knowing when he was going to attack. We charged around the town at breakneck speed, and I was looking around me all the time, but we returned home safe and sound. Thankfully, the two dead horses had gone.

There was now a builder bending down rummaging in the debris. Taking several measurements, he had a quick discussion with Ben, and said he'd phone him tomorrow morning with his estimate.

When the builder left, Ben came up to the house and asked casually if we'd had any problems. I assured him we hadn't.

I spent the rest of the day getting the boys interested in painting and trying to distract them from asking awkward questions. Surprisingly, 'art' captured their attention for several hours. Harry painted a horse, Alex painted a willow tree, and Rory painted a bacon sandwich and a chocolate bar! He was hungry, he said.

We cleared away the watercolours, and the boys washed their mucky hands while I cooked our tea. We had the lamb chops I'd got out of the freezer yesterday. It was Rory's favourite, except for the vegetables. Ben was adamant they eat vegetables. Harry and Alex didn't have a problem with this; however, Rory hated them, so he devised a way of getting them down. He would pour himself a glass of orange juice, and, swallowing his sprouts or whatever veg we had, would quickly follow it with a large mouthful of juice, rather like taking a tablet. Ben found this a constant source of amusement.

Ben kept the boys occupied in the evening, trying to teach them how to play chess, while I showered and got ready to go out.

When I walked into the drawing room, where they were all congregated, Rory wolf-whistled at me, while Ben just stared.

'You look nice,' he said.

'Thank you.' I was only casually dressed in trousers and a shirt, and felt enormous relief that Ben was so easily pleased.

'Right, you lot,' I said, giving the boys a kiss, 'I'll see you in the morning.' Crossing the room, I kissed Ben quite hard on the mouth. 'I'll see *you* later! I won't be late.'

'Don't you dare say, "And don't wait up, dear!"' he drawled, shooting me a dark look.

A horn was hooting outside.

'That'll be my taxi.' I waved and headed for the door.

'Take care,' said Ben. 'And have a good time.' I smiled and nodded, then trotted out to the waiting car.

As Loxton was only about a mile away from the Yard, within minutes I was sitting in the pub with a large gin and tonic.

Sam was already there when I arrived, and we were soon idly chatting about the general goings-on of the townsfolk. She was blissfully easy to talk to, and very sweet.

I told her about the fire.

'God, how awful,' she said, biting her lip. 'Did one of the tourists drop a cigarette or something?' Intrigued, she took a hearty mouthful of wine.

'I expect so,' I murmured, not wanting to talk to her about Matt. As it all seemed hardly believable to me, someone on the outside could hardly be expected to understand.

'Anyway,' I smiled brightly, trying to distract her, 'I do have some *good* news.'

'What?' she asked, leaning forward impatiently.

I took a deep breath. 'Ben and I are getting married.' Her face slowly creased into a radiant smile.

'Penny, that's marvellous. Oh, you are so lucky. He's absolutely gorgeous. You've only known each other a short time. How romantic! Love at first sight!' She gazed wistfully at the far wall, then, sighing, she looked back at me. 'When did he ask you?'

'Last night,' I replied, thinking it was nothing of the sort.

'Am I the first to know?' Rummaging in her bag, she produced a dog-eared purse.

'Yes. Obviously the boys know, but, come to think of it, we haven't even told the lads in the Yard yet.' I frowned, making a mental note to tell them. I supposed they'd like to know.

'How did the boys take it?' Curiosity burned in her eyes.

'Thrilled to bits, fortunately,' I said, knowing I sounded relieved.

She grinned. 'Same again?' Pointing to my empty glass, she didn't bother waiting for an answer, and with indecent haste charged at the bar and brought us two more drinks. She'd only just sat down again when Dominic and Finn walked into the pub.

Dominic got himself a beer, and came over to our table. Finn went and sat down by the door, and began talking to a man already sitting there.

'Hi, Pen, mind if I join you?' asked Dominic.

'No, take a pew,' I said, pushing a chair in his direction.

Sam was gazing openly at him, practically drooling. I smiled into my drink.

'Dominic, do you know Sam?' I asked, nodding at her.

Dominic swivelled his large dark eyes in Sam's direction. 'No, can't say as I do.' Taking a sip of beer, he left a white foam moustache on his top lip.

Sam virtually shook herself, and said faintly, 'I'm Sam West. I work for the Harrises.'

'Oh? What do you do?' enquired Dominic, having a stab at being polite.

'I'm their nanny.'

'Are we meaning Archie here, or his parents?'

Sam giggled. 'Both!'

Dominic didn't seem to be aware of the effect he was having on Sam. He was one of those beauties who, adorably, didn't know he *was* beautiful.

Turning back to me, he said, 'How's Ben? About the fire, I mean. Has he any idea what started it?'

'One or two.' Catching sight of the interest on Sam's face, I quickly added, 'I have some news you might like to hear.'

'Oh, what's that?'

'Ben and Penny are getting married!' interrupted Sam, excitedly.

Dominic raised his eyebrows. 'Really? Since when?'

'Since last night.' I went pink and took to rattling the ice in my drink, for something to do.

'Good on yer!' He shot me a rare smile. Then Dominic's eyes slid past mine and the smile was suddenly wiped off his face. He was watching two people who had just come into the pub.

140

Turning my head, I saw Adam and Will saunter over to the bar and order two beers. Dominic had gone very still. I studied him with interest. He caught me staring at him, and hastily took a swig of his beer.

Adam and Will were glancing casually around the pub. Their eyes caught mine and, nodding in recognition, they picked up their drinks and made their way over to us.

'I think I've died and gone to heaven!' sighed Sam rapturously.

I laughed, I could see her point. Being surrounded by three dark beauties was every girl's dream! A pity she didn't know that dreams were all they were.

Dominic surveyed her sourly.

Will and Adam sat down, and Sam told them about Ben and myself.

'That's great news,' said Adam, grinning. 'You look good together.'

'All the best to you.' Will raised his glass to me.

'Thank you.' I smiled. 'Anyone for a refill?'

'Yes, please,' said Sam, thrusting her drained glass under my nose.

I looked at Dominic enquiringly. 'Er – yeah, thanks,' he said, suddenly looking grumpy.

Picking my bag up off the floor, I went to the bar and ordered another round of drinks. Fishing my purse out of my bag, I paid for the drinks and carried them back to the table, wondering what had ruffled Dominic's feathers.

Adam and Sam were by now deep in conversation. Dominic was studiously ignoring Will, who looked thoroughly miserable.

'Will, are you OK?' I asked, setting the drinks down on the table.

141

'Fine,' he replied, forcing a smile.

'Excuse me,' Dominic suddenly announced and, glancing at Will, strode off towards the gents.

'I could do with some air,' said Will, sidling off towards the door. 'I don't feel that well.'

Adam looked up sharply, cutting Sam off in mid-flow. 'Will, what's wrong?' he asked, obviously concerned.

'It's just so hot. I'm fine, really. I just need to cool down. I won't be long.' And with that he shot out of the door.

'Well, I could do with a break, too,' I said, getting to my feet. 'I won't be long.'

Once in the lavatory, I heard voices outside the window. They were instantly recognisable to me as Dominic and Will.

Feeling horribly guilty, I put the lid down on the loo and stood on it, peering out of the slightly open window.

'Stop being so nasty to me,' Will was saying quietly, looking close to tears. 'It's not my fault, I just couldn't get out.'

'You would have managed it somehow, if you had really wanted to,' snapped Dominic.

'What was I supposed to say? I never go out without him. I've had an awful job getting out to see you. He must think I've taken up fishing, the number of times I've been down to that canal!'

'Oh, for heaven's sake! He's not your keeper. Just tell him you're going out!'

'I can't go out on my own too often, he'll get suspicious. You know what he's like.' Will glanced around anxiously.

Dominic ran a hand through his hair in irritation. Suddenly grabbing Will by the arms, he pushed him against the wall, and hugged him fiercely. Will, curling his fingers into Dominic's hair, hugged him back equally hard. Finally, taking a deep breath, Dominic said, 'I want you all the time. You've no idea what it's like, watching you with Adam. Not being able to touch you, or kiss you. You just think how you would feel, watching me with someone else.'

Will looked as if he would rather not.

'Will, I love you. When are you going to leave him? When can we finally be together?'

Dominic was almost pleading with Will. Will kissed him lightly.

'Soon. We'll be together very soon. Let me tell him in my own good time. I don't want to hurt him, he doesn't deserve it.'

Dominic sighed impatiently. 'And me, what do I deserve? You're not being fair to either of us.'

'You weren't so interested in being fair when we were alone together in his house,' snapped Will.

Dominic's face twisted with rage, and, bringing his hand back, he slapped Will none too gently across the face. Taken off balance, Will fell to the ground.

It had happened so suddenly, it made me flinch, and I very nearly fell off my precarious perch.

Dominic wrenched Will to his feet and held him tightly, apologizing profusely for hitting him.

'No, I'm sorry,' Will said, rubbing his eyes with the back of his hand. 'I shouldn't have said that. You're right, I'm not being fair. I'll talk to him tonight.'

Dominic gazed at him, and took hold of his hands.

'Just be sure which one of us you want. I don't want to lose you three weeks after I've found you, because you suddenly realize you're still in love with Adam.'

Will shook his head. 'I've made my choice.'

As he slipped his arms around Dominic's neck, I realized I couldn't watch any more because I was getting cramp from standing so awkwardly. At least this explained Will's blatant show of concern towards Dominic during the fire.

What had happened, I wondered, between now and the night of the barbecue, when Will and Adam had seemed so happy?

I now understood the comments Dominic had made that night, when Ben had asked him what he was doing near the stables. He'd been to see Will.

I was just about to return to the bar, realizing that Sam must have thought I'd been kidnapped by now, when Adam appeared round the corner of the wall, no doubt thinking Will was sicker than he'd let on, judging by the length of time he had been outside.

Adam stopped dead in his tracks and stared at Will and Dominic, embracing passionately.

My stomach dropped to my feet, and rolled into the next cubicle. I scrabbled down from my perch and belted out of the pub, nervously anticipating a punch-up.

When I got outside, Adam was demanding to know just what the hell Will thought he was doing.

'And how long has this been going on?' he spat, glaring at Will.

'Since the week of the barbecue,' mumbled Will, looking at his feet.

'And to think I invited that bastard to the cottage for a drink, thinking perhaps I'd bury the hatchet. Well, I know where I'd like to bury it now!' snarled Adam.

'I was going to talk to you tonight.' Will wrapped his arms around his body as though trying to comfort himself.

'Don't bother,' snapped Adam. 'I think I've got the message. As far as the cottage is concerned, you can pack your things and clear off. I'm not moving out, why should I? You're the one who's mucked up, no pun intended, so you can find somewhere else to live! I'm sure,' he hissed, glowering at Dominic, 'you and lover-boy here can find somewhere. I mean, you can't live with Finn and Mark any more, can you, Dominic? Just like Will and myself, we can't have our little secrets getting out.' He smirked nastily.

Adam and Dominic glared at each other.

Finally, Will said, 'I'm sorry, Adam, I really didn't want you to find out like this.'

'Oh, how touching. Were you really going to tell me tonight? Or were you hoping to avoid any unpleasantness, and just let me catch you at it?'

Will winced. 'Adam, I know you're angry and upset, but please believe me, I didn't want to hurt you.'

Adam, because he *was* hurt, just became more vicious.

'Don't worry, I'm glad I know now. It turns my stomach to think I've been living, with you, when you've been with *that*.' He shot a contemptuous look at Dominic. 'I wouldn't want you now if you paid me.' Adam then called Will disgusting and any other insulting names he could think of.

Will swallowed, and nervously bit his lip.

'That's enough!' snapped Dominic, putting his arm around Will.

'And you can shut up!' roared Adam. 'You cheating bastard!'

Will looked up at Dominic. 'Where am I supposed to sleep tonight?'

'Perhaps I can help,' I said quietly, behind them.

Startled, all three of them spun round.

'Will can come and stay at the Yard, in the house. I'm sure Ben wouldn't mind for a while.'

Dominic glared at Will, terrified their secret was out.

'She's known for a while about me and Adam,' Will explained. 'And she hasn't told a soul. Our secret's safe enough with her.'

'It won't be a secret for much longer, if you don't stop arguing outside the pub,' I reminded them.

Adam looked back at Will. 'You can stop by the cottage tomorrow and collect your things. I want rid of you as soon as possible.' And, turning on his heel, he strode off to his car.

Wrenching open the door, he got in and sped off into the night.

Dominic put his arm around Will's shoulders. 'You go with Pen. I'll find us somewhere to live in the next few days. Do you want me to come with you tomorrow, to the cottage?'

Will shook his head. 'No,' he said wearily. 'Adam won't be awkward, that's not his way.'

I left them briefly, to go into the pub and phone for a taxi.

Apologizing to Sam, who was standing at the bar talking to a group of her friends, I said I was feeling unwell and Will was very kindly taking me home.

I picked my bag up off the floor and said I'd wait outside for the taxi.

'I'm sorry you're not well,' said Sam, looking at my stomach and clearly thinking I must be pregnant.

I smiled to myself, and asked if I could drop her anywhere.

'No, it's all right, thanks, Pen. One of my mates'll take me home.' Apologizing again, I said goodnight, and walked out of the pub into the cool night air. Will and Dominic were at least being a little more discreet, and were now standing two feet apart.

Within a couple of minutes, the taxi had arrived. We dropped Dominic off on the way, as he'd left his motorbike at home, and as he got out, he looked at me.

'What'll you tell Ben?'

I shrugged my shoulders. 'I'll sort something out,' I replied.

Nodding, Dominic strode off towards the house he shared with Finn and Mark, giving us a wave as he went up the path.

Reaching the Yard, I paid for the taxi and led Will into the house.

Ben was in the kitchen, making himself a drink. The boys were in bed.

'Hello, you're back early,' he said, glancing at Will, mildly surprised.

'I did say I wouldn't be late.' And, padding over to him, I kissed him lightly. 'Ben, would you mind if Will stayed here for a few days?'

Ben looked at Will and shrugged.

'No, I suppose not. But what about the cottage?'

'Er – Will and Adam have had words,' I muttered, plonking my bag down on the table. 'They're not even speaking at the moment, so Will's moving out, but he needs a few days to find somewhere else to live.'

Will stood by the door, looking uncomfortable and miserable.

Ben eyed him steadily, not making him feel any easier. Finally, he said, 'I'll show you to your room.'

Mumbling his thanks, Will followed Ben upstairs.

Two minutes later, Ben was back in the kitchen. I sat at the table, drinking a large mug of coffee.

'OK. What's going on?' Folding his arms, he fixed me with a beady stare.

I looked at him under my lashes. 'How broad-minded are you?'

Ben coughed. 'Two of my stable lads are gay, is that broad-minded enough for you?'

My head snapped up, and I looked at him, open-mouthed. He smiled at me gently.

'How long have you known?' I asked.

'Quite a while, actually,' he said, watching me with amusement. 'I saw Will and Adam kissing in one of the boxes, oh, about six months ago. I must admit, they shocked me a little. I never let on I knew – none of my business. It had no effect on their work, and I personally don't have a problem with gay people.'

Getting to my feet, I crossed the kitchen and put my arms around Ben.

'I didn't know whether to tell you or not. I didn't want anyone losing their jobs.' I felt like a traitor; I should have told him.

'Well, don't keep any secrets from me in future; I'm not that bad, you know. And anyway, I want us to be able to say anything and everything to each other. I don't want to be shut out, not from you.' Gently nipping me on the neck, he asked, 'When did *you* find out, anyway?'

'It was at their barbecue. I went into the cottage and literally bumped into them. They were kissing. It didn't particularly shock me, as I already had my suspicions about Will.'

'So why are Will and Adam splitting up? What's happened?'

Ben slipped his hands under my shirt and began kneading my back with his long fingers.

'Dominic and Will are having an affair, and Adam found out. Tonight, at the pub, Adam caught them together and it was clear what was going on. He's told Will to collect his things from the cottage tomorrow. Dominic's going "house-hunting". He's still living with Finn and Mark, who don't realize Dominic is gay.'

Ben blinked. 'Neither did I.'

'I sort of guessed he was. I noticed him gazing at Will quite a lot. That's why he always seemed bad-tempered. He was desperately unhappy, watching Will with Adam. He was jealous, that's why he's always hated Adam. I don't suppose Adam particularly likes Dominic now. Lord knows how Dominic finally got around to doing something about asking Will out.'

Ben raised his eyebrows. 'Well, I have to admit, I didn't notice. I just thought Dominic was moody and bad-tempered, even though he's a bloody good horseman.'

'What bothers me is what happens now?'

'What do you mean?' he asked, looking lost.

'Well, how are they all going to get on in the Yard, working together?'

Ben grimaced. 'Perhaps one of them will decide to leave. I don't want to lose any of them, though, they're all good lads. Oh, damn it,' he said irritably. 'Why, when things blow up, do they land *me* in trouble!'

I snorted. 'That's Sod's Law.'

'No, it isn't,' he said crossly. 'That's Ben's Law.' Then he sighed resignedly. 'We'll just have to wait and see how it all turns out.'

I nodded and asked him if he'd had any problems getting the boys to bed.

'No, they know they can't get away with anything where I'm concerned.' He scowled at me.

I laid my head on his chest, and very slowly, very gently, reached up and kissed him in a comical, grovelling way.

Ben laughed, and, murmuring that he still had to get me back for knocking him over at the races, chased me upstairs to our room.

I was sure I heard muffled sobbing coming from the spare room.

Why was human nature so fickle? I wondered sadly. I suppose we would now have *three* moody, bad-tempered lads about the Yard.

CHAPTER 12

Leaving the boys with Mrs Travis, I wandered down to the Yard to see if Dominic or Adam had showed up for work. If they hadn't, I would have to step in; it would be terribly unfair to expect Mark, Finn and Will to manage all the work on their own. Dominic and Adam, however, were mucking out as usual. I decided to hang around for a while, to see how they got on.

I had kept the boys out of the way, just in case there was any awkwardness. I didn't want them seeing Dominic and Adam bashing each other's brains out. Children, being quite shrewd creatures by nature, would be inclined to ask probing questions.

I went and sat in the tack room. Noticing a rather grubby bridle hanging on a nail, I decided to clean it.

Ben had gone into town to see a chap he knew about some wood, and other raw materials. The builder had phoned that morning with his estimate, and when Ben had heard what he was going to charge, he'd nearly fainted, and decided that he would pay the builder for putting up the new hay store and stable block, but that he'd see to the building materials he needed himself. He would have preferred to do it *all* himself, I knew, but with so much to do in the Yard he just hadn't the time.

After feeding and mucking out the horses, the lads had their coffee break as usual. Will came and sat with me in the tack room.

'How are you?' I asked.

'All right,' said Will unconvincingly, and stared down at his feet. I looked at him steadily. Although he'd slept in the house last night, this was the first chance I'd had to ask him; he'd let himself out of the house before any of us were even up.

Finally, I said, 'You don't honestly expect me to believe that, do you?'

Sighing, he raised his head, and looked at me with huge sad eyes, which were red from crying. He looked exhausted, and had obviously been sobbing his heart out all night.

'I couldn't stop thinking about Adam, all alone in the cottage. It must have been a terrible shock to him. I suppose he hates me now.'

I looked at him sympathetically. 'Would you like me to take you to the cottage, to collect your things?'

'You wouldn't mind?'

I shook my head. 'No, I don't mind. And anyway, how else are you going to do it? You don't have a car. I'll take you this evening, when you finish here.' Walking over to him, I rubbed his shoulder affectionately. You couldn't help liking Will.

The tack room door opened, and Dominic walked in, shutting it behind him. Moving swiftly over to Will and catching hold of his arm, he asked him how he was. Dominic looked nervous and uneasy, as though half expecting Will to have changed his mind about Adam. He too looked pale and tired.

Will, after glancing shyly at me, moved closer to Dominic, and buried his face in his neck.

I turned, and suddenly took a great deal of interest in the bridle I was cleaning.

Dominic hugged Will briefly, and said, 'I'm going to see a house later this evening. I phoned up about it this morning. It's not much more rent than you and I are paying now. I'm not sure about the state of it inside, though, but we can always do it up. There's one snag.'

Will frowned. 'What's that?'

'It's just down the road from the cottage.' Dominic looked at Will intently, trying to gauge his reaction.

Will swallowed. 'I don't see that we have much choice. We'd better take it.'

Dominic nodded. 'Don't worry, it'll be all right. Everything will calm down eventually.' Stroking Will gently on the cheek, he let him go, and picked up the grooming kit.

Heading for the door, he stopped and turned towards me. 'By the way, thanks for looking after Will. I don't quite know how we'd have got on last night if you hadn't been there.'

I nodded. 'It was Ben really. He let Will stay.'

Dominic looked at me meditatively, and then, after one last fleeting smile at Will, let himself out of the tack room.

He hadn't been gone more than a minute when Adam walked in. He'd obviously waited for Dominic to go, so he could talk to Will in private.

Adam looked awful, just as pale and tired as Dominic. One look at his face told me Will wasn't the only one who'd sobbed his heart out all night. He stood by the door, gazing longingly at Will. I expected anger, even aggression, but he just stood there quietly, his face stricken and hollow-eyed.

Heavens, how did you deal with that? I thought miserably. Anger, hate, frustration, you knew where you stood with those base emotions.

Finally, Adam walked across the tack room and stopped in front of Will, who, not knowing what to say, gazed down at his feet again.

Adam put his hands in his pockets.

'Will,' he mumbled, 'I'm sorry for the things I said to you last night.'

Will nodded, and continued to gaze at his feet.

I began to feel uncomfortable, and wondered if I ought to push off and leave them to speak in private, but Adam barely acknowledged my presence.

At last, Will lifted his head and looked at Adam sadly. 'I'm sorry if I've hurt you. I really didn't mean to do that.'

Adam blinked several times and nodded, struggling to keep his composure. 'D'you love him?' he blurted out.

Will sighed and nodded. 'Yes, I think so.'

I glanced at Adam's face, and quickly looked away again. It was like looking into a tortured soul.

Turning abruptly, he simply walked out of the tack room, letting the door slam shut behind him.

Will looked at me dumbly.

'It's always been my experience that you don't ask questions like that unless you want the truth,' I said.

'Do you think he'll ever forgive me?' asked Will in a tight voice.

'I don't know.' I squashed the soapy sponge, watching the little white blobs appearing in serried ranks all along the surface of it. 'I don't know if he'll ever get over you.'

'You must think I'm horrible, doing this to him.' Will was close to tears again.

I shook my head. 'No, I don't. We've all done things in our time that we wished we could have avoided, and I'm not here to judge anyone.

'I was guilty of doing the very same thing to somebody a couple of years ago. It's sad when you fall out of love with someone, but it happens. You made the same mistake as I did – you didn't finish the old relationship before embarking on another – but there are a lot of people guilty of that particular crime. Adam would still have been hurt, just, maybe, not feel quite so betrayed. I'm sure, in time, he'll learn to live with it.'

Privately, I didn't think Adam could or would face a life without Will. But Will nodded, hastily rubbed his eyes, and mumbled that he'd better get back to work.

'I'll see you later, and take you to the cottage,' I said. Thanking me, he let himself out of the tack room.

I finished cleaning the bridle, and surveyed the Yard's activities out of the window. Adam and Dominic were managing to ignore each other.

Mark and Finn, aware something was amiss, tactfully said nothing and simply exchanged meaningful glances. Fortunately they didn't have long to ponder on this problem, as Ben drove into the Yard, back from seeing the chap about his building materials.

I watched Ben ask Will where I was, and when the lad pointed to the tack room, Ben made his way over to me. He stepped inside, and closed the door behind him. That door would be off its hinges before the day's out, I thought. It had been opened and shut more times than an umbrella in a rainstorm!

'Well, how are things this morning?' he enquired, leaning against the wall.

I wrinkled my brow doubtfully.

'Well, Adam and Dominic are doing a good job of ignoring each other. Dominic's going to look at a house this evening, so I think Will's going to be moving out shortly.

'Adam has apologized to Will for the things he said to him last night. I think he wants him back. Will seems to be sticking to his guns, and appears to be serious about Dominic. I'm taking Will over to the cottage later to collect his things.'

Ben sucked his bottom lip thoughtfully. 'It's early days yet. We'll see what happens. If things get too bad, I'll have to ask one of them to leave. To be honest, I'd prefer to keep Dominic; he's more versatile in helping to break the horses to drive.'

'Adam's fairly handy, though,' I said defensively, starting to feel sorry for poor Adam. All of this mess wasn't even his fault. To lose your lover *and* your job, in quick succession, would be almost too cruel, I thought.

I went on, 'He can drive the horses, and he has broken horses to drive before. Admittedly, he doesn't have Dominic's experience, but it's not as though he's never been around driving horses either.'

Ben looked at me reflectively.

'Don't worry, Adam's a big boy. He can look after himself; he's tougher than you think.'

I looked at Ben with a mixture of doubt and concern. I wasn't entirely sure Adam *could* cope.

Sighing involuntarily, I moved over to the door.

'I'll go and fetch the boys. The local gymkhana's on Saturday. Their ponies could do with a bit of attention.'

'I have noticed,' said Ben. 'I made the mistake of patting them the other day and thought I'd aged ten years!'

I looked at him, frowning.

'I went to the bathroom and caught sight of my white hair in the mirror. I was covered in dust. I think they could all do with a bath.'

I grinned, and remarked that he would probably look more sexy with grey hair. Ben gave me a disgusted look, and said, being so dark, when he went grey he would no doubt resemble a badger.

I laughed, and said it could be worse. A skunk, for example. As long as he didn't smell like one!

I went up to the house and found the boys in the kitchen, trying to help Mrs Travis prepare a casserole for our dinner that evening.

I padded over to Mrs Travis and put an arm around her plump shoulders.

'Have they been good boys?' I asked, comically glowering at them.

Mrs Travis gave a hearty chuckle. 'Right as rain,' she said, looking at them fondly and wiping her hands on her apron. It was a daft question really. In her eyes they could do no wrong.

'Right, you lot!' I commanded, rubbing my hands together. 'Let's go and get those ponies cleaned up.'

The boys, predictably, groaned and pulled faces.

'Do you want to go to the gymkhana on Saturday?' The boys nodded eagerly. 'Well, you'd better make them presentable, then, hadn't you?'

The boys charged off to put their boots on and I flashed a grin at Mrs Travis. Shaking her head and chuckling, she got to work on a bread and butter pudding, one of the boys' favourites.

The boys and I caught the ponies and gave them a bath. Merrylegs, with his ears laid back flat down his neck, took it in bad part, and, mildly protesting, stood on Rory's foot. He then shook water all over the place. Badger and Flicka, Rory's and Alex's ponies, heaved great sighs, and resignedly put up with soap in their ears and water up their noses.

Finally, after an hour or so of scrubbing, cleaning and polishing, I despatched the boys off to the tack room to clean their saddles and bridles. I didn't see why the stable lads should have to take care of either the boys' ponies or their tack. They had quite enough to do, and a little responsibility for the boys wouldn't hurt.

I was rewarded with a grateful smile from Finn, who didn't appear to be himself lately. He seemed distracted.

In fact, we spent all afternoon in the Yard, doing little odd jobs the lads were just too busy to get around to. We cleaned the grooming kit, scrubbed the shovels, forks and brushes they used to muck out with, washed bandages and tugs, and finally swept out the tack room.

The boys will sleep well tonight, I thought, smiling to myself.

That evening, as I'd promised, I drove Will to the cottage. Once there, I parked myself in an armchair, feeling awkward.

Will stood in the middle of the little sitting room, gazing about him. Finally, he said, 'I'll just go and get my things, I won't be long.' He went off around the cottage, gathering up his possessions.

Within twenty minutes, he'd finished. We were just about to load my car with his luggage when Adam arrived.

He leapt out of his car, and burst into the cottage, practically falling into the sitting room. There followed an uneasy silence. Once again I felt as though I was intruding.

Will took the key to the cottage off his key-ring, and laid it gently down on the table. Gazing at Adam, he said, 'I'm sorry. I was hoping to be done and out of here by the time you got home.'

Adam's eyes flickered. 'Is it really that awful, being in the same room as me?'

'No!' Will almost wailed. 'I'm trying to make this as easy as possible. I think I've hurt you enough already, don't you?'

Adam nodded. 'Yes, you have. More than you'll ever know, but I still love you, Will, and I always shall do. You can come back any time you want, you know. I could forgive you anything.'

Adam looked at Will, his longing and pain almost tangible. It was not lost on Will, who was clearly feeling horribly guilty and upset, and snapped, 'Adam, stop. Don't you have any pride?'

Adam walked over to the table, sat down heavily and slumped forward, his head in his hands.

'Not where you're concerned. I've never loved anyone the way I love you.' He sighed. 'I know it may sound like an old cliché, but it's the truth. Nobody has ever brought me to my knees before.' Adam laid his head down on the table, and very quietly began to cry.

Rather than feeling embarrassed, I felt close to tears myself. Will had broken him in every way.

I looked down at my hands, swallowing hard.

'I'm sorry, Adam.' Will stumbled out of the cottage and got into my car.

I clumsily got to my feet, and, picking up Will's luggage, loaded it into the car. It took three agonizing

159

trips, as each time I returned to the cottage Adam was sobbing helplessly.

On my last trip, I went up to him, put my arms around him, and gently stroked his head.

Burying his face against my waist, he croaked, 'Oh, Penny, what am I going to do? I barely managed to get through last night. I can't face this forever. I can't eat, I can't sleep. I miss him so much.'

'I know you don't want to hear this right now, but it does get easier in time.'

Adam shook his head, and said, almost irritably, 'You don't understand. He was the only one for me. He'll always be the one for me.' Adam was clinging to me, shivering, desperately seeking comfort.

'You'll still get to see him at the Yard, you'll still be able to talk to him. Who knows what may come of it in time?'

I began to rock him, as if he were one of the children. I didn't want to build Adam's hopes up, just to have them come crashing down again, but I was seriously concerned for him. I felt that some distant hope would at least be something for him to cling to. At least until he was stronger, more stable, able to cope better having got used to being without Will.

I really had to force myself to leave Adam there, all alone in the cottage, with his misery.

As I drove away, Will sat beside me, gazing listlessly out of the window, tears streaming down his face.

When we got home, I helped Will up to his room with his luggage. I tried to persuade him to have dinner with us but he declined, saying he wasn't hungry.

I went downstairs, feeling very subdued.

Ben scowled at me, and said he wouldn't have me dragged in on their problems and upset. In future, he

160

announced, Will could fetch anything else he wanted himself!

'I offered,' I protested weakly.

'Well, stick to fretting over me and the boys!' he ordered in a mixture of concern and pure irritation. It suddenly dawned on me that he was jealous of the attention Will, Adam and Dominic had been getting. Ben leaned against the Aga, arms folded, sulking. Swiftly crossing the kitchen, I put my arms around him, kissed him tenderly, and apologized for neglecting him.

'I should think so too!' he said, sniffing and smiling tenderly at me. 'And we do have problems of our own. Like my dear brother.' His voice took on a serious note.

'I know,' I said, sighing heavily, 'but Adam is worrying me. He's in an awful state – distraught.'

'I'll keep an eye on him when he's in the Yard. If I think he's really that bad, we'll have him here in the house where we can keep watch over him, OK?'

I smiled up at him. 'You really are a very kind man, under all that bravado.'

'That's just a vicious rumour,' he said airily.

Laughing, I let him go and called the boys. Dishing out the casserole Mrs Travis had made for us, I found that the boys' lively chatter soon perked me up again.

They were mildly curious as to why Will was staying with us, so Ben told them it was while Will was having his house done up, as he'd now got one of his own.

Later that evening, Dominic called in to see Will. They went off to look at the house Dominic had found for them, Will riding pillion on the back of Dominic's motorbike. Faced with three pairs of inquisitive eyes, Ben again explained that Dominic was helping Will to do

161

up his house and move him in. Ben could lie quite well, I noted, feeling slightly disturbed!

Will came back a couple of hours later. I had just put the boys to bed, and passed him on the stairway, as he was going to his room.

'How d'you like the house?' I asked.

Will nodded. 'It's quite similar to the cottage, actually. It's not in too bad a state, either. We're moving in tomorrow.'

'So soon? You could stay a while longer if you want to tart it up a bit,' I offered.

Will smiled and shook his head. 'Thanks, Pen, but Dominic's a bit impatient. He wants us to be together like yesterday.'

I smiled. 'Well, I hope it all works out for you.'

'Yeah, thanks. So do I.'

He didn't seem to have cheered up much, though. He looked at me sadly. 'I still can't stop thinking about Adam. He was so upset. I knew he loved me, but I didn't realize quite how much.' Will blinked several times, tears threatening to overtake him again.

'Didn't you? I did. Be kind to him, Will. I know you're not a nasty person. Speak to him when you're in the Yard. Don't shut him out too soon, and help him to adjust to being without you. Try not to be too affectionate with Dominic when he's around. You'd better talk to Dominic, explain what you're trying to do. It'll stop any jealousy if he happens to see you talking to Adam. Reassure Dominic that he has nothing to worry about. I don't think a fist-fight would help matters.'

Will nodded slowly and bit his lip. 'Well, I think I'll turn in.' He ran a tired hand down the back of his head.

162

'Goodnight, Will.'

In fact, it wasn't much later when Ben and I went to bed. The stint in the Yard had really taken it out of me. Ben seemed weary too, but I had a feeling this had more to do with the problems concerning Matt. His silence regarding Matt since the fire made me horribly uneasy. Ben was doing a fair imitation of someone who was being 'quietly dangerous'.

The boys and I rose early the next morning, and tramped down to the stables. The blacksmith was due that day, to shoe several of the horses in the Yard. The Thelwells were also having nice new shoes. What would happen if one of them threw a shoe, and couldn't go to the Ball tomorrow, I dreaded to think!

As the blacksmith was leaving, a lorry drove slowly into the Yard, and the driver, jumping down from his cab, came over to me and asked for Ben. He had the building materials Ben wanted.

'Oh, right, I'll just go and find him; he's here somewhere,' I said, and wandered off to locate Ben.

I found him in the little meadow at the back of the stables, giving a rare riding lesson. The Yard didn't go in for much of this – Ben preferred to do as he was now, teaching individually rather than in groups, and there wasn't much call for this, as one-to-one tuition cost a small fortune these days.

I called out to him.

He turned, and called back to me, 'OK, I've finished here. I'll be right over.'

Ben said something to the young girl he had been teaching, and pointed towards the stables. She gently walked the pony over towards them, and Ben sauntered over to me.

163

'What is it?' he asked, his eyes narrowing against the bright sunshine.

'Your chap's here with your building stuff.'

'Oh, right. I'll give him a hand to unload it. The builder's coming on Monday to start on the stable block.'

He wiped his arm along his forehead. I turned and made my way back to the stables, with Ben following me.

I left Ben to deal with his 'chap', while the boys and I had a few practice games in the little paddock, in readiness for the gymkhana tomorrow.

When the boys and I turned out the ponies, Mark and Finn strolled over to me and leaned on the paddock rails.

'I gather congratulations are in order,' said Finn, his eyes crinkling with the huge grin he gave me, which we hadn't seen much of lately.

'You've heard, then?' I grinned back at him.

'Yes, Dominic did mention it,' said Mark, watching Merrylegs rubbing his bottom against a tree.

'Personally,' said Finn airily, 'I'm heartbroken. To think I've been having the most erotic dreams about what you were going to do to me when we finally got it together!'

'I heard that!' said Ben, suddenly appearing at my side.

Mark and Finn burst out laughing, and Ben, pulling me against him, said tartly, 'She's mine! Clear off and find your own woman!'

'May I kiss the bride?' asked Mark innocently, trying to keep a straight face.

'No, you damned well, may not!' howled Ben indignantly. 'You keep your hands off her, you cheeky little swine, or I'll sack the pair of you!' He wrapped his arms around my body, prodding me in the ribs. 'And that reminds me. You haven't given me a date yet.'

'I'm working on it!' I sighed.

Ben bit me gently on the ear, and I playfully jabbed *my* elbow into his ribs.

'I hear Dominic's moving out?' I yelped, dodging his fingers.

'Yeah, he's moving into his new house tonight. Will and Adam don't seem to be speaking at the moment, so Dominic has agreed to put him up. I think he wanted to live on his own really, but he wouldn't see Will on the streets,' said Finn.

Your secret still seems to be safe, Dominic, I thought, smiling faintly. Mark and Finn obviously thought Will's sharing with Dominic would be as platonic as it had been when Dominic had lived with them.

'Will you find somebody else to take Dominic's place?' I asked.

Mark shook his head, 'No. Dominic was only ever a temporary measure, until he found his own place. Now that he has, we'll keep it to just us two. We can manage the financial side of things, and at least I might get a shave in the mornings now!' Mark grinned and rubbed his chin ruefully.

Mark and Finn wandered off back to the stables, with Ben reluctantly following them.

I felt slightly apprehensive about the gymkhana tomorrow. Matt seemed to be stepping up his campaign. The whole thing was beginning to seriously unnerve me. In fact, it was on my mind all evening.

Ben, seeing that something was obviously bothering me, demanded to know. Feeling silly, I told him. When we went to bed, he said he knew of something that would take my mind off it, and pounced on me. Rolling around on the bed, I felt so frustrated, I took it out on him, and, pushing him on to his back, I climbed eagerly on top of him and rode him as if I were on the home straight in the Grand National!

After some time, Ben rolled me on to my back, and urgently, passionately drove me on to delicious oblivion.

Lying with my hand on his chest, he gently stroked me, murmuring that if that was how I behaved when I felt nervous about something, he'd take to leaping out at me from behind doors!

I laughed sleepily, and yawned. Within two minutes I was fast asleep. But very soon that night, I had a most disturbing dream about Matt. It was so vivid. Everywhere I went he was there too, grinning evilly at me. I tried to turn and run but my feet seemed to be glued to the floor. My legs felt like heavy lead weights, as they struggled to get away from him. As I saw him closing the gap between us, I fought harder, trying to release my feet, and just as his hand reached out to grab me I awoke with a start.

Breathing heavily, I kicked off the duvet. I felt so hot. I put a hand up to my forehead and found I was sweating profusely.

Ben seemed to be sleeping peacefully. Relieved that I hadn't woken him up, I eased on to my side, and with a shaking hand turned the clock radio to face me. It was four o'clock in the morning. I watched its illuminated face flick over for another two hours before I finally drifted off again.

CHAPTER 13

Saturday dawned hot and sunny, without a cloud in the sky. The boys were rather over-excited, as they'd been looking forward to the gymkhana all week.

We spent an hour or so in the Yard, polishing ponies and tack (yet again!) in readiness for the day. The gymkhana was to be held in the same field as the fête had been.

The boys rode their ponies down the lane, with me following on foot with Bracken, who adored gymkhanas.

When we arrived at the gymkhana, the field had been transformed. Three arenas were roped off, one for the games, one for the jumping competition, and one for the showing classes. There were several vans, selling burgers, doughnuts and fish and chips. There was also a tea tent, a beer tent, and a bright orange tent, strongly resembling an enormous Spanish navel orange, where you registered for the day's events.

I paid for the boys to take part in the games and the jumping competition. They drew the line at showing.

'All that trotting around with plaits and things,' snorted Rory, with a disgusted look.

I turned and ruefully surveyed a little girl with freckles and pigtails getting a ticking-off for having brown dusty

167

patches on her jodhpurs. Her mother was frantically trying to rub the marks off with a dandy brush.

I sighed involuntarily. Why didn't parents allow their children to be children? I thought irritably.

Looking across the field, I spotted the vicar, desperately trying to get away from Mrs Harris, who was holding a fat grey pony with Archie perched on top. I couldn't see Sam anywhere; perhaps it was her day off. Scanning the names on the programme, alongside the day's events, I noticed that, along with a Mrs Prodworthy, who worked at the dry-cleaners, the vicar was one of the judges. Mrs Harris was obviously putting a little pressure on him, perhaps by threatening to poke holes in every slate on the church roof if he didn't place Archie first.

The tannoy hiccuped, and announced that the showing was due to start in a couple of minutes. The boys and I wandered over to have a look at the entrants. There were only three children who could be bothered to enter. Nobody, it seemed, liked showing.

The three entrants shuffled into the ring, and lined up in front of the vicar and Mrs Prodworthy from the dry-cleaners. Mrs Prodworthy was a large woman in a purple frock, and had 'various veins', as Rory called them, to match.

Archie, sitting askew his fat pony, who was appropriately called Dumpling, started fidgeting with boredom.

'Archie!' screeched Mrs Harris, 'sit up straight, and stop fiddling with yourself!'

Archie went scarlet, scowled at his mother, and promptly poked his tongue out at her. The boys and I howled with laughter.

My gaze wandered to the second entrant. It was the little girl with freckles and pigtails. She was sitting very upright on a beautiful chestnut pony, which had a fine head, long elegant neck and dainty legs, and went by the name of Fantasy.

There's your winner, I thought idly, since standing next to her was a short, fat, coloured pony, who looked as if he lived in a lay-by and in his spare time pulled the milkman's float. His name was Charlie, and indeed, he looked a proper one. He was supposed to be black and white. Every white patch was stained green, where he had evidently rolled in the wet grass. His head hung down, and he rested a hind leg, his tail lazily swatting flies along his sides.

The vicar and Mrs Prodworthy walked around the ponies, pretending to take an interest. As Mrs Prodworthy was talking to 'Pigtails', Archie leaned over and, with his whip, slowly lifted up her dress, revealing vast white pants. Cackling evilly, he lowered it.

The vicar and Mrs Prodworthy decided on 'Pigtails' as the winner; the milkman's they put in second place, obviously impressed because he was still standing, and Archie third.

Mrs Harris turned purple with rage, and stomped into the ring to collect her pride and joy. Barging through Mrs Prodworthy and the vicar, she swept out of the ring, dragging a shuffling Dumpling.

I found I couldn't stop laughing, and, sniffing weakly, told the boys they'd better get themselves over to the ring, where they were starting the games shortly.

The first game was the egg and spoon race. There were four heats in all. Harry was in the same heat as Archie, which didn't bode well.

As they lined up, Archie stuck his tongue out again, this time at Harry, who, putting one arm across the other, jerked it up and blew a raspberry.

The vicar, dropping a handkerchief, started the race. Harry hurtled forward on Merrylegs. Archie, flapping his legs into Dumpling's sides, sluggishly ambled after the rest.

Merrylegs reached the end of the ring first, and Harry, flinging himself off his pony, bent down and picked up his egg and spoon, and sauntered back to the start, winning easily.

I cheered and clapped my hands, and was rewarded with a baleful glare from Mrs Harris. Hastily coughing, I watched the rest of the heat finish the race.

Archie was tiptoeing down to the start, his tongue peeping through his teeth in concentration. Dumpling decided he was hungry, put his head down sharply, and began eating the grass. As his reins were hanging over Archie's arm, he wrenched him backwards, making him drop his egg, which Dumpling promptly ate.

Archie jumped up and down with rage in the middle of the ring, viciously kicking Dumpling on the leg. Dumpling had just about had enough of Archie, and kicked him back, knocking Archie flat on his back.

Harry was laughing so hard, he fell off Merrylegs in a crumpled heap, giggling feebly.

Rory and Alex were racing against each other in the same heat, with three others. Rory and Alex were neck and neck going back to the start, until Rory dropped his egg. Deliberately, I was sure. Alex was chuffed to bits, as he put it; he'd actually won his heat.

I gazed at Rory. That boy really knew how to humble one, I thought fondly.

Rory gazed steadily back at me, gently smiled, and sat down on the grass to watch the last two heats. I sat down behind him, putting my legs around him, and he leaned against me, scratching Bracken's head.

The last two heats were won by 'Pigtails', and a little boy with flowing white hair and buck teeth. With his teeth and Mrs Harris's rear end they could win the Derby, I thought!

Alex, Harry, 'Pigtails' and 'Buck Teeth' lined up for the final. Off they went again, charging up to the end of the ring, neck and neck, all leaping off their ponies simultaneously, grabbing their eggs and spoons. Coming back down to the start, Alex and Harry were doing fine, I noticed proudly.

'Buck Teeth' dropped his egg, and, putting his spoon into his mouth, he bent down to retrieve his egg.

That'll be the last we see of that spoon, I thought with a snort.

Plonking his egg back on to his mangled spoon, 'Buck Teeth' continued on his way, just as Harry reached the start again. He'd won.

I hugged him tightly and said excitedly, 'Harry, you won! Well done!' You'd have thought, by my reaction, that Harry had won the lottery!

Harry was a natural on horses, as was Rory, just like their father. Alex however, had to work very hard at it. He was more academic than his two brothers. He came in third, which he seemed perfectly happy with.

'Buck Teeth', surprisingly, although he'd dropped his egg, came second, and 'Pigtails' last. Next came the 'bending' race. The vicar and Mrs Prodworthy, who'd been worthy of a prod from Archie, began putting traffic cones intermittently spaced, the length of the ring, for the ponies to bend in and out of.

Archie was obviously going to be the day's entertainment, as he did hopelessly in this race as well. Dumpling went one way, and Archie the other. He gracefully bounced twice, knocking his cone over.

Mrs Harris screeched loudly, making me jump, and be thankful that the glasses in the beer tent were plastic. Had they been the genuine article, she'd have shattered them!

The boys and I were hysterical with laughter, much to the annoyance of Mrs Harris.

Rory won the bending race in effortless style. I smiled at him happily. He really did deserve to win, after what he'd done for Alex.

As the entrants fought their way through the sack-race heats, I idly glanced around the milling crowd. My eyes travelled over the faces, then quickly jerked back to one particular face.

It was Matt.

Standing by the beer tent, a drink in his hand, he realized I'd seen him and raised his glass to me, grinning nastily.

Hastily, I turned my face back towards the ring, just as Archie executed a perfect forward roll in his sack.

He gave a muffled wail as Dumpling stepped on him. Mrs Harris strutted into the ring, crying, 'Archie! Archie, my poor boy!' Disentangling Archie from his sack, she set him on his feet.

Archie sniffed noisily, and howled 'Stop touching me, you revolting old witch!'

Mrs Harris furiously compressed her lips, and, grabbing him by the arm, virtually dragged him out of the ring, to a gentle round of applause.

I bit my lip in indecision. What should I do? As I watched Harry win his second race of the day, I knew I couldn't possibly spoil their fun and drag them home.

172

Then I remembered what Ben had said. Matt wouldn't do anything silly in front of a crowd of people. He didn't want any witnesses. Relaxing a little, I decided to ignore him.

The tannoy announced that there would be a half-hour break for refreshments. Glancing at my watch, I realized it was lunchtime. I bought the boys burgers and cola, which they hungrily demolished.

'I've just spotted Uncle Matt,' said Harry, his mouth full of burger.

'Yes, I know he's here. I've seen him too,' I said, keeping a close watch on him out of the corner of my eye.

Rory looked at me nervously. 'We can stay, can't we?'

I nodded and smiled. 'Yes, of course we can. We're not going to let him drive us away. We're here to enjoy ourselves, and that is exactly what we're going to do!'

Mrs Harris, holding Archie by the scruff of his neck, marched up to the burger van, where the boys and I were standing. Giving me a frosty stare, she announced sharply, 'One burger, please, young man, and be quick about it!'

The burger vendor raised his eyebrows, parked his chewing gum behind his ear, winked at me, and handed over a burger.

'Well, really!' she bellowed. She was just about to launch into him when Archie interrupted her.

'I want chips as well, and a doughnut!' he said, petulantly.

'Yes, all right!' snapped Mrs Harris. 'I'll get you some when you've eaten that.'

Archie, wanting them all now, threw his burger down on the grass, and stamped on it.

173

Harry fell about laughing. Archie, his pug face a mask of spite, lunged at Harry, knocking him down.

'Get that delinquent off my Archie!' screeched Mrs Harris, rushing forward and slipping slightly on Archie's discarded burger.

Grabbing Archie by the seat of his pants, I dragged him off Harry.

'Right! that does it!' Mrs Harris spat, froth appearing at the corners of her mouth. My goodness! She's rabid, I thought hysterically. 'I'm going to see to it you do lose your job this time. I shall be speaking to Ben Carmichael this evening.' And with that she flounced off, dragging a protesting Archie after her.

Sourly watching her march away, I checked Harry over for any damage.

'When I'm bigger, I'm going to smash his face in,' said Harry, cheerfully.

I gently scolded Harry. He had been the one doing the taunting, I reflected.

Harry looked at me under his lashes. 'I'm sorry,' he said sulkily. 'I just don't like him.'

'Neither do I,' I muttered under my breath.' And that goes for his mother as well.'

We walked back to the games ring. The apple-bobbing race was due to start shortly. The vicar and Mrs Prodworthy were busily parking buckets of water at the end of the ring, dropping apples into them with a loud plop!

Glancing around, I caught Matt staring at me from six feet away. Looking away, feigning indifference, I gave the boys a leg-up on to their ponies.

I didn't like the way Matt was devouring me with his eyes. It was slightly disturbing.

The apple-bobbing race was going tremendously well, until Bracken did his party-piece and slipped his lead. Deciding he was thirsty, he stuck his head into the bucket Archie had his head in, and drank noisily, making Harry curl up with hysterical giggles.

Archie, coughing and spluttering, aimed a kick at Bracken, who rolled his eyes and pinched one of the apples, and hurtled back to me, to show me what he'd got.

Harry, furious at Archie for trying to kick Bracken, threw an apple at him, which bounced off his head, splitting on impact and reducing Archie to noisy sobbing.

Harry was disqualified, at which he merely shrugged, and trotted out of the ring.

The apple-bobbing race was won by 'Buck Teeth', which wasn't surprising really, when he could skewer his fruit to get it out of his bucket.

The flag race could hardly be called a success. Archie, revenge on his mind, barged into Harry on his pony, to which Harry responded to by hitting Archie repeatedly on the head with his flag. It resembled an old-fashioned jousting match! Fortunately, when I called to Harry, he trotted obediently back to me.

This time, both Harry and Archie were disqualified. I steeled myself as I saw Mrs Harris bearing down on me.

'Well?' she barked. 'What d'you have to say for yourself?'

I sucked my teeth thoughtfully. 'I'd say Harry had the upper hand. One more minute and he'd have had him off!'

Mrs Harris thrust her bosom out at me. You could lose an eye doing that to someone, I thought.

'Are you going to punish that child?' she demanded, staring at me coldly, veins standing up in her neck like telephone cables.

I surveyed her calmly. 'Mrs Harris, what would you have me do? Tie him up and drag him along behind his own pony at full tilt?' I smiled sweetly.

After much puffing and wheezing, she finally gulped out, 'Well! Of all the rude . . .' And stopping abruptly, she brushed past me, and strode straight up to the vicar, no doubt to try and persuade him to have the race again.

A little girl with long blonde hair had already won the flag race, and the vicar decided to leave the outcome as it was. Mrs Harris looked as if she would spontaneously combust any minute.

The boys and I went off to have another drink. I was conscious the whole time of Matt watching us closely.

A little later, the jumping competition started. By this time most of the children were hot and bothered and tired.

There were only half a dozen entrants in the 12.2 section, one of whom was Alex.

'Buck Teeth' was the first to go into the ring, and had three refusals; one at the gate, one at the wall, and one at Mrs Prodworthy, who stood in the middle of the ring with a clipboard. I suppose, being that close to Mrs Prodworthy, the horse had a point.

The next two entrants, 'Pigtails' and a ginger-haired boy, both went clear, to boos and hisses from Rory and Harry.

The last two riders before Alex, both sickly-looking girls, had three fences down apiece, and trotted out of the ring to loud wailing.

176

I held my breath as I watched Alex cantering around the ring, little Flicka with his roan ears twitching, listening to Alex murmuring encouraging words.

As Flicka soared over the fences, I suddenly realized I felt quite faint, and hastily began breathing again. Two jumps from home, and Flicka rapped a pole quite hard. Hearing a muffled croak, I glanced down, and realized I'd got Harry in a suffocating clinch.

'Sorry,' I mumbled, and felt about fit to burst as Alex completed a clear round.

'Oh, Alex!' I crowed, and swung Harry round by his armpits.

In the jump-off, which was against the clock, both 'Pigtails' and 'Ginger' had a fence down apiece, which meant Alex could take his time.

'You've only got to clear,' Harry said, sounding like a miniature trainer talking to his jockey. Alex nodded, and walked into the ring.

Harry, being a bright child, kept out of arm's reach where I was concerned, and shoved a protesting Rory in front of me so I could throttle him during the tense bits.

I could hardly bear to watch and buried my face in Rory's neck. Peeping around his ears, I watched Alex calmly complete a second clear round.

'You won! You won!' I cried, deafening Rory. Pulling Alex off his pony, I gathered him up into a huge bone-crunching cuddle. I was so proud of him, I seriously embarrassed myself, and snivelled all over his nice clean jacket. As Mrs Prodworthy dished out the rosettes, it was to the accompaniment of loud honking noises in a sodden tissue, coming from my direction. Rory sighed heavily, while Harry merely raised his eyes to heaven.

The 11.2 section had about ten entrants all told. Archie had to follow Harry.

Most of the entrants didn't even complete the course because they were so young and forgot which fence came next.

Harry tore round the ring like a demon, Merrylegs attacking the fences with ears laid back and his little legs going like merry pistons.

He went clear, to a lot of rapturous yelling from me, and a tight-lipped glare from Mrs Harris.

Archie shuffled into the ring on Dumpling, who decided to stop and have a look at the other ponies lined up around the ring. Archie kicked him on, and, totally ignoring him, the pony put his head down and began eating the grass. He liked his grub, did our Dumpling!

Kicking like mad, and getting absolutely nowhere, Archie decided to give him a sharp crack with his whip. Dumpling's head shot up, and, hitting Archie smartly on the nose, he succeeded in knocking his hat off.

Dumpling then took off with a speed I wouldn't have thought possible if his backside had been on fire. The G-force of Dumpling's nought to sixty in one and a half seconds threw Archie backwards, so he was lying horizontally on Dumpling's back, his legs stuck straight out in front of him, his feet wiggling around Dumpling's furry ears.

Terrified, Dumpling stopped dead and with a series of bucks threw Archie off, depositing him on the ground with a dull thud.

Archie got to his feet, having ripped his breeches around the gusset region, and stomped across the ring to fetch his hat.

I know I shouldn't have laughed, but I couldn't help it. The vicar, looking not unlike a large crow, charged into the ring waving his arms about at his sides, trying to catch a rampaging Dumpling.

Dumpling didn't quite know what to make of this apparition flapping towards him, and veered off sharply, very nearly flattening Mrs Prodworthy, who with a screech dived for cover behind a brush fence.

Harry and Rory were weak with laughter. In fact, looking around the ring, all I could see were laughing faces. I would have felt quite sorry for Archie and his awful mother, if they weren't so self-opinionated, conceited and all round disgusting.

The vicar gave Archie a leg-up, and, not realizing his own strength, succeeded in chucking him straight over the top of Dumpling. Archie called the vicar some rather unpleasant names, and was finally hoisted back on to a snorting Dumpling by Mrs Prodworthy.

With his face set, Archie flapped his legs into Dumpling's sides, and trundled off around the ring.

I think Dumpling's energetic and sudden spurt had rather exhausted him, and with three-legged hops and various other peculiar gaits he managed to heave himself over the fences.

Unfortunately, Dumpling ran out of steam three fences from home, and simply stampeded the obstacles in his way, knocking poles and wooden bricks flying.

Mrs Harris, being a raging snob, was so embarrassed she keeled over in a dead faint, seriously endangering the lives of a a dozen small children standing nearby.

There were only three riders in the jump-off and Harry was due to go last. At least he was assured of a rosette of some kind.

Both of the entrants before Harry went clear. Harry rode a superb round, but Merrylegs pecked on landing at the wall, and lost valuable seconds.

Harry came second, with a pretty dark-haired girl coming first, and a little boy with beer-bottle-bottomed glasses in third place.

All three lined up in the ring to get their rosettes. Harry was surreptitiously eyeing up the pretty girl. She blushed and giggled into her hand. Harry fluttered his eyelashes and grinned a lot.

God, he's only five, I thought in horror. He's going to be a real ladies' man, that one.

Harry got quite impatient with the vicar when he blocked his view of the little girl with his rather large body.

The vicar called out their names and asked us all to give the 'brave little ones' a round of applause. Apparently, according to the vicar, the little girl's name was Annie Croft.

While Rory took on nine entrants in the 13.2 section, Harry and Annie were casting surreptitious glances in each other's direction.

'Harry, close your mouth,' I muttered, watching Rory struggling with a tired Badger.

Somehow, Rory, through sheer skill and determination, managed to get around the course. Unfortunately, so did seven of the nine entrants.

The jump-off was a fierce contest with some excellent riding. Five entrants had gone clear again with the fastest time being twenty-two seconds. One more before Rory, I thought, nervously wringing my hands.

Harry, I noticed, was sidling closer to the sumptuous Annie. Seizing his hand, I shoved him in front of me, much to his disgust.

A skinny girl with long blonde hair completed the course in twenty-three seconds.

'Come on, Rory!' I shouted, as he cantered into the ring.

'Yeah, come on, bro!' chorused Alex and Harry.

Badger knocked, clipped and rattled poles all the way round, which just about shattered my frayed nerves to breaking point. Two from home, and I just couldn't watch any more. I turned my head away to face Harry, and found Annie shoulder to shoulder with him, shooting doe-eyed looks in his direction.

Harry suddenly did something I'd never seen him do before. He went all shy, and seemed at a loss for words.

Alex let go the most ear-splitting scream, as Badger and Rory sailed over the last fence in twenty-four seconds. He'd come third.

Rory patted a tired Badger, tweaking his ears in proud affection. He collected his rosette with a red face and a toothy grin. Needless to say, he was promptly crushed to death by myself in a paralysing cuddle, and, looking embarrassed, he called Harry a roaring sissy as he caught sight of his youngest brother holding hands with the luscious Annie.

Harry scowled. Rory was at an age when all girls were silly, and did 'girlie' things like crying and kissing, usually in that order.

Rory, I reflected, could be quite a sissy when he hurt himself or when he felt a little poorly, and could cry and kiss any girl under the table, if you'll pardon the expression.

Prising Harry away from Annie, I promised she could come and play with him some time. In a few years, I thought, I would have to be careful about saying something like that.

Finally the gymkhana was at an end. I have to say, I was relieved to be going home. It had been a long day, and Matt's constant hovering in the background was making me increasingly nervous.

I didn't think I'd done too badly. I'd given a fair impression of someone who didn't have a care in the world, so there!

We gently walked the ponies home. When we arrived at the Yard, we washed the sweat off them and turned them out into the little paddock, which they now shared with several of the riding horses.

We made our way up to the house, and, stepping into the kitchen, I heard Ben on the phone, saying in an icy voice, 'That woman . . . is to be my wife, and I don't care for your attitude towards her!' Ben winced and held the phone away from his ear. I could hear Mrs Harris's muffled squawks from where I was standing.

Ben started to laugh; she was obviously telling him what I'd said to her.

Finally, when Ben couldn't stop laughing, she clearly slammed the phone down on him.

Ben, doubled up, finally spluttered, 'Had a nice day, dear?'

I looked at him under my lashes. 'I'm sorry about that, Archie and Harry had a disagreement. She stood up for Archie, I stood up for Harry. That's really all there is to it.'

Ben sniffed. 'Pen, you don't have to explain. Stop treating me as if I'm still your boss. I'm not. I'm well aware of how unreasonable Mrs Harris can be. I quite enjoyed it really. She felt rather put down when I said you were going to be my wife. I think she feels a bit silly now, talking to you the way she did. The only way I could sack you is by not marrying you, and that, my darling, will never happen.' Ben grinned broadly at me.

I crossed the room and put my arms around his waist, and looked up at him.

'Ben, I have something to tell you,' I stammered.

Ben frowned. 'Yes?'

I bit my lip anxiously. 'I saw Matt at the gymkhana – but don't go mad!' I added quickly, as Ben's face grew hard and his whole body tensed. 'He didn't speak to us or anything. He kept his distance. I just thought I'd better mention it.'

Ben relaxed a little and grunted, 'Well, I'm glad you did. I want you to tell me if that bastard comes anywhere near you or the boys.'

'I will.'

All three boys, having been busy changing their clothes, had not been to see their father yet. Noisily, they burst into the room and charged up to Ben, showing off their rosettes.

'Look, Dad!' said Alex excitedly. 'I won my section in the jumping competition!'

'Well done!' he said, rubbing Alex's head affectionately.

'I've also got a third!' gabbled Alex, waving his yellow rosette in Ben's face.

'What did you get that in?' enquired Ben, smiling fondly at him.

'Egg and spoon race.' Stroking his rosette, he took hold of the string hanging off it and, trying the two ends together, hung it over his ear, rather like an enormous ear-ring.

'Oh, that's definitely you,' said Harry solemnly.

I caught Ben's eye and couldn't stop laughing. Ben dutifully inspected Harry's two firsts and the second, which Harry grumbled would have been several more, if it hadn't been for Archie.

Rory pinned his two rosettes on the noticeboard in the kitchen. Ben was asking Rory what he'd won them in, as I whispered in his ear just what Rory had done for Alex.

Ben gazed at his eldest son, and clearly felt so proud of him that he was speechless. Rory blushed at his father's doting expression, and hastily informed him that Harry had a girlfriend.

'Really?' Ben laughed.

Harry shot Rory a filthy look, and flounced off to irritate Alex.

As I was dishing out our dinner, Mark and Finn came up to the house. They were helping Will and Dominic move into their house and they'd come to collect Will's luggage.

They began loading it into the car. Will thanked Ben profusely for putting him up.

Ben merely nodded. 'My pleasure.'

When he'd gone, I asked Ben how Adam had been in the yard.

'Distracted,' he said, thoughtfully.

When we'd finished dinner, I loaded the dishwasher, and went off for a long soak in the bath. Relaxing in the scented water, I must have dozed off for a while, because when I came to the water was stone cold. Shivering slightly, I added a little hot water, and quickly finished bathing.

I made my way downstairs, and joined Ben in the sitting room, where he and the boys were watching television.

'What happened to you?' asked Alex, slightly miffed. 'You've been gone ages.'

'I'm sorry, I didn't mean to be. I fell asleep in the bath.'

I sat down next to him on the sofa. Alex snuggled up to me, wanting some attention.

'It's all that fresh air!' said Ben mockingly.

I wrinkled my nose at him.

'Pen didn't know what it was like to work until she came here,' he drawled.

Leaping off the sofa with an indignant snarl, I shot across the room and jumped on him. I called the boys to help me and they charged up to their father. Rory grabbed Ben's arms, while Harry and Alex sat on his legs, as I tickled him mercilessly.

Harry, seizing the chance to get some of his own back, dug his knuckles into Ben's ribs, saying to him, 'Now what do we say?'

Ben had a ritual when the boys got a little cheeky. Instead of spanking them, which he didn't believe in, he would stretch them out on his knees, and tickle them ceaselessly. The boys got so hysterical with laughter, they would scream out the same three lines dictated by Ben. This was what Harry was now doing to Ben.

'Well?' said Harry, digging his knuckles into Ben's ribs again. 'I can't breathe.' Harry put his head on one side.

'I can't breathe!' gasped Ben, laughing helplessly at Harry's comical expression.

'I wanna be sick!' said Harry, blinking.

'I wanna be sick!' croaked Ben.

'I'm gonna burst!' said Harry solemnly.

'I'm gonna burst!' said Ben hoarsely, barely able to speak.

The meaning of this being, when Ben did this to the boys, they were terrified they'd have a heart attack, throw up or explode!

Ben started to cough. Thinking he might be choking, we sat him up.

He eyed Harry under his lashes, then he quickly grabbed his son, and performed the ritual all over again.

Harry very nearly did explode! Finally, when we thought Harry had had enough, Ben let him go.

When the boys caught their breath, the conversation, predictably, veered round to the day's events at the gymkhana. Alex couldn't stop touching his rosettes. I don't think he could quite believe he'd actually won something.

Ben offered me a drink, and when I nodded in agreement, he fixed me a gin and tonic, and a scotch for himself. Handing me the drink, he flopped down on the sofa beside me. I leaned against him, watching the boys, feeling loved and contented.

'What's gin taste like?' asked Alex, looking at me hopefully.

'Aftershave,' said Ben, sticking a finger into my drink and dabbing it behind his ears.

'It's an acquired taste,' I said, slapping Ben on the back of his hand. 'Would you like to taste it?'

Ben raised his eyebrows and looked at me as if I'd flipped. 'Perhaps you'd like to ask them if they'd like something for the weekend, sir?' he drawled.

Laughing, I replied, 'There isn't any harm in it. Just watch.'

Alex, tentatively, came over to me, and took a sip of my drink.

'Ugh! It's disgusting!' he wailed, working his mouth like he'd got a toffee stuck to his teeth.

'There you are! One person who won't be a raging alcoholic!' I grinned.

Harry and Rory, thinking it couldn't be that bad, had a sip, and also decided my taste-buds must have died at some point.

They then all tasted Ben's scotch, and asked him if he'd got it mixed up with something else. They were convinced it was the same stuff he used to clean the car.

'I'm never going to drink alcohol!' said Alex stoutly.

'How's that?' I said, smiling gently at Ben.

Ben snorted. 'You wait until they're eighteen and their taste-buds reject anything that *isn't* alcohol, and they stagger home roaring drunk!'

I laughed. 'I know it won't put them off for ever, but by not making an issue out of it, they'll not fall over themselves to try it again.'

Ben looked at me meditatively. 'You make a good mother.' He paused, eyeing me. 'I'd like a large family.'

I choked on my gin, and blinked a lot.

'Yes, well. If it happens, fine. If it doesn't, then that's fine too.'

'Wouldn't it bother you if you couldn't have children of your own?' he asked, obviously shocked.

I shook my head. 'No, not really. Besides I already have three little boys.' I gazed at them fondly. Ben gazed into his drink and said nothing.

Going to bed that night, Ben was quiet and subdued.

'What's wrong?' I asked.

Ben surveyed me steadily. 'It would bother *me*, if you couldn't have children.'

I looked at him, slightly taken aback. 'Why? You already have three beautiful sons.'

'I know, and I love 'em to death, but I want a baby you and I have made together.' He looked at me, his face softening. 'The boys see you as their mother now, and I think that's great, I really do, but it's not the same as having our own baby.'

I scuffed the carpet with my foot, and, sighing heavily, returned his gaze, feeling slightly hurt. 'I see.'

'No, you don't!' said Ben agitatedly.

'Ben, I didn't say I wasn't ever going to have a baby. I will if I can, but if I can't, then that's that. I'm not the sort of person who dwells on problems. If it doesn't happen, then tough. It's just one of those things. For your sake I hope I can, because if I can't, I'll now know you won't be happy. I thought this relationship was all about you and me. Now I realize it's you, me, and having a baby.'

Ben shot across the bedroom and pulled me against him.

'I'm sorry. I don't mean to upset you, or put any pressure on you. I'm just speaking my mind.'

'Well, your opinion has been noted. And the moment you put pressure on someone to have a baby, they invariably don't conceive. Perhaps it would have been kinder just to wait and see, don't you think?' I stared at him stonily.

I pulled away from him, and, slowly undressing, got into bed. What a stupid, thoughtless thing to say, I thought irritably. What if I couldn't have a baby? Apart from feeling a complete failure, now that I knew Ben wanted one, I would have all sorts of additional doubts and misery to cope with. Perhaps he wouldn't want me any more? I was also hurt by the way Ben clearly thought about me in relation to the boys. I knew

Annabelle was their biological mother, but now she was dead, I thought I'd been accepted not just by the boys, but by Ben also as being their substitute mother.

Ben got into bed, and I presented him with my rigid back.

'Penny,' he said softly, 'turn over. I want to talk to you.'

I was screaming a protest in my head, even while I said calmly out loud, 'Ben, I'm tired. Go to sleep.'

'No! I will not. Now turn over and talk to me!'

Sighing impatiently, I snapped, 'I think you've said quite enough already, don't you? I now know your feelings on the subject of babies, not to mention how you think of my relation to the boys – now drop it!'

Ben, slipped his arms around me, turned me bodily on to my back, and leaned over me, so that I couldn't turn away again.

'What d'you mean by that? How *do* I relate you to the boys?'

'I mean you see the boys as yours and Annabelle's, which they were, but you haven't adjusted yet. You still see things as yours and mine, as though we're in two separate worlds. Then and now, I wish you'd get used to seeing me with the boys, rather than Annabelle, because let's face it, pal, I'm all they've got now. If the boys can adjust – and they have, as they don't seem to have a problem with my being their new mother – then you can!'

I looked away in agitation.

Ben looked at me sadly. 'Is that how I come across to you?'

189

'Ben, you stood in this room, not more than a few minutes ago, and told me that the boys and I are not the same to you as if we had our own, shared baby. Frankly, I see the boys as yours and mine. I don't have a problem with the fact that someone else looked after them before I came here. It's now that matters.'

Ben gently stroked my cheek, 'I'm sorry. I've been hurting you. I swear I didn't mean to. I've just had so many years of seeing the boys with Annabelle, it's difficult trying to see another person as their mother. I'll see to it that I put that right. And about the baby, I have to admit I would be disappointed if we didn't have one, but I'll keep reminding myself what life would be like without you, and compared to how I would feel then, it would seem a small price to pay.'

Ben looked at me rather calculatingly, I thought. 'Perhaps I'll find it easier to see you as the boys' mother when we're married.' He grinned.

I slapped him playfully on the back. 'Don't you dare pressure me into setting a date for the wedding!' I bleated.

Ben laughed. 'All right!' All right! I won't push it.' He paused, and muttered into my hair, 'For now!'

I scowled, and pinched him. Shooting me a sidelong glance, he asked, 'I really am sorry – am I forgiven?'

I sniffed. 'I suppose so.'

'Well, prove it!' he said, his eyes full of laughter.

Expecting me to fall into his arms, he was pleasantly surprised when I said, 'August.'

He looked at me warily. 'August? Is that when we get married?'

'Yes.' I smiled gently at him.

Ben was beside himself. 'Right, you start making lists of anything you want: invitations, caterers,' and he was off!

When we finally got to sleep after Ben's constant chatter about weddings, we were woken abruptly, for the second time in as many days, around four o'clock in the morning.

CHAPTER 14

Ben sat bolt upright, putting his head on one side, listening for whatever had disturbed us. There it was again. It sounded like a bucket being kicked about outside the house.

Leaping out of bed, Ben pulled his clothes on, and so did I, albeit in a slightly wobbly fashion. As we were dressing, we heard a scrunching noise on the gravel outside. There appeared to be a horse loose, out of its box or one of the fields.

Our hearts pounded as we galloped downstairs, where we pulled on our boots and shot out of the house. We caught sight of Merrylegs plodding calmly down the drive. Instead of veering right, towards the stables, curiosity got the better of him, and he walked straight on, through the gate that led on to the road.

Ben always shut the gate, in case of this very thing happening. It had obviously been opened deliberately, and Merrylegs trotted out into the road and, turning left, set off towards Loxton.

'Oh, God, no,' said Ben in horror, 'he'll get killed on that road. Or kill someone else.' Ben sprinted across to the stables, and taking out a fistful of keys, unlocked the tack room door. Grabbing a bridle, he ran back to one of the boxes. Putting the bridle on Lurch, who looked extremely put out at being woken up at such an ungodly hour, Ben vaulted on to his back.

As he clattered out of the Yard, he told me to phone the police: if anyone saw a pony, it was ours, and they should try and catch him and hold on to him. Nodding, I shot back into the house to make the call, while Ben cantered down the drive, pointing Lurch's nose towards Loxton.

Sitting at the kitchen table, I fidgeted nervously. Suddenly, going very still, I realized we hadn't checked the paddock, to see just exactly where Merrylegs had got out. I had visions of all the horses in the paddock out on the road.

I dashed out of the kitchen, raced down the drive towards the Yard, and shot across to the little paddock. The gate was wide open.

Hastily I shut it, and holding my breath, made a quick count of the horses in the paddock. Merrylegs was the only one out. Relieved, my breath came out in a groan, and I trotted back up towards the house.

I was halfway up the drive when I heard in the distance a clattering of hooves on the road. Spinning round, I ran towards the road.

Ben, gently steering Merrylegs from behind, got him level with the gateway. Just as Merrylegs was about to turn into the drive, however, a bird rustled in the hedge, startling Merrylegs, and he shied violently, and set off down the road in the opposite direction to the town.

'Oh, no!' I wailed, giving chase.

Merrylegs hadn't gone far when a lorry came around the bend and ploughed into him with a sickening crunch. Letting out a piercing scream, Merrylegs fell to the ground, trembling all over, his nose swinging round to his shoulder as he lay on his side. Two of his legs were at awkward angles.

Ben on Lurch, and myself on foot, just stood and stared disbelievingly.

The man in the lorry jumped down from his cab, and, rushing to the front of his vehicle, surveyed Merrylegs in horror. Finally, he stumbled over to me, and said almost tearfully, 'I'm sorry, he was right in front of me. I couldn't stop in time.'

In all fairness to him, Merrylegs had been on the bend, and a pony in the middle of the road at four o'clock in the morning was surely a pretty rare sight.

Sliding off Lurch, Ben gave his reins to me to hold, and went over to Merrylegs, who kept on trying to get up, squealing in pain whenever he put any weight on to his broken limbs. Ben knelt down and inspected the pony. Realizing at once the extent of his injuries, he stood up abruptly, and said to me harshly, 'I'd better get my gun.' And with that, he ran up to the house.

While he was gone, I asked the driver if there was any damage to his lorry. He walked over to it and had a quick inspection.

'One smashed headlamp and a dented bumper,' he informed me as he walked back towards me. He then gave me the name and address of the insurance company.

Ben returned with his gun, and, telling me to go and put Lurch away, went over to Merrylegs. Kneeling down beside the terrified pony, he gently patted his neck, talking to him softly, stroking his pert little ears.

Ben got to his feet, and, seeing me still frozen to the spot, shouted at me to go.

'And telephone the vet. We'll need his help!'

As Ben took a step towards Merrylegs, I turned abruptly, and led Lurch back to his box. I was removing his bridle when his head jerked up sharply and he literally lifted me off my feet as a loud bang rang out. Swallowing hard, I locked the bridle away in the tack room, went up to the house and phoned the vet, explaining that we needed him to come now with his tractor, as Merrylegs was blocking the lane.

'I'll be right over,' said Dick Fox, in his usual calm, unruffled manner.

I ran back down the drive, taking an old blanket with me. When I reached the road, Ben was sitting on the grass verge, his gun lying across his knee, his head in his hands.

I heard retching sounds, and, glancing along from Ben, saw the lorry driver throwing up in the hedge. I handed the blanket to Ben.

He slowly got to his feet, walked over to Merrylegs and spread the blanket over him. Ben gazed down at the lifeless pony, and, throwing back his head, he yelled, 'You bastard!'

The lorry driver jumped violently, and looked suitably frightened and guilty all at the same time. He thought Ben was yelling at him. I touched his arm lightly, making him jump again, and, shaking my head, I said quietly, 'It's all right, he doesn't mean you.' The driver blinked quickly several times, and nodded.

After what seemed like twenty minutes or so, Dick Fox arrived with his tractor and trailer, and placing several straps around the pony's body, he winched him up off the ground and put him into the trailer, which he then reversed into our drive. The lorry driver got back into his vehicle, looking pale and shocked, and drove away.

'Do you want to have him here?' Dick asked Ben matter-of-factly.

Ben shook his head. 'No, you take him. Sorry about the time of night. Send me the bill.'

Dick looked at Ben consideringly for a minute, and said, again matter-of-factly, 'Have you told the police about this? I think you ought to report it.'

'Why bother?' Ben said vehemently. 'They'll not do anything.'

'What do you mean?' asked Dick, totally lost.

'My brother! That's what I damned well mean!' shouted Ben, and stormed off into the Yard. He spent the next twenty minutes padding up and down the drive with buckets of water out of the water trough, washing the blood off the road. It was going to be difficult enough for Harry, without having the evidence left behind for him to see.

I left Ben to his cleaning up and took Dick up to the house for a drink, explaining about Matt.

Dick listened quite calmly, as he always did. I sometimes wondered what it would take to ruffle his feathers. 'So that's four horses he's killed,' said Dick ruefully.

'Yes, Mistral he poisoned, Arthur and Barney he burned to death, and now Merrylegs.' I gazed into my drink.

'But why destroy a business he half owns?' Dick asked, logically.

'Because Ben has control over this place and Matt hates that. He wanted to have a say in running this place, but he hasn't got a head for business, so, feeling shut out, he's obviously decided to destroy what he can't have.'

'That's bordering on psychotic!' Dick said, raising his eyebrows a fraction.

We've got him now, I thought! He's obviously shocked! I looked at the vet nervously. 'He scares me. I have a feeling he's only playing with us at the moment. He's being a nuisance, an irritant. I dread to think what he'd do if he was deadly serious.'

'Why hasn't Ben called the police about all this?'

'What can they do? You can bet your life they won't find any evidence, and I'll also bet Matt'll have someone who'll vouch for him, say that he was somewhere else when we had the fire, and all the other incidents.'

Dick looked rueful. 'I see what you mean. You know it's him, but how do you prove it?'

I nodded miserably.

Hearing footsteps on the gravel outside, Dick glanced at the kitchen door. Ben walked in, strode straight into the drawing room, and returned holding a glass of scotch. Leaning against the Aga, his favourite spot, he downed it in one gulp and banged his glass down. He stonily surveyed the far wall.

I looked at Dick, who sighed and got to his feet, saying he'd better be off.

'I'll walk down with you,' said Ben. 'I've got two padlocks in my study; I'll just go and get them.'

Ben went off to fetch the padlocks, and then walked down the drive with Dick.

I heard the tractor start up, and, sighing, I pondered on the task ahead, of having to tell Harry his pony was dead.

Within five minutes Ben was back, slightly calmer and quieter than before. He'd put the padlocks on the gate leading to the road and the gate to the paddock.

'I suppose that's how it's got to be in the future, although he could let the whole bloody Yard out if he wanted to,' he said wearily.

197

I looked at my watch. It had just gone five o'clock.

'Do you want to go back to bed?'

Surprisingly, Ben said he did. I thought he might be too wound up to sleep.

Climbing back into bed, Ben pulled me against him quite roughly, and, with him holding me tightly, we fitfully dozed on and off.

On waking, mid-morning, we heard the boys downstairs, chattering away to each other. I gazed at Ben steadily, and we both sighed as we decided to get up.

Harry had to be faced.

I kissed the boys as I always did as I walked into the kitchen, Harry was singing Merrylegs' praises for the gymkhana. I was just about to speak when Ben put his hand lightly on my arm.

'I'll do it.' Giving me a brief smile, he picked up Harry, and carried him off into his study.

I told Alex and Rory. Alex, predictably, burst into tears. Rory swallowed hard, and gazed at his feet. I'd emphasized the point that Merrylegs had been the only one hurt; their ponies were safe.

I could hear muffled sobbing coming from the study, and within a couple of minutes, Ben carried Harry back into the kitchen. The child reached his arms out to me, so I took him from Ben, and Harry wrapped his arms and legs around me like a little monkey as he clung to me, whimpering softly.

I sat down at the table and gently rocked him back and forth. Alex came up to us and tenderly patted his brother on his back, trying in his gauche fashion to comfort him.

Harry decided he wanted to be in the Yard, which I wasn't sure was a good idea, but in the end I relented.

198

When we walked into the Yard, Finn and Mark had nearly finished mucking out. The lads worked alternate Sundays, so they had every other Sunday off. There was no riding or driving for visitors, so the horses got a day off too, except, that was, when Dominic worked, as he was generally breaking in or training one of the horses. Having lost two driving horses in the fire, Dominic had started to break two of the riding horses to harness. Sundays involved feeding, mucking out, and turning all the horses out for a few hours to let them graze, and generally have a little freedom to do as they wished.

Harry poked his head through the paddock rails, and sadly surveyed the absence of Merrylegs. Alex and Rory tactfully didn't go over to see their ponies.

Finally, heartbreakingly, Harry turned away and, stuffing his hands into his pockets, wandered back up to the house, absent-mindedly kicking pebbles as he went.

Mark, aware that Merrylegs wasn't in the paddock, asked where he was. I told him what had happened, and about Matt. If the stable lads know, I thought, there's a few more pairs of eyes and ears keeping watch.

'Bastard!' howled Mark in disgust.

'How's Ben?' enquired Finn, more calmly.

'Angry, fed up, disgusted, take your pick. He can't quite get his head around the fact that Matt knows how the boys feel about their ponies, and yet he let them out. Harry, as you've seen for yourself, is terribly upset. I couldn't hurt any child like that, certainly not intentionally.'

Mark and Finn nodded soberly.

'Well, I'd better get back up to the house. I want to keep an eye on Harry.' Steering Alex and Rory in front of me, I noticed Finn looking almost tearful.

Walking quietly back into the house, I wandered into the drawing room, where Harry was sitting cross-legged on the floor, his teddy bear on his knee.

Alex, brushing past me, sat down next to him, handing him a jigsaw puzzle. Harry scowled at him, and looked as if he was going to tell him to clear off. Alex calmly took back the jigsaw puzzle and emptied the pieces out on to the floor.

He began putting the pieces together, and Harry, noticing a bit he'd got wrong (accidentally on purpose, I guessed), swapped it for a piece that did fit. I watched them, smiling faintly. Ben came up behind me, and, taking my hand, led me into the kitchen. I glanced at the newspaper he was holding.

'What do you want with that? It's yesterday's.'

Ben tiptoed to the door and quietly shut it.

'I've just phoned up about a pony that's for sale. I'm going to see it now.'

'Don't you think it's too soon? I mean, he might need a little time to get over Merrylegs.'

Shaking his head, he said, 'In a child's world, emotions shift rapidly. If I give him another pony immediately, it'll be sure to help him get over Merrylegs.' Giving me a light peck on the cheek, he strode off towards the Yard.

Two minutes later, Ben drove off in the horsebox. He returned an hour later, and, leaving the horsebox in the drive, he came into the house looking pleased, then ushered us all outside.

Tied to the horsebox was a chubby grey pony, with a cheeky face and bright, intelligent eyes. Catching sight of us, he peered inquisitively, lazily blinking in the sunlight.

'Harry, meet Tinker!' announced Ben, holding an arm out towards the pony.

Harry's dull eyes began to sparkle with interest. Slowly, he walked up to the pony, and gently stroked his neck. Tinker, obviously deciding that he had an itch, rubbed his head up and down Harry's arm, very nearly knocking him over. Harry giggled.

'Take him to the paddock,' said Ben, looking slightly relieved. 'Let him get used to his new home.'

Harry untied Tinker and led him gently to the paddock. As Tinker was turned loose, the riding horses took absolutely no notice. Flicka and Badger, however, eyed him suspiciously. After a few snorts and tail-flicking squeals, they appeared either to lose interest or accept him. Either way, they resumed their grazing.

Harry, delighted with Tinker, perked up considerably, and couldn't stop sidling off to the paddock to have a gawp at him.

When Ben and I went to bed that night we heard muffled giggles coming from Harry's room. Creeping in, Ben whipped back the duvet, and found Harry, Alex and Rory huddled at the bottom of Harry's bed, listening to the radio.

Harry and Alex guiltily tried to hide behind their teddy bears. Rory tried to hide behind Alex. Ben, scooping up Rory under one arm and Alex under the other, walked into their respective rooms, and unceremoniously dumped them on to their own beds, bellowing, 'If I hear one peep out of you. I'll ground the lot of you!'

Coming back into our room, Ben grinned at me. 'I see Harry's back to his usual self, corrupting his brothers.' He raised his eyes to heaven.

Ben was secretly quite pleased Harry was playing him up. The damage Matt had done had, hopefully, been repaired.

Monday morning brought bright sunshine and a loud clanking lorry. The builder had arrived to start on the new hay store and stable block. The boys and I were in the Yard grooming the ponies. Harry was impatient to try out Tinker. I noticed the builder had several tough-looking men helping him, all with tattoos (which, incidentally, were spelt wrong) and they all spoke with a Welsh accent. Dominic, for reasons best known to himself, sourly referred to them as the 'Lilac Army' – an expression *I* soon adopted, too.

By the end of the day, the 'Lilacs' had made good progress. The structure and foundations of the building were coming along at a furious rate. Two of the 'Lilacs' couldn't take their eyes off Will, much to the annoyance and acute irritation of both Dominic and Adam. The two 'Lilacs' were obviously not gay, it was just that Will was so pretty. Everyone stared at Will, including me.

Harry and Tinker, having parted company twice, were now getting along famously, and Harry informed me he was a 't'riffic bender', whatever that meant! When I put him to bed that night, his excited chatter about Tinker made me think Merrylegs was already a distant memory.

The rest of the week passed pretty uneventfully, until Friday.

Matt seemed to be keeping a low profile. The boys and I rode every day. One of the 'Lilacs' was finally on speaking terms with Will, who flirted a bit, and Dominic and Adam were out of the Yard most of the time with their driving tours.

Adam seemed to be functioning on automatic pilot. His manner towards Will, as it had been from the beginning, was to gaze at him, longingly. His manner towards Dominic, however, was changing by the day. Having ignored him to start with, he now glared at him at every opportunity.

On Friday, things came to a head. As the boys and I finished breakfast, Mrs Travis waddled into the kitchen to start work for the day, puffing and wheezing about how hot it was.

'It makes my feet swell, and the cat's behaving very strangely,' she complained, wiping her face on the hem of her frock.

'Is it still OK for you to babysit the boys tomorrow night?' I asked, pouring her a glass of ice-cold orange juice.

'Of course it is,' she said, beaming at me. 'Where is it you're off to?'

'To have dinner with John, my brother,' I replied, cramming Tinker's sweat rug into a groaning washing machine.

'Oh, yes, you did mention it.' She hitched her frock up over her mottled knees and sat down heavily, her legs apart, at which Alex quickly looked away, and Harry quickly looked up.

Ben walked into the kitchen to get himself a drink, and, seeing Harry, gently tapped him on the shoulder.

'Morning, Mr Carmichael,' said Mrs Travis, grinning broadly. 'It's turned out hot again, hasn't it?'

'Very,' said Ben, taking a can of beer out of the fridge.

'OK you lot,' I said to the boys, 'let's go for a ride.'

Eagerly the boys pulled their boots on, and we tramped out of the house, and down to the Yard. We rode for miles alongside the canal, the heat making us feel drowsy. It was so hot, a shimmering heat haze distorted the horizon, the sky a beautiful aquamarine, with little cotton-wool clouds dotted here and there.

When we got back to the Yard, Adam and Dominic were facing each other, hands on hips, glaring, obviously having a disagreement of some sort. Over Will, no doubt. Hastily I led the boys with their ponies around the corner of a stable block, leaving them to hose them down.

I went back to Dominic and Adam. Dominic was accusing Adam of trying to get back together with Will.

'I was only talking to him,' said Adam coldly.

'No, you bloody weren't,' spat Dominic, 'you were playing on the sympathy angle. "Oh, Will, I can't live without you! Please come back to me!" I know the sort of stuff you were talking about.'

Will, having walked out of the tack room, caught sight of Dominic and Adam facing each other with obvious hostility, and shot over to them.

'What's going on?' he asked the other two men nervously.

'It seems that Dominic has a problem with my even speaking to you,' said Adam mockingly.

'That's not what it's about and you know it!' snapped Dominic.

'Oh, yes, Dominic here seems to think I'm trying to take you away from him, which is pretty insulting really. More his style, don't you think, Will?' Adam eyed Will balefully.

'Just stop it, both of you!' snapped Will, starting to get upset.

'Why? You started all this,' hissed Adam, viciously turning his anger on Will. Will blinked and looked away, biting his lip.

'You bastard!' roared Dominic, and smashed his fist into Adam's face. Adam staggered backwards, then righted himself and lunged at Dominic, knocking him to the ground. They rolled over and over, hurling insults and fists into each other.

Will, desperately trying to stop the fight, got hit in the face, and retreated to sit dazedly on the water trough.

All I could do was watch helplessly. There was no way I was going to step in between them, and the 'Lilac Army' were being no help at all. They downed tools and had a tea break, idly placing bets between them as to who would win.

I looked around me in agitation for Ben, or Mark or Finn, but they all seemed to have temporarily disappeared.

Dominic managed to get to his feet and, grabbing Adam by his arms, slammed him up against one of the boxes, bringing his knee across Adam's body to deflect any blows his opponent might aim at him.

Adam, determined not to be defeated, head-butted Dominic, who with a bloody nose staggered backwards, releasing Adam. Adam seized a disorientated Dominic and pushed his head into the water trough, evidently trying to drown him. This, thankfully, was when one of the 'Lilacs' decided enough was enough, and pulled Adam off Dominic, who erupted out of the water trough, gasping for air.

Shaking water out of his hair and eyes, he glared at Adam in a murderous rage. The 'Lilac' was still holding on to Adam, with his arms behind his back, and Dominic took full advantage of this. Charging up to him, Dominic smashed his fist into Adam's already battered face.

Adam's legs buckled, and Dominic, dragging him over to the water trough, stuck his head in it, asking savagely how *he* liked it. When Dominic showed no signs of letting Adam up, the 'Lilac' hit him on the back of the head with a broom, and Dominic slithered to the ground, unconscious.

Adam exploded out of the water trough, just as Dominic had done, and weakly sank to the ground.

Will and I gazed at each other, shocked and trembling. Adam sat on the ground, head hanging, breathing heavily.

It was several minutes before the 'Lilac' managed to bring Dominic round. Owing to the length of time Dominic had been out, I insisted on taking him to hospital. Will insisted on coming with me.

Ben and Finn wandered around the corner of a stable block, discussing one of the horses. In one swift glance they took in what had happened. Ben was furious. This couldn't go on. He'd been patient and understanding beyond the call of any boss. He would speak to them all shortly.

I said I was taking Dominic to the hospital; I thought he might have concussion.

Ben remarked that if he didn't have concussion, he'd see to it that Dominic did when he got back from the hospital! Then he knelt down in front of Adam, tilting his chin up with his finger. Adam winced.

'It sodding well serves you right!' snapped Ben. Adam looked at him with a mutinous expression. The 'Lilac Army', now with the fun over, resumed their sporadic banging of hammers.

I helped Dominic into my car, leaving the boys with Mrs Travis. Ben had quite enough to do around the Yard as it was. Neither Adam nor Dominic were in any fit state, and Will was still insisting he come to the hospital with us, which meant that his help wouldn't be forthcoming either.

As I was leaving for the hospital, Ben took Adam into the house, no doubt presenting his battered face to Mrs Travis to clean up.

At the hospital, they confirmed what I'd thought. Dominic had slight concussion.

'Interfering Taff!' spat Dominic, gingerly rubbing the back of his head.

'Dominic, you were killing Adam,' I reproached him mildly. 'What was the other chap supposed to do?'

'Let me,' said Dominic, acidly. Will still hadn't said much. He looked at me sadly.

'This isn't working out, is it? I think perhaps I'd better leave.'

'Well, you don't seem to have the problem. I mean, you get on with both Adam and, obviously, Dominic.'

Dominic surveyed me steadily. 'I suppose I'll go. But Will comes with me. I'm not leaving him to work in the Yard on his own. Without me there, Adam would be all over him like ivy up a vicarage wall.' Shifting his legs irritably on the bed, he moodily inspected his bloody knuckles.

Will smiled faintly, and then winced. He'd cracked the cut on the corner of his mouth, where Adam or Dominic had thumped him one. Thinking back, I felt sure it had been Adam.

The nurses thought Dominic, and especially Will, utterly gorgeous, and couldn't stop fiddling with their wrists, which was pretty amusing when Will wasn't even there as a patient!

Dominic scowled at them. 'Can I go now?' he barked, dodging a prodding finger wending its way towards his cheekbone. His face, like Adam's, was quite battered. They had really meant it.

'Yes, but take plenty of rest,' said a large bossy nurse, whom Dominic referred to as 'the roadblock', and Will, out of sheer nerves, had called 'sir'.

On our way back to the Yard, Will made Dominic promise him there would be no more quarrelling. He took no pleasure in seeing the two people he most cared about fighting over him.

Dominic said he'd try, but if 'that bastard' tried anything he'd finish the job next time, and kill him, which all in all wasn't much of a promise!

When we got home, we walked wearily into the Yard. Ben, Finn, Mark and, surprisingly, one of the 'Lilacs' had finished the chores for the day. Ben, beckoning to Will and Dominic to join him, marched them up to the house, with me trailing behind them.

Ben took them straight into his study. When they emerged, some twenty minutes later, it had been decided that Adam should leave, apparently at his own suggestion. He'd sat in the study, waiting for Will and Dominic to return, and quite openly admitted to Ben that he couldn't stand to see Will with Dominic. He'd been thinking about leaving anyway.

Dominic looked awkward and uncomfortable. Will looked miserable and horribly guilty. Adam, giving a brief smile, told me to keep in touch.

'And where do I do that?' I asked, feeling a wave of desolation sweep over me. I was very fond of Adam.

Adam shrugged listlessly. 'There are a few stables around these parts. I might try those. I might move

208

away altogether, I haven't decided. I'll let you know.'

I nodded, gazing at him. I was sincerely sorry for the mess he'd found himself in.

Ben came over to me, and slipped an arm around my waist. 'I'll give you a good reference, and send it to you in the post, along with any wages you're owed. You're a good worker, Adam. Reliable and trustworthy. I shall miss you.'

Adam's eyes flickered, and, gruffly saying goodbye, he walked out of the house, and down the drive to his car.

Will and Dominic looked embarrassed, and fidgeted nervously. They apologized again for the trouble they'd caused, and sidled out of the house, back to the Yard to collect Dominic's motorbike.

The boys wanted to know why Dominic and Adam were fighting.

'A difference of opinion,' said Ben blandly.

'What about?' enquired Alex, sticking his thumb in his mouth.

'Football,' said Ben. The boys looked undecided for a few moments, and I thought Ben might have to do better than that, when their faces cleared, and acceptance registered. Mrs Travis smiled knowingly.

Sighing heavily, Ben said, 'I'd better get an ad in the paper for a new lad. If I get moving now, it'll be in Monday's edition. I need one as soon as possible. That stable block'll be finished by tomorrow, and then there'll be another four horses to muck out.' Using the phone in the kitchen, he called the local rag.

Before going to bed that night, Ben walked down to the paddock, and to the main gate at the bottom of the drive, to check he'd put the padlocks on.

We could do without another sleepless night.

CHAPTER 15

I awoke to bright sunshine streaming through the window, and a now familiar clanking noise. The 'Lilac Army' had arrived to finish the stable block.

Ben was already up and out of the house, or so his note told me. He was down in the Yard helping the lads feed and muck out. In effect, he was taking Adam's place until he got a new lad.

The boys and I spent the best part of the day in the Yard with the ponies.

Around lunchtime, the 'Lilacs' packed their kit and trundled out of the Yard.

The atmosphere was different around the Yard. Mark and Finn seemed fairly subdued at Adam's departure, though Finn had been 'off' for a while now. Will appeared to be in shock, and Dominic was the most relaxed he'd ever been. The boys were missing Adam dreadfully.

In the evening, Mrs Travis took care of the boys' tea, while I got ready to go out to John's for dinner. Ben came up to our room just as I'd finished.

'I'll just dive through the shower, then we'll be off,' he said, pulling his shirt off, dropping it on the floor, and galloping off to the bathroom.

I was sitting in the drawing room, listening to the boys' chatter, when Ben walked in, tucking his shirt in.

'Ready?'

I nodded, and looked him up and down. He was wearing chinos which emphasized his long legs, and a loud shirt.

Apart from the shirt screaming obscenities at me, he looked gorgeous and I told him so. He smiled, and remarked, 'Ditto,' looking appreciatively at my legs, which were crossed under a skirt several inches above the knee, and then his eyes moved, equally apprecia- tively, to my tight, clinging top.

As I walked past him, he ran his hand lingeringly over my thigh, and found what he was searching for, the little nobbles indicating that I was wearing stockings and suspenders.

Ben pulled a pained face and coughed. Reaching up, I licked his ear and murmured, 'Shall we go?'

Ben looked at me as if he didn't want to go anywhere but the bedroom, but we made it out to the car, kissing the boys and thanking Mrs Travis again for babysitting.

John lived some forty minutes or so away from the Yard, and we arrived just after seven.

John and I hugged each other almost to death, while Ben held out his hand, and John shook it, smiling gently. Ben ran his hand over the back of his head, and apol- ogized to John for his terse manner towards him when he'd come to see me.

John grinned broadly. 'Forget it. It's not important. Penny did explain why you were so obnoxious.'

Ben gave a lop-sided grin and, looking slightly em- barrassed, glanced down at the carpet, stuffing his hands in his pockets.

John laughed, while I gently reproached him for being so wicked. John introduced his lady friend, who it had to be said was very pretty, but rather slow. John obviously only wanted her for her mind. The point being, she obviously *wouldn't* mind! Ben and I shook hands with Carolyn Burton.

'Pleased to meet you,' I said, catching John's eye as he winked at me.

We settled down in the sitting room, which still felt like home to me, with its funny little characters painted on the walls and the simple modern furniture.

John poured us all a drink. Ben asked for just one beer, as he was driving. I had my usual gin and tonic. Carolyn decided to be daring, and had a bottle of flat ginger ale that John found at the back of the drinks cabinet.

John kept disappearing into the tiny kitchen to check on the food, while Ben and I made polite conversation with Miss Burton. Ben's stomach gave a loud rumble.

'Andrew's Liver Salts,' said Carolyn, kindly. Ben looked blank and blinked at her.

'Wind,' she said, pointing to his stomach.

I started to laugh, but, catching sight of Ben's stony face, hastily smothered my chuckles with a cough. Ben turned his stony stare towards Carolyn.

'I do not have wind. That was hunger.'

Fortunately, John reappeared to call us into the rather sparsely furnished dining room, where he'd laid out the starter, a salmon mousse, one of my favourites.

We sat around the table, which was only just big enough for the four of us. I turned to speak to Carolyn and very nearly got jabbed by her rather bony elbow.

'You really should get a bigger table,' I told John.

'I know. I had friends over for dinner last week and had this same problem. So in the end we linked arms and fed each other.'

Ben and I fell about laughing, while Carolyn took to holding her fork on the very tip and, pivoting it on its axis, managed to twist her head so she caught it on its way round.

The conversation moved on as John asked Ben how business was.

'Fine, fine,' he smiled. 'Who painted your walls with those cartoons?'

'I did,' John replied.

Ben choked on his mousse and Carolyn missed her pivoting fork and had to go round again.

John laughed. 'Didn't Penny ever tell you what her good-for-nothing brother does for a living?'

Ben, looking slightly watery-eyed, shook his head. 'Are you a cartoonist?'

'Amongst other things. I do a feature in a national magazine called *Man's Monthly*.' John grinned, and, leaning back towards a bookcase, pulled out last month's edition. He flicked through to the back of the magazine and handed it to Ben.

'Are you still using the same character?' I asked, looking at it over Ben's shoulder.

John nodded. He had used the character called Mabel Thorpe for years. She was an old northern lady, who had a nameless friend, and they discussed life's little quirks and old sayings. They both wore large duffel coats and coal miners' boots. Ben and I creased up into hysterics.

'It's very good,' said Ben, looking impressed. 'Do you sketch?'

'Sometimes, but I prefer to paint. I've done a few of Penny. Perhaps you'd like one?'

'John!' I muttered, going pink.

'I'd love one. We could hang her in the hall.' Ben grinned.

'Charming,' I replied, watching Carolyn bobbing and weaving with her fork.

We'd just finished our starter when the phone rang. John went off to answer it, and returned almost immediately, to tell Ben it was for him.

'For me?' Ben looked both surprised and bewildered.

'Your housekeeper,' John informed him, holding out the receiver.

I looked at Ben, slightly alarmed. I hoped it wasn't one of the boys. I'd left John's number in case of any emergencies.

Ben, taking the receiver off him with a brief smile, said hurriedly, 'Yes, hello?'

Mrs Travis was obviously explaining the problem to him. Ben's face relaxed, and, looking at me, he shook his head. Relieved, I sat back in my chair, sipping my drink. Finally, Ben came off the phone.

'I'm sorry, I've got to go back to the Yard. One of the horses appears to be ill, apparently making a hell of a lot of noise. Probably in a lot of pain. I'm sorry to muck up dinner.' He looked apologetically at John.

'Don't worry.' John waved a hand. 'I understand. Twenty-four hours a day, aren't they?'

Ben nodded ruefully, and, looking at me, said gently, 'You stay for a while – no need to ruin your evening. Get a taxi home.'

Fishing his wallet out of his back pocket, he laid several notes down on the table.

'Are you sure?' I asked, looking at him doubtfully. It didn't seem fair to me, but he insisted I stay. Pecking me on the cheek, he let himself out of the flat and drove away.

John cleared away the dishes, and returned from the kitchen buckling under the weight of a huge beef wellington he'd made. John was a marvellous cook, far better at it than I was. He loved cooking. I hated it. Just another chore to me, like cleaning the loo.

John's beef wellington lived up to his usual standards, absolutely delicious. As we ate, I told him Ben and I were getting married.

'Really!' he said, incredulously. 'I was beginning to worry about your shelf-life. I was thinking of branding you with a "best before" date.' He grinned, wiping pastry off his lips with a crumpled napkin. 'So when do you actually become Mrs Carmichael?'

'August the first,' I replied, watching Carolyn going to great pains trying to scrape pâté off her beef.

John, following my gaze, asked her, 'Don't you like pâté?'

She shook her head. 'No, I'm afraid I don't.' She wrinkled her nose in disgust.

John, working his food over to the other side of his mouth, considered her for a moment. 'Never mind, have some more wine.' And he filled her glass to nearly overflowing.

He's out to get her drunk, I thought. Personally, I didn't think she needed it.

'There, get that down yer neck,' Grinning unashamedly at me, he watched her taking great gulps of wine.

John and I continued to discuss the wedding, and Carolyn continued to drink. By the time we got to

215

dessert, a mandarin and kiwi-fruit pavlova, Carolyn had developed a bad case of hiccups and a slightly cross-eyed expression. Over coffee, her elbow kept on sliding off the table, and I thought John had overdone the wine a bit. I know my brother likes passionate women; unfortunately this one was now semi-comatose.

I couldn't help giggling as I helped John clear away and load the dishwasher, which chore was punctuated by several apologies as we kept on bumping into each other.

We'd taken so long over dinner, I felt I ought to be getting back to the Yard, I phoned for a taxi. Ten minutes later it arrived, and, thanking John for a lovely meal, I kissed him and trotted out to the waiting car. I didn't bother saying a farewell to Carolyn because she was face-down on the table with smudged lipstick all over her face and was most definitely out for the count.

I arrived back at the Yard, complete with the taxi driver's phone number – just in case I changed my mind, he said, and decided to go for a drink with him. Waving him off, I locked the gate and walked up the drive.

Entering the house, I found all the lights were out. All in bed. I quietly called to Ben. No answer; perhaps he was still down at the stables, looking after the sick horse.

I made my way down to the Yard, and had a quick glance about. Shrugging, I guessed he'd also gone to bed, and returned to the house.

Creeping into the kitchen, I light-footedly made my way into the hall and, stopping dead, gave a startled gasp then relaxed, heaving a great sigh, Ben was standing in the doorway to the drawing room, silhouetted by the moonlight behind him.

'God, you made me jump!' I whispered hoarsely, rushing over to him and slapping him playfully on his

216

arm. Reaching up, I put my arms around his neck and pressed against him. His arms came around my waist, and squeezed me tightly. Curling my fingers into his hair, I gently kissed him, moving my hands down to stroke his face.

Something wasn't quite right. Ben didn't have a scar on his cheek. Going briskly into reverse, the hands gripped my arms and jerked me to within an inch of the face. Matt grinned evilly at me.

'Don't stop now!' he said, almost caressingly. 'I was enjoying that.'

I gazed up at him dumbly. I began to shake. His black eyes bored into me. I just froze, rooted to the spot.

'Where's Ben?' I finally croaked out.

'Somewhere he won't be coming back from,' said Matt, menacingly.

I gave a strangled moan, and closed my eyes. My scrambled brain was frantically trying to work. My first thought, as with any trapped creature, was to run. Try and escape. Yes, that's it. Try and raise the alarm, get the police.

Matt shook me gently and I opened my eyes, gazing at his shirt unseeingly. Licking my dry lips, I asked shakily, 'What have you done to the boys?'

Matt glowered at me. 'I haven't done anything to them. They're all in bed.'

'I don't believe you.' With an enormous effort I raised my eyes to his.

'Well, that's easily settled.' Grabbing my hand, he dragged me along behind him, stumbling up the stairs. He led me into each of the boys' rooms. They were all sleeping soundly, thankfully oblivious to what was going on around them. He led me quietly back to the landing.

'See,' he whispered, 'all safe and sound.'

'And Mrs Travis?' I asked, my eyes darting around me for any signs of a struggle.

'Ah, yes, well, I'm afraid she got rather unpleasant.' Putting his head on one side, he eyed me with amusement.

I gazed at him in horror. 'What have you done to her!'

'I've only locked her in a bedroom.' He led me to one of the spare rooms, opened the door and pushed me in.

Sitting in an armchair was Mrs Travis. I rushed over to her, and gently asked her how she was. Matt was quickly beside me, and seized my arm.

'I'm just checking she's OK,' I snapped, wrenching my arm free. I glared at him, suddenly very angry.

'How are the boys?' she asked, obviously very upset.

'They're fine,' I replied, turning to face her, 'they're all asleep.'

Suddenly, she burst into tears. Gently, I hugged her, patting her eyes with my handkerchief.

'I'm so sorry,' she wept, 'he made me do it.' She lowered her head in shame.

'Made you do what?' I asked, rocking her back and forth, rather as I would have done to one of the boys. She sniffed several times, and wiped her nose on the back of her hand.

'That swine –' she jabbed a porky finger at Matt '– made me phone your brother, to fetch Mr Carmichael back here. I had to say one of the horses was ill. He said, if I told you one of the boys was ill, you'd come too, and he didn't want that. He wanted Ben on his own.'

'I think that's enough chit-chat for now,' said Matt, and yanked me away from Mrs Travis. 'See you later.'

218

He gave her a little wave. Seizing my hand again, he dragged me out of the room, locking the door behind him, and, forcing me to walk briskly, he took me back downstairs and into the drawing room. He pushed me down on to the sofa, quite hard.

'Sit there and do as you're told and I won't hurt you,' he barked, pointing his finger at me.

I looked down at my hands, which were nervously wringing my handkerchief. Finally I asked in a quavering voice, 'What did you do to Ben?'

'I hit him very hard, with something very blunt, and threw him into the canal,' he replied, looking quite pleased with himself.

I swallowed hard several times. 'What do you intend to do with all of us?' I wasn't sure I wanted to hear the reply.

He crossed the room and stood looking down at me, his eyes wandering all over my body.

'Well, you and I are going to have some fun for starters.'

For starters salmon mousse, I thought hysterically. I looked up at him. 'What do you mean?'

'Oh, I think you know.' He started to rock back and forth on his heels.

I quickly looked away, shifting uncomfortably. I felt revolted, and terrified. He'd bumped off my future husband; who knew what else he was capable of? How could someone who was almost the spitting image of Ben be so different?

'What about the boys?' I asked, not sure whether I was trying to distract him or myself.

'As long as they behave themselves, they'll come to no harm.' Folding his arms, he watched me, obviously trying to work out what was going on behind my frightened eyes.

'You wouldn't hurt them,' I whispered, shaking my head. 'You couldn't hurt a child.'

Matt examined his fingernails.

'Believe me, if I can kill my own brother I can kill one of his brats.'

I gazed at him, shocked, speechless. He knelt down beside me. 'I would rather not hurt anyone else, but if I have to, I will. Do I make myself clear?'

'Perfectly,' I said, faintly.

'Good.' He slid on to the sofa beside me.

'Why are you doing this?' I asked, blinking back tears.

'Oh, I think you know!' he snapped. 'I've just about had enough of Ben and his damnable lording it over me. I've tried to get through to him so many times and he doesn't want to know. So I've sorted him, once and for all.' His face was inches from mine. Apart from the scar, he could almost be Ben.

'But you can't just waltz in here and take over from Ben. I mean, most people know how you and Ben feel about each other. They know he'd never give you this place. Besides, people will start asking questions, like where he is, for instance.' I cringed back against the sofa.

Matt surveyed me stonily. 'I haven't decided yet whether to sell the property or just blow the whole useless place up,' he snarled, 'but either way, you come with me.'

'And what if I don't want to?'

'Well, it's either that, or I bump you off as well. I mean, I can't have you, or anyone for that matter, being a witness as to what went on here.'

I gazed at him disbelievingly. 'You're mad!'

He leapt off the sofa and, hauling me to my feet, shook me vigorously. I collapsed on to the sofa, sobbing quietly.

'Oh, Ben,' I wailed, and got a china horse thrown at me for daring to want Matt's brother. Fortunately it missed me and hit the far wall.

Grabbing me by the arms, Matt yelled at me, 'Don't you ever mention his name to me again. He didn't want to hear about me, so I don't want to hear about him! Right?'

I held my breath and, nodding, looked at him with what must have been huge frightened eyes, feeling the blood trickle out of the corner of my mouth, where he'd slapped me.

Taking a deep breath, he snatched the handkerchief out of my hand and dabbed the corner of my mouth, looking into my eyes as he cleaned up the blood. He hadn't actually split my mouth; I'd bitten it on the inside when he hit me.

Suddenly, I remembered the remark Dick Fox had made, about Matt's behaviour bordering on the psychotic, and felt faint.

Matt, finished with his dabbing, sat back on his heels and surveyed me through dark, surprisingly sorrowful eyes. Finally, he said abruptly, 'Penny, you don't have to be afraid of me. I told you, if you do as you're told you'll be fine.'

Completely out of my control, a large tear spilled over and rolled slowly down my cheek. Matt caught his breath and ran his hand through his hair in an impatient gesture. His sharp, sudden action made me flinch and cower in the corner of the sofa. Strangely, this didn't irritate him, as I feared it might, but seemed rather to appal him.

Reaching over, he lifted me up in his arms as if I were as light as Harry and sat down on the sofa, sitting me on his lap. Through gritted teeth, he moaned, 'I'm sorry,' and held me tightly.

He looked at me expectantly, and, suddenly realizing his meaning, I put my arms around his neck. I found I couldn't stop shaking. Shock, I suppose.

'Now, calm down, stop crying and relax.'

I'm sitting on the knee of a psychopath and he's telling me to relax, I thought hysterically. I sniffed, noisily.

'Right. This is what I have in mind. You and I are going to hide out for a while, until I sell this place, or whatever. Actually, I know of someone who would be interested in buying it. It wouldn't take too long to sort out.'

He scratched his nose and went on, 'Now, the boys stay here with Mrs Travis. If she thinks anything of you, she'll tell no one what's happened here. She'll tell the stable lads that Ben had to go away and he's taken you with him. That should take care of any curious questions. Then we'll just have to see what happens.'

Why do I get the feeling he's making this up as he goes along? I thought.

'Why are you taking me with you? Why can't I stay here like the boys and Mrs Travis?' I asked, fresh tears filling my eyes.

'Because you are my insurance policy. And if you do anything silly, I'd not only have to bump you off, but also Mrs Travis . . .' He paused for effect. 'And the boys.'

'But the boys don't even know you're here,' I protested.

'They might do. If they suddenly decide to nip to the loo or something, I can't afford to take the risk.'

I swallowed, and said shakily, 'When d'you want to leave?'

He glanced at his watch. 'In a few minutes. That should be long enough for you to pack a few things. I want to be away long before the boys get up or any of the stable lads arrive.'

Nodding slowly, I sighed resignedly. 'I'd better get a few things together, then.' And I went to get off his knee.

Tightening his grip on me, he said in my ear, 'Before you go . . .' and kissed me.

Deciding to play along with him, I kissed him back, hoping I didn't have to go to any more extreme lengths just to stay alive.

Finally, he let me go, and I got off his knee. He followed me upstairs to the room Ben and I shared. I grabbed a few clothes and toiletries, tiptoeing about, hoping, praying I didn't drop something with an almighty clatter and disturb the boys.

I parked my holdall on the landing. Taking a piece of rope from around his waist, Matt tied it around mine, knotting it several times, so tightly it would have to be cut off me, and then tied the other end to his belt.

'What's this for?' I asked, wiggling the rope.

'To stop you running off,' he explained, and, smiling gently, he turned and picked up my bag and set off down the stairs. I meekly followed him. There wasn't much else I could do, seeing as I was joined at hip and handbag with him.

I thought really unpleasant thoughts, like pushing him down the stairs, but I'd only go crashing down behind him. He glanced over his shoulder at me and smirked. Bastard! I thought savagely. He knows what I'm thinking.

He plonked my bag into Ben's car, the Jaguar. He patted the car gently.

'I might as well have this also.' He grinned nastily.

I turned away in disgust. Just rub it in, why don't you? I thought, silently screaming for Ben.

Turning abruptly, Matt strode off back into the house, giving the rope a sharp tug. I stumbled after him.

Going up the stairs, I asked him where *his* car was. He stopped dead, and stared at me as though I was the one off my head.

'Do you honestly think I'd drive here and leave it parked out the front like a sodding calling card?' he spat, clearly most insulted.

I shook my head, dumbly. 'But your fingerprints are all over the house,' I said, affording myself a little inward gloat. It quickly dissolved when he said calmly, 'I should think so; I half own it!'

He must have seen the dismay on my face because he grinned, then laughed. He actually laughed! I looked away, desperately wanting to slap his mocking face. He tugged on the rope again, and led me sniffing into the spare room where Mrs Travis was still locked in. Amazingly, she'd nodded off. It's bizarre, but I actually felt the stirrings of hysterical laughter in my throat, which I managed to smother.

Matt had no such restraints, and slumped against the wall, shaking helplessly with silent laughter. To me, he had never looked more like Ben, and blinking back tears, I gazed at the carpet.

Matt, gaining control of himself, the pig, wiped his eyes and sauntered over to me, tilting my head up with his finger under my chin.

'Why the tears?' he asked.

I shook my head, and averted my eyes from his face. Cupping my chin, he put his face close up to mine. 'Tell me, or I'll make you.'

'Er – you don't want to know,' I mumbled.

Matt's eyes narrowed. 'Yes, I do. Now tell me.' He glowered at me and waited. I realized I'd have to tell him.

I took a deep breath, 'It's when you – er – were laughing, you so reminded me of Ben.'

His face grew hard and angry, and he seized me by my hair, making me yelp in surprise.

'Thinking of Ben, were you? Crying for him, were you?' Pushing my head back, he placed his other hand on my throat. 'What have I said about mentioning that name to me? From now on you'll see only me, cry only for me. D'you understand?' His eyes stared into mine.

'Yes,' I whispered, not taking my eyes off his. Abruptly, he shoved me away and strode over to Mrs Travis. He gave her a nudge, and she awoke with a start and a muffled squawk. He told her what he'd said to me. If she thought anything of me, she wouldn't say anything to anyone.

'I shall be watching this place closely, but you won't know from where. Remember, if you think a lot of Penny, you'll think very carefully about talking to anyone,' he repeated.

He told her how to deal with the boys and the stable lads. Mrs Travis looked at me, and, transferring her gaze to Matt, nodded slowly. Licking her lips primly, she gave him her word that she wouldn't contact anyone. She gave me a huge bear-hug, and smiled encouragingly.

'You're free to move around the house now. But stay in this room until we've gone,' Matt said, not looking her in the eyes.

Why should that make any difference? I wondered.

Yanking on the rope, he nearly pulled me off my feet, and I fell against him, clutching at his shirt to steady myself.

Without another word he dragged me out of the room, down the stairs and out to the car.

He shoved me on to the back seat, instructing me to lie down, which I did. He then tied my hands and feet together at the back of me with the rope from around my waist. He tied a handkerchief over my mouth and another over my eyes.

He doesn't want me to see where I'm going, I thought in terror. He's going to take me miles away from here and kill me too.

I heard Matt get into the car, and starting it up, he drove down to the gate. He switched off the engine, and I heard him fumbling with the keys, searching for the one that fitted the padlock on the gate. He appeared to find it, and, getting out of the car, I supposed, unlocked it.

He got back into the car and drove out of the gateway, turning right, away from the town.

As I lay in the back, I felt panic rise in my throat like bile, and tried desperately to push any thoughts of Ben out of my head, terrified I would cry and give myself away. Any mention of Ben in any way made him explosively angry, and also, it seemed, a little frustrated. I must not cry. It would only bring me more trouble. He'd probably hit me again. It really was a bit too much. He'd already killed the man I loved. He didn't have to hit me to scare the living daylights out of me!

It was a pity he didn't know that.

CHAPTER 16

It felt as if we'd been driving for about an hour when the car slowed up, and we turned off down, I supposed, yet another lane. After a little while, we turned off again, down what appeared to be a dirt track, full of potholes, which the Jaguar made a fairly smooth ride of.

We came to a halt, and Matt switched off the engine and got out of the car.

He opened the back door and removed my blindfold and gag, and then, producing a pen-knife from his pocket, he cut the rope round my waist.

He dragged me out of the car, and I stood blinking as my eyes adjusted to the moonlit night. Matt retrieved my bag from the boot, and jerked his head towards a small, badly run-down cottage, indicating that I should lead the way.

Walking down the path, I noticed the cottage had shutters at the windows, hanging off their hinges like an odd false eyelash hanging off an eyelid. It was once honey-coloured stone, but was now a dirty grey, with a hint of green around the edges. The thatched roof looked as if it had had a nasty bout of alopecia. The lawn had been cut. A few rose bushes were dotted here and there.

Reaching the door, Matt unlocked it and I stepped inside. Shoving me further into the room, he slammed the door shut and locked it, pocketing the keys. He switched the lights on.

I found I was standing in a small sitting room, with an archway at one end, that led into a tiny kitchen. Glancing to my left, I saw there were stairs. I guessed it had a bedroom and a bathroom on the second floor.

Surprisingly, the cottage was clean and tidy. I looked around the room. A table and chairs, a two-seater sofa, a television standing on a table in one corner and a stereo on a shelf in the other. A small sideboard stood under the window facing me; a lamp with its shade askew had been placed on top of it.

'You'll get to know this cottage extremely well,' said Matt, giving me the impression that I was to be here for quite some time.

I didn't say anything. I couldn't quite believe all this was happening to me. I walked over to the window, and, shading my eyes against the light in the room, I peered through the glass. There were fields all around, and horses idly grazing. I wished I were one of them.

Matt joined me at the window and, peering out also, said softly, 'One of those is mine.'

I glanced at him. 'Really? I didn't know you had a horse.'

He glared at me balefully. 'I have another twenty, at the last count.'

Oh, God, we're back to the Yard again, I thought nervously. Sighing involuntarily, I looked out of the window again, and saw my own pale, frightened reflection.

'Well, I do apologize! Am I boring you?' he snapped, wrenching me round to face him.

As it happens, dog's-breath, you are, I thought irritably. Clutching at his shirt, I replied wearily, 'No, I think I've got the message. The Yard, and everything in it, is half yours, and you're angry that you can't be there.'

'Don't sound so damned patronizing!' he yelled, again shaking me like a rag doll.

I'd had enough. Putting my hand up to my forehead, I burst into tears, saying over and over, 'Just stop it!'

I think that was when he realized how much he'd frightened me. Gathering me up in his arms, he held me so tightly that I could hardly breathe, soothing me as you would a badly frightened horse.

I couldn't stop sobbing, and trembling all over. It took him a fair while to calm me down. The whole bizarre night had finally caught up with me. Finally, with me whimpering like a wounded puppy, Matt picked me up and, carrying me up the stairs, put me to bed.

He actually looked quite upset, and horribly jolted. He carried me as though I were a child, and tripped on the last step.

'You'll give yourself a hernia,' I murmured, wondering if I could be that lucky!

He smiled, and after a slight pause kissed me on the forehead. Kicking open the bedroom door, he gently placed me on the bed and stood looking down at me with an expression I couldn't quite read. Finally, he blurted out, 'I'll get your bag,' and, turning abruptly, belted out of the room and down the stairs.

Within thirty seconds he was back in the bedroom, and dumping my bag on top of an ottoman that stood under the window.

'Do you mind if I go to the loo?' I asked. He shook his head.

I took myself off to the bathroom, which led off from the bedroom, rather like an en-suite. I noted the clean bath, shiny taps and polished mirror, and again felt surprised. Just because you were a nutter, it didn't mean you have to be dirty, I supposed. Yawning, I had a quick wash, pinching his toothbrush to clean my teeth. Habit rules even in times of terror, I supposed.

Going back into the bedroom, I found Matt leaning against the door, smoking and blowing smoke-rings. I padded over to the bed, and with a resigned shrug I undressed as far as my bra and knickers. His eyes nearly fell out of their sockets at my stockings and suspenders.

Well, that's something the two brothers had in common, I thought soberly.

Launching himself off the door, he swung round, locked it and bolted into the bathroom, slamming the door shut behind him. I blinked, and, realizing my mouth was open, I shut it. I took off my stockings and suspenders, hid them under my skirt, and got into bed.

A couple of minutes later, Matt tentatively emerged from the bathroom, peeping round the door. Seeing that I was in bed, he padded round to the other side of it and got on top of the sheet. I lay with my back to him, close to the edge of the bed.

After a minute or so, he gave an impatient sigh, got up off the bed and, unlocking the door, left it wide open and stomped down the stairs.

I made no move to escape. That was the sort of stuff a heroine would have done, and that certainly isn't me!

After a few minutes, Matt stomped back up the stairs, carrying a tray with two mugs of coffee on it. Setting it down on the bedside table, he pushed the door shut and locked it.

I felt, rather than saw, Matt plonk himself on the bed. He shunted himself up the bed, resting his back on the wall. Tapping me on the shoulder, as if I had some awful disease, he said, 'Here, have some coffee. You must be thirsty.'

Slowly, I turned over and wriggled to a sitting position, tucking my long legs under me and pulling the sheet around me.

He handed me the coffee, and I timidly took it from him. Crying always left me feeling thirsty and drained, and I went to take a huge gulp of my coffee. Matt hastily put his hand over my mug.

'Go steady, you'll burn yourself.'

I clutched the sheet and looked at him apologetically. I looked away, not knowing what to say, and then looked back at him again. He took the mug from me, and put it on the bedside table.

I huddled deeper into the sheet, and rested my head on the wall. I think he must have found something touching in my face, or perhaps my behaviour, or both, because he suddenly looked extremely guilty, and cross with himself.

When my coffee had cooled down a little, he gave it back to me, and I drank as if I hadn't had a drink in a week. Matt scowled at the door, seeming suddenly to hate the thought that he'd made me uncomfortable.

You're not really cut out for this type of stuff, I thought. For starters, you've got a conscience.

I handed my mug back to him, and he snatched it out of my hand and slammed it down on the tray, which rather made my point.

231

I retreated further under the sheet, and after a couple of minutes yawned, and cautiously, slowly, I snuggled down the bed, bringing my knees up like a foetus, resisting an urge to suck my thumb like Alex.

Matt put his mug down on the tray and, getting up, he took a blanket out of the ottoman, and then lay down on the floor.

After much sighing and fidgeting, he finally dropped off to sleep. Only then did I feel I could too. It was a welcome release.

When I awoke, I knew something wasn't right. This bed's softer than usual, I thought, and I'm facing the wrong way. When I sleepily opened my eyes, I found Matt wide awake, watching me intently from the foot of the bed.

'Are you OK?' he asked, looking quite concerned.

I nodded, rubbing the sleep out of my eyes. I asked him if I might have a bath. It would be better to keep out of his way. He said I could, but he'd have to lock the bedroom door. I nodded, and waited for him to go.

Once he'd locked me in, I got up, made the bed, thinking that would please him, and opened my bag. Gathering together a few toiletries and fresh clothes, I locked myself in the bathroom.

As I lay in the bath, I began to think of ways to escape. Drug the swine, I thought savagely, then realized I had no transport to get away. The crafty pig had hidden the keys to the Jag. I idly thought about the horses in the field, and decided that, without so much as a headcollar to steer one with, I didn't stand much of a chance. Perhaps I could make one out of belts and suchlike.

There didn't appear to be any pills about the place. Bang went one theory, which was probably just as well really. What if it didn't work, and he came round from his drug-induced slumber and came looking for me? That was one thing I could be sure of: he would try and find me. What then?

I thought about the boys, and shivered. If I escaped somehow, he'd drive to the Yard and kill the boys. I didn't know where I was, except that I was in the middle of nowhere. He'd get to the Yard before I did. Because he'd already said he'd killed Ben, and I saw no reason to doubt him, I feared for the boys' safety.

I wondered if he was schizophrenic. He seemed like two different people, one nice, one nasty.

Ben drifted back into my mind, and I began to relive the past few months. Very quietly, in case Matt should hear me, I sobbed my heart out. I thought about John, and pulled myself together, cursing myself for being a weak drip.

Telling myself I had to be strong for Ben and the boys, I finished bathing, got dressed in cool cotton trousers and shirt, and sat on the bed. I looked around the room, and decided it was hot in there. I tried to open the window, but found I would need a key to unlock it. Matt was always locking and unlocking doors and windows. I began to wonder if he was a frustrated prison warder!

I opened the wardrobe door and had a peek inside. Nothing of interest, only what should be in there, Matt's clothes. I wandered over to the chest of drawers, and had a peek inside those too. Again, more of his clothes, the top two containing his underwear. Boxer shorts, with reindeer doing what they do naturally, all over them.

Putting my bag on to the bed, I rummaged in the ottoman, and found only bedding: sheets, blankets and duvet covers. Closing the lid, I heard the key turn in the lock, and Matt stepped into the room.

I glanced at the window. 'Could you possibly open that? It's very hot in here.'

He stared at me, totally deadpan.

Oh, dear, Mr Nasty's back, I thought nervously. Finally, he nodded, and, locking the door, unlocked the window.

I lifted my chin slightly, breathing in the fresh air. Taking hold of my hand, he unlocked the door again and led me downstairs. He left me at the table in the sitting room. Tea and toast were laid out. I drank several cups.

Fearing I might say the wrong thing, I said nothing at all.

'Eat!' he ordered, pushing a slice of toast towards me. I ate.

I looked out of the window, watching the horses grazing, swatting flies with their tails, tossing their heads in agitation as flies dive-bombed their eyes.

Matt's eyes followed my gaze.

'The black one is mine,' he told me, lighting a cigarette.

'What's his name?' I asked, pouring another cup of tea.

'Merlin.' Narrowing his eyes through the cigarette smoke, he noticed that I sat bolt upright with a jolt. I nearly dropped the teapot. A sharp pain ran through me as I saw Ben's face, and the boys laughing at the lop-eared Merlin at the races.

With a shaking hand, I sipped my tea, praying my face was giving nothing away. It must have been God's day off. I failed miserably.

'That name reminds you of something,' he stated, studying my face. 'What is it?' He stubbed his cigarette out, waiting for my reply.

'It was a pony I had as a child,' I mumbled, looking down at my hands, desperately trying to hide my face.

'Liar!' he spat, getting abruptly to his feet, 'I hate being lied to!'

Oh, God, I thought, my stomach contracting in fear, here we go again!

He moved around the table, and, bending over, said very quietly into my ear, 'It's Ben, isn't it? It's something to do with Ben.'

'No,' I whispered. 'I told you it was one of my ponies.'

Matt straightened up and walked over to the window, and stood with his back to me. 'You *will* tell me.'

I was so scared, I didn't know what to do. Leaping to my feet, I ran upstairs and locked myself in the bathroom. I could hear Matt pounding up the stairs after me. I sat down in the corner, drawing my knees up to my chin, whimpering in terror.

Matt kicked the door in and, seizing me by the arms, dragged me into the bedroom and threw me down on to the bed. He got on top of me to hold me down.

I was almost breathless with fear. He's really going to hurt me now, I thought in panic.

Matt began to shout at me. If I didn't tell him about Merlin, he said he'd hit me, once for running away from him, and the second time for lying to him.

Again, he asked me what the name Merlin meant to me. Crying and trembling, I told him, and got a shake for thinking of Ben.

'Don't you dare hit me!' I screamed. 'You don't have to do that to scare me!'

I got threatened with another vicious slap for making a sarcastic remark, and daring to tell him what to do. I then got slightly hysterical.

235

Matt, who must have realized, as he had done the previous night, that he'd gone too far, spent the next hour trying to calm me down. Murmuring soothing noises, he looked so appalled at himself, I thought at one point *he* was going to burst into tears.

Matt fetched a bowl of water and a wad of cotton wool, and began dabbing at my face. I'd bitten my lip, and with all the crying I'd done, my tears had trickled into the blood, which was running down my neck in pink streaks.

He gently mopped up the blood, and then my tear-stained face. I found I couldn't stop shaking.

Matt had a stricken look about him, and explained that he was going to lock me in, as he had to go out. He got up off the bed, locked the window, and, letting himself out of the room, locked the bedroom door too.

I heard him walk down the stairs and out of the cottage.

Once he'd gone, I allowed myself to think about Ben. I said his name, and finally cried for him, as if in some sort of defiant gesture.

It only seemed a matter of minutes when I heard Matt unlocking the door. He stomped into the room, slamming it behind him. I buried my face in the pillow, thinking he was still in a bad mood, and instinctively put my hands over my head, preparing to protect myself, certain he was going to hit me again.

I was shaking so violently that the bed shook too. Matt walked over to me, and grabbed my arms, pulling them away from my head.

'No!' I screamed. 'Don't hit me! Leave me alone! Stop hurting me!'

'Penny!' he yelled, 'I'm not going to hit you. Now calm down.' I gazed up at him, scared out of my wits. 'Now calm down,' he repeated shakily.

Whimpering, I found I couldn't take my eyes off his face. He looked terribly pale, and extremely disconcerted.

Letting my arms go, he went downstairs to the kitchen, and returned with a large jug of water and a glass. Pouring me a drink, he sat me up, and held it to my lips. I drank deeply, watching him all the time.

'Nobody's ever hit you in your life, have they?' he asked quietly, as though that wasn't normal.

I shook my head. Funnily enough, no, they haven't, I thought. Matt gazed at his hands. Finally, he said evenly,

'Don't you ever run away from me again. I'm really not that bad.' And, getting abruptly to his feet, he strode out of the room, locking the door behind him.

I stayed where I lay all day, only moving to use the loo. I remembered reading somewhere that if you personalized yourself with the hostile person, they would find it more difficult to hurt you.

I decided I would be as nice to him as I possibly could be, that I would try not to antagonize him, and do as he said, when he said, within reason. And if that didn't work, I could safely say I was a goner!

I hastily squashed the thought that you couldn't get more personalized than being brothers! Matt seemed not to care about bumping off Ben!

That evening, Matt brought me soup and sandwiches, and a mug of coffee. He opened the window. I hadn't noticed the heat in the room this time.

'I'm sorry. If you want the window to stay open, I'll have to be here with you.'

237

I nodded, and gazed unseeingly at the wall. Matt ran his hand through his hair in an impatient gesture. His conscience seemed to be taking a few well-aimed stabs.

'Eat your food!' he snapped.

I sat up stiffly, and, picking up one of the sandwiches, I nibbled at it, but found I couldn't swallow. Blinking hard, I tried desperately not to cry, but, lifting the back of my hand to my sore mouth, I couldn't stop the tears that began to fall again.

Matt sighed impatiently, and moved round to my side of the bed.

'I'm eating!' I said tearfully, hastily taking another bite of the sandwich, thinking that I'd annoyed him by showing little interest in the food. Matt took the sandwich from me, putting it back on the plate, and handed me the coffee.

'Here,' he said gently. 'This'll help it to go down.'

I drank the coffee. Matt put his hand to my face, I realized later, to wipe away the tears. I flinched, not seeing it until he had nearly touched my face. His hand stopped abruptly, and then fell away. I cowered against the wall, not looking at him, thinking I'd antagonized him. I really couldn't help it.

Matt looked down at the carpet. 'I won't ever threaten you, not ever again.' Getting up, he locked the door, and told me to get into bed. I did as I was told.

He parked himself on the ottoman, looking miserable and uncertain. I think I'm getting to him, I thought, a tiny flicker of hope beginning to course through me. My muscles ached from trembling. I must have dozed off, because when I came to it was dark outside. The room was nice and cool. I tentatively tried to get out of bed.

Matt's head popped up from the side of the bed, making me jump.

'Where do you think you're going?'

I'd thought he was asleep.

'I need the loo.'

He grunted some comment, and I got out of bed and padded into the bathroom. When I got back into bed, I snuggled down under the sheet.

Matt seemed to have trouble getting back to sleep, and sitting on the ottoman, his favourite spot, he lit a cigarette. Obviously, if he couldn't sleep, I wasn't going to be allowed to either.

Finally, he said softly, 'I meant what I said.'

'What about?' I asked, thinking he meant he was going to bump me off. I started to shake.

'When I saw you in the woods that day, and I told you I could quite easily fall in love with you.' Getting up, he plonked himself on the bed. He gazed down at me, and murmured, 'You're very beautiful.'

What was that I'd told myself about personalizing yourself with the hostile person? I think I've cracked it, I thought. Trouble was, I realized I might have overdone it! Anyway, people always look beautiful in the dark!

Matt reached out and gently ran his finger down my face. With a heroic effort, I didn't flinch. He smiled.

'Why is it my brother always falls on his feet?' he murmured.

Was he on about Ben's way of life, or how he'd landed when Matt threw him in the canal? I thought hysterically. Either way, back on dodgy ground. Don't mention Ben, I reminded myself. I said nothing.

Matt fidgeted nervously. He sighed, and leaning over, flicked the bedside lamp on, the scar on his face in shadow. Apart from that scar, he and Ben could have passed for twins. A shame their characters were so different, I thought.

I took a crafty peek at him, trying to work out his mood. I was slightly shocked to see him slumped forward, the expression on his face so haggard that I actually plucked up the courage to talk to him.

'Matt,' I wriggled into a sitting position, 'Are you OK?'

He looked at me miserably. 'No, not really,' he replied in a low voice. He lowered his head and began picking at a chipped fingernail. 'Is there anything you want?' he asked, not looking at me.

'No, I'm fine, thanks.'

A long, awkward silence followed. I decided to take the plunge.

'Matt, what's this all about? I mean, really all about?'

He nibbled his bottom lip. 'To show Ben how it feels when you lose somebody you love very much.'

I cursed myself for not going to university. It might have sharpened up my excuse for a brain. Slowly, it began to work.

'Are you talking about the problems you and Ben had, and the fact that he wouldn't talk to you?'

He nodded and quickly swallowed several times.

'You miss him, don't you?' I murmured. Frankly, he wasn't the only one.

'Yes,' he croaked. 'I've tried talking to him, but he just won't listen to me.'

'Well, I hate to say it, but you did clear off with his wife.'

Matt shook his head. 'That really wasn't how it was, I can assure you.'

Suddenly, I realized he'd made a bit of a slip-up. I began to tremble with suppressed excitement.

'You said you wanted to show Ben how it feels to lose someone you love. How can he suffer, when he's supposed to be dead?'

Matt shot me a lop-sided grin. 'I'm no good at this, am I?'

'You haven't bumped him off,' I cried. 'I think the only thing you've bumped is your head at some point.'

I felt so relieved he hadn't hurt Ben that I felt a rage sweeping over me I didn't know I was capable of. I shot across the bed, and slapped him hard around the face.

'Have you any idea what you've put me through!' I howled, I was so angry, I cried all over again.

I went to slap him again, but he was ready for me this time, and caught my arm. So I tried clouting him with the other hand, and the pig got hold of that one too. I considered head-butting him, but it wasn't particularly ladylike and anyway I didn't fancy knocking myself out.

Pinning my hands behind me, he pushed me back on to the bed and sat on me. Arms folded, he calmly waited until my frantic struggles and sniffles ceased.

'Did you honestly think I could bump off my own brother?' he snapped.

'Yes!' I restorted, thinking, how the hell would I know? I didn't really know him that well, and what I'd seen hadn't been very reassuring. He could have done for all I knew!

Matt's face had a wounded look about it. 'What do you think this is all about?' He waved a hand at me, looking cross.

241

'Personally, I think you've flipped!'

I tried releasing my hands from underneath me by feeble wrigglings, but only succeeded in getting slightly out of breath and cramp in my fingers. Matt raised his eyes to heaven with a heavy sigh.

'Are you going to listen to me, or spend all night fidgeting?' he asked, eyeing me in what looked suspiciously-like amusement.

Scowling at him, I had to admit defeat. Matt took a deep breath.

'I'm sorry for doing this to you, but I was desperate and I know how my brother feels about you. I thought this would make him sit up and take notice of me, listen to what I have to say. Perhaps you're right. Maybe I did flip out for a while.' Matt sighed and went on, 'I went to the Yard on the spur of the moment really. I just had to speak to Ben. When I realized he was out, I just went crazy. I'd been psyching myself up so much to talk to him. So I got Mrs Travis to phone your brother's place and tell him one of the horses was ill. I knew he'd come back for that, and I wanted him on his own. But when he got home, he still refused to talk to me, banging on about how a worthless lowlife like me had ruined his night out.' Matt gazed down at his hands. 'Have you any idea how much that hurt me?'

Yes, I had an idea. It was written all over his face.

'So what *did* you do to Ben?' I asked, hoping they hadn't had a fight.

'I locked him in the tack room.'

'Is he still in there?' I asked, thinking frantically that Ben might be dying of dehydration or starvation!

'Don't worry. Mrs Travis'll have let him out once we'd gone.'

242

That's why he'd kept her locked in the spare room. In case she snuck off and let him out before we'd left. Crafty devil, I thought.

'Matt, you obviously adore your brother, so what made you have an affair with Annabelle? You must have known how much that would have hurt him?'

'It wasn't like that!' he snapped. 'I didn't even like Annabelle! For years I watched her putting him down, pulling him down, making him miserable. All right, I admit my methods might have been a bit extreme, but I had this mad idea that I was somebody who could vouch for him in a courtroom. She'd had dozens of affairs, but I was someone who could prove she'd committed adultery. I thought, with me being her husband's brother, it would look even worse for her. I even had taped conversations of her actually admitting to me she didn't really want the boys. She wanted to take them away from Ben just to hurt him, and for no other reason. You don't understand, Penny, she was the most evil bitch I'd ever met.' Matt's eyes pleaded with mine to believe him. I did.

'How come Ben put up with her?'

'Ben was prepared to live with her until the boys were old enough to decide themselves who they wanted to be with, and he was also scared to death that he'd lose them. You know the courts usually favour mothers.'

'So what happened to the tapes you made?' I asked, and winced. One of my arms was on fire. Hastily, Matt got off me and sat next to me.

'I didn't manage to give him the tapes – well, not properly anyway. I underestimated how much Annabelle hated him. I was all set to go to him with them when she suddenly grabbed me and kissed me, right in the middle of the High Street.'

243

Painful, I thought.

'I mean, she really kissed me, in front of everyone, broadcasting the fact that we were having an affair. Well, Ben wouldn't listen to a word I said, and, snatching the box out of my hand, he threw it on the fire. I think he thought it was some sort of peace offering. Unfortunately, it had the tapes in. Then he threw me out of the house and told me he never wanted to see me again.

'I stayed in a hotel for a while. Trouble is, I had to carry on with Annabelle to make new tapes, otherwise she was going ahead with her plan to take the boys away from him.'

Matt's head drooped. It looked as if we'd all seriously underestimated his feelings for his brother, including Ben himself. He obviously worshipped the ground Ben walked on.

As always, curiosity got the better of me.

'How come Annabelle hated Ben so much?' I asked.

Matt grimaced. 'Annabelle knew she was guilty of trapping Ben. She'd got pregnant deliberately. She actually admitted that much to me. Very swiftly, she realized Ben didn't love her – not that she loved him, but she expected every man to adore her – and he'd only married her out of a sense of duty. Hardly the right reason for marrying someone.

'Our Dad drummed responsibility into Ben all his life. He thought it was the right thing to do. Annabelle never forgave him for not loving her, and yet she never accepted that you can't force someone to love you. But what she couldn't understand was that Ben would have stayed loyal to her forever. She ruined their marriage, not me.' Sorrowfully, he gazed at the pillow, his eyes mirroring what he felt. He wished Ben still loved him.

'Then you had the accident,' I murmured, sitting up and tucking my legs underneath me.

Matt nodded. 'When Ben didn't come to see me in hospital, I was gutted. I nearly died, and he didn't care. I cried, I actually cried.'

He looked suspiciously as if he was going to now. I surveyed him thoughtfully.

'I have to admit, Ben may have been wrong about you. But I can understand why. And I have to say too, you haven't helped matters by scaring his housekeeper half to death – someone, incidentally, whom you've known since you were a child – and then kidnapping his future wife!'

Matt's head snapped up. 'Are you two getting married?'

I nodded, and watched him, trying to gauge his reaction. If he didn't like what I'd told him, he was clearly capable of anything. Maybe he'd chop off my little finger and send it off to Ben by recorded delivery, I thought wildly, remembering all the kidnapping cases I'd read about or seen movies about. Needless to say, I felt quite relieved when he gently smiled.

'I take it you don't mind?' I drawled, shooting him a sour look.

'Oh, I think he's got the right woman this time,' he grinned.

'Well, that is encouraging,' I replied, a tad tartly.

'Believe me, I don't go around ruining my brother's life for him. Annabelle was a one-off, thank God. She'd have scared the Bogey Man. I'm not really a bad chap, honestly.' He eyed me from under his lashes.

'If you're not so bad, why try and ruin Ben?' I fixed him with one of my baleful glares. 'Why have you been bumping off the horses?'

'Eh – what are you talking about?'

I stared at him, noting the genuine bewilderment on his face. Oh, God, I thought, suddenly realizing we'd all made a terrible mistake.

I opened my mouth, and shut it again. My eyes darted around the room. I told him about Mistral, the fire and Merrylegs.

'And you all thought it was me?' he asked, incredulously.

'Well, yes! You can't blame us!' I retorted defensively.

He gazed at me, appalled. 'Yes, I bloody well can!' he exploded. 'What sort of crank do you think I am?'

I squirmed, feeling angry, hot and uncomfortable.

'I'm sorry, but Ben seemed to think you were out to get him. And on the evidence of your behaviour towards me, can you blame us?'

Matt got off the bed and took a turn around the room, and then went round the other way. Stopping dead in front of me, he quietly smouldered, tapping his foot.

'Look, I'm sorry,' I repeated. 'But we didn't know any of what you've just told me. Ben still doesn't.'

Matt shot me a filthy look, and flopped down on to the bed. 'Oh, God, Penny!' he moaned. 'I want my brother and the boys back!'

I sighed. He really was suffering.

'I think they miss you too,' I said, giving him a shove.

'No, Ben doesn't. You're just saying that!' With his sulky expression, he suddenly reminded me of Harry in a bad mood.

'I'm not. Ben has actually told me he was so hurt when you cleared off with Annabelle, but it wasn't because of her, he said it was you who'd hurt him. He told me he thought he meant more to you than that. He says

Annabelle's still hurting him, even though she's dead, because you and he would never be close again.'

Matt blinked several times, looking slightly undecided.

'Why don't we go back to the Yard right now, and I'll talk to him?'

Matt sighed irritably. 'I've tried that. He just won't listen to me.'

'No, not you, but he might just listen to me.'

Suddenly, Matt started to look both nervous and excited all at the same time. Leaping off the bed, he shooed me off it and quickly straightened the sheets. I adjusted my rather crumpled trousers and shirt, and zipped up my bag.

'Ready?' I asked, noticing that he'd gone extremely pale.

'As I'll ever be.'

I followed him down the stairs, feeling just as nervous as he was. Matt's idea of helping his brother might have been slightly off the wall, but his heart was in the right place. His only crime was to love his brother dearly. Was that so wrong?

CHAPTER 17

Matt locked the cottage, and, dumping my bag on the back seat, got in the car, and we drove off.

As we were cruising along the lanes, I spotted a signpost for Loxton. I frowned, feeling slightly confused.

'I thought we drove for about an hour when you took me to the cottage?'

Matt grinned and looked sheepish.

'I just kept on criss-crossing around the lanes, trying to make you disorientated, in case you were making a map in your head. I wanted to give you the impression that you were miles away in the middle of nowhere. Then you wouldn't have been so keen to escape.'

He began to giggle. I surveyed him sourly.

'Pig!' I retorted, and sulked the rest of the way home.

When we reached the yard, Matt began to shake. He looked almost ill with nerves.

I walked into the kitchen, where I found Ben sitting at the table with a large scotch in front of him. He looked exhausted. Mind you, it was three o'clock in the morning.

Ben leapt out of the chair, and, grabbing hold of my hands, pulled me against him, and kissed me fiercely.

Finally, when he'd let go, he asked awkwardly, 'How are you? I mean, did he hurt you?' He looked at me searchingly.

I shook my head. 'No, that wasn't the point. Matt took me to force you to listen to him. I think you need to talk to him. There are a few things you need to know. He misses you desperately; that's what all this is about – a sort of protest. To shock you into listening.'

Ben sat down at the table. 'How can you expect me to talk to him, after all he's done to you? Am I also just supposed to brush aside what he's done to my horses?'

'He hasn't done anything to the horses. I confronted him with it, and he honestly didn't know what I was talking about.'

Ben gazed at me, speechless. I shot out of the kitchen and found Matt leaning against the wall, looking green. Seizing his hand, I led him into the kitchen.

Ben got to his feet and slapped him across the face. That's his second slap of the day, I thought idly.

'That's for taking Penny!' he snapped. Then he sat down again, and nudged a chair in Matt's direction. I went to leave them to it, but Ben shoved me down next to him, keeping a tight grip on my hand.

'This better be good!' he snarled, glaring at Matt. 'I was going to ring the police in a minute and let them know what's been going on.'

Matt sat down opposite us, and wearily told Ben all that he'd said to me. Matt gazed at his hands, as he hoarsely told Ben how much he'd missed him, that he wanted to be part of his life again, that he loved his brother and his nephews and wanted them back. It was painfully obvious that he meant every word.

Ben was visibly shaken. Sighing heavily, Matt slowly raised his head.

'It's not me who's been topping the horses. Why would I? They're mine as well. *And* I've just been sick in a rose bush!' He looked owlishly at Ben.

I burst out laughing, and amazingly so did Ben. Scratching his head, Ben gazed at me softly, looking suspiciously bright around the eyes. I guess he'd missed his brother more than he'd let on. Turning to face Matt, he muttered, 'I'm sorry.'

'What for?' Matt asked, knowing full well what!

'Annabelle, this place, blaming you for the horses.' Ben paused, looking down at his hands. 'For not going to see you in hospital.'

'Yeah, so you should be,' Matt complained with an indignant sniff.

Ben smiled. 'Why don't I make it up to you? We're a lad down in the Yard. I could do with some help – I mean, if it's not too degrading, acting as a stable lad.'

Matt shot him a filthy look. 'Stop being an utter . . .! I'd like to very much, and you know it!' He folded his arms, sulking. Grinning, Ben told him to put his bottom lip in, because he was really quite pretty when he smiled! Then Ben glanced at his watch.

'Look, do you want to stay the night – well, what's left of it?' Ben shifted awkwardly, and eyed Matt guiltily.

'Yes, please,' his brother mumbled, shuffling his feet under the table, which no doubt would remain firmly under it now.

Ben got to his feet, and, nipping out of the back door, checked on his beloved Jag. He came back carrying my bag.

'Sorry about that,' Matt muttered, waving a hand, and got to his feet. I suppose he was thinking that if Ben was going to thump him one, he'd like to be standing up. But Ben strolled over to him and rested an arm on his shoulder.

'You ever take my car again without asking, and I'll make you wash it for the next fourteen years!' And if you ever take *Penny* anywhere again without my knowledge, I'll kill you!'

Matt blinked, grinned, and, planting a great wet kiss on his brother's nose, he turned and belted off, heading for the stairs, with Ben in hot pursuit, muttering under his breath.

Sighing, I locked the back door and padded off after them.

When I got upstairs, Ben and Matt were in the peach spare room, trying to see who could get the other in a half-nelson first.

'Does my salary go up, with another child in the house?' I asked, and, giving a yelp, tried to make a bolt for it.

Matt and Ben caught hold of an arm each and, chucking me on to the bed, mercilessly tickled me until I could hardly breathe. Finally, sniffing weakly, I crawled off the bed.

On the landing, Ben stuffed his hands in his pockets and scuffed the carpet. Matt hovered in the bedroom doorway, scratching his head and looking at the floor.

Ben heaved a great sigh, and suddenly seizing Matt by his shoulders, he gave him a back-slapping cuddle. Matt buried his face in Ben's neck. I decided to leave them to it, and silently crept off to bed.

Soon afterwards, Ben snuggled up behind me and curled himself around my body. 'I've missed you so much,' he murmured, nuzzling around my ear.

I hope my ears are clean, I thought, and turned over to face him. 'I missed *you*.'

He kissed me tenderly.

'I'm sorry you were dragged into this, and yet, if you hadn't been, Matt and I would very probably have never resolved the problem.'

'Well, you've got him back now. Just don't go falling out again, and if you do, for God's sake talk to each other!'

Gently, I nipped him on the lips. Throwing a leg over mine, he pressed himself into me, and yawned. We were both so tired.

'I can't quite believe I've got you and Matt back in one night,' he mumbled, with a sleepy grin on his face.

I knew how Ben felt. I had a very close relationship with my brother. I really didn't know what I'd do without John. I hoped I never had to find out.

We got up early, because the boys didn't realize I was back, and I was desperate to see them. Ben, Matt and myself, were sitting, bleary-eyed, at the kitchen table eating boiled eggs. We'd only had about four hours' sleep apiece.

The boys tramped into the kitchen in single file, with Rory at the front. When he caught sight of Matt, he stopped dead, causing Alex and Harry to cannon into the back of him.

Three pairs of innocent, inquisitive eyes calmly surveyed Matt.

'Say hello to Uncle Matt,' said Ben gently.

'Hello to Uncle Matt!' the boys chorused, collapsing into hysterical giggles. It certainly broke the ice.

Alex didn't know whether to greet me first or Matt.

Harry, typically, being the nosiest, padded over to Matt and gazed up at him.

'Is your head better now?' he asked, in a serious tone.

Matt looked at him, speechless. I caught Ben's eye and quickly looked away, trying not to laugh.

'What have you been telling 'em?' asked Matt suspiciously.

Ben scratched his nose. 'Well, because we thought it was you who had knocked off the horses, we told them you were ill.' Ben looked at his brother apologetically. Matt raised his eyebrows and grunted.

'Yeah, Dad said it was yer brains!' said Alex, nodding solemnly.

Ben closed his eyes, slowly put his hand over his face, and peeped out through his fingers.

'My brains?'

Ben nodded, grimaced, and fidgeted awkwardly. Matt looked back at Harry.

'To answer your question, my head's fine, thank you. I think I can safely say I'm not off my rocker!'

Harry, deciding his uncle was normal as far as he could see, clambered on to his knee and flopped down with his legs swinging. Clasping his hands together in his lap, he proceeded to tell Matt all about Tinker.

When Matt could finally get a word in edgeways, he said, 'I'm sorry about Merrylegs. He was a good pony.'

'I know,' said Harry, 'but Tinker is better!'

I caught Ben's eye, and grinned.

Alex and Rory, tentatively, went over to Matt, eyeing him like a wild animal they'd just shot and were not quite sure whether it was dead or not. They walked slowly round him, giving him a wide berth, and, after a fleeting eye-meet, decided he wasn't going to leap up and bite them.

253

I had to hand it to Matt, within five minutes he had them all eating out of his hand, which was better than I'd done.

Alex was quite miffed with me because I'd left him, he said, looking indignant, but soon came round (after much grovelling), when I reminded him of our promise.

The boys took Matt off to the paddock to see their ponies. Ben made a call, and cancelled his ad in the paper, remarking that Matt couldn't have picked a better time to come back!

We took a walk down to the Yard to see how Matt was getting on with the ponies. Apparently, to howls of mirth from the boys, Tinker had bitten him.

Matt came over to us and stood behind Ben, peering over his shoulder, warily surveying the stable lads. He'd already had several dirty looks.

'I suppose you told them you thought it was me, knocking off the horses?'

'Erm – yes, we did,' said Ben, and coughed. 'But don't worry. I'll sort that out now.' And he strode purposefully over to the lads. They were having a coffee-break, and kept glancing at Matt in disgust. Ben spoke briefly to them, and after a few resigned nods and shrugs they got back to work, looking slightly disconcerted.

Hearing the boys howl with laughter, I spun round to see Mrs Travis, chasing Matt with a large French stick. He shot up a willow tree, apologizing profusely. Ben was doubled up with laughter.

'Don't think you're too big to go across my knee!' she bellowed.

'Ben, don't just stand there laughing, help me! And stop talking dirty,' he said, looking down at Mrs Travis.

'I'll give you dirty, you cheeky little devil!' she barked, hurling a tin of peaches at him.

'Less of the little!' said Matt, dodging the tin.

'Come down from there this instant!' She gave the tree an almighty whack with the French stick.

'Not bloody likely!' he snorted, and huddled deeper into the tree.

Ben sauntered over to Mrs Travis, and as she giggled feebly, put an arm around her plump shoulders, and gave her a huge and noisy kiss on her cheek.

Mrs Travis patted Ben affectionately on his cheek, and, bending down, picked up the bag of groceries, grumbling that she ought to take to Matt with a big stick, then she waddled off into the house to start on the day's chores.

Matt jumped out of the tree, eyeing the house warily. 'A mite disgruntled, do you think?'

'A fair assumption,' said Ben, as Matt started to laugh again.

Ben took Matt on a tour of the Yard, showing him the new stable block. I took the boys back up to the house, deciding to give the brothers a little time alone together.

As we stepped into the kitchen, Mrs Travis beamed at me, and asked how I was.

'I'm fine,' I replied, smiling at her fondly, and switched the kettle on. 'I like the way you got stuck into Matt!'

She shook her head in exasperation. 'He's always been a devil!' She chuckled, and winked at me, 'Mind you, it's nice to see the two of 'em back together. That brazen hussy, splitting 'em up like that. I couldn't believe it when they went their separate ways; they've always been so close. It's about time someone sorted 'em out!'

255

'Just a few crossed wires,' I murmured, eyeing my reflection in the window. Not a bruise in sight; how infuriating!

Mrs Travis chuckled. 'Fancy taking you off like that! What on earth was he thinking of?' She shook her head again.

She'll need two aspirin shortly, I thought.

'He was desperate. He thought Ben might listen if he had me with him.'

'He thought right, then, didn't he? Is he coming back to live here?'

'I don't know.' I was slightly taken aback. The thought hadn't occurred to me. I'd only seen as far as getting Matt on speaking terms with Ben.

Matt and Ben came back up to the house, and helped themselves to a couple of cans of beer. Mrs Travis cornered Matt by the Aga, and mercilessly swiped him several times with the tea-towel. Finally, she sniffed, 'Is his Lordship stopping for 'is dinner?'

Matt looked at Ben questioningly.

'Yes, he is,' he said, smiling gently.

Mrs Travis nodded and grinned, giving Matt a final stinging whack across the backside. Matt yelped and rubbed his bottom.

Ben was studying Matt thoughtfully. Looking across at me, he jerked his head towards the study, and, nodding, I padded off. Ben joined me shortly after, shutting the door behind him.

'I've got something to ask you,' he said, fiddling nervously with a pen he found on his desk.

'What?'

He took a deep breath, 'Would you have any objections to Matt's moving back in here?'

'No, none at all. This is his home, after all; I mean, he is a joint owner.'

Ben let out a relieved sigh. 'I thought you'd say that. I just wanted to check.'

Ben and I returned to the kitchen, where we found Matt and Mrs Travis drinking sherry, and swapping racy stories. Ben strode over to Matt, and, placing an arm around his shoulders, asked, 'How would you like to move back in here?'

Matt's head snapped round to Ben, and then to me, then back to Ben.

'You mean it?'

'Of course I do!' he snapped. 'I wouldn't have asked you otherwise!'

Matt hastily took a huge belt of his sherry, and nearly choked.

'When?' he croaked.

'Well, today. Now, if you like,' said Ben, flapping a hand.

'I like!' said Matt, and bolted to the door, 'I'll go and get my things. Can I borrow your car?'

'Well, it's so nice of you to ask!' said Ben, tartly. Finishing his beer, he gathered up his car keys. 'Come on, I'll take you. It'll be quicker with two of us.' Ben kissed me lightly on the cheek, and ushered Matt out of the door.

I wandered down to the Yard, and dodged probing questions from the lads as to where I'd been.

'My brother was ill,' I muttered, not looking any of them in the eye.

Ben and Matt returned a couple of hours later and unloaded Matt's gear, taking it up to the peach spare room. He couldn't have his old room; Harry had pinched it.

257

Mrs Travis clucked over Matt all evening, saying it was just like the old days, except they now had a 'smashing gel' in me, and not that revolting evil witch, meaning Annabelle. To welcome Matt back 'into the fold' as she put it, she'd cooked a huge roast dinner. Nobody had the heart to tell her it was too hot to eat such a heavy meal.

After dinner, we all tramped stickily off to the sitting room to watch television. Alex, as usual, was sprawled across my knee. Matt, I felt sure, given the chance would have parked himself on Ben's knee. Wherever Ben sat, Matt lounged close to him, rather like a besotted puppy.

Ben's gaze often rested on Matt, contented, affectionate, and with a trace of something else I couldn't fathom.

Alex was still not his normal self with me, so I told him a thumping great lie and said John had been ill. It had worked for the lads in the Yard! He forgave me instantly, and Rory and Harry seemed a lot happier, and forgave me too.

I felt a rotten fraud, but sometimes you just had to do these things, I told myself.

None of us was late going to bed that night. From the moment we'd got into bed, Ben and I were all over each other.

Shoving him on to his back, I slowly moved down his body, kissing, licking, nipping, and gently sucking the skin just inside his hipbone. Knowing where all his sensitive areas were, I mercilessly tortured him!

Ben, breathing heavily, threw an arm across his eyes. Sucking his inner thigh, I moved along the top of his thigh, along his sides and across his ribs, avoiding the very important area which was just screaming for attention!

As I planted feathery kisses up his neck, Ben peeped out from behind his hand.

'Stop teasing me!' he growled.

I shook my head, and grinned. Swiftly seizing me by the shoulders, he pushed me down beside him, and then proceeded to torture *me*!

He kissed, licked and sucked his way down my body, caressing my ribs, hips and inner thighs.

I moaned softly, as, very gently parting my legs, he slipped inside me, moving slowly. Murmuring loving words, Ben rolled on to his back, and I began to move just as slowly on top of him.

Taking hold of my hands, he pushed me backwards, making me arch my back. Sitting up, he wrapped my legs around his body. I wound my arms around his neck, kissing him tenderly, as his tongue duelled with mine.

Ben tipped over on to his side, and, turning me on to my back, he drove into me, harder and faster, becoming more urgent, more passionate every second.

Ben practically went into a frenzy, paying me back for all my teasing, driving himself into me, making me moan, making me breathless, until finally we climaxed together.

We lay, still wrapped around each other, for some time, feeling happy and totally spent. Ben kissed my shoulder.

'Oh, God, Penny, I love you so much,' he whispered.

'And I love you,' I murmured sleepily, stroking his strong, broad back.

To gentle petting from Ben, and final reminders to get moving on our wedding arrangements, I sank into peaceful oblivion, and fell fast asleep.

CHAPTER 18

The next fortnight turned out to be very hectic. I did as Ben asked, got busy and began planning the wedding. Several rows ensued, because Ben wanted a church wedding and I wanted a register office one: a sort of 'he does, I do, we do, crack on, son' type of do. After several heated exchanges, he finally relented, and I went ahead and booked the register office.

We'd been squeezed in on the thirty-first of August, as we'd wanted, at 3pm. Ten minutes and I'll be married, I thought in satisfaction. The thought of our guests sitting in a church, getting goose-bumps, or just plain getting goosed by Uncle George, while I supposedly glided down the aisle filled me with horror. I'm not one for the limelight, and if two witnesses hadn't been absolutely necessary I'd have done away with those as well. As it was, Matt and John had said they'd do it, mainly because, Matt being Ben's brother, and John being mine, if we'd have asked anyone else I had a strong feeling it would have been our funeral rather than our wedding.

I wanted a light-hearted do, which I felt would be more 'me'. The reception, again, brought a few differences of opinion. Ben had got on his high horse, and wanted to book a function room in a five-star hotel. I wanted a marquee in the little paddock, among all the trees, here at the Yard.

'Why don't we just roll up in jeans, a punk rocker hairdo apiece, and have a swift 'alf down the Cock of Hope!' Ben spat, snatching the Yellow Pages from me.

'Now there's an idea!' I retorted, snatching back the Yellow Pages. I was hunting for a firm that supplied and erected marquees.

Ben glowered at me, hands on hips.

'I take it you do want to get married! This isn't some sort of protest, whereby you're trying to put me off the idea? Because if it is, you've failed. Miserably. Whatever you want, I'll go along with, but if you could try not to be so outrageous I'd be very grateful!'

'I do want to get married, but without all the "pomp and ceremony". Shove up a marquee, have buckets of champagne, stick a plateful of grub in front of everyone, then see what happens!' I said, nervously flapping a hand.

Ben surveyed me scornfully.

'Then see what happens? What's that supposed to mean?'

'Well, I thought, once everyone had eaten, we could set up the music and bop the night away. I was also toying with the idea of having a barbecue, just in case the guests felt peckish later on.' Smiling brightly, I awaited his reaction.

Ben closed his eyes and sighed. I went all hot and bothered and cross.

'Don't look like that!' I snapped. 'It's what I want!' and scowled at him.

'And the grub? What's that going to be? Jellied eels and black pudding!'

261

'Actually, yes. Why not?'

'It sodding well isn't,' Ben exploded, looking at me in horror.

'Ben,' I said gently, 'I'm only joking!' and I collapsed into hysterical giggles.

Finally, Ben hired a firm of caterers, which, with a rueful shrug, I agreed to. They would also see to the cake.

The next row was over the guest list. I wanted to invite the Harrises, purely for the entertainment value, and Ben said he didn't want them there.

'What if they bring that revolting creature?' he snapped, pulling a face.

'I don't think Archie can come without his mother,' I replied, vaguely.

Ben had invited most of the town, the stable lads, and several relations I hadn't met yet. I hadn't got many relations left who were alive. We could hold always the reception in the cemetery, I supposed! Other than Uncle George and my grandfather, the rest of my guests were old friends. John asked if he could bring some of his friends. I agreed, much to Ben's annoyance.

'This is going to be a wedding reception, not a sodding rugger scrum!' he barked at me, irritably running a hand through his hair.

'Lighten up, would you? Weddings are always so formal and boring. I want ours to be fun!'

'Well, I'll just go and hire a bouncy castle!'

I stormed off and sulked in our bedroom, until boredom got the better of me, and I began to dust Harry's room with a pair of Ben's clean underpants.

What to wear? I wanted to bob into the town and buy something. Ben went berserk.

'You will not!' he bellowed. 'You're going into Chalfont to buy your dress! Lots more choice, and choose something traditional. You come back with something that resembles a belt, and it goes straight back!'

I sulked again, and stomped off down the Yard to vent my rage on the weeds growing at the foot of the drive.

After several minutes, and as many expletives, Will sauntered over to me and asked what he should wear to the wedding.

'Nothing!' I retorted hotly. 'Come in the buff. In fact, let's all go in the buff!' My voice rose hysterically. Will surveyed me nervously.

'Is it all getting a bit of a strain?' he asked, nodding solemnly.

'A strain!' I screeched, making him jump. 'No! No strain! Just an allergy to overbearing husbands-to-be and long frocks!'

Will looked at me open-mouthed, and suggested a lie-down.

I can't, I thought savagely. Ben had remarked that I had lost some weight recently, which I couldn't afford to lose, and I thought that if I did lie down, the dog would bury me in mistake for his favourite bone! Sighing, I looked at Will apologetically. Then I had an idea.

'Will, would you come shopping with me?'

'Eh?' he muttered, blinking.

'I need to buy an outfit and I want your opinion.' I swatted a midge on my arm with a loud thwack. 'I mean, just tell me what looks appropriate. Anything I choose, Ben'll send it straight back whence it came.' And I gave an hysterical snort, clouting Will on his arm.

'Er – yes, alright.' Gazing at me intently, he was obviously wondering if I was on something illegal.

263

Only on the brink of a nervous breakdown, I thought.

'Tomorrow?'

'I can't – what about the Yard?' he replied, frowning at me.

'Oh, don't worry about that. I'll have a word with Ben. Say ten o'clock?'

Will nodded, and said he'd come up to the house to collect me. That sounded apt; I felt like a bit of old baggage.

After another row, this time about Will, and my taking him away from the Yard. Ben finally, heaving a great sigh, relented yet again.

'Well, it's your own fault!' I snapped. 'All this fuss! I'm sure I could have found something in Loxton!'

'And just how d'you think Will can help you?' His face was an exasperated mask.

'He's got very good taste in clothes!' I said defensively.

Just after ten, Will came up to the house and we set off in my car for Chalfont St Giles. When we reached Chalfont, we parked and headed for the shopping precinct. Will steered me into a very chic, very expensive boutique, and, rifling through a rack of suits and dresses, picked out a handful and despatched me off to the changing rooms.

I put each one on, and stepped out to show him. He chose a lightweight black and white suit. The skirt ended just above my knee, and the jacket stopped at my waist.

He added a white camisole, black high-heeled shoes, a handbag and a black and white broad-brimmed hat.

Grinning mischievously, he threw a pair of black crotchless knickers at me, which I bought, along with the suit and accessories, much to the obvious disgust of a toffee-sucking, middle-aged shop assistant.

I was very pleased we had managed to find something in the first shop we went in. I loathe shopping, and wanted to get it over and done with.

Realizing we hadn't spent much time in the store, I felt a warm glow running through me as I thought about what we could do to kill time. Ben was expecting us to be gone most of the day, so I obliged him.

Driving home, I shot past the Yard and straight into Loxton, screeching to a halt outside the pub. Will surveyed me in mild shock. I practically fell out of the car and into the pub.

Will and I spent all afternoon getting steadily drunk. Bert, the landlord, eventually phoned for a taxi to take us home.

Giggling feebly, we arrived back at the Yard, and weaved our way up the drive, slap into Ben, who appeared from behind a tree and glared at us.

'No need to ask what you've been doing!' he snapped.

I hiccuped, and staggered back a couple of paces. Ben's gaze transferred to Will, who looked everywhere but at him.

Fortunately, he was saved from a severe ticking off by the appearance of Dominic, who stomped over to us and, throwing Will over his shoulder in a fireman's lift, stormed off to his motorbike. Goodness knows how Will's going to stay on that, I thought.

I looked owlishly at Ben, who, much to my surprise, started to laugh.

'You're not cross?' I asked, looking at him under my lashes.

'Absolutely furious!' He doubled up into hysterics. 'I presume your car is at the pub?' I nodded and hiccuped again.

'Right, Matt and I will collect it.' Giving *me* a fireman's lift, he carried me into the house, up the stairs, and dropped me unceremoniously on our bed, where I promptly passed out.

When I surfaced around lunchtime the next day, with a pounding head and double vision, I found my new suit hanging up in the drawing room, with a note pinned to it, saying 'It'll do'.

Wincing my way into the kitchen, I found Ben on the phone ordering vast amounts of potted plants and flowers. Catching sight of the obvious look of distaste on my face, he snapped that that was what we were having, like it or lump it, and, knowing me, I'd have probably preferred nettles from the banks of the canal!

Because I was clearly in a highly nervous state, Ben suggested I do something to take my mind off our approaching wedding.

'Penny, all the arrangements have been made, so do something that isn't even remotely connected to weddings. In fact, try not to have any thoughts about it at all!'

I couldn't get my soggy brain to function normally, so I did what any rational person would do and consulted a five-year-old.

'Harry, what shall we all do?' I asked, slapping cheese and pickle on to wilting slices of bread.

'We could go hunting for treasure!' he replied, suddenly looking quite excited.

'Oh, yeah! Like where?' snorted Rory, with half a crust poking out of his mouth.

'The attic!' said Alex, licking pickle off his fingers.

'I didn't think there was anything in the attic,' I muttered, surreptitiously wolfing down two aspirins.

'Dad says it's heaving with loads of old stuff,' said Rory, handing Bracken a sandwich. I sat down at the table and three little faces gazed back at me expectantly.

'OK,' I sighed. 'I'll ask Ben if he minds.' This could be fun, actually, I thought, and absent-mindedly handed a drooling Bracken yet another sandwich. Unfortunately, Ben walked into the kitchen and caught me.

'Penny, stop feeding the dog. He'll be so fat soon, we'll have to push him everywhere in the wheelbarrow.'

'Sorry,' I mumbled, wishing he didn't sound so loud.

'Dad, can we go hunting for treasure in the attic?' asked Harry, gazing hopefully at him.

Ben shrugged. 'Yeah, if you want to. God knows what you'll find up there. Probably a relative. It's full of old junk mainly.'

At the top of the stairs, facing us, was the door to the attic. We all filed through it, and I realized it led on to an old staircase which creaked worryingly at every step. There was another door at the top which obviously opened into the attic itself.

The door was stiff and heavy and hadn't been opened in quite some time.

'This is spooky,' whispered Alex, as Rory and I shoved, pushed and cursed at the door. With an almighty crunch, the door finally gave way and Rory and I practically fell into the attic.

It was quite dark and smelt musty. The attic ran the whole length of the house. I spotted a light switch on my right and, flicking it on, felt quite surprised when all the bulbs lit up.

'Look at all this stuff!' cried Harry, his little face alight in wonder.

The attic was full of old furniture, tea chests brimming with an assortment of items, and wardrobes spilling out decades of changing fashions. Thick dust coated everything with huge cobwebs like a paper chain along the beams of the roof

A large spider with at least forty-two legs ambled along the edge of a tea-chest, and had a spot of difficulty negotiating the corner.

All the way along the sloping roof, on my left, were about half a dozen windows, all terribly grimy and dull from not having a scrub in goodness knows how long.

An old gramophone sat on a table under the window nearest to me and appeared to be riddled with woodworm. Harry wandered over to it, and after a brief inspection came to the conclusion that it was an old-fashioned ear-piercer.

'You lay your head on this bit, and then let this sticky-out bit drop, and then it puts a hole in yer ear!' He shot me a toothy grin, highly impressed with his own deduction.

'Harry, that is an old record player!' sighed Rory, raising his eyes heavenwards.

'Are you sure?' Harry murmured, looking down the huge pink horn with a disappointed sigh.

Alex, I noticed, was mesmerized by a piebald rocking horse. The paint was coming off it all over the place from where generations of Carmichaels had ridden it, kicking it on to escape some loathsome baddie. He had a sparse mane and tail, and appeared to be giving a ride to a very old teddy bear wearing a pith helmet.

Rory began happily turning out the contents of a tea-chest.

'Ugh! How gross!' Rory held up a little blue baby-gro.

'Obviously yours!' I laughed.

I decided to have a rummage through myself, and found the chest to be full of baby clothes, all once belonging to the boys; they were far too modern to have been anyone else's. I produced two pink booties, and, holding them up, raised my eyebrows at Rory.

'They weren't mine!' he retorted indignantly. 'They were Harry's. Mum wanted a baby girl.'

Harry scowled, and, disappearing into another tea-chest up to the waist, emerged entangled in a trombone. He then proceeded to make the most awful flatulent noises on it, very nearly taking Alex's ears off as his arm shot in and out.

Giving Harry a wide berth, Alex made his way over to a large scratched wardrobe which stood behind me. Harry's awful din wasn't doing much for my head.

'Harry!' I wailed. 'Do you have to do that?'

'No,' he replied, and chucked the trombone back into the chest.

I turned to see what Alex was up to, and nearly fainted. He'd put on a black lacy shawl, high-heeled shoes and a black hat with a veil. He strongly resembled a grieving bee-keeper.

I peered along the length of the attic. There were so many tea-chests scattered about. I wandered along the threadbare carpet which stretched the length of the attic. It was so old and dirty that it was difficult to say what the pattern had once been. The attic had obviously been used at some point in time as sleeping quarters, probably for servants and such like, as several wooden beds and an assortment of yellowing mattresses were slumped against a mahogany bureau. I stopped to inspect a wooden crib which looked as if it had cradled many little Carmichaels through the years, and had rows of tiny teeth marks along the rim. A bad case of teething trouble, I thought, and smiled. A tea-chest had been parked next to it, and I decided to have a rootle through it, and found it was groaning under the weight of various books. There were a lot of children's books, poetry, Horatio Hornblower, a Bible and Rupert the Bear.

I moved on to the next chest. Hearing a teeth-clenching shriek, I turned to see what the boys were up to and saw Harry feeding a deerstalker through a rusty old mangle. Alex fell about laughing, and then fell off his high heels.

Rory was trying to see himself in a tall free-standing dusty mirror. He'd found a trench coat and a trilby hat, and looked like a miniature Alain Delon!

Resuming my foraging in the tea-chest, I came across several old photo albums, and creased brown paper bags containing a few more photographs. I opened one of the albums and found they had pictures of all the boys as babies and toddlers. I parked myself on an antiquated sewing machine.

'Rory, come and look at these.' I waved the album.

Rory padded across to me and flopped down on the filthy carpet.

'Oh, I think that's one of me as a baby,' he said, looking not altogether quite sure. I decided he wasn't much help and thought I'd take them with us when we'd finished in here and ask Ben. I plonked them by the door.

We found several more chests crammed full of children's toys. Rory seized a plastic gun and, taking aim at Harry, fired. A small plastic pellet shot out of the end, and, totally missing Harry, got lodged in Alex's veil.

'Oi!' wailed Alex. 'You could have had my eye out!'

'Rory, don't shoot your brother. It's not nice,' I said, and lifted a velvet bag out of the chest.

'What's in there?' asked Alex, teetering towards me in his high heels.

'Well, let's see, shall we?'

I emptied the bag out on to the floor. Dozens and dozens of stripy coloured marbles rolled on to the dirty carpet.

'Cripes, look at all those!' breathed Alex, his eyes out on stalks. If he wasn't careful he'd get those lodged in his veil as well, I thought. Harry, not wanting to miss anything, came for a gander.

'Can we take these with us?' asked Rory, gently rolling one of the marbles in his hand. 'These are real treasure!'

'I suppose so, but you'd better check with your father. They might have been his and Uncle Matt's when they were little boys.' They looked quite old, and I found it hard to imagine either Ben or Matt as vulnerable little people.

As we worked our way down the chest, we came across stamp albums, an old spinning top with a stick, paint sets, and what appeared to be a Noah's Ark. It was made of wood, as were the dozens of little animals, which had hardly any paint left on them.

I was enchanted by it, whereas the boys displayed little interest and attacked the next chest having barely glanced at it.

'This is great!' cried Alex, and lifted out an old train. It was green, made of tin and appeared to be clockwork. It had received many knocks and bumps during its lifetime, and had dents all over it.

Rory dived into the chest and came out wrestling with a sailing boat, again made of wood, with peeling blue and white paint. The sails were torn and crumpled.

271

I left the boys to their boats, trains and planes, and wandered off to have a look at a rather worn general-purpose saddle. The leather was worn so thin on the seat, it was down to the tree running along the length of it.

I glanced towards one of the windows and noticed several bicycles with flat tyres and rusty handlebars parked front-wheel-first in a fire grate.

I had a closer look at one of the wardrobes, and again found it was full of woodworm, with brightly coloured attire spilling out of it. I made a fatal mistake and opened the doors, and very nearly got buried alive.

Black, pink and blue ballgowns fell on top of me, heavy and stiff as though someone still stood up in them. The boys howled with laughter as I struggled underneath them and felt as if I was having a horizontal tango with one of them.

Rory, with a disapproving look, inspected a black pram with huge wheels and a ripped hood. Suddenly, seizing Harry, he picked him up and plonked him in the pram and then proceeded to wheel him up and down the attic.

Harry was bellowing to be got out, while Alex was eyeing up a frilly pink ballgown. I bent down to retrieve the dresses, and let out a shriek. I swung round to see what had goosed me and spotted a black elephant with a long, wrinkled, phallic-looking trunk.

Alex had now ditched the shawl and veil, and was struggling into the pink ballgown.

'Alex, you big jessie!' screamed Harry. 'Help me out of this thing!'

Alex calmly ignored him, and swapped his high heels for a pair of hobnail boots. Rummaging in the bottom of the wardrobe, he emerged holding a jewellery box, and added beads, sparking clip-on ear-rings and a bent brooch to finish his outfit.

Rory was laughing so hard, he let go of the pram, which hurtled off on its own with Harry holding on to the sides in a white-knuckled clench. Yelling his head off, he crashed into a tatty gold chaise-longue, knocking off a tea-chest which was perched precariously on top of it. Tin soldiers, barometers, kites, oil-lamps, fishing tackle and several stuffed toys flew out all over the place.

I made an undignified dash to try and catch Harry as he sailed out of the pram. So did Rory, who tripped over Alex in his long frock, and succeeded in tipping them both over. We all landed in a crumpled heap, buried alive under half a ton of miscellaneous antiques.

'What on earth is going on here?' asked an amused voice.

Disentangling arms and legs from mine, I got to my feet, realized it was Ben and went pink.

'We were looking for treasure,' I mumbled, feeling very silly. Much to my irritation, Ben found it terribly funny and couldn't stop laughing.

'That's right! Mock the afflicted!' I snapped, clutching my head.

The boys, giggling feebly, got to their feet. Ben doubled up in hysterics at the sight of Alex.

'Could I take you to dinner one evening, my darling?' he croaked at him.

Alex smirked and found he was hooked up on the elephant's trunk by his beads, and nearly succeeded in garotting himself.

Ben sniffed, and, wiping his eyes, staggered over to the wardrobe near the door. Slipping a hand behind it, he

273

produced four very dirty, very beautiful paintings. John would be in his element here, I thought.

'These are my grandparents, Charles and Evelyn,' said Ben, and turned the paintings around. It was immediately apparent where the brothers got their looks from. Charles Carmichael had dark hair and eyes and a Clark Gable moustache. The painting had been done when he'd been a young man and only had the head and shoulders, but the man had a presence about him, rather like his two grandsons. Charles was utterly gorgeous.

I consciously shut my mouth and swivelled my eyes to Evelyn. She was undoubtedly one of the most beautiful women I'd ever seen. She had long dark hair piled up on her head, showing off her elegant neck. Diamonds glittered around her throat and on her ears. The eyes were large and dark, and radiated a warm kindness. She wore a black dress with a neckline plunging between her breasts. Her skin looked smooth and creamy, which was pretty good considering the state of the painting.

'They ought to be cleaned up and shown off,' I remarked, feeling about as sophisticated as a bag lady at a Hunt Ball. 'What happened to Charles and Evelyn?'

'My grandfather died quite young. He had an infection of some sort. It's all a bit hazy really. Evelyn died giving birth to Sid, my Dad's youngest brother.'

Ben stacked the paintings against the wall, and turned the two remaining pictures around.

'These are my parents, and Matt's, of course,' he muttered, surveying them through narrowed eyes. I knew Matt didn't particularly like his father.

'And what did they answer to?' I asked, noticing that all the portraits had been done when they were all young. Mind you, who wants to ogle an old fossil?

'These are Henry and Emily. Dad died a few years ago, as you know. He had a heart attack and died quite young, although not as young as his father. My mother had a riding accident, and while recovering from that she caught a fatal bout of pneumonia.'

It seemed to me that none of the Carmichaels lived very long. I look quite good in black but didn't fancy being a young widow.

Ben gazed at his mother's portrait, a slight sadness in his expression. Perhaps children never get over the loss of their mother. I often thought about mine, whom I'd lost as a child.

I glanced at Alex, who was trying to extract himself from the frilly pink ballgown with a little help from Rory. I looked back at the paintings. Henry Carmichael looked a lot like his father. He wasn't quite so good-looking, but had inherited the same dark features.

Emily was gorgeous, had long dark hair worn around her shoulders. Her dark eyes were full of laughter.

Henry's, however, were not. He looked cold and unapproachable, and I began to wonder what sort of life she'd had with him. I could imagine him striding around the house bellowing at Emily, demanding his dinner and his pound of flesh.

Although Henry and Emily were absolutely ravishing, they didn't have that refined beauty that Charles and Evelyn had had. It had skipped a generation and had been passed down to Ben and Matt. They both looked the spitting image of their grandfather, minus the Clark Gable lip-rat.

Looking past Ben, I spotted the corner of another painting peeping out from behind the wardrobe. Intrigued, I wandered over to it and found there were another three paintings, much to Ben's intense embarrassment.

The first one was of Ben as a very young man. He looked barely twenty, and was perched on the edge of a desk, arms folded, looking none too comfortable at having to pose. Ben appeared at my side.

'Oh, God! I wish you hadn't seen those!' he moaned, and ran a hand over his face.

'I think this is lovely.' I gazed at Ben's handsome face, looking not straight at me but as though watching something behind the artist. He looked not unlike how I'd first seen him, perched on the edge of his desk in the study.

Ben looked at my face, and, seeing what I was thinking written all over it, smirked smugly.

'Oh, clear off!' I mumbled, and hastily stacked it against the wall with the others. Then I slowly turned the second one around.

'Oh, yes. Very mean and moody!' I remarked, and grinned. Matt was seated on the edge of a desk in exactly the same pose as Ben had been in, and, instead of looking slightly uncomfortable like his brother, he wore a bad-tempered scowl.

'He enjoyed himself, then!' I laughed.

Ben shot me a sidelong glance. 'We both absolutely hated it. "Don't move, sit this way, look over there, hold your head up!"' He pulled a face and shuddered. 'It took four days of poncing about to get these done.'

I looked at the last portrait carefully. It was Ben and Matt as small boys. Matt had been parked on the gold chaise-longue which was now in the attic, while Ben was standing at the back of it, leaning down slightly, with his head quite close to Matt's. They'd been virtually identical, even as boys.

They wore black trousers and white shirts, and looked as though they'd just got home from school.

'Ah, now that is nice,' I murmured, holding the picture out at arm's length.

Ben grimaced. 'I remember having to sit for that. I insisted on whispering filthy comments into Matt's ear, making him laugh, which the artist said put him off his finer strokes!'

'Mm, sounds rather unfortunate.' I smiled and stacked the canvas with the others.

I decided we'd had long enough up here, and rounded up the boys.

'Come on, you lot. I think we've just about demolished the place. Time to go.'

A few groans and whinges were uttered, and, seizing the marbles, they eventually complied. Harry wanted to bring the trombone and I said yes, knowing I'd regret it later. Alex I put my foot down with.

'You are not wearing a frilly pink frock around the Yard!' I snapped.

'You can have the blue one,' said Ben, and collapsed into hysterics.

Alex decided to be awkward and said he wanted to take the rocking horse.

'Can't you find anything smaller?' I asked, getting a tad impatient. He finally settled on a book about a pit pony and a broken kite.

Ben took the paintings for me, while I carried the photo albums.

'Did you have to bring these down?' he grumbled, as he stacked the paintings in the drawing room and turned his to face the wall.

'Yes!' I snapped, turning his picture back again. 'Besides, I've noticed a few cracks appearing in the walls and these'll cover them nicely.'

After dinner, Matt took the boys off into the sitting room to watch television, while I cornered Ben in the drawing room.

'I want to decide where to put these.' I dragged him back over to the paintings. Ben, predictably, pulled a face. 'You're not really thinking of putting them up, are you?'

Nodding, I replied that I hadn't seen anything as lovely as him in a long time!

Ben smiled. 'Stop grovelling!'

'I'm not. I mean it. I think they're all marvellous. I'd love one of the boys, actually, just as they are now.'

Ben snorted in disbelief. 'What, that rabble? I can't see that lot sitting still for four days!'

'They don't have to. When John does a portrait of anyone who's – er – let's say difficult, he takes a good quality photograph, then paints them from that.' I grinned, and waited for his reaction. I would dearly love a picture of the boys.

Ben looked rueful. 'Well, if you really want one, we'll get you one. But you might have a few problems getting the photos done; they don't like that either!'

'Don't worry. John's brilliant with a camera! And that reminds me, I've found some photo albums, and a load more in paper bags. Do you fancy taking a peek?'

Ben shrugged. 'Yeah, if you like.'

Bowled over by his enthusiasm, I parked myself on the sofa and grabbed an album. Ben flopped down beside me.

The first album I'd picked up was the one I'd briefly flicked through in the attic with the boys as babies and toddlers.

'That's Rory,' said Ben, pointing to a photograph of a beautiful baby who appeared to spend his entire life fast asleep. Nearly every photograph of Rory had him flat on his back, legs akimbo and in a comatose state. Alex, however, was never asleep in his photographs, and gazed into the camera with huge sad eyes and a pouty expression. He also had been a beautiful baby, or perhaps that was just my biased viewpoint.

Harry resembled a little monkey, with eyes the size of saucers and hair which stood up on end in a permanent peak, rather like John in the bath. He wore a happy smile in every photograph.

The second album contained photographs of Ben and Matt as little boys, which reduced Ben to agitated squirms and pained expressions. They always stood or sat very still, on their best behaviour. No spontaneity was allowed. Our Henry, I thought. Ben looked like Alex as a little boy, whereas Matt looked like Harry. Rory was growing to look more like Ben every day.

The third album was full of old yellowy-looking photographs of his parents, grandparents and Henry's two brothers. Sid was the youngest and Roger was the middle brother, whom Ben perked up at the sight of.

Sid looked boring to me, whereas Roger looked a bit of a hoot.

'You'll meet those two and their wives when we get back here for the reception. You might even see my cousins,' Ben informed me.

'How many children did they have?' I asked, thinking that this family got larger by the day.

'Two each.' Ben was starting to fidget. He was getting bored.

The fourth and last album gave me such a kick in the stomach, I could hardly breathe.

'Oh, God, Penny! I'm so sorry. I thought I'd got rid of this.' Ben was so appalled with himself, he didn't quite know what to say.

It was his and Annabelle's wedding album. Hastily, he went to whip it away.

'No! No, I'd like to see it,' I stammered, wondering if I wasn't some sort of masochist on the side.

I gazed at the photos, paying a lot of attention to Annabelle. Lord, she really had been a beautiful woman. A great thick mane of dark wavy hair, huge nut-brown eyes, dainty little features with a wide sexy mouth. She was long and lean and looked absolutely ravishing in her off-the-shoulder wedding dress. You wouldn't have known she was three months pregnant.

Slowly I turned the pages, noticing how happy Ben had looked that day, even though he'd told me he hadn't wanted to marry her. He had a funny way of showing it. He looked positively ecstatic, the devious louse.

Ben seemed to be getting more and more uncomfortable, and resorted to wriggling and coughing a lot.

The last two pages were of Ben and Annabelle kissing. I looked closer to see if she'd got him in a half-nelson, but he seemed to be a willing partner. Didn't want to marry her, my foot!

'Well, I have to say, she was lovely,' I murmured, and dropped the album into his lap, feeling like doing something very unladylike and thwacking him around the head with all four albums. Consecutively.

'You think so, do you? Well, I'll show you how "lovely" she was!' he snapped, and, upending the crumpled bag, feverishly hunted through it, muttering that there just had to be one in there.

I sat in a daze, feeling sick, wishing I hadn't peeked. Jealousy's an awful thing, I told myself, and felt another wave of the stuff sweep over me.

'Ah! Here we are. Get a load of that!' he snorted, with a look of triumph over his face. He handed me a photograph I wasn't sure I wanted to see. A woman with short brown hair, lank and greasy into the bargain, sat on a wall. She had half a dozen chins, a fleshy face and small mean eyes. The whole face had a spiteful look about it, and she was bursting out of her jeans all over the place.

'Don't tell me this is Annabelle!' I croaked, peering closely at the photograph.

'The very same.' Ben grinned. 'Hideous, I know. That was taken a year after we were married. Rory would have been about six months old.'

Frankly, I was overjoyed! 'But what happened?' I tried very hard to keep the silly grin off my face.

'She took her face off and didn't wash,' he snapped.

I could hardly believe the transformation in her, but it was undeniably Annabelle.

'Course, I got the blame for her looking like that. My fault I'd got her pregnant. My fault she was depressed. My fault we had a bad winter that year!' Ben raised his eyes heavenwards. 'I tried to help, to be understanding, but she hated me. And she hated the baby.'

'She did look nice on her wedding day, though,' I conceded.

281

'Penny, she spent three *days* getting ready for that! She had all the best professional people in to do her hair and make-up. I'll bet it was the biggest challenge of their careers!'

'Don't be nasty,' I said, giggling in spite of myself.

'But that's one of the things I love about you,' he murmured, shuffling towards me on his knees. 'You look beautiful without all that muck.'

'Oh, I think a bit more grovelling and we can call it a day,' I replied, and nodded solemnly. He grinned and, leaning over, kissed me lingeringly. There's one like this in that photo album, I thought, and tried desperately hard to forget it.

Abruptly, Ben got to his feet and belted off out of the room. He shot back a minute later with several newspapers.

'Ben, what are you doing? Don't tell me you're going to burn that album.'

'The best place for it!' he snapped, and hastily twisted sheets of newspaper together. Chucking them on to the grate, he had a rootle in the wood basket and found some kindling sticks. Ben lit the fire and sat back on his heels waiting for it to catch.

'Ben, is this fair? I mean, what about the boys? She *was* their mother.' I hated saying it, but I would have hated myself more for not saying it.

Ben snatched up the album and, tearing out the photos, threw them on the fire.

'Penny, you know how she felt about the boys. She was a bitch to them, and she never really wanted them. She even told Matt as much!' Ben glared at me in a cold fury, but hastily shut up as he caught sight of my face. He swung round, following my gaze, and saw Alex hovering in the doorway.

Without a word, Alex padded across to me and, bending down, retrieved the photo of Annabelle looking not at her best. He stared at it, his little face twisting in rage.

'I hate her! I hate her!' he cried, and, taking the photo between his fingers, tried to tear it.

When he couldn't, he scrunched it up, threw it on the floor and stamped on it. Bursting into tears, he hurled himself at me and clambered on to my knee. I let him cry. Better out than in, I thought. Didn't know what else to do. A bit out of my league, all this.

Ben picked up the photograph and calmly placed it on the fire, watching it brown and curl around the edges.

'I'm sorry,' he said softly. 'I didn't mean for you to hear that. Ever.'

'I know she didn't love us,' said Alex in a choked voice. 'And I'm glad she's gone!'

'Now don't say things like that. You don't mean it.' Gently, I patted his back.

'Yes, I do!' he gulped. 'She used to say horrible things to us, like she wished she'd never had us.'

I winced, as Alex went on, 'She said we were bad boys, and she really hit Rory once, and made him cry. He always got the worst of it.'

I could imagine. I suppose she blamed Rory for the mess she'd put herself in. He'd meant to be the one thing that would force Ben to love her. She'd compelled Ben to marry her, and then resented him for it. Poor little Rory. A lifetime of spoiling for you, my lad, I thought. I would make it up to him. Somehow.

Alex sniffed and clutched my shirt. Ben padded over to us. 'I'm truly sorry you heard that,' he repeated, and looked at me, shaken. He hadn't wanted to make his son cry. He'd hurt him and he hated himself for it.

Personally, much as it hurt me to see Alex so upset, I felt at least now the dreadful ghosts could finally be laid to rest. But why was I always in the thick of it? I wondered.

'How do Rory and Harry feel about all this?' I asked, rubbing my chin against his cheek.

'They knew it too,' said Alex, and peeped out from under my chin at Ben. He sighed, and flashed his father a watery smile. Ben flashed one back.

A tiny cough by the door alerted me to Harry, Rory and Matt standing in the doorway.

'Why are you having a fire in the middle of August?' asked Rory.

'I'm getting rid of some old junk.' Ben leaned across and, picking up the photos, began hunting through them for any more of Annabelle. He found two more and they also got thrown on the fire.

Rory and Harry wandered over and plonked themselves on the floor, gazing at Alex with sombre expressions.

'Alex tells me Annabelle used to clout you,' Ben blurted out, and watched his eldest son intently.

'Mm, sometimes.' He shrugged. 'Didn't bother me. I didn't like her anyway, and she smelled funny.' He wrinkled his nose, then he and the other boys wandered into the kitchen for a drink.

When they'd gone, I raised a brow at Ben and Matt. 'She *smelled* funny?'

Ben grunted. As an aside to me, he muttered, 'Oh she liked her drink, right enough. 'Unfortunately, alcohol became her best friend.'

'Her only friend,' said Matt savagely.

'I was scared of her,' said Harry, coming back into the room and subconsciously edging closer to Rory.

We all sat quietly for a while, as we digested this rather taboo subject we'd just hit head-on. I felt as if somebody had hit *me* head on. A trip to the attic hadn't been meant to end like this. Still, it was all out in the open, and I supposed it was even good for Matt in a way. It would tie up the loose ends for him also.

Alex had returned to sit on my knee and Rory and Harry suddenly decided they'd like a bit of what Alex was having, and padded across the floor on their hands and knees. A couple of coy looks were exchanged before Rory flopped down on Ben and Harry collapsed on Matt, both with their heads in the men's laps. Ben and Matt smiled faintly, and gently rubbed the boys' heads.

I felt a sense of enormous well-being wash over me. These people around me who'd all suffered their own private misery could now move on, while I took a job in the Foreign Office as a diplomat! No, that wouldn't do. I couldn't speak French and anyway I was far too scruffy.

Later that evening, when I'd put three calm and happy little boys to bed, I received a phone call from Sam West.

'Hi, Pen. How are you?'

'Oh, fine, thanks. Apart from the pre-wedding nerves, that is. I've already bitten my nails down to the quick, so I've started on Ben's.'

Sam cackled down the line. 'Well, I have a slight problem. It's Archie's birthday tomorrow and I need children. Lots of them. Mrs Harris wants to give him a party.'

'At this short notice!' I interrupted.

'Yeah, exactly,' she sighed. 'So I was wondering if you'd bring your three and help to pad it out a bit?'

'Mm, but what about Harry? I mean, he and Archie don't see eye to eye, so to speak.' I had visions of a blood bath.

'I think it just might be what's needed.' She sounded desperate. 'Y'know, bury the hatchet an' all that.'

'Yeah, OK,' I replied, not convinced it would make the slightest bit of difference.

'Bring them round about four o'clock, OK?'

'Fine. But what about Mrs Harris? She's not too keen on me.'

'Oh, don't worry about her. She'll be away with hubby, business or something. She'll be gone all day.'

'Well, if you say so. We'll see you tomorrow, then.'

I plodded back into the sitting room, where Ben and Matt were watching television.

'Who was that?' asked Ben, as I flopped down beside him on the sofa.

'Sam West. You know, the Harrises' nanny. Archie's having a birthday party tomorrow and she's invited the boys.'

Matt started to laugh. 'Is that wise, do you think?'

'No,' I replied, and started smiling myself.

'Well, just don't leave Harry on his own with him,' said Ben, snuggling down into my lap.

'I'm hoping Harry's girlfriend'll be there. That should keep him occupied.'

Matt raised an eyebrow. 'Girlfriend?'

'Mm, Annie Croft. He met her at the gymkhana. Eyes met across the steaming dung piles and that was it. Madly in love!'

Matt started laughing again. 'But he's not even in

286

double figures yet! I can see you two are going to have to watch him as he gets older.'

Ben grinned. 'Aren't we just!'

I began to ponder on the fact that it wouldn't be long before Rory was a teenager and getting all clammy-handed and dewy-eyed over the local talent. And perhaps Alex, with his penchant for pink frilly frocks, ought to talk to Will!

CHAPTER 19

During breakfast the next day, I broke the news to the boys that they were going to Archie's birthday party. Rory dropped his spoon with his cornflakes still on it, Alex choked on his toast, while Harry shot me a wicked grin.

Ben and Matt fell about laughing as I told Harry that in no circumstances was he to kill Archie or inflict pain of any sort.

Harry went into a serious sulk, which reduced Matt and Ben to raging hysterics. I wagged a sticky finger at them both. 'Don't encourage him.'

'Perhaps I should give you a pep talk on the subject of Mrs Harris!' Ben gazed at me, wearing what he thought was an innocent expression.

'There's no need,' I sniffed. 'She won't be there. Apparently Mr and Mrs Harris have gone away for the day on business.'

'It must be horrible not having your mum at your birthday party,' said Alex, slopping jam on another slice of toast. 'I would hate it if Penny wasn't at mine.'

I caught Ben's eye and felt mine filling up.

'Not when it's Archie's mum!' said Rory, and shuddered. 'Can you imagine coming home from school every day to that?'

Ben and Matt couldn't stop laughing and, deciding they couldn't take any more of the boys' banter, they got up from the table and said they'd better get some work done. Ben planted an extremely affectionate kiss on my sticky mouth and loped off out of the door with Matt and Bracken in tow.

The boys and I cleaned up the kitchen before Mrs Travis saw it, and wandered down to the Yard. With the party not until the afternoon, we could have a ride first.

We took the ponies into the meadow at the back of the stables to practise their jumping. Harry wanted to see just what Tinker was capable of.

I decided to give the riding a miss for a change and watched the boys from my chosen vantage point, perched on the fence.

Harry was 'popping' Tinker over a few poles when Will appeared at my side.

'Coffee-break time already? Heavens, where does the time go?' I murmured, watching Tinker refuse to jump a six-inch fence.

'Tinker!' Harry bellowed.

Tinker shot over the fence, doing a fair imitation of a stag, jumping it on all four feet. Landing with a jolt, Harry wailed that he'd bitten his tongue.

'It might shut you up, then!' said Rory, kicking Badger over the little fence.

I glanced at Will, who clambered on to the fence beside me. He looked pale and drawn.

'Are you OK?' I asked, noting that he also seemed thoroughly miserable.

Will gazed at his hands.

'Will . . .'

He sighed heavily. 'Blast! It seems all I ever do is moan.'

'Is it Dominic?' I studied his lovely face, noticing how his eyes darted around when I said the other man's name.

He nodded. 'He's nothing like Adam. He's not as gentle or as loving as Adam.'

'That's because he isn't Adam. He's Dominic, with his own personality. Let's face it, Will, apart from their looks, they couldn't be more different.'

Will's head sank into his hands. 'Why am I so stupid?' he snapped, which didn't sound like Will at all. He was obviously desperately unhappy.

'What'll you do?'

'What can I do?' His eyes looked feverish, almost. 'Adam hates me, and Dominic would kill me if he knew I was talking to you like this.'

'Will, Adam doesn't hate you, and I'm pretty certain he'd take you back like a shot, but you'd better decide what or who you want. If I were you, I'd live on my own for a while. I mean, don't leave Dominic to go straight to someone else. Spend some time on your own, then try and approach Adam.'

'But where would I go?' he whispered, shooting nervous looks over his shoulder. 'I can't make decisions on my own. Adam's always taken care of me. I can't even open a letter without getting a paper cut at the moment!'

'Oh, Will.' I sighed. 'You're in a right pickle, aren't you?'

He nodded miserably.

'Will!' He jumped higher than Tinker when Dominic called to him.

'Just coming!' he called back, and tried to arrange his features into a happy smile. He failed, miserably. Frankly, I thought he resembled the Joker in Batman.

'See you later,' he mumbled, and scarpered. Poor Will. Didn't know what he had until it was gone. I suppose his gentle nature made him a target for being easily led. I wondered if I ought to phone Adam, as no doubt Will wanted me to, but common sense prevailed. It wasn't my place to interfere.

An hour later, we were scrubbing three tired ponies with the yard brush and the hosepipe. I caught Dominic watching me. I smiled and averted my eyes. Dominic was suspicious by nature and his deadpan gaze was making me nervous. I knew exactly how Will felt. I tried to put on my everything's-fine-and-dandy-face, and obviously failed. Dominic walked towards me, narrowing his eyes.

'Penny, can I have a word?'

'Er, yeah. Sure.' I watched him watching me, and hoped I appeared calm and unruffled. I didn't feel it. I thought of Dick Fox and tried to adopt one of his expressions. I wasn't sure which one, but I was working on it.

'What was Will talking to you about? Anything I should know?'

'No, no. He just wanted to know how I was. Y'know, wedding nerves an' all that.' I cracked a smile through stiff lips.

Dominic grunted. 'And how *are* you?'

'Nervous, scared, happy. In that order.'

Dominic's steady gaze held mine, and, nodding, he turned and strode off to the tack room.

I spotted Will loitering with intent by the water trough. I shook my head and winked. Will nodded and shut himself in a box.

After a lunch of ham sandwiches and fruit cake, the boys all had a bath in readiness for Archie's party. I caught Harry pinching some of Matt's aftershave.

'Harry, if Matt caught you in his room he'd go nuts!' I snapped, dragging him out by the scruff of his neck. Harry stank to high heaven. 'I think you've overdone it,' I remarked.

'I want to smell nice,' he replied with an indignant sniff, which was more than I dared do. He ponged like someone who lived with hordes of cats.

We had some time to kill so I took them to Loxton to buy Archie a present. Harry suggested a loaded gun without any instructions because then he could show the birthday boy himself how to use it, by firing straight at him.

I settled for various gift vouchers for books and CDs. I didn't really know Archie that well, and didn't have a clue what his likes and dislikes were, apart from Harry, of course.

Rory chose a card for him with a disgusting porky warthog rummaging in a dustbin plastered across the front. I had to hold Harry down to get him to sign it.

We arrived at the Harrises' large white house just after four o'clock. It was situated at the end of a long gravelled drive with fenced-off paddocks to the left and right, with a grumpy-looking gardener pottering around with a lethal-looking pair of secateurs. I tooted Bloody Mary's horn, making him dive for cover behind a tub of marigolds. He tentatively emerged, looking shocked and disorientated. Obviously been terrorized by Archie, that one, I thought.

Two thick white pillars framed the huge carved front door, which had a great knocker in the shape of a dolphin hanging off it like a well-fed slug with *rigor mortis*. I tried to rattle it, and realized the *rigor mortis* had spread to the hinge. I tugged it out and there it stayed. It point-blank refused to lie back down again, so I took to bashing it with a large stone I found on the drive.

Fortunately, we'd made enough noise for Sam to realize we were there. Grinning, she led us into the vast hall with doors leading off all over the place. A wide carpeted staircase you could have driven a bus up dominated the hall.

'Thanks for coming.' Sam pulled a relieved face. 'We're all in here.' She turned and walked towards the second door on the left. Harry was sulking.

'Try and be nice!' I whispered hoarsely in his ear.

'Why?' Harry stuck his bottom lip out.

'Because I said so!' I snapped, and ushered him through the white-panelled door.

As soon as we got into the room, Harry fell about laughing. Archie, dressed in his flowered dungarees and frilly white shirt, was nose to nose with Annie Croft, the little girl from the gymkhana. Harry stopped laughing.

Her large eyes swivelled towards Harry. She wore a deep blue dress which matched her eyes. Her long dark hair tumbled around her shoulders. Harry was mesmerized. Alex suddenly came over all shy and tongue-tied and Rory was looking bored.

Archie's face contorted in a hideous scowl at the sight of Harry.

'What's he doing here?' he howled, and seized Annie's hand.

'I asked him to come,' replied Sam, and shot him a warning look, to which Archie promptly responded by blowing a raspberry.

Annie brushed him off, and, tweaking the ends of her hair, she sidled over towards Harry, who was straining at my hand, dying to get at her. I shrugged and let him go.

Little Annie and Harry gauchely bumped into each other and, giggling, sat on the floor, casting coy looks all over the place except at each other.

'Get me a bucket,' muttered Rory, glaring at Harry.

Archie didn't take too kindly to losing Annie, especially to Harry, and stamped his foot. He swung round and grabbed the first girl he saw. She would have been about his age, had red curly hair which clashed horribly with her pink frock, and he practically gave her a rugby tackle on to the leather sofa, which made the most awful noises, rather like Harry on the trombone.

Rory and Alex spotted a group of children they knew from school. Sam hadn't done badly to get this many kiddies in such a short space of time, especially considering whose party it was. I idly wondered if vast sums of money had exchanged hands.

There appeared to be two groups of children, one of boys and the other of girls. All of them were between five and eleven, or thereabouts. The room seemed to be heaving with Sarah-Janes, Lauras and Alices, all in bright summer frocks. Unfortunately, the boys weren't much to shout about and looked very much like Tarquins, Jeromes and Nigels.

Rory strode purposefully towards the boys, while Alex hovered somewhere in the middle. He liked boys, a lot, but had lots in common with the girls too. He liked talking about broken fingernails and having his hair done.

'We'll start the games soon,' said Sam in my ear. 'Then they can have their tea.'

'Sam, have you come in disguise?'

'Eh?'

'You've shrunk! Have you been dieting?'

Her face creased into a huge grin. 'You mean you can tell?'

'I'll say.' I looked her up and down. Her jeans clung to her slim body, showing off her curves and flat tummy. Her open-necked shirt strained against her ample bosom. She was now most men's idea of the perfect figure. Unlike me. John was forever telling me to keep out of the cupboards, as I might get mistaken for the ironing board.

'You've made my day!' she crowed, and kissed my cheek.

'You look beautiful,' I said truthfully.

She went pink. She'd lost so much weight, I discovered she had cheekbones I didn't know she had and her eyes looked enormous.

'When are you hoping we'll all push off?' I asked, trying to spare her blushes. And I didn't particularly fancy running into Mrs Harris. Taken quite literally, I'd never survive the impact!

'Well, most of the nannies and a few parents who can be bothered are coming to collect the kids around six o'clock.'

'I'm quite surprised Mrs Harris has allowed this party,' I murmured, gazing around the room.

'Oh, Gwen says she felt she ought to do something nice for Archie.' Sam snorted. 'More likely to stop him howling and screaming at her. He wanted a party and she wanted a quiet life!'

I laughed, taking in the dust-sheets thrown over the furniture at the far end of the room.

'Her prized collection of porcelain is in that walnut china cabinet,' Sam said, following my gaze. All the other ornaments and several clocks had been moved to at least four feet off the ground. There appeared to be great gaps around the room.

'Gwen, or rather George, moved out some of the antique tables and chairs. He's been complaining about his lumbago ever since.' Sam rolled her eyes. 'He's scared to death it'll all get damaged in the scrum.'

'He may have a point,' I muttered, as Archie, imitating a baboon, shot across the room after the little girl with red curly hair. It was most realistic. He finally cornered her by a sad-looking fern.

Harry watched him with a disgusted look on his face. I noticed that Harry and Annie had progressed to the 'holding hands' stage. Sam grinned.

'Aren't they sweet?' she sighed.

'Hardly!' I muttered, as Harry suddenly lunged at Annie, deciding he'd have a stab at kissing. Alex stopped talking in mid-sentence, blushed, and gazed at the grey carpet. Rory pulled a face, not sure which one, and nearly fainted in horror as a girl approached him. His eyes flew to mine. Apparently, according to Alex, I was the only girl Rory considered a bit of all right. I felt quite honoured and reassured.

'Be nice to her!' I mouthed at him. Rory scowled and parked himself up against the wall, trying to merge into the grey stripy wallpaper. The girl finally cornered him by the scarlet curtains, which Rory blended into extremely well. I could almost feel the heat of his blush from where I was standing.

'Right, you lot!' bellowed Sam. 'Let's have the first game.'

Excited chatter filled the room.

'Harry!' I shrieked. 'Stop gnawing Annie's face off!'

Reluctantly, Harry let her go, but kept a tight grip on her hand, which was turning blue like her frock.

Archie was eyeing Annie up again. Harry adopted a stern look which plainly said, 'I'll stand and fight for my woman!'

'Annie, come and sit next to me,' said Archie, flashing his wonky teeth at her. 'It is my party after all.'

'Offside!' I said, wagging a finger at him. Annie slunk behind Harry.

'Right. Pass the Parcel,' said Sam, producing an object wrapped in brown paper with half a ton of sellotape.

She did marvellously well in rounding up all the children and parking them in a circle on the floor.

'OK, when the music stops, the person holding the parcel can unwrap one layer, and so it goes until one of you will actually find the gift,' she explained, and turned on the ghetto-blaster.

Noddy, the man in a little red and yellow car, warbled around the room. Rory couldn't stop laughing, while Alex was deep in conversation with one of the Sarah-Janes about pleated skirts.

Harry chucked the parcel, without bothering to whip off a layer, into the lap of a little boy sitting next to him, simply because he would have had to let go of Annie's hand. I didn't blame him. Archie was seated on the other side of Annie.

The game had to be abandoned when several of the boys got bored and started a punch-up with each other. I think Sam had wrapped the parcel with too many layers and the boredom threshold had kicked in. I never did find out what was in that parcel!

We tried musical chairs next, which didn't go too badly, until there was only Archie and Harry left. Archie was still in the running because he'd cheated. He'd pushed, shoved or bashed anyone in his way.

They prowled around the lone chair, glaring at each other, both fighting for the hand of little Annie. *The Good, the Bad, and the Ugly* theme tune wafted around the room. Rory's idea of a joke, and one I found terribly funny.

The moment the music stopped, they pounced on each other, kicking, biting and punching, having totally ignored the chair.

Sam and I had to part Archie and Harry forcibly; they were still aiming kicks at each other. Alex hid behind Annie. Sam and I took to the wine.

'OK.' Sam mopped her brow. 'I want you all to pair off, and here's a pad and pencil for each pair.'

Needless to say, Harry hung on to Annie, while Archie seized one of the Sarah-Janes. She was a lovely little girl, blonde and very frail-looking, and would be a little older than Archie. I guessed she'd be about seven.

She had obviously been brought up extremely well because she was far too polite to tell Archie where to get off, and put up with his erratic groping in a very dignified manner.

'Archie!' scolded Sam. 'Leave her alone and play nicely!'

Archie stuck his tongue out, while Harry suddenly looked extremely menacing with his sharpened HB2.

'Isn't he a darling?' said Sam, through gritted teeth. 'Right. Has everyone got a pad and pencil?'

Alex was still nose to nose with the girl with the pleated skirt; the conversation had now moved to the use of slides in the hair. He seemed happy enough to have her as a partner.

Rory, however, was still cornered by one of the older girls, and was cringing against the wall trying hard not to brush up against her.

'Rory, I see you have a partner,' I said pointedly, and fixed him with one of my beady looks. Sullenly, he flopped down on the floor and point-blank refused to look at the girl.

'Here's a tray of items.' Sam pointed behind her and realized she hadn't brought it in. 'Er – there will be a tray of items. Shortly. And you get one minute to study it, and then I take it away and you have to write down as many of the things as you can remember. The pair with the highest number wins. And gets a prize.'

Sam scuttled off, and reappeared a minute later with the tray, which held items such as cotton reels, key-rings, an assortment of plastic cars and animals and an apple core.

She caught me looking at the apple core. 'My lunch,' she muttered, and plonked the tray down.

After a minute, or roughly thereabouts, she whisked the tray away.

'OK, get scribbling.'

Little heads bobbed down over their pads, writing furiously, while Sam and I attacked the bottle of wine. Mrs Harris, much to my surprise, had left a crate of the stuff to give to the nannies and parents when they came to claim their delectable little offspring and charges.

While the children were busy, Sam wheeled in an easel with a huge sketch-pad on it, with what appeared to be a camel drawn on it.

'Shouldn't that be a donkey?' I murmured.

'It is!' she snapped, and held up a pathetic-looking tail with a nail protruding from the end. 'I'm no good at drawing,' she sighed. 'Best I could do, I'm afraid.'

'It's fine, honestly,' I replied, patting her hand.

'OK, everyone.' She clapped her hands together, and scanned the eager little faces. 'Let's see who remembered the most items.'

Each pair read out loud what they'd written down. Because Sam couldn't remember what was on the tray, she awarded prizes to everyone, including me. It was a 'Lucky Dip' bag of goodies. Alex came to show me what he'd got.

'I wonder what's in it!' he breathed, and, opening the bag, he found several sweeties and a pair of dangly ear-rings, which he insisted on wearing.

'Alex, you're beginning to bother me!' said Rory, shooting up behind me in a vain attempt at escaping his rather persistent partner.

Sam herded all the children into a single file in readiness for the 'Pin the tail on the camel, sorry, donkey' game, which Harry seemed hell-bent on sticking into Archie. I had to take drastic action and barred Harry from playing purely because I feared for Archie's eyesight.

Several heavily blindfolded children missed the board completely and left nasty foot-long scratches on Mrs Harris's antique sideboard.

A prize was awarded to Annie for managing to stick the tail in its ear, which was the nearest any of them got to the board at all.

Sam decided on a final game of 'Hide and Seek', which was a complete disaster. We found Harry and Annie under one of the beds, canoodling next to a pair of moth-eaten slippers.

'Harry!' I bellowed. 'What am I supposed to tell her mother?' which sounded as though he'd got her pregnant or something.

Rory I found in the kitchen, bellowing to Archie to lose weight as he battled to get him into the flip-top bin.

Back in the sitting room, a few of the children were colouring in the stripes on the wallpaper. Sam and I were fast losing control, and not just of the children. Seizing the wine, Sam poured herself another huge drink. I squinted at it, and decided I'd better phone Ben to come and collect us all later.

Ben grumbled that he'd have to bring Matt as well to pick up my car. I apologized and managed to get round him by making gooey noises which reduced Rory to embarrassed disapproval. I apologized to him for being 'girlie'.

Sam, at a slight list, ushered all the children into the kitchen and seated them around a large round table heaving with food and supporting a waterproof table-cloth. Very wise, I thought.

Silence prevailed as the children tucked into sausages on sticks, cheese and pineapple chunks, ham sandwiches, crisps, jelly and ice-cream, trifle and an enormous iced birthday cake.

The children had barely begun to eat when several rather done-up mothers and nannies in high-necked frocks arrived to collect their precious little darlings. Sam and I handed out glasses of wine.

I found I was talking to Annie's mother, Fiona. She was petite, had light brown hair and appeared to be very easy to talk to. Unfortunately, by her second glass of wine her tongue was considerably loosened, and she promptly blurted out her life story. She was a single parent, since Trevor ran off with that – that TART!

Automatically, I produced a handkerchief which she snatched out of my hand and blew in alarmingly loudly. I made soothing noises for a bit, patted her hand and said I'd better see if Sam needed a hand in the kitchen.

I turned and fled, straight into a leering, lecherous local in dun-coloured trousers and a left-of-centre parting.

'Sorry,' I muttered, and tried to go around him, as he tried to go around me. The same way. We must have looked as if we were doing some kind of tribal dance.

'May I butt in?' said a familiar voice. I glanced up and felt enormous relief to see Matt grinning down at me.

'Yes! You may!' I snapped.

Seizing my hands, he very kindly waltzed me out of the room. 'Who on earth was that?' I whispered hoarsely.

'Roy Battey. He owns the local garage.'

'I didn't ask what he was . . .' I shuddered, and belted off to the kitchen with Matt in tow.

We found Sam removing vast quantities of jelly from Archie's frilly shirt. The boy was bawling his head off. I felt that sinking feeling wash over me and turned to face Harry, who was peeping around Annie. Matt got the giggles and didn't shut up for a full five minutes.

Ben strode into the kitchen and with one swift glance at Archie took in what had happened.

'Harry, did you do that?' Ben's lips twitched. Harry, sensing his father's weakness, flashed him a toothy grin.

'Well, don't do it again,' Ben ordered lamely, and coughed.

Harry came out from behind Annie, and, padding over to Ben, tugged at his trousers. Ben obliged him, and picked him up.

'So, who's your friend?' Ben asked, smiling gently at little Annie.

'That's his girlfriend!' said Rory in disgust.

'At least I've got one!' howled Harry, glaring at Rory.

'I don't want one. All they ever do is cry!' snorted Rory.

'I'll make you cry in a minute if you don't belt up!' snapped Ben, watching Annie's face bordering on what little girls were always doing according to Rory.

'Now, don't cry. Look, Mummy's here,' I said, kneeling down beside her. Annie sniffed and gave me a watery smile.

Unfortunately, Fiona was still sobbing, and between herself and her daughter they really weren't doing much for our gender's credibility.

Rory at least had the good grace to look mildly disconcerted for upsetting Annie. I gave up, and in desperation poured myself another glass of wine.

Matt, I noticed, had gone rather quiet. I realized why. He couldn't take his eyes off Sam. The problem was, every time Sam glanced in his direction he would quickly look the other way. I felt mildly surprised. Matt didn't strike me as the shy type.

Smiling faintly, I gave Ben a nudge. He followed my gaze and grinned unashamedly at an awkward-looking Matt.

'Sam, do you know Ben's brother, Matt?' I asked, sidling over to her.

'Oh, goodness!' Goodness, I thought as Mae West once said, has nothing to do with it. 'Yes,' she stammered. 'You do look a lot like Ben.' Going pink, she wiped her hands on her bottom and held her hand out.

'Matt, this is Sam West. She has the unfortunate job of Looking After Archie,' I said, watching the horror himself flicking icing at Harry.

'Oh, I *am* sorry,' Matt drawled, and shook her hand in jerky little movements. Sam giggled as Archie pulled a face at him. Matt pulled one back and reduced Ben to helpless laughter.

'Don't tell me you actually enjoy looking after that!' he murmured, looking as if he had a nasty smell under his nose.

Sam looked bleak. 'What else is there?'

'Well, can't you find another job?'

'Like what?' Blushing furiously, she resumed her mopping up of Archie.

'Have a look round. There must be something. For your sake, find something else, anything else!' Matt looked almost serious.

I turned to say something to Ben and realized he'd been cornered by three amorous mothers and a ferocious-looking nanny.

Ben took to making frantic hand signals at me, which I chose to ignore, and instead watched him unashamedly, convulsed with mirth.

'Penny! Don't be rotten! Go and rescue your beloved!' Sam gave me a shove towards him.

'Hello, darling!' said Ben, through gritted teeth, and, grabbing my arm, pulled me against him.

'Hello, O light of my life!' I replied, grinning sweetly at him.

Four round, red-veined faces glared at me, and, turning abruptly, his admirers flounced off.

'And about time too!' he snapped. 'You are heartless! How could you leave me to that lot?'

'Oh, stop grumbling. You're obviously so drop-dead gorgeous, they felt impelled to impale themselves on your beauty!'

'Stop grovelling,' he sniffed. 'Harry!' he bellowed. 'Stop that!'

I glanced over my shoulder and caught Harry practising his kissing on Annie's forehead. I scanned the kitchen, and located Alex, still wearing the earrings, talking to another little boy who was wearing a bow in his hair and carrying a handbag, which he'd mentioned at some point that he'd won for his sister.

Rory was cowering by the Aga trying to avoid a gaggle of little girls. Matt and Sam seemed to be suffering from longer and longer pauses in their conversation, neither sure what to say to the other.

I drained the last of my drink while Ben rounded up the boys.

As we were leaving, Matt and Sam seemed at a total loss for words, and each stood fidgeting from foot to foot. I considered drawing squares around their feet for a game of hopscotch.

I promised to call Sam, and we dragged off a totally smitten Matt.

When we got home, Matt didn't say a great deal and only picked at his dinner. Mind you, so did the boys. I think they'd overdone the jelly a bit.

Ben studied Matt and raised an eyebrow. 'Obviously in love,' he muttered to me under his breath.

In fact, Matt pined away all night, and seemed very quiet and distracted. It got so bad that Ben and I dared not touch each other for fear of upsetting him!

CHAPTER 20

Matt was still dewy-eyed by lunchtime the following day, so I suggested to Ben that we have Sam over for dinner.

'In fact, let's ask John and – er – whoever, and have a little dinner party. We ought to really, after ruining the dinner party he gave for us.'

'Penny, haven't you got enough to worry about with our wedding, without throwing dinner parties?'

'Well, someone has to help your lovestruck brother.'

'Let him sort it out!' Ben noisily rummaged about in a cupboard looking for a teabag. 'I think we need to do some shopping,' he remarked, and, finding a *bouquet garni*, began to pour boiling water on it, clearly under the impression it was some sort of teabag.

'Mrs Travis is in the town doing some shopping as we speak. And don't change the subject. It won't hurt to give Matt a gentle shove.'

Ben heaved a great sigh. 'Are you trying to run yourself into the ground?' he barked.

'I need to keep busy!' I retorted, shooing a skulking Bracken through the door.

'Penny, you've just shut the dog in the pantry.' Ben dragged a mildly protesting Bracken out of the cupboard.

His twitching red nose idly inspected a packet of biscuits on the way, his hairy bottom scuffing the tiles.

Ben looked at me assessingly for a minute. 'OK, if you want a dinner party, then we'll have one.'

I wrapped my arms around his neck and kissed him tenderly. 'I promise it won't be anything fancy. Very informal. You know, elbows on the table, children present and only two crates of wine, that sort of thing.'

'Well, I'll leave you to sort it out. I'm off down the Yard.'

He gave me a quick peck, which completely missed my cheek and got me in the eye. I watched him saunter out of the kitchen through watering eyes.

Bolting to the phone, I rang John. He took so long to answer, I thought he must be out.

'Yeah, hello,' drawled the familiar voice.

'John, it's me.'

'Oh, hi!' I loved the way his voice became softer, more animated when he spoke to me. Feeling a warm sensation sweep over me, I asked what he'd been doing.

'I was in bed.'

'At this hour?'

'Mm.'

'John, are you alone?' I asked, my brain finally switching on.

'No,' he laughed.

'Oh, dear! Have I interrupted something?'

'Yes, but I forgive you! She's not come to the boil yet!'

I screamed with laughter. 'Well, whoever she is, do you fancy coming for dinner, both of you, say, tomorrow night?'

'I'll be there.' He paused. 'Is it all getting a bit much, this wedding thing?'

'I just need to keep busy,' I replied, tweaking the telephone wire.

'OK, what time?'

'About seven?'

'Yeah, great. See you tomorrow.'

It took me five minutes to pluck up the courage to phone Sam. I was dreading hearing the dulcet tones of Mrs Harris on the other end. Fortunately, Sam answered. She sounded a little breathless and I idly wondered whether she'd thought I might be Matt calling. I told her about our little dinner party the next night.

'So, do you fancy coming?'

'Yes!' she replied, sounding thoroughly overexcited. 'Well – er – will Matt be there?'

'Of course, and I'll park you next to him so you can play erotic footsie under the table all night!'

She giggled. 'Oh, that'd be lovely.'

'See you at seven, then?'

'I wouldn't miss it for the world,' she breathed.

I spent an hour discussing what to feed them all with Mrs Travis.

'Would you like me to help you make it?' she asked, hauling a bra strap up a large white shoulder.

'Er – I thought I might have a bash at going it alone.'

Giving my hand an affectionate rub, she stomped off to fetch her assortment of cookery books.

'Now, then, let me see,' she murmured, flopping down at the table. She began flicking through the pages. 'Ah, yes. How about watercress soup?' She peered at me over the top of the book.

I nodded, wondering if I could possibly louse that up.

'Right, and how about moussaka for the main course, followed by . . . chocolate mousse?'

I nodded again. Well, at least the boys would find the pud remotely edible.

'If you need a hand, give me a shout.' She beamed at me encouragingly, and stomped off to wrestle with some pink sheets flapping on the washing line.

I had a feeling I'd be yodelling from the rooftops for her much needed help before too long.

I made a shopping list. Watercress, double cream, aubergines, minced lamb and plain chocolate.

I checked the cupboards, and realized we'd got all the other ingredients loitering at the back. God bless Mrs Travis and her well-stocked cupboards! Mind you, it meant I couldn't back out at the last minute. Shame, that.

If this was an informal meal, heaven knew what I'd have to cook for that really special occasion! Suckling pig, I thought with a shudder.

I nipped into Loxton and spent a frenzied hour sweet-talking the butcher into mincing the lamb, while the greengrocer rootled in the back of his shop hunting for more aubergines.

'Just how many are you feeding?' he asked, brandishing the bulbous vegetable in my face.

'Nine,' I replied, blinking.

'Well, I can safely say, you've got enough here to feed a regiment!'

'Oh, right. I'll take that lot, then.'

Nervously surveying me, he stuffed them into my shopping bag.

When I got home, I quickly unpacked the groceries before Ben saw how much I'd bought.

I thought I'd better see to the dining room, and realized it could do with a bit of a clean up. I whipped off the tablecloth, and watched sourly as a cloud of dust flew up and decided to settle on every available surface.

I plugged in the vacuum. It decided to behave very strangely, and made the most awful whining noises. A flashing red light finally alerted me to the fact that the bag needed changing.

I forgot to switch it off first, and as soon as I lifted the lid the bag shot off in a perfect arc and landed in the fruit bowl, coating the table in yet more fluffy dust.

'Oh, no!' I wailed.

I heard the sound of muffled giggles, and, glancing up, I saw three little boys creased up in hysterics watching me from the doorway.

'It's not funny!' I snapped. 'And seeing as you're here, you lot can help me clean it up!' That wiped the smiles off their faces, I can tell you.

Alex wasn't much help, and took to drawing faces in the dust on the table, while Rory and Harry had a game of noughts and crosses.

I turned to fetch a cloth and bucket from the kitchen, and froze. A large section of wallpaper had a huge tear in it and was flapping about like one of the sheets on the line.

'Oh, my God,' I muttered, and, twisting around to pierce the boys with a fierce look, caught sight of Harry studiously ignoring me.

'Harry, did you do this?' I pointed at the V-shaped tear in the corner of the room.

'I didn't mean to!' he wailed. 'I fell over and put my hands out and ripped it!' Harry burst into noisy sobbing.

'All right. Calm down.' I sighed, and beckoned to him. Harry galloped towards me and took a flying leap. I caught him and sat him on my hip.

'Have you been scared to tell anybody?' I asked, hitching him up.

'Yes!' he sniffed. 'Dad would've shouted at me.'

'I knew he'd done it,' said Rory, cheerfully. 'But I didn't tell on you, Harry.'

'I know.' Harry afforded his brother a tiny smile.

'Well, we'd better do something about repairing it,' I murmured, and, setting Harry down on his feet, slunk off to the kitchen.

The only thing I could find was a roll of opaque sellotape, but the walls were quite damp, and it just wasn't holding.

I had an idea. It wasn't the ideal solution but it would do for now.

Five minutes later the boys and I were noisily chewing gum.

'OK, here goes.' Grimacing, I stuck four pink blobs of gum on the wall and pressed the paper against it. Funnily enough, it worked! Harry was overjoyed.

I finished cleaning the room with more energy than success, and laid the table with a fresh white tablecloth. I then qualified for the Olympics running up and down the table bunging down place mats, coasters and finally the cutlery.

I went hunting for some candles to put in the silver candlesticks, which quite frankly could have done with a polish, and eventually located some in a drawer in the kitchen. Unfortunately we only had bright yellow ones, so they had to suffice.

I polished a few wine glasses and plonked them on the coasters, and even gave the leaves on the potted plants a bit of a wipe. Satisfied, I turned the radiator on just to take the chill off the room, and threw open a small window to try and get rid of that musty smell.

I spent the rest of the day in a state of panic. My culinary expertise, as John would have confirmed, was practically nil. What if I poisoned everyone? My wedding was only two days away. What if we were all attached to drips and things and couldn't attend?

John would say that's what a wedding was: attaching yourself to a drip.

I didn't sleep well, and kept on having nightmares about an aubergine hell-bent on killing the world. I got up early to start on the food. By lunchtime, I'd managed to get the soup done. The nightmare with the aubergines was coming true, and by mid-afternoon Mrs Travis took pity on me and my pathetic whimpering, and did the moussaka for me while I attacked the mousse.

By teatime the food had been prepared and I was exhausted. I rewarded myself with a long, hot soak in the bath and nodded off. Ben woke me, and I then had a frantic few minutes doing hair and make-up and then slipped into a red stripy dress which made me feel just about as sexy as the faded Regency stripe in the drawing room.

John arrived with Carolyn Burton, which was surprising considering that he changed his girlfriends as often as I changed the sheets.

I took them into the drawing room to have a drink while we waited for Sam. Matt and Ben, looking almost identical in black trousers and white shirts, were breathtakingly handsome.

John looked gorgeous too, in his grey brushed cotton trousers, but had the unfortunate habit of attracting any bits of fluff floating about, which stuck to him as if he were a piece of Velcro. Carolyn looked lovely in her lemon summer dress with her blonde hair bobbing around her shoulders, shiny and thick. Not unlike her personality, I thought meanly.

Matt was getting increasingly nervous and prowled around the room, surreptitiously peeping out of the window.

After ten agonizing minutes, when Matt had reduced the carpet to an even more threadbare state, we heard a scrunch on the gravel and saw a taxi pulling up.

I met Sam at the kitchen door. She looked absolutely gorgeous and I told her so. She wore a loose-fitting short-sleeved blue dress which seemed to make her green eyes a turquoise colour. I whisked her into the drawing room. Matt took one look at her and nearly fainted. The colour drained from his face.

'Hello,' he croaked.

'Hello.' She smiled.

Ben, looking highly amused, watched his brother with interest.

'Right. Shall we go through?' I muttered, thrusting a sizeable gin into Sam's hand. I bolted into the dining room, and realized to my horror that I hadn't switched off the radiator. Hastily, I turned it off and opened all the windows to let the heat out. I could feel my palms getting damp and clammy, rather like the walls.

As they all trailed into the room, Ben shot me an exasperated look. I shrugged apologetically. Mrs Travis ushered the boys into the room, all wearing little grey trousers, quite similar to John's and stripy shirts. They all wore scowls and looked decidedly uncomfortable in their smart attire.

Ben parked himself at the end of the table. Carolyn sat opposite Rory. John sat opposite Alex, Sam opposite Harry, and Matt was opposite me. They all had a lovely view of the garden, while the boys and I got a boring view of the far wall.

John started to laugh. 'I do like the candles. Reminds me of Heathrow's runway!'

I giggled. 'They're all I could find.'

Mrs Travis helped me to carry the soup in from the kitchen, and starting from opposite ends, we began serving ladlefuls of watercress soup to everyone.

The boys, predictably, pulled a face. Ben poured everyone a glass of wine.

The boys took one mouthful of the soup and very nearly spat it out.

'It's cold! You've forgotten to cook it!' accused Harry, eyeing me in disgust.

'It's meant to to be cold!' I snapped, snatching up my glass of wine. I took a great gulp and tried to remain calm. They hate it, I thought in panic. Everyone hates it!

Alex, God bless him, told me it was lovely and forced down as much of it as he possibly could. Rory, sarcastically, requested a knife and fork. Ben patted my hand and remarked in a most convincing voice that he didn't think there was anything wrong with it.

Matt and Sam appeared not to notice the food and seemed to be edging closer towards each other with every mouthful.

John, in between pained expressions at my miserable attempt at cooking, took a great deal of interest in the portraits of Ben and Matt's various relations hanging off the walls. I followed Carolyn's gaze out of the window into the garden, and saw that she was watching Bracken

315

have a daft half-hour rubbing his face on the apple trees and Mrs Travis's nice clean washing.

I felt enormously relieved, that everyone, except the boys, had managed to get the soup down and was doing a grand job of keeping it there.

Again, Mrs Travis helped me lug in and hand out great platefuls of moussaka and garlic bread, at which the boys merely enquired as to whether they'd been given Bracken's dinner.

John was helpless with laughter, and I'd downed enough glasses of wine to simply not care any more. Besides, when they tasted it I knew they'd love it. Because Mrs Travis had made it.

We'd nearly finished the main course, and were noisily discussing the approaching wedding, which through a haze of alcohol didn't seem half so frightening, when I caught something out of the corner of my eye.

To my horror, the wallpaper in the corner flopped down, and, bobbing gently, revealed four pink blobs of gum. My hand flew to my mouth, as my gaze flew to John.

He swung round in his chair and choked into his napkin. Ben followed his gaze, raised an eyebrow, and shot me a sidelong glance.

'Do you want to enlighten me?' He waved a hand at the flapping wallpaper.

'Er . . .'

Harry forked up a piece of aubergine, ate it, and immediately regretted it.

'I did it!' chorused Rory, Alex and I simultaneously.

Both of Ben's eyebrows went up this time.

'Really? All three of you?' He shot me a lop-sided grin. 'So what happened, Harry?' Ben eyed his son with badly concealed amusement.

Harry dropped his fork, as his eyes darted all over the place. 'I slipped and fell,' he muttered, looking suspiciously moist around the darting eyes.

Ben started to laugh. 'Why do I get the feeling there's some sort of conspiracy going on around here?'

The boys looked momentarily blank. Too many letters in that one. Didn't know what it meant. But I did. John and Matt fell about laughing. Ben grinned.

'Sometimes my family make me feel such a rotten monster!' He smiled at John. 'Did you know that on the first day of every month I round them all up, with Penny at the front, and beat them, repeatedly, until they beg for mercy.'

Harry stole a quick peek at his father, and received a wink for his trouble. The little boy shot him a toothy grin back. Ben got up from the table and came and stood behind me.

'I do wish you'd tell me these things!' he muttered in my ear.

'Sorry,' I mumbled. 'I think it really was an accident. He didn't mean to do it.'

'I believe him.' Ben smiled, and gently nipped my neck.

'If you'll excuse me . . .' murmured John, flashing me a grin.

Chucking down his napkin, he shot out of the room, and reappeared a couple of minutes later as I was dishing out great dollops of chocolate mousse. The boys perked up considerably at the sight of it.

'Now don't get cross with me,' said John, kissing my cheek, and watched my face intently.

I frowned, spoon aloft. 'What?'

John padded back to the doorway, and produced two paintings he'd done of me a couple of years ago.

317

'Oh, John!' I wailed, brandishing a sticky spoon at him.

Ben was beside John and happily inspecting them before I could say Bob's your uncle.

'Oh, yes. I like these,' he breathed, holding one out at arm's length.

Going pink, and feeling completely flustered, I dropped a dollop of chocolate mousse on Carolyn's knee. She gave a shriek as ice-cold mousse slid down her thigh.

'Oh lord! I'm so sorry!' I said, appalled.

'Not to worry.' John grinned, and, bending down, licked it off her leg.

Ben and Matt fell about laughing again. Harry, who'd been taking a great deal of interest, suddenly lunged at Alex, knocking him off his chair. He then surveyed Alex thoughtfully, flicked a dollop of mousse at him, where it landed with a splat on his cheek, and, grabbing his head between his two hands, frantically sucked at Alex's face.

'Harry!' I bellowed. 'Stop molesting your brother!'

'I'm practising for Annie,' came the muffled reply.

Matt, grinning, separated them.

Ben continued to stare at the paintings. One was of me looking out of a window with my hands tucked into the back pockets of a tatty pair of jeans. In the other, I was dolled up to the nines in a black frock. John often worked from photographs and I hadn't been aware at the time that he'd taken them.

'Penny did say you do paintings from photos,' Ben remarked.

'Mm – can you imagine her sitting for a portrait?' John jabbed a thumb in my direction and snorted.

'Actually, I want some done of the boys. Penny wants a portrait of them all together.' Ben glanced at his sons and was met with three heavy scowls.

318

Personally, I knew how they felt, and dearly wished John and Ben would put the paintings away. My toes were curling up in embarrassment.

'Oh, Penny. This is delicious,' sighed Carolyn, making agonized faces.

'Well, I thought so, and the mousse isn't bad either,' John grinned.

'How much do you want for these?' Ben waggled the paintings.

'Don't be daft!' said John, looking quite affronted. 'They're a wedding present.'

Ben murmured his thanks. 'When could you photograph the boys?'

'Tonight,' replied John, and shot off to fetch his camera from the car.

For the first time during the whole meal the boys had finally found something they liked, and heartily tucked into the mousse. Matt and Sam, I noticed, still seemed to be hitting it off extremely well, and had now reached the touching of fingertips stage.

Although Matt looked just like Ben, he didn't have his self-assurance, and kept absent-mindedly touching the scar on his cheek. If Sam noticed, she tactfully didn't say anything.

Sam helped me clear the table, while Ben herded everyone back into the drawing room.

In the kitchen, I switched the coffee percolator on, which Mrs Travis had kindly prepared for me. Ben adored 'proper coffee', as he called it.

'Well, you and Matt seem to be getting along nicely.' I shot Sam a look under my lashes and she grinned. 'I had a feeling you were up to something! And I have to say, he's absolutely gorgeous.'

319

'I know,' I agreed.

Sam tentatively shuffled towards me. 'I – er – didn't want to say anything, obviously, but that scar. How did he get it?'

In all fairness she looked pretty uncomfortable at asking me, but curiosity had probably got the better of her. And I suppose she might have thought he was a bit of a thug and received it in a punch-up.

'He got it in a car accident. A very bad car accident. I'm sure he'll tell you about it one day when he's good and ready. He's very conscious of it, though.'

Sam snorted. 'Well, he needn't be! Take more than a scar to damage *his* looks!'

'Now that *is* reassuring.' We swung round to find Matt stood in the doorway. Hastily, I began clattering cups and saucers into a tray.

'Matt, I'm sorry. I asked Penny because . . . well, it doesn't bother me but I know it does you.' Sam wrung her hands, nervously.

Matt smiled. Fortunately. 'It's OK. I heard you and Penny talking, and she's right. I'll tell you about the accident one day.'

'You don't have to. I don't care.' She paused. 'I think you're gorgeous anyway.' Sam gazed at her feet.

In two strides, Matt had reached her, and, gathering her up in a tight embrace, proceeded to kiss the life out of her.

I coughed, bunged the percolator on to the tray, and scuttled off out of the kitchen.

I staggered into the drawing room, buckling under the weight of the tray, and found Carolyn listening owlishly to Alex's ideas on make-up.

John grinned. 'Is he muscling in on my woman?'

I laughed. 'Alex'll talk to anyone, especially if it's about fashion.'

Matt and Sam wandered through the door, holding hands. Ben hid a smile as he bent down to pour the coffee.

'Are you sure you don't want a drink, Carolyn?' I asked, trying to rescue her from Alex's incessant chatter.

She shook her head and smiled. She'd been on orange juice all night. 'I'm driving, I'm afraid.'

'You're all welcome to stay the night,' said Ben, handing out cups of coffee. Was that a ghost of a wink I saw him flash at Matt?

'Thanks, but I've got an early meeting tomorrow morning,' said John. 'My editor at the magazine wants to see me. Otherwise . . .' John shrugged.

'Never mind. You'll be staying the day after tomorrow,' I said, and felt nervous again. I'd just reminded myself of the wedding. I felt sick with nerves. John watched me, knowing me better than I know myself.

'Listen, you'll be fine,' he murmured, gently stroking my face.

I'd had so much to drink, I actually believed him.

Ben parked the boys on the sofa, and began arranging them like scatter cushions.

'No, that's not right,' he murmured, and, picking up Harry, sat him on the arm of the sofa. Harry scowled, knowing what was coming.

'Rory, stand behind the sofa and lean down.' Rory heaved a long-suffering sigh, but did as his father asked.

'Alex, stop gassing and stretch out on the sofa. That's right, lean on the arm of it, near to Harry.'

Alex loved all this attention and posed quite happily. Rory and Harry shot him a disgusted look which reduced John to uncontrollable laughter.

John took several photos of the boys, and really had to coax them to smile. Alex wore a permanent grin. Rory and Harry were getting increasingly agitated. John took another two photographs and called it a night, to their visible relief.

An hour later, and the boys were yawning their heads off. I turned to say something to Ben and caught John taking a photo of him. Oh, no, I thought, don't tell me he's been surreptitiously snapping away for the past hour?

I crept up behind him and, snatching the camera out of his hand, chased him around the drawing room, taking photos of him. John, like me, hated having his photograph taken.

In desperation, he hid behind Ben and refused to come out.

'I hope you all realize,' I drawled, 'that my darling brother has been clicking away for the past hour.'

'Really?' said Ben, and, grabbing John's arm, lowered him down into his arms and bent his head close to John's. It looked as if Ben was kissing him!

'Take a photo of this, Penny. Strictly for blackmail purposes, of course! Then we've always got him!'

I took the photo, and was laughing so hard, I doubted whether it would be in focus.

'Ah, but . . .' John sniffed. 'That goes for you too!'

'You have a point,' Ben conceded, and dropped John on to the floor.

John, weak with laughter, crawled on to the sofa and collapsed on it. I handed him his drink.

'Sneak!' he muttered, and drained his glass.

As we kissed John and Carolyn goodnight, Matt phoned for a taxi to take Sam home.

I put the boys to bed, and just caught Sam as she was leaving.

'Thanks, Penny. I've had a lovely time, not to mention getting a head start with that gorgeous creature.'

'My pleasure,' I replied, and left Matt, literally, hungrily devouring her, much to the weary, bored-looking cab driver's irritation. I supposed he saw a lot of that.

I padded back into the drawing room and, flopping into a chair, kicked my shoes off and rubbed my aching feet.

'Why don't you go up?' murmured Ben. 'Matt and I'll take care of the clearing up.'

I smiled sleepily, and, giving him a lingering kiss, teetered off to bed. I must have gone out like a light because I can't remember Ben coming to bed. I spent the best part of the following day swinging erratically between whimpering terror and manic high spirits. The boys didn't know quite how to deal with me, so they took to either ignoring me or showering me with affection.

Matt spent half the day on the phone drooling lustfully at Sam, and wore a silly grin the other half of the day.

That evening, after I'd tucked in the boys, I shut myself in the drawing room with a medicinal brandy. Ben was in his study taking care of a mountain of paperwork.

Personally, I thought the nerves were getting to him too.

Matt wandered into the drawing room later and fixed himself a drink. He surveyed me from the depths of the sofa. Finally, he blurted out, 'It's nice seeing Ben so happy. He's spent so long being miserable. I'm glad he's found you.'

I smiled. 'Thank you.' What else was there to say? A long, heavy silence followed.

When Matt had first moved back in here, we had been very polite towards each other, but remained strangers. The time in the cottage, although unacknowledged, never talked about, had stood between us.

I'd felt uneasy around him at the beginning. Wasn't sure I liked him. He had kidnapped me, after all! Mind you, I reflected, I'd slapped him. Matt wore a permanently guilty look on his face whenever I walked into a room. He'd put me through hell, but what he didn't know was that I understood his reasons, his motives for doing something so stupid, so frightening, so desperate.

I liked him, I realized. I didn't hold anything against him. If it had been John, I'd have done anything to get him back; I'd have sold my soul. Still would, if John needed me to. If I'd do that for John, I knew I would do it for Ben. Hadn't Matt done just that?

I gazed steadily back at Matt. 'I couldn't bear to lose John,' I said. 'I mean, I'd do anything to get him back.'

Matt understood my meaning, swallowed, nodded and shot me a watery smile. 'I'm sorry,' he mumbled, picking at the rim of his glass.

'I know.'

'You seem to understand.'

'Absolutely.'

Matt took a great gulp of his drink, which he held with a trembling hand.

'I see you and Sam were – er – getting on well.' I grinned. Matt looked relieved that I'd changed the subject and shot me a grateful smile.

'I think I have you to thank for that. Ben told me it was your idea. He said something about giving a gentle shove!'

'Did he now? Ben shouldn't sneak,' I muttered, and buried my face in the brandy.

Grinning, Matt got off the sofa and knelt down beside my chair. Tentatively, he wiggled a finger on my knee-cap.

'Penny, I just want you to know. If you ever need anything, need *me* to do anything for you, you only have to say.' Matt gazed at the arm of my chair.

'Ditto,' I murmured.

Matt slowly raised his eyes to mine. They were full of affection. As, I'm sure, were mine. I held my arms out and he flopped into them, desperately seeking my forgiveness – or was it my approval? He had both.

Matt never quite forgave himself, I felt, for the night he took me away, and bent over backwards ever afterwards to show me how he felt about me: that I was accepted, adored and cherished.

Matt would become one of my closest friends.

CHAPTER 21

Finally, it was the day before my wedding. All the invitations had been sent out and replied to. The caterers, having supplied us with a menu, were coming first thing in the morning to set up the tables and bring the food, including the cake.

Several gorgeous men in shorts, big boots and with deep suntans came and erected the marquee in the little paddock, and began placing huge potted plants all around it, both inside and out.

The DJ would be arriving around six o'clock. I'd borrowed him from one of the nightclubs in Chalfont, which went by the name of the Rollicking Kneecap.

The boys were highly excited, overtired and emotional. Ben had sent Mrs Travis into Chalfont to buy three little suits. He didn't dare send me, thinking my nerves might divert me to the lure of the pub!

So I spent the day alternating between cowering in an armchair in the drawing room and surreptitiously watching the rippling muscles of the bronzed chaps hauling up the marquee. I haven't even got the boys to keep me company, I thought.

Ben, Matt and the lads were all exceptionally busy in the Yard, and I kept on bursting into tears when I thought of the conversation Matt and I had had the previous night.

John arrived in the evening wearing a huge grin and carrying two enormous bottles of wine. I felt better already.

'Just a little light relief,' he drawled, waving the bottles at me. Oh, dear, I thought. And I'd hoped to look so nice on my wedding day.

After a leisurely dinner, of which I didn't eat much, the boys decided to spend all evening tormenting John, desperately wanting his attention. I knew how they felt. Times like these you really need your brother, I thought, and felt close to tears again.

Going up to bed that night, I frightened myself to death, reminding myself that this was my last night as a single woman. I put my head between my knees and breathed deeply. It didn't help at all. I very nearly fainted.

Everyone got up early, except me. I slept in until nearly eleven o'clock, having had a restless night. Strung up tighter than my uncle's banjo, I wandered aimlessly about the house. At one o'clock in the morning, John and I had been playing poker on his bed, until Ben woke up, and, realizing I wasn't next to him, came looking for me. With several expletives, he dragged me back off to bed by the scruff of my neck.

I took an age to get ready, with only one small mishap, which occurred when I was in the bath. Because I was shaking so much, being a complete bag of nerves, the soap shot out of my hands, bounced off the wall, and smashed the light bulb and a china tooth-mug.

When I finally walked into the kitchen, holding the roses Ben had sent up to my room earlier, Ben, Matt,

327

John, Mrs Travis and three identically dressed little boys in grey suits gazed at me wide-eyed and open-mouthed. With a shaking hand, I drank a cup of cold coffee. Everyone remarked on how beautiful I looked. Personally, I felt like regurgitated lasagne.

Matt went off to fetch the Jag from the garage while I locked myself in the downstairs lavatory. Harry rattled the door, and said accusingly, 'Penny, come out of there! We're ready to go.'

I gritted my teeth, and had the greatest difficulty in getting out of the lavatory. The lock seemed to keep on dodging my fingers. Blind terror about summed it up, I think.

I cautiously emerged from around the door, where upon John grabbed my hand and gently steered me outside and into the back of the Jag. Ben sat in the front, next to Matt, who was being chauffeur for the day.

When I'd had the dinner party, John had gently told me it wasn't too late to back out if I really wanted to. Hardly the most encouraging thing to say to someone who was having a bad enough time of it anyway.

Having had the seed of doubt planted in my mind, I'd calmly walked into the sitting room and huddled in an armchair and started swigging scotch, which I hated.

Ben had caught me, and forcibly removed the bottle, reminding me how much he loved me and wanted to be my husband.

I sat rigid, gazing at the back of Matt's head, while the boys clambered into the car. Harry climbed on to my knee, and Alex sat on John's. Rory sat in between John and me, and made sure the child locks were on – not to stop his brothers falling out, but to stop me making a run for it.

When we arrived at the register office I refused to let Harry go, holding on to him tightly, like a live teddy bear. Finally, making soothing, encouraging noises and no sudden movements, John coaxed me out of the car.

'I should have brought a carrot to give her!' he grinned.

John and Ben frogmarched me into the register office, which was sparsely furnished with several rows of wooden chairs with arms, and a large desk with a phallic-looking candlestick on top. It smelt musty and unused. I'll bet the divorce courts don't smell like this, I thought, nervously fiddling with John's lapel.

The Registrar, Mr Oftenthwaite, was a balding, middle-aged man with BO and a nervous twitch. Breezing into the room, he clapped his hands together and suggested we get cracking. He spoke very fast, and had a habit of grinning inanely after each sentence. I looked at John, then quickly looked away, terrified I was going to burst out laughing.

'Take your places, please,' said Mr Oftenthwaite, grinning and jerking convulsively, and parking half-rimmed spectacles on the end of his nose. Are we going to do the Do-Se-Do? I wondered. Ben and I stepped forward and John stood behind me, slightly to one side, and Matt, likewise, stood behind Ben, with the boys standing in between John and Matt.

Ben, catching hold of my hand, kissed it, and gazed at me adoringly. I shot him a gritted-teeth look, and tried to smile, which must have made me look as if I was baring my teeth. Mr Oftenthwaite cleared his throat noisily, and launched into his spiel.

I said Alexander Brenda instead of Ben Alexander, and dropped his ring. Diving under the desk, pulling my skirt over my bottom as I went, I retrieved it from a pile of fluff and emerged with my hat askew.

John couldn't stop laughing, and, as he'd always been able to do, he set me off. Ben's stony face only served to make me worse, purely out of nerves, I might add.

Mr Oftenthwaite twitched and pressed on. I was shaking so much, Ben could hardly get the ring on my finger. Clamping it to his chest, he slipped it on, and we were pronounced 'man and wife'.

I shook Mr Oftenthwaite's hand and made an indecent bolt for the door, which only prolonged the whole thing, as I was dragged back to sign the register.

John and Matt took several photographs of Ben and me kissing, signing the register and smiling engagingly at Mr Oftenthwaite.

Stepping outside into the fresh air, I breathed deeply, and felt faint with relief. The boys had behaved impeccably, far better than I had, and I told them so, at which Ben acidly remarked that even a five-year-old could behave for fifteen minutes without getting bored. He was still smarting over the fact that I hadn't wanted a church wedding, which, considering the short amount of time we'd had to plan the whole thing, was rather fortunate, I felt.

John and Matt took several more photographs outside the register office. I think this was the detail that had taken our rows into double figures. I didn't want a stuffy photographer, just John with his Olympus 35mm. Ben, from then on, had referred to our wedding as 'The Pantomime'. I detest having my photograph taken anyway, and fidgeted a great deal.

Ben and I together, then John and I together, then with all the boys, then with all the boys individually, and finally, with Matt, who remarked in my ear that John knew now how it felt to be totally Pennyless. After twenty agonizing minutes of infernal clicking and whirring, we all piled into the Jag, and headed back to the Yard.

By the time we arrived, so had most of our guests. Mrs Travis and one of John's cronies were doing a sterling job, having seated everybody and handed out champagne. As we entered the marquee, everyone shot out of their seats, which swayed recklessly back and forth, and in one big mass surged towards us. It took us a fair while to greet everyone, so I took to holding two conversations at once, which meant I said 'yes' and 'no' in totally the wrong places.

I was introduced to Ben's Uncle Roger, his late father's brother.

'Roger . . . Penny,' said Ben, beaming with pride. Roger Carmichael was an absolute scream, and we hit it off immediately. He was wearing plus-fours, a monocle, and pipe tobacco in his handle-bar moustache. Rumbling in his throat, he gathered me up, and gave me the biggest bear-hug of my life. He would come to be one of my favourite relatives.

Sid Carmichael was the youngest brother of Ben's late father, and was totally different from Roger. He had been a military man, and walked, stood, and sat very erectly, and judging by his wife's grim expression, Sid obviously never relaxed his military bearing. Sid Carmichael wore a similar suit to Ben's, Matt's and John's, a sort of dusty charcoal, which showed off their long legs. He shook my hand as his face creaked into a sort of smile. Obviously wasn't used to doing that, I thought. In a low voice, he introduced me to his wife, Clarissa.

She was a slim, kind-looking woman, knocking on for sixty, and she had two-tone hair, rather like a skewbald pony, I thought hysterically. Her blue eyes smiled into mine, and her voice was rich and husky. She wore a pale blue frock, and earrings you could have opened a tin of beans with.

'It's all over now,' she purred, patting my hand. 'Don't mind Sid, I have to iron him every morning to put the creases in!'

I screamed with laughter, which awarded me a stern look from old Sid.

'Madge!' a voice barked.

Startled, I swung round to see Roger steering a plump lady in a bright pink frock, with swollen ankles, in my direction.

'Meet the wife!' boomed Roger. 'And don't laugh, she can't help it!' Twirling his moustache, he shot her a playful wink. Madge sighed, and raised her faded brown eyes heavenwards.

'Nice to meet you, Penny.' She smiled, and proceeded to apologize for the 'obnoxious old devil' on her left. 'I left him on platform three at Cheltenham station once, but he bought a map.'

Roger roared with laughter and clapped her on the back. She gave a delicate cough.

'Did you bring my cousins?' asked Ben, looking highly amused.

'Er – no,' said Roger, extracting his monocle. 'They're both working abroad now. Peter's in America. Works in advertising, y'know.' He nodded at me. 'Both of 'em do, although Andrew's in Australia. He seems to have developed an unhealthy interest in wallabies.' Roger snorted, and, muttering under his breath, dragged off a protesting Madge.

'What about James and Richard?' Ben asked, grinning at Sid.

332

'Both in the Middle East. They're soldiers,' he explained to me.

Of course, I thought. What else?

Sid was revving up to give us the complete history of the British Army, when mercifully Clarissa bawled, 'Eyes right!' and double-timed him back to their table.

We talked at length to a few of my old friends, mainly Sue and Karen. Sue I'd known from a job I'd done a few years ago. We'd met in Ibiza's capital, San Antonio, where we'd shared digs. We'd had a whale of a time. Ben showed enormous interest and asked her if she'd kindly divulge any juicy bits about my somewhat hazy past. She remarked that if he offered a four-figure sum and multiplied it by five, she might consider it.

I was fond of Sue. We'd got out of more scrapes together than I cared to remember. Her short red hair framed her face, emphasizing the big green eyes in the lily-white skin. She was tall, slim, and about my age, and I thought her very attractive. Sue also had a sense of humour like mine, and could put a rugger player to shame.

We chatted for a while about her new job. She'd been married, had a baby, had got divorced and now worked in a hotel on the coast. Ben's attention began to drift to my other friend, Karen.

If truth be known, Karen was my bestest, bestest friend. We'd gone to school together and went all the way back. I patted Sue's hand, told her I'd see her later and introduced Ben to Karen.

Ben looked at Karen with badly concealed excitement, hoping to glean more snippets about my past, but got no joy from that direction either.

Where did this desire to know about my past come from? I wondered. Ben studied Karen with a peeved expression. Her nut-brown eyes danced in her rather ruddy complexion. She was quite a large lass, but not what you'd call fat. Her brown hair hung in a straight curtain down her back. I would have done anything for Karen, and vice versa.

Karen informed me that she wasn't married yet. She couldn't find anyone rich enough, daft enough or short-sighted enough to want her.

'Oh, Karen. Stop putting yourself down!' I snapped. I'd always hated her doing that, and as far as I could remember she'd always done it. I thought her very pretty and a lovely person. She had a thing about her large feet, which, on reflection, did have a tendency to trip everyone over.

'So, what are you doing now?' I asked, wondering whether she was being boiled alive in that heavy black frock she was wearing.

'Same thing, roughly. I'm teaching in a riding school, mainly children.'

'What's the place like?'

'Oh, that's pretty much the same thing as well. Some drip of a chap, knows absolutely nothing about horses, except for the teeth in one end and tail at the other.' She wrinkled her nose and grimaced.

Ben looked slightly put out. 'We're not all like that, you know!'

Karen laughed. 'I know. I just always seem to get them!'

'D'you have any plans to move on again?' I asked.

She shook her head. 'No. I think I'll stay. I'm growing accustomed to stability. It's quite disturbing actually!'

I laughed, and, giving her an affectionate pat, took Ben off to meet some of John's cronies. Ben surveyed them with a wary expression.

David politely shook Ben's hand. He was dark and very good-looking, that no doubt being the reason why Ben kept a watchful eye on him as he kissed my cheek. He'd been a friend of John's for years and I knew him quite well, as I'd always lived with John in between jobs.

David was a journalist and had met John through the magazine they both worked for. I always remembered him having hordes of women chasing after him, and he would often hide out in John's flat, which didn't help much considering the amount of women John always had after *him*! They exchanged brief greetings and I introduced Ben to Simon, who was blond, blue-eyed and gentle-looking. He was an artist and had met John at a party a few years ago, and had been madly in love with John from first meeting him. Whether John minded or not, he never said. Ben shook the offered hand, and immediately transferred his gaze all the way up the six-foot-four-inch frame of Robbie. He wrote for a sports magazine and had met John at some mind-numbingly boring awards ceremony. He played rugger in his spare time and looked as if he did. With his crew cut and bulging muscles, he looked a bit of a thug.

Robbie gave Ben a knuckle-crunching handshake and beamed at him, crinkling the corners of his dark eyes, one of which was darker than the other where someone had more than likely thumped it. He gave it a prod. 'A size eleven did this last Saturday. Good game, though!'

Ben smiled. 'What d'you play?'

'Rugger.'

'How long have you played?'

'Since I was at university, Great excuse to get out of lectures, actually.'

Ben laughed, and, taking my hand, said we'd see them later.

I spotted John talking to Carolyn. She'd obviously managed to get here all right on her own, despite John's sarcastic remark that all she used maps for were to stop the table wobbling.

Matt and Sam were nicely ensconced with each other, and waved to me from across the marquee. Matt had a protective arm around her shoulders, which Sam was thoroughly enjoying. And who could blame her? I thought.

Jack, my quietly bewildered grandfather and my rampant Uncle George were seated at a table eyeing up all the young and attractive women milling about. I'd introduce them to Ben later on, when he'd had more to drink. Cowardice is a shameful thing, I told myself.

We stopped to briefly chat to the stable lads, who couldn't stop fidgeting and looked extremely uncomfortable in their lightweight suits.

Ben cleared his throat, thanked everyone for coming and suggested we eat. Several relieved faces peered back at us.

Ben and I, along with John, Matt, Mr and Mrs Travis and the boys, sat at the top table. The caterers had surpassed themselves. The food was not only delicious, it also looked pretty. Smoked salmon, roast quail, strawberries and profiteroles. The boys started to take an interest around the strawberry stage.

The marquee soared and dipped with conversations, and I felt the tension gradually seeping out of me.

I spotted the Harrises, complete with Archie. Mrs Harris looked larger than ever in her dun-coloured long skirt and billowing top. There were possibilities there if we should encounter any problems with the marquee! She'd had a mauve rinse on her hair, which Archie couldn't take his eyes off, and it appeared to have gone all frizzy and stuck out all over the place, strongly resembling a loo brush.

She dwarfed Mr Harris, who was wearing a navy pinstriped suit, just like his little son, and looked like something out of *The Godfather*.

Archie wore a permanent scowl and refused to eat his smoked salmon. Mrs Harris scooped it up, plonked it on her plate and shovelled in great mouthfuls in between her constant yakking.

Mr Harris always wore a resigned expression, and now I understood why. He glanced in desperation at the vicar, who was seated next to him, but Reg was not to be drawn, and kept his eyes firmly fixed on his plate.

Mr Harris (George) caught me looking at him, and gave me a little coy wave, at which Mrs Harris (Gwen) slapped him with her napkin, shooting me a baleful stare. I grinned, and caught Matt staring at me.

'All right?' I mouthed to him.

He flashed a look at Sam across the marquee and grinned at me. I guessed he was.

After we'd all finished eating, the caterers cleared away the debris and half of the tables, while the DJ set up his equipment.

Ben and I, John, Matt and the boys tramped up to the house to get changed. I slipped into a cool white loose-fitting dress, while Ben swapped his suit for a pair of chinos and a shirt. Kissing me lingeringly, he reluctantly let me go, and returned to our guests, taking the boys with him, who'd all changed into jeans. I went into the bathroom and repaired my face.

I was just about to wander out of our bedroom and on to the landing when I heard Matt and John talking in hushed voices, which immediately alerted me to the sensitivity of the conversation. I hovered inside the doorway, listening.

'Ben doesn't want Penny worried or upset. You know how strung up she's been about this wedding, and everything going OK.'

'Mm,' John murmured. 'When did it happen, this incident?'

'A couple of days ago. Ben nipped into town to pay some money into the bank and someone damn near flattened him. He's certain it's something to do with the trouble we've been having here recently.' Matt was trying very hard to keep his voice down, and was succeeding. I was having to strain to catch what he was saying. But hear him I did.

'Can't Ben go to the police?' asked John.

'With what? He didn't get a licence number or anything. What could he tell them?'

'Are you sure it's something to do with what's been going on here? I mean, they could have been trying to rob him,' reasoned John.

'After he's paid it in?' Matt snorted.

John let out a long, slow breath. 'Point taken. Will Ben tell Penny what happened?'

'What would be the point? It'd only worry her, upset her.'

'I agree, but better that than have her wandering about in ignorance, which I hasten to add is seldom blissful. She might not be safe.' John's concern was most apparent in his voice.

'Don't worry. We'll look after her,' said Matt soothingly.

'You'd better. That's my sister we're talking about.' John's tone wasn't exactly unfriendly, but held the warning all the same.

'Look, I think the world of her too!' said Matt, a tad defensively.

I put my hand to my mouth and blinked.

'Do you honestly think,' Matt went on, 'that I'd let anything happen to her? I'm telling you, they'd have to go through me first!'

A slight pause followed, and then I heard them heading for the stairs, still muttering in low voices, while I shot behind the door.

I sat on the bed, pondering. They had both been right. Yes, I'd had enough to cope with lately, what with the wedding and everything, but what if *they* came after me? What if they tried to get to Ben though me?

Well, at least I now knew about it, if nothing else. And yes, I was worried. Matt's rather sudden declaration had shocked me a little. I knew we were getting closer as a family, but I didn't realize how fast.

I sighed. So many people who genuinely loved me, cared about me. I considered myself very fortunate. I understood Ben's reasons for not telling me, and I knew he loved me so much that he didn't want to worry me, frighten or upset me, but I still felt curiously peeved.

I decided I'd better get back to our guests, and had a go at a couple of karate kicks out on the landing to get rid of my anger, and damn near ruptured my prospects. I decided I'd be no threat to the villains, whoever they were. Better to stand behind Matt and do as he said: let them go through him.

CHAPTER 22

Composing my ruffled karma, I stepped into the marquee and got ambushed by the vicar.

'Ah! The lovely Mrs Carmichael!' he boomed, making me draw back in horror. 'Please have this dance with me!' And, advancing towards me, he cornered me by a huge cheese plant.

As I protested feebly, he tangoed me into the centre of the marquee, and proceeded to disco-dance energetically to the latest hits. I use the term 'disco-dance' loosely. Flailing his arms around like a windmill, and thrusting his hips forward, he began to sing along to the record, very loudly and out of tune. The old boy could really go, I reflected in amusement. Our vicar was a real hoot! I danced another two records with him, constantly fearing I might get a black eye, when rescue came in the form of Adam.

'Adam!' I cried, overjoyed. 'You got the invitation, then?'

He nodded, grinning. 'Yes, I'm still at the cottage. I work for Bob Chester now.' He looked at me under his lashes. 'I have – how shall I say – a new partner.'

'But that's great!' I replied, kissing him on his cheek. 'Let's go and sit down, have a drink, and then you can tell me all about him.'

340

We found a table in the corner, and sat down with a bottle of champagne.

'Well? What's he like?'

'Oh, a couple of years younger than I am, dark, beautiful – and very kind,' he said, a touch acidly.

I gazed at him steadily. 'You still miss him, don't you?'

Adam blinked, and stared at the bubbles rising in his glass. Finally, he lifted his head and looked at me sadly. 'Yes. Yes, I do.' He sighed. 'But Paul helps. He's someone to talk to, someone to hold, to wake up with.' Groaning, he raised his eyes to heaven. 'Don't start me off! This is your wedding day! Be happy! You don't want to hear me whining on about Will. Drink up and enjoy yourself!'

I smiled at him, and idly watched the vicar patting Mrs Harris's bottom. I laughed, and Adam, turning to see what I'd laughed at, doubled up into hysterics. Several people close by heard us, two of whom were Will and Dominic. I saw Will shake off Dominic's hand from his arm and walk purposefully over to us.

'Hello, Adam,' he said softly. 'How are you?' Will gazed at him intently, seeing if the cracks had been filled in, I suppose.

'Fine, thanks,' Adam replied, smiling gently.

'Where are you working now?'

Adam explained where he was working, and how nice everyone was, and at that point, bang on cue, the un-nice Dominic sauntered over to us, sucking his teeth in ill-disguised irritation.

He nodded curtly. 'Adam.'

Adam inclined his head. 'Dominic.'

All very polite, I thought, mildly surprised. I supposed messing up wedding days was still considered bad form.

341

'Made any new – er – friends?' asked Dominic, nastily.

'As it happens, yes. One special new friend in particular.' Adam smiled engagingly.

Will looked as if he was going to faint. Dominic made a sarcastic remark implying that the poor boy was obviously desperate, stupid or blind, or possibly all three. Adam looked down at his hands, and, shaking his head, gave a snort of laughter. Looking up at Dominic, he drawled, 'Dominic, shove off!'

Dominic glared at him, and, turning abruptly, snapped at Will, 'Are you coming?'

'In a minute,' Will mumbled, gazing at Adam. Dominic stormed off in a filthy temper. Will continued to gaze at Adam.

Fidgeting, Adam muttered, 'You'd better get going. He seems to be in a bit of a huff.'

'So what?'

Adam and Will gazed at each other for a long time. Finally, Adam said gently, 'Goodbye, Will. Take care.'

Will blinked, swallowed and, turning on his heel, strode off back to Dominic.

'That took some doing, didn't it?'

'Well, put it this way, I don't think I could do it again,' he said, gazing into his drink. I looked across to where Will and Dominic were standing. They seemed to be having a tight-lipped row, speaking out of the corners of their mouths in order not to attract anyone's attention. Adam burst out laughing.

I spotted Roger revving up around the marquee, twirling around his long-suffering wife, Madge. He had Mrs Harris puffing and wheezing in disgust as he pulled Madge against himself and deliberately dropped his monocle down her enormous cleavage.

'I'll never see that again, at least not alive!' he roared, and reduced Mr Harris to fits of laughter. 'Well, not unless . . .' He gave a low rumble in his throat. 'Not unless I dig it out here and now!' And Roger's hand shot towards Madge's frock, at which she merely sighed, and calmly removed the eye-piece herself.

I nearly didn't notice Sid. He stood as straight as one of the poles holding up the marquee, and looked as if he was giving them a hand.

With a bored expression, he watched his wife, Clarissa, having a bop with Matt. Mrs Harris approached Sid, fluttering her eyelashes like a dozen hysterical spiders, and only succeeded in frightening him. Personally, I could see his point. I supposed he'd rather face a charging army of Scotsmen with bayonets aloft than that apparition hurtling towards him. He swallowed.

Seizing him by his rather thin shoulders, Mrs Harris dragged him off for a dance. Sid deliberately stepped on her feet, then escorted her back to her table, buckling under her weight as she hobbled along complaining that he'd trampled a corn.

I heard a deafening shriek, and swung round in my chair to see Carolyn being subjected to the most appalling mauling from my Uncle George. He barged into the middle of the marquee, dragging a protesting Carolyn in his wake. He insisted on keeping both hands on her bottom, and steered her around the marquee by her tightly clenched buttocks.

'How about a dance with me, Mrs Carmichael?' John, looking slightly cross-eyed, grinned down at me.

'Oh, go on, then. You'll do!' I laughed. I got to my feet and told Adam I'd see him later. John waltzed me into the centre of the marquee. Cheek to cheek, we sailed past my friend Sue, who was getting highly over-excited with our Robbie.

'Can't take him anywhere!' John drawled. We shuffled past Simon doing the charleston with Mrs Travis. I fell about laughing, and cannoned into the vicar.

Ben emerged from the throng, and asked where I'd been.

'Mingling.' I absent-mindedly waved a hand over the crowd. John patted my hand and wandered off to placate Carolyn. Actually, I haven't done much mingling, I thought, guiltily.

'Well, come and mingle with me,' he said, indignantly.

I decided I couldn't postpone the inevitable and introduced Ben to my Uncle George, who wore odd socks, braces, a blue suit several sizes too big for him, and a permanent lecherous grin. He shook Ben's hand, while gazing at Sally from the hairdresser's at the same time. He was a tall thin man, with a full head of rather unruly hair, which I wished he had brushed at some point. Uncle George told Ben he was very lucky to have me, did he know who that girl's name was, and what won the 2.15 at Thirsk!

'Haven't a clue,' shrugged Ben, smiling gently.

'No, I didn't back that,' said Uncle George, and shot off after Sally.

My grandfather, Jack, was five feet two inches, skinny, bald as a coot, of a nervous disposition and had a nasty habit of taking his teeth out and leaving them on any available surface. He sidled over to us, and informed me in a frozen whisper that the DJ was using Japanese speakers. Didn't I know I had to be careful?

'You can't trust 'em, y'know!' he whispered, eyes darting everywhere.

I patiently explained to Ben that Jack had been in a Japanese POW camp. Ben sympathetically asked him what it was like there.

'Shocking weather!' he retorted, and wandered off to have a closer look at the DJ who sourly surveyed him with a set of headphones perched on top of his head, looking not unlike Mickey Mouse.

The champagne was going down at a hell of a rate. John rapped the table, and said it was about time Ben and I cut the cake. I glanced over at it, having forgotten all about it, and felt slightly surprised to see that it was still intact.

Taking my hand, Ben led me over to it, and handed me the knife. Having never cut a wedding cake before – you don't think I'd go through this twice, do you? – I was about to attack it in a fair imitation of something out of the shower scene in *Psycho* when Ben hastily put his hand over mine, and to more clicking and whirring we sliced into the cake, accompanied by half-hearted cheers. We then spent the next half-hour dishing out pieces of the stuff.

I desperately needed a drink, and went off in search of a glass of champagne. Hearing a piercing scream, I swung round to find Rory and Alex stuffing cake down Archie's underpants. Harry was trying to lift a bottle of champagne, to crack it over Archie's head. Belting over to them, I seized the bottle from Harry, and in no uncertain terms asked them what they thought they were doing.

'Annoying Archie,' said Rory, smiling sweetly.

'Do you realize, if you had hit him with this,' I brandished the bottle at them, 'you could have killed him!'

Three little faces gazed placidly back at me.

'Give me strength!' I muttered, grabbing Archie by his sticky hand.

I delivered him to his father, who made the most ferocious pass at me. I was saved from giving him a stinging slap in the face by Matt, who told him if he ever did that again he'd do worse than hit him, he'd tell Mrs Harris. Mr Harris swallowed audibly, and visibly paled. Muttering apologies, he slunk off, and hid behind one of the potted plants, peering out through the foliage.

'Thank you,' I said, shooting Matt a grateful smile.

Matt took me off for a bop, while poor Sam had to put up with my Uncle George's probing hands. Sam decided to keep him at arm's length. Easier said than done! I thought. He kept on edging closer, until he had her in a tight clinch, his hands wandering all over her bare back in the strappy apple-green dress she was wearing. She clearly wouldn't be wearing it for much longer if he had his way!

I watched Ben with a great deal of interest, trying to fend off both Mrs Harris and Sally from the hairdresser's. I giggled and hoped Ben wouldn't notice. Matt, seeing that my eyes were watching something across the marquee, looked over his shoulder, just in time to see Mrs Harris lunge at Ben.

I collapsed into hysterics, with Matt joining in. Ben's face was a picture! He was absolutely terrified. Sally was stroking his arm, or so she thought. Actually, she was stroking Mrs Harris. Hardly surprising. Everyone, by now, was three parts plastered. People were now letting their hair down (one or two literally!).

346

I had one more dance with Matt, then decided I needed some fresh air.

When I got back to the marquee, somebody had set up several barbecues, and John, Ben and Robbie, the rugger player, were charring sausages, chops and burgers. I couldn't stop laughing. When I'd mentioned the barbecue, I hadn't been serious. Still, why not? I thought hysterically. Anything goes at my wedding!

Ben, waving his fish-slice at me, called me over to him.

'Why didn't you rescue me?' he snapped, savagely thwacking a pork chop.

'I needed some fresh air,' I hiccuped, thinking he didn't seem remotely tipsy; 'besides, it was so entertaining to come back and discover that you'd taken me at my word about the barbecue!'

He surveyed me, looking irritated.

'Ben, this is a day when you're supposed to enjoy yourself,' I said, watching one of his burgers catch fire.

'I know, and I am.' Calmly he extinguished it, and, putting it in a bun, he gave it to the vicar.

'I just don't seem to have seen much of you today, apart from fifteen minutes in a disgusting building with an even more disgusting creature that was doing a bad imitation of a human male!'

'Let me fetch one of John's friends to do this,' I waved an arm at the barbecue, 'then we'll find a nice quiet corner, sit in it, and fondle each other!'

I shot off into the marquee, and, catching sight of Simon, made my way over to him. I felt mild surprise to see him burrowing clumsily in Sally's blouse, while the rest of the townsfolk were singing rugger songs, to the accompaniment of loud cheering.

347

Calmly removing Simon's hand from Sally's cleavage, I led him outside, and parked him at the barbecue, promising him a Bonio and John's help. That put the smile on his face.

I took Ben off for a walk around the Yard. Strolling hand in hand, listening to the snorts and rustlings coming from inside the boxes, we sat on the water trough, murmuring fondly to each other, relieved to have some time alone.

'I know I shouldn't say this, but I hope everyone pushes off home soon,' he murmured, nibbling at my neck.

'Mm. Been a long day, hasn't it?'

After a little quiet canoodling, we decided we'd better get back to our guests. We hadn't seen the boys for some time either. Better see what they were up to.

Back in the marquee, we found Rory, and, surprisingly, Alex, slumped on a chair, giggling inanely, and squinting.

'Where's Harry?' I asked.

Snorting with laughter, they pointed to the table. Glancing at it, I registered their meaning, and looked under it. Harry was fast asleep snoring gently. Ben picked up Harry, shoved him under one arm, and with Rory under the other he then stalked out of the marquee, and up to the house. I carried Alex.

We put them to bed without waking them.

'They're going to hate us in the morning!' I observed ruefully. 'They'll say we should've woken them up and let them stay till the end of the party.'

'We'll have enough people staying on to the end of the party,' observed my new husband grimly.

Then, muttering under his breath, Ben strode back to the marquee, leaving me to repair my face.

Going back downstairs again, I heard voices coming from the kitchen. Tiptoeing closer, I peered cautiously through the crack in the door, and saw Adam and Will standing quite close to each other. Oh, lord! Not again! I thought wearily. It seemed that Will was determined to test the water of his old relationship.

'What's his name?' Will asked, looking as if he'd rather not know.

'Paul,' replied Adam, scuffing the floor with his foot.

'It didn't take you long to find someone else, did it?' snapped Will, folding his arms.

'Well, at least I waited until I was single again!' retorted Adam.

With a loud crack, Will slapped him round the face. Adam calmly licked his lips, rubbed his chin, and went to walk out of the house.

'Don't you dare walk away from me!' Will yelled, and lunged at Adam, beating his fists into Adam's chest, calling him an ignorant pig. Adam, seizing Will by the arms, held him against the door and shouted, 'Just what the hell do you expect from me? You've made your choice. I'm entitled to have a lover, and I intend to keep him!'

Will started to cry.

'Don't you dare start crying!' bellowed Adam. 'Will, stop it!' Adam looked guilty and shaken. The sight of Will in tears was obviously something he couldn't stand. Will, using Adam's guilt like a weapon, redoubled his sobbing. Adam, swearing constantly, stomped across the kitchen, then back to Will.

'Just what are you trying to do to me?' he asked shakily. 'Haven't you got what you wanted?

Aren't you happy now?' Adam looked at Will searchingly.

'No!' he wailed. 'I'm not happy! Dominic isn't what I thought he was, and I don't love him. I love you, and I miss you so much, Adam.' Will gazed at him longingly, gently sniffing.

Adam impatiently ran a hand through his hair, and chewed his bottom lip thoughtfully. 'So, what are you saying?' He looked at the door, rather than at Will, I suppose steeling himself, waiting for the answer he so desperately wanted.

'I'm saying I want us to get back together.' Will gulped tearfully.

That appeared to be all Adam was waiting for. Smiling joyfully, he hugged Will to him passionately, which Will responded to eagerly. After an awfully long time, Adam came up for air. Gently he stroked Will's face.

'What are you going to say to Dominic?'

'How about, It's all over, pal?' Will ran a finger along Adam's shirt collar. Oh, dear, not more punch-ups, I thought bleakly. Finally I coughed and deliberately walked into a few pieces of furniture as I padded into the kitchen.

'Hello,' I said brightly, 'it's nice to see you're still good friends! Er – where's Dominic?'

Will glanced at Adam. 'I really don't know, or care. Adam and I are going to try again.'

'Have you told Dominic yet?' I asked, absent-mindedly shutting a cupboard door where we kept some glasses.

'I'll take him home and tell him there, and then meet Adam at the cottage later.' Will didn't take his eyes off Adam.

I looked at Adam, wondering if Paul was waiting for him at the cottage. As if reading my thoughts, Adam explained, 'I'm not seeing Paul until tomorrow. I'll straighten it out with him then.'

Poor Paul, I thought. Why does there always have to be a loser?

'We'd better go now. I don't want any unpleasantness to spoil your wedding day,' smiled Adam, and, coming over to me, he kissed my cheek. 'Thanks for the invite. I've had a much better time than I thought I would.' And he looked at Will.

'I'll walk down with you,' I said, thinking about Will and Dominic working together in the Yard. I couldn't see it myself. It was a good job we were leaving the honeymoon until later in the year, when the Yard was quieter. I supposed Will would leave to be near Adam, and Ben would have to take his place in the Yard.

I watched Adam get into his car and drive off, while Will found a fierce-looking Dominic, and after a few minutes they left on his motorbike.

Sighing, I walked back into the marquee. A hand shot out and grabbed my arm.

'Penny!' Karen shrieked. 'We've hardly spoken all night! Come and talk to me.'

I smiled, and we settled ourselves at a table, with yet another bottle of champagne sitting on it. I'd lost count of how much everyone had drunk. I'm sure they'll all know tomorrow, I thought sourly.

'I must say, you haven't lost your touch. That husband of yours is gorgeous!' she breathed, giving me a dirty grin and a wink.

'I know,' I replied, glancing round, trying to spot him. 'Actually, have you met his brother?'

'Mm. Spitting image, apart from that scar on his cheek. I'd quite like a bop with him.'

'Well, he's got a girlfriend, but I'm sure she won't mind. Just don't go making a play for him?' I grinned back at her.

Pulling a peeved face, she sighed. 'Fair enough!'

I peered round the bodies desperately clinging to each other. I supposed that was why they always have the smoochy dances at the end of the night: to help everyone hold each other up.

I spotted Matt dancing with Sally, and decided he needed rescuing anyway. She wore a very low-cut red spotted dress. I remember what my mother told me about women in red dresses, I thought, or was it a red hat? I got to my feet, somewhat unsteadily, and, marching up to him, asked if he would come and meet an old friend of mine.

Sally hung on to him tighter, a pathetic, dreamy expression on her face. No, don't upset her, I thought. The next time you want a haircut, she'll only cut your fringe too short, and you'll have to put your eyebrows up for a fortnight.

'Excuse me,' said Matt politely, and with some difficulty disentangled Sally's arms from around his neck. I strode back to the table, cannoning off a potted plant on the way, with Matt following me.

'Matt, have you been introduced to my old friend Karen?' I asked, pointing at her.

'No, I don't think I have.' Matt politely shook hands with her.

'Matt, Karen would like to have a bop. Why don't you give her a twirl?' I grinned as he obligingly whipped her away. I belted off, to look for Ben.

I found him trying to defuse a potentially fatal situation between Mrs Harris and my Uncle George.

'What's the problem?' I asked, of no one in particular.

'Apparently,' said Ben heavily, 'your Uncle has made a most indecent pass at Mrs Harris.' He looked at Uncle George disapprovingly.

Uncle George coughed, and muttered rudely, 'Bloody lucky someone took an interest, if you ask me!'

I smothered a giggle. 'Mrs Harris, he was only being kind!'

Mrs Harris turned beetroot, and started spluttering that she might have known she wouldn't get any sympathy from me, as I had the same disgusting mind! They obviously ran in our family! Fortunately, Mr Harris appeared at my side carrying a sleeping Archie, and gently reminded her that it was my wedding day. Thanking me for inviting them, he ushered his wife, who looked slightly mollified, in front of him. Uncle George shrugged, and weaved his way over to a table, flopping down on to a chair, blinking. Ben took me off for a smoochy dance.

'Looks as if most people are leaving,' he remarked, glancing around the marquee. 'How's your Uncle George getting home?'

'He isn't,' I replied, yawning. 'He's staying in a hotel in Chalfont. There's a taxi coming to pick him up, and my grandfather. They'll go home tomorrow.'

Because quite a few of our guests didn't live near us, they'd also booked into hotels. The drive resembled a taxi rank. Nobody, it seemed, liked going to a wedding and not being able to drink. Let's face it, you have to have some sort of help to get you through it!

I snuggled up to Ben, grateful that he was holding me up. I doubted I could have supported myself for much longer. We swayed on for another record, and then decided we'd better see off the remaining guests.

Twenty minutes later, everyone had gone. Wearily, Ben and I made our way up to the house and headed straight for the bedroom.

My wedding night was one I would rather forget. I was sick in the bidet, and passed out on the bedroom floor. Ben had to put me to bed.

When I came to, around mid-afternoon, I felt the worst I've ever felt in my life, and, galloping off to the bathroom, was horribly sick, for what seemed like hours. Then I somehow cleaned my teeth, and staggered weakly back to bed.

I surfaced in the evening, feeling a lot better. I had a bath and washed my hair. Creeping downstairs to get a drink, I was so thirsty that I couldn't wait for the kettle to boil, and drank some juice straight out of the carton from the fridge. Ben caught me, and, forcibly removing it, took great pleasure in my state of collapse.

'Morning!' he said acidly, looking pointedly at his watch.

'I'm sorry,' I muttered, sidling over to him, 'I know I messed up our wedding night. I promise I'll make it up to you later.'

'Oh, that you can be sure of!' He grinned. Rotten pig, I thought irritably. I hadn't been ill on purpose.

'How are the boys?' I enquired.

'Poorly!' He laughed like a drain. 'The same goes for your brother! I found him this morning, in the stables

354

with his cronies, curled around Bodmin, muttering about halitosis and big ears. I put him to bed, and nobody's seen him since!'

I laughed, which made my head bang. 'Anything else happen today?' I asked, wondering if Dominic and Will had had a domestic in the Yard.

'Dominic's leaving, or rather, he *has* left.' He rubbed his eyes wearily. He looked exhausted. 'You'd have thought he'd have given me a week's notice at least. I shall have to do his share of the work now! I really don't want to lose him either. He's a bloody good horseman. Oh, damnation!' He slammed his hand down on the table, which my head took in very bad part.

So, Will and Adam seem to be on again, I thought, and felt very happy for them both. I supposed Dominic couldn't face working with Will, seeing him, and not being part of his life, rather as Adam hadn't been able to.

'Why don't we try Adam?' He might come back now Dominic's gone,' I suggested. Ben looked at me doubtfully.

'I wouldn't mind having him back, but I don't think he'll come. What about Will?'

'They're back together.'

'Give me strength!' he snapped. 'I can't keep up with that pair! I suppose that explains Dominic's rather sudden departure!'

'Do you want me to phone him? I could do it now.' Looking at Ben hopefully, I began sidling over towards the phone.

Ben, smiling gently, said, 'You like him, don't you?'

I nodded. 'Yes. Yes, I do. Very much. I've missed him, and I know the boys have. He so reminds me of John.'

Taking hold of my hands, he kissed me. 'Go on, then, phone him!'

Grinning, I shot across the kitchen and called Adam. Yes, he'd be delighted to come back. It meant he could be near Will twenty-four hours a day! I heard Will laughing in the background.

'He'll be in tomorrow,' I said, with a silly grin on my face. Ben raised his eyes to heaven at my obvious pleasure.

'Are you up to to having something to eat?' he asked, gently squeezing me.

'Mm. I think so,' I said brightly, trying to disguise how bad I felt, and only succeeded in making myself feel sick again.

'I'll phone for a take-away.' Slapping my bottom, he then ruffled my hair, which really didn't help matters.

I padded off upstairs to see if my brother was still breathing. He was, just. He lay with an arm thrown over his head, looking green and making little whimpering noises.

'How d'you feel?' I asked.

'Don't shout!' he replied shakily.

'I didn't!' I giggled. 'D'you fancy some Chinese take-away?'

Throwing back the sheet, he shot out of bed, and galloped to the bathroom.

'I'll take that as a no,' I muttered, shuffling out of the room.

As I cautiously made my way along the landing, Matt stepped out from his room, looking disgustingly perky.

'Hello! You're alive, then!' he grinned.

'I think so,' I mumbled. I don't believe death is this painful, I thought. I swayed, feeling dizzy, and clutched my pounding head. Matt hastily shoved his arm across my back and, steering me into his room, he sat me on the bed. He looked at me, frowning.

'Why did you drink so much?' he asked.

'It was my wedding day!' I snapped. 'I'm entitled to quaff!' I winced, wondering if my head was going to explode. 'How come you and Ben are so nauseatingly healthy?'

'We usually drink scotch. We're not that keen on champagne really, so we didn't have too much of the stuff.'

'Bully for you,' I muttered, scuffing the carpet with my dangling feet.

'You look terribly pale. Can I get you anything?'

'A new head would be nice.' Waves of giddiness kept on washing over me.

Matt started to laugh. Grudgingly I giggled, then wished I hadn't.

'I heard you talking to John.' I glanced at Matt, and quickly looked away.

Matt closed his eyes and ran a hand over his face.' So, you know, then. About Ben's – er – incident.'

I nodded gently. Frankly, I dared not do anything else; my head might fall off.

'And . . .?' Matt flapped a hand.

'And yes, I'm scared, worried, upset but very aware.'

He folded his arms, nibbled his bottom lip, and looked extremely uncomfortable.

'Look, I know you're probably very angry that Ben didn't tell you, and that John or I didn't tell you, but you know why.'

'I know. In a bit of a dilemma really, weren't you?'

'You could say that.' He grinned.

'Lord, Matt, what's going on? Who is this nutter?'

Matt shrugged and sighed. 'I honestly haven't a clue. But don't worry. We'll get this sorted out.'

Hearing a loud crash and a muffled 'oof', I guessed my brother was having a few problems. 'That'll be John. I'd better go and see what he's done.'

I staggered off into John's room and found him sprawled on the floor, with Carolyn standing over him, wrapped in a towel.

'What happened?'

Gingerly, he sat up. 'I tripped over my bag!' He looked at me apologetically.

Sighing, and raising my eyes to heaven, I told him and Carolyn to get dressed and come down when they were ready. I told John he really ought to try and eat something. I made my way back downstairs, taking each step very slowly. This is seriously unfunny, I thought savagely.

Shuffling into the drawing room, I was greeted enthusiastically by the boys, who felt very grown-up at having been to their own father's wedding.

When the food arrived, I found I couldn't eat much. Neither could John. Both of us kept going hot and cold, and we exchanged stricken glances from time to time. I'm really not up to this, I thought, pushing congealed noodles around my plate. Carolyn tucked in as if she hadn't been fed for over a week. John and I watched her in horror.

Peering at his watch, John eventually said they'd better get going. We all tramped outside to see them off. I watched him drive away, feeling pathetically miserable. What is wrong with me? I thought crossly. I should be swinging off the door-handles, and talking non-stop about my 'husband'! You're obviously very tired, I told myself. You'll feel better in the morning.

It couldn't have been more than an hour or so later when Ben and I went to bed. He was impatient to make it all legal, as he put it. I think a corpse might have moved more than I did, at which Ben remarked if it hadn't have been for the fact that the dishes were done, he would have thought I had died earlier in the day! Still, it did my headache the power of good!

CHAPTER 23

Ten days into my marriage, and I found it rather disappointing. It wasn't a bit different, being married. Life had gone on in its usual way. Not a whiff of violins and harps, or roses growing round the back door.

Ben seemed absurdly happy, as did the boys. Matt took his brother-in-law role very seriously and I only had to clear my throat to get him leaping up asking if everything was OK.

Once I'd got over my monumental hangover after our wedding, it'd left me feeling washed out and drained. My nerves were stretched so tightly, I felt physically sick.

I felt a warm glow sweep over me, however, as I sent off my passport, driver's licence and bank details, to have 'Carmichael' plastered across them. At least now I was no longer named after an antiquated bicycle.

I was overjoyed to see Adam back in the Yard; in fact everybody was, especially the boys, who hounded him to death at every available opportunity.

Apart from Mark, nobody else was remotely bothered that Dominic had gone. Where to, no one knew; he'd just disappeared. He hadn't even been in touch requesting references and the wages owed to him.

'Good job!' Ben had snapped. 'If he couldn't be bothered to give a week's notice, then I can't be bothered to pick up a biro!'

Because Dominic had always done the 'driving tours' alongside Adam, Matt now did them, which worked out rather nicely.

John had called in with Carolyn to give us the lowdown on how the paintings of the boys were coming along. Personally, I think he was just checking that nothing untoward had happened to me.

'I'm afraid I shall have to paint in a smile,' he remarked ruefully, and went on to explain that Harry wore a heavy scowl on every photograph.

'You know . . .' he mused. 'All this wedding lark . . . I might just have a bash. See if I'm any good at it.' John grinned. Carolyn nearly fell off her chair.

'Well, I can highly recommend it,' said Ben, crushing me against his body.

John smiled, watching us. He thought a lot of Ben, he'd told me, because he knew how much Ben loved me. John swivelled his eyes towards Carolyn, who was looking slightly dazed.

'Well? What d'you reckon?' John tapped his ring finger.

'John! Ask her properly, in private!' I said, slapping his arm.

'I can't. My bottle might go!'

Carolyn giggled, and, hurling herself at John, mumbled a 'yes' into his neck.

'Right. There's only Matt left and then it'll be a hat-trick!' said Ben.

John didn't stay very long after his rather sudden proposal, and spent most of the time talking to Ben. I watched them, feeling happy and contented. John and Ben were becoming good friends, and Matt had taken to John right from the word go. I wouldn't mind Carolyn as a sister-in-law. Frankly, anyone could get on with her, and she was basically a good-hearted lass.

I woke up late, feeling awful, as I tended to do lately, and I'd barely opened my eyes when the phone rang beside me, making me jump.

'Hello,' I mumbled, rubbing the sleep out of my eyes. A long silence followed. I suddenly felt wide awake.

'Look, if you're a heavy breather or a pervert or something, you're not remotely sexy or frightening.' I snapped. 'In fact, you sound asthmatic!'

A sniff, then a croak. 'Penny,' wailed a voice.

'Sam! Is that you?'

'Yes.' She burst into tears.

'Whatever's the matter?' I struggled into a sitting position.

'I'm in the pub. Can you meet me?'

'Yes, of course. Give me fifteen minutes.'

I leapt out of bed, in a fashion, had a quick wash and brush-up and fell over in my haste to get my jeans on. I shoved on an old, faded T-shirt and galloped off downstairs without brushing my hair, which looked as if it was imitating the points of a compass.

I found Ben in the Yard wrestling with one of the horses as he tried to worm it. A great syringe poked out of its mouth like an obscene cigar.

'Keep still, you devil!' Ben growled.

'Ben, I have to go out.'

'Why? What's the panic?' He dodged Bodmin's head as she tried to wipe her yellow mouth all over his jeans.

362

'It's Sam. I think she's in trouble of some sort. She's just called me from the pub in an awful state.'

'What's she doing drinking at this hour?' he snapped.

'She's not drunk! She's crying. I'd better go and see what she wants.'

'Mmm, all right. But don't be long.'

He wasn't keen on my going anywhere on my own. He hadn't said, but I knew why: that business when he'd nearly got flattened. I hadn't told him I knew. How could I, without getting Matt and John into trouble for letting me overhear them? It wasn't their fault, but I knew Ben would say they should have been more careful. He wanted to wrap me in cotton wool, which wasn't a bad thing but could sometimes be a dangerous hindrance.

Ben stuck his head over the door, wanting a kiss, which he got before I belted off up the drive to get my car.

I arrived at the pub, and was in such a hurry to get to Sam, I nearly throttled myself with the seat belt. Impatiently pushing it aside, I scuttled off into the cool gloom of the pub.

Bert, the rotund, ruddy-complexioned landlord, had seated Sam at a table with a vast brandy. She looked deathly pale and shook like a leaf, clutching her drink.

'Oh, Penny!' she wailed, and collapsed into hysterical sobbing at the sight of me.

I slipped an arm around her shoulders and looked at Bert with raised eyebrows, silently asking the question. He merely shrugged and stomped off to polish a few glasses.

I let her cry for a bit, and produced a rather grubby handkerchief. She took it and noisily blew her nose.

'Why don't you tell me what this is all about?' I murmured.

'God, it's so embarrassing,' she sniffed. Oh, dear, I thought, has Mr Harris been a bit over-friendly? But it wasn't anything of the sort.

'Mrs Harris seems to think I've . . . I've . . .' She dissolved into tears again.

'She thinks you've done what?' I prompted.

'Stolen some money!' she howled, making Bert jump and drop a glass.

'OK, calm down.' I waited until she'd got to the gulping stage.

'She left forty pounds in the kitchen for the butcher, so she says. He came to deliver a load of meat for the freezer; she stocks it right up every so often. Well, he sent her a bill a few days later for the meat he'd delivered. Mrs Harris rang him, ranting and raving, saying she'd already paid him with the money she'd left for him in the kitchen. Well, he says he never saw any money in the kitchen.'

'So she assumed it must have been you who'd taken it,' I muttered, feeling a slow burning in the pit of my stomach. I knew Sam well enough to know that she was as honest as the day is long.

'So what happened? Did she come right out and accuse you?'

Nodding, she wiped her eyes. 'She shouted at me, accused me of taking the money. I didn't even know she'd left some money in the kitchen. I tried to tell her that, but she just told me to go. So, I packed my gear, carried it downstairs and then tried to talk to her again, but she just threw me out of the house, saying I was lucky she didn't call the police.' Sam gulped and went on, 'I think Mr Harris stopped her doing it. He wasn't convinced I'd taken that money, but she was having none of it. I was going and that was that.'

364

I pursed my lips thoughtfully. 'I think it must have been Archie. I mean, the butcher wouldn't steal, he'd never get any more business from her, and anyway, he's a good old boy. I'd say that's why no police were called, because deep down she knows it was her own blasted son.'

'That's what Mr Harris said, but she wouldn't hear of it. She said her darling baby would never do anything like that, and then they had this huge row. I just ran out to my car and drove here.' She flashed me a watery smile and shrugged. Her eyes were filling up again. 'Oh, Penny, I swear I didn't take it! I couldn't!'

'I know, I know,' I assured her, patting her hand.

'But what am I going to do?' she wailed. 'I don't have any money. She threw me out, telling me I wouldn't get paid and I could live off the forty quid I'd pinched.' Sam blew her nose again.

'Look, why don't you come home with me? We'll talk to Ben and Matt, and take it from there.'

'I can't do that! It's not their problem. I shouldn't have called you really, but I didn't know what else to do.'

'Sam, if I didn't take you home and Matt got wind of it, he'd never speak to me again!'

She giggled, but it got stuck in her throat, and she burst into tears again. That old witch had really upset her.

'Come on, where's your gear?'

'Still there, at the Harrises'. When they started arguing, I just ran out of the house.'

'OK, first of all we'll go home, then get your gear later.'

I got to my feet, flashed a smile at Bert and walked outside to my car, with Sam getting into hers.

We chugged up the drive, with 'Bloody Mary' alerting everyone to the fact that I was home with an ear-splitting bang. Sam got out of her car, and started shaking again. 'Penny, are you sure about this? I don't want Matt feeling responsible for me.' She gazed at me, sadness and worry clouding her eyes.

'Sam, I'm surprised this wasn't the first place you came to rather than the pub. You know how Matt feels about you. Now stop worrying. Has it occurred to you that he would *want* you to come to him?'

I parked Sam in the drawing room. Mrs Travis buzzed around her, calling her 'petal' and thrusting cups of tea into her trembling hands, while I went hunting for Ben and Matt in the Yard.

I found both of them, with their shirts off, looking unreasonably gorgeous, hauling hay-bales off a trailer and chucking them into the new hay store.

'Ben, Matt, could you come up to the house?'

'What's the problem?' Ben surveyed me through narrowed eyes.

'Er – Sam's here.'

Matt perked up sharpish, and enquired, 'Is she all right?'

'Er – not really. She's terribly upset. She's had a spot of bother with Mrs Harris. I think you'd better see her.'

Matt didn't need telling twice, and, snatching up his shirt, he threw it over his shoulder and set off up the drive with Ben following him.

Oh, dear, I think she's going to have a bit of an audience, I thought, as the boys came hurtling towards me.

Back in the drawing room, Sam was in tears again, being comforted by Mrs Travis. Matt shot over to her, clearly concerned. Gently, he pulled her against his body, and her sniffles soon stopped as she encountered all that gorgeous bare flesh!

'Penny said something about a spot of bother with Mrs Harris.'

Ben was leaning against the wall with his legs crossed and his arms folded, his shirt hanging off his jeans where he'd poked it through a belt loop.

I flopped into an armchair, still feeling slightly sick, with the boys strewn across my knee, my feet, and the arm of the chair. Buried alive in children, I thought.

'Do you want some privacy with Matt?' I asked, realizing this was highly embarrassing for her. She shook her head,

'No, it's OK, thanks. I don't have anything to hide, or to be ashamed of.'

'So what's all this about?' asked Matt, bending his head close to hers.

In between sniffs and gulps, she told Matt and Ben all she'd told me. Matt was absolutely furious.

'Evil bitch!' he howled, leaping off the sofa, and was all for going round there and giving Mrs Harris a piece of his mind. No prizes for guessing which piece. It took all of Sam's, Ben's and my powers of persuasion to calm him down and talk him out of it.

Alex got off my knee, padded over to Sam, parked himself next to her on the sofa, and, clasping his hands together in his lap, told her not to worry because we had loads of bedrooms.

Matt suddenly stopped his pacing of the room and shot Ben a questioning glance. Ben shrugged, and stared steadily back at Matt. I understood Ben's reaction. It

367

was Matt's decision really. He'd only just met her, but if he felt she was the right one, then why not? Might have happened soon enough anyway.

Matt swivelled his eyes to mine. I shrugged, and stared steadily back at him, making the same point.

'Sam, would you like to stay here?' asked Matt, looking awkward and embarrassed. 'You know, until you decide what you're going to do? I mean, we have a couple of spare rooms. You – er – don't have to move in with me or anything.' He coughed, while Ben and I grinned unashamedly at him. Matt scowled at both of us.

'I don't want to be a burden,' Sam muttered, holding on to Alex's little hand.

'Don't be silly!' said Matt, irritably. 'You're not a burden!'

'Right. That's settled, then,' said Ben, suddenly launching himself off the wall.

Sam looked at me guiltily. 'I have to get my luggage, but . . .'

'You don't want to go on your own?' I finished.

She nodded, and nervously bit her lip.

'No problem. I'll come with you,' I said, not really relishing the thought of seeing an irate Mrs Harris. I had a delicate tummy as it was.

As it turned out, we all went, mob-handed, leaving the boys with Mrs Travis. Matt had insisted on coming with us, and Ben, in turn, responded by saying he wasn't letting Matt go unsupervised. He was obviously concerned that his brother's temper might get the better of him.

We took the Land Rover. Pulling up outside the Harrises' large white house, Matt didn't even bother to knock. He just strode straight in with Ben close on his heels. The Carmichael Twins, I thought, and nearly laughed. Sam and I trailed in behind them.

'OK, where's your gear?' I asked, noticing that Sam had started shaking again.

'It's in the drawing room,' she mumbled.

'Right. Let's go and get it.'

Second door on the left, I told myself, as I remembered Archie's birthday party.

We found her two suitcases and two holdalls, and grabbed one of each between us.

Suddenly, a door opened and Mr and Mrs Harris stomped out into the hall, still arguing. They stopped abruptly when they caught sight of us all.

'What do you think you're doing?' she spat, glaring at each one of us in turn.

'Collecting Sam's gear,' I replied, calmly heading for the door.

Archie hurtled up behind his mother, clutching at her mauve skirt, and nearly succeeded in pulling it down.

Mr Harris shuffled from foot to foot, looking extremely uncomfortable. Matt just couldn't help himself. 'I suppose you get your kicks from terrorizing your staff,' he barked, and stared at Mrs Harris in a cold rage.

'How dare you . . .?' she spluttered, turning puce to match her skirt. 'That girl stole from me. I can't have someone like that in the house, leading Archie astray.'

'Don't give me that!' Matt howled. 'Leading Archie astray – that's a laugh! You know damn well she didn't take that money. And because you know who did, that's why there's been no police called.' Matt transferred his icy gaze to Archie, who blinked and burst into noisy sobbing.

'There, there, my pet,' she cooed, and bent down to scoop up her baby. She crushed him to her rather ample bosom and began thumping his back. Mr Harris swallowed, and turned to face his son.

'Archie, did you take that money?' He fixed him with a piercing stare. Archie redoubled his sobs. Mr Harris asked him again.

'Yes!' he wailed, kicking his feet in frustration.

'So why tell Mummy Sam took it?'

'Because I didn't want to get told off!' he howled.

'Hush, hush,' soothed Mrs Harris, and glared at her long-suffering husband. 'How can you expect him to tell the truth when she's standing here glaring at him!'

She transferred her frosty gaze to Sam, who appeared to be looking at the floor nowhere near Archie.

'Oh, come on!' Ben snapped. 'The boy's just admitted he took it! How the hell do you hope to raise a decent lad when you continually make excuses for him? He stole from you, not Sam. I know who I'd be punishing!'

'Don't you dare speak to me like that!' she screeched, her bottom lip wobbling all over the place.

'Oh, for Pete's sake, woman!' yelled Matt, starting to lose his temper. 'Why do you think nobody likes him, eh? You tell me he has lots of friends? No, don't bother. I'll tell you why he hasn't got any. Because nobody likes a spoilt brat, and that is exactly what Archie is!'

Matt's face twisted in disgust. Mrs Harris opened her mouth very wide and screamed in rage, perforating a few eardrums into the bargain.

'You just can't walk in here and tell me how to raise my child!'

'I wouldn't dream of it!' spat Matt. 'You seem to be ruining the boy all by yourself! It's pathetic! You're so

370

typical! You obviously had Archie very late in life and I'm sure you were relieved to have him. But now you've completely and utterly spoilt him, forever! The saddest thing of all is, it isn't the boy's fault. It's yours!' Matt looked her up and down contemptuously.

Mrs Harris burst into tears, obviously hearing the ring of truth, which was more than could be said for the rest of us with perforated eardrums.

'George!' she wailed. 'Do something!'

He shrugged. 'Like what? He has a point. Frankly, I'm sick of the pair of you?'

Mrs Harris stopped in mid-bawl and looked at her husband in acute shock.

'What are you saying?' she whined in a quavering voice.

'I'm saying you're both as nasty and thoroughly odious as each other. Personally, I'm embarrassed I've got a wife and child like you two. You've treated this young girl abominably. You knew she didn't take that money, yet you threw her out on to the street. Anything to protect that – that monster you've created!' Mr Harris's voice rose angrily. I'd never seen him cross before, and I have to say, he went right up in my estimation for finally daring to tell his loathsome wife what he thought of her.

'Archie,' said a small voice. 'Why did you do that to me?' Sam gazed at him sadly. 'Is it because you hate me?'

'No,' he replied tearfully. 'I like you lots, really I do.'

Sam nodded, as though this answer satisfied her, and went to walk out of the door.

'Don't go!' screamed Archie, struggling to extract himself from his mother's suffocating clench. Mrs Harris kept a firm grip on him, her lips tightening in suppressed anger.

Perhaps that had been an underlying problem, I thought. Mrs Harris was jealous of how Archie felt

371

about Sam. Mr Harris shuffled forward, placing a shaking hand lightly on Sam's arm.

'Sam, I'm so dreadfully sorry about all this. Why don't we try again, eh? Please come back and work for us.'

Ben and Matt snorted in unison. Sam turned to face him, and flicked a quick glance at Mrs Harris.

'Thanks for the offer, and for sticking up for me, but I can't work for her.' She jabbed a finger at Mrs Harris, who stubbornly refused to look at her, and was wearing a wounded expression, no doubt as a result of what Mr Harris had said to her. Sam went on, 'If you were on your own then I might consider it. But in these circumstances, no.'

Sam turned on her heel and stalked out to the Land Rover. Ben and Matt picked up her luggage, and, shooting one last disgusted look at Mrs Harris, ushered me out in front of them.

Sam was very quiet on the way home, and listlessly gazed out of the window. Matt insisted on sitting next to her and held her hand all the way home.

Back at the Yard, the stable lads knew something was going on because of Ben and Matt's abrupt departure from stacking hay-bales. Tactfully, they asked no questions. Ben and Matt would no doubt fill them in later, leaving out the stealing bit.

Puffing and grunting up the stairs with Sam's luggage, I took her to one of the spare rooms. She could always shift into Matt's room later on, I thought.

Sam stood in the middle of the room, gazing about her at the cream walls and double bed, and wandered through to the bathroom as if in a daze. I suppose she felt awkward with everything new and strange.

'Well, I'll – er – leave you to unpack.' I muttered, and turned to go.

'Penny . . .'

I hovered in the doorway. 'Yes?'

'Thanks, for everything.'

Mrs Travis took great pains to make Sam feel welcome, but nothing was familiar, and she whispered as she asked if she might have a glass of water.

'Sam! Help yourself to anything you want. Don't stand on ceremony!'

She gazed at her hands, looking uncomfortable. 'I just can't help feeling I'm in the way. You know, as if I've been forced on to you all.'

'Sam, you are most welcome, and if you don't believe me, just take a look at Matt. He couldn't be happier.' I grinned unashamedly at the deep blush spreading down her neck.

The boys pestered her to death all night, including Rory, which was surprising seeing that he wasn't keen on those 'girlie' people. They all read her a story, told her about their ponies in great detail, and wanted the general low-down on Archie.

Matt sat very close to her all night, and practically had to see off the boys as competition to get a look-in. 'Have you got everything you need?' Ben asked Sam, watching his brother gazing openly at her.

'Yes, thanks. You've been very kind,' she mumbled.

'Hey, don't mention it.' Ben smiled.

'I'll be looking for another job tomorrow. See if I can find another live-in position somewhere. I might try an agency. They're usually quite quick at placing nannies.' I noticed Sam looked calmer, happier, and relieved, in a way.

'I'm sure you'll be able to find something around here,' I said, trying to look encouraging.

373

'But what if you don't?' asked Matt, suddenly looking extremely disconcerted.

Sam shrugged. 'Then I suppose I'll have to move away.' She gazed at her hands, biting her lip.

'I need a word,' Matt mumbled, and, catching hold of her hand, he hauled her to her feet and belted out of the room, practically dragging her along after him.

Ben grinned at their departing backs. 'Methinks he's not going to let her go,' he murmured.

As I put the boys to bed, I heard muffled voices coming from Sam's room. Perhaps she wouldn't be in that room for very long, I found myself thinking.

I read the obligatory stories and settled the boys for the night. Padding along the landing, I realized the talking had stopped. I smiled, and thought if they were making love then I would too!

With everyone out of the way, or otherwise engaged, Ben and I spent some time murmuring 'girlie' words at each other. The gentle petting became more intense.

Abruptly, Ben got to his feet, and led me over to the rug in front of the fireplace. Slowly, deftly he undressed me, then himself, as I lay back watching him, desperately wanting that strong, muscled body.

We both lay on the rug, totally naked, and the thought of someone walking in on us made it all the more exciting.

Ben kissed every inch of my body, working his way up, and stopping to bury his face between my legs. I gave a low moan, and entwined my fingers into his silky, dark hair.

Slowly, he continued to work his way up my body, gently sucking and licking at my breasts, kissing my throat as he slipped inside me.

I gave a surprised squeak as something cold trickled

down my neck. Ben was happily tipping scotch all over me, and enjoying himself enormously licking it off.

I suppose it's a change from ice-cream or chocolate sauce, I thought, and gently caressed his broad back, creeping downwards to cup his bottom, pressing him deeper into me.

Ben ran his hands down my sides, and, slipping them underneath my body, wrapped my legs around his waist. He moved rhythmically inside me, murmuring loving words, until suddenly he stopped, and, removing himself, pushed me on to my belly. Seizing me by my hips, he lifted me on to my knees and plunged back inside me, making me catch my breath.

Ben began to thrust himself into me, harder and faster. We were both so excited by this new position, and I was totally astonished at this new, passionate side to my husband's nature, that all too soon we both moaned, and collapsed on to the rug.

Ben lay on top of me, breathing heavily, totally spent. Panting, I entwined my fingers into his, and putting them to my mouth, gently sucked the tips.

We didn't spend too long lying on the rug, aware that we were still naked. Tiptoeing up to bed, we clutched our clothes in a bundle next to our bodies, nervously anticipating insomniacs roaming the hallway.

I glanced at the dining room door, and idly wondered about the dining table. I looked at Ben, hopefully, but he shook his head and shuddered. He said he couldn't do it with his father watching him from his vantage point hanging on the wall!

CHAPTER 24

The next morning I woke up early, belted to the bathroom and threw up in the bidet, which brought back awful memories of my disastrous wedding night. I felt ill all the time lately, and, having niggling doubts, I took myself off to the doctor.

As I'd guessed but hadn't admitted even to myself, I was several weeks pregnant. I was suffering from morning sickness, and not alcohol withdrawal as I'd first thought!

I went home, studied the calendar and felt faint. Rushing into the drawing room, I did everything the doctor tells you not to do. I poured an enormous gin and tonic, and lit a cigarette. Ben caught me, and icily demanded to know what I thought I was doing drinking at this time of the day, also reminding me that I don't smoke.

'I've had a bit of a shock,' I said shakily.

Ben frowned at me. 'What do you mean?'

'I'm pregnant,' I mumbled, lifting the drink to my lips. Ben leapt forward, and, snatching the drink and the cigarette out of my hand, he pulled me to my feet and kissed me fiercely. He was shaking all over. Finally, he let me go and started telling me how wonderful it was, that I

376

wasn't to drink any more, and that I must be careful coming down the stairs. All I could think of was waddling instead of walking, stretch marks, and getting wedged in the bath! I would have to buy an enormous shoe-horn to help me in and out!

'When's it due?' he asked excitedly, patting my tummy.

'April.'

I couldn't quite take it in. We were going to have a little bundle of joy of our very own.

Taking me by the hand, Ben led me down to the Yard, and to my acute embarrassment announced to everyone that I was pregnant. I received several wet kisses and a request from the boys for another brother, apart from Harry, who wanted a spaniel.

'That's great,' said Matt, and dutifully kissed my cheek.

'Where's Sam?' I asked, idly scanning the Yard.

'Job-hunting,' Matt responded.

Ben chased the boys around the Yard, absolutely beside himself, threatening to dunk them in the water trough. I watched fondly, thinking what a great father he was.

'When's it due?' asked Will, looking slightly broody.

'April,' I replied, watching Ben holding Harry upside-down over the water trough.

'That's the problem with being pregnant,' said Adam grinning, 'everyone knows what you've been up to!'

I gave a snort of laughter, and slapped him playfully on his bottom. Glancing at Will, I saw that he had a bruise along his cheekbone. I hadn't noticed it before.

'Where did you get that from?' I asked, almost accusingly.

'Well, not from me!' said Adam indignantly, looking extremely put out.

'I didn't think anything of the sort!' Gently I prodded him in his ribs. 'Dominic did that, I'll bet.'

Will looked at his feet in embarrassment, and bit his lip.

'Did Dominic hit you?'

Will swallowed nervously, and nodded. 'He said I'd done exactly what he was afraid of,' he mumbled, glancing at Adam. 'I left him to go back to Adam. He said I'd hurt him on purpose, and then he hit me.'

Will's bottom lip trembled. He looked suspiciously as if he was going to cry.

'I'm sorry. It's none of my business. I didn't mean to upset you. I was just concerned. And don't cry, you'll set me off! Pregnant women are highly emotional, and do strange things like listening to seventies music and drinking engine oil!'

Will laughed, and rubbed his eyes.

'Watch out!' cried Adam, as Alex came tearing up to me, trying to avoid his father. Screaming with laughter, he shot behind me and peered out from around my elbow.

'Dad's trying to dunk me!' he squealed. 'Don't let him, Penny! I can't swim!'

'Can't you?' I was slightly surprised. And to think of all the times we'd walked and ridden by the canal, I thought.

Harry charged up to me, and stuck his head up my T-shirt, trying to find the baby. He emerged looking bemused.

'Where is it?' he enquired.

'It's inside my tummy. It doesn't hang off the outside like a monkey!'

He pondered on this for a bit, then, deciding it was all beyond him, asked if we could go for a ride.

'Absolutely not!' snapped Ben, appearing at my side. 'You can, Harry, here in the paddock, or the meadow at the back, but Penny will not be riding for a while. Not in her condition!'

'Don't be silly!' I said irritably. 'It won't hurt the baby if I carry on riding!'

'Well, you can't carry on riding!' he retorted, getting all domineering on me! 'What if you fall off?'

'Then I'll bounce!' I said, crossly. I'd only known I was pregnant for about an hour, and already I was reduced to eating, sleeping and knitting, I thought savagely.

'You'll do as you're told!' he howled. 'And if I find out you've been riding, I'll lock you in the house for the whole duration of your pregnancy!'

He glared at me, daring me to argue. I opened my mouth and shut it again. I decided not to argue, and stalked off up to the house to sulk.

Ben just about drove me mad during the next week. Several times he caught me surreptitiously trying to saddle one of the horses and promptly tore huge strips off me.

Matt found the whole thing hilarious, much to my intense irritation. Especially when I told him about the dreams I'd been having.

I dreamt I was in labour, in excruciating pain, when suddenly the baby burst out of my stomach, rather like the creature in the film *Alien*, and, making little 'rivet-rivet' noises, shot across the delivery room and bit the doctor! What Matt found even more funny was the fact that I was deadly serious.

'Did you know it's my birthday tomorrow?' he said, changing the subject. He didn't look terribly excited. Mind you, who does when you're hurtling through double figures at the rate of knots? I thought.

'No, I didn't,' I replied. 'Is there something you want that I can get for you?'

'You don't have to get me anything,' he said, settling himself on the kitchen surface.

'Well, why tell me it's your birthday tomorrow if you don't want me to get you anything?' I snapped.

'I was just telling you, that's all. Lord save us! Are all pregnant women this awkward?'

'I wouldn't know. I've never been out with any!'

Matt started to laugh, the rotten swine. So I decided to aggravate him, and made myself a banana sandwich with mustard and mango chutney. Matt looked at me with a slightly pained expression, and, standing right in front of him, I bit into it.

'Would you like me to make you one?' I asked.

'Not right now,' he replied faintly. My sandwiches were a constant source of amusement, except at meal-times, where I received several disgusted glances.

'We could take you out for a meal,' I said, licking chutney off my fingers.

'Yeah, that'd be nice. As long as the menu isn't anything like yours!'

I shot him an old-fashioned look, and asked him where he'd like to go. He decided on a restaurant in Chalfont. I asked him whether Sam would have any objections, to which he said he hadn't told her it was his birthday. I suppose, with Sam having no money, he didn't want to make her feel awful. I decided I'd lend her some money to get him a present with.

I called the restaurant and made a reservation, unaware then that we'd never get to that meal.

I wandered down to the Yard looking for the boys, and found them playing in the meadow at the back of the stables. When I called to them to come and get their tea, they plodded across the meadow, grumbling and pulling faces, which they kept up all the way up the drive and into the house.

'You can go out and play again when you've eaten,' I promised, ushering them into the kitchen.

They wolfed down the pasta I'd made for them and looked at me expectantly, rather like a quivering spaniel waiting to be told to fetch his ball. I hesitated for a couple of seconds, then nodded. Scraping back their chairs with an awful screech, they belted off back to the meadow.

Sighing, I cleared the table and loaded the dishwasher, vaguely remembering what it was like to be wanted!

While Matt was in the study, catching up on the paperwork, I was asking Ben what he thought we should get for his birthday when Sam walked in back from job-hunting.

'Any luck?' I asked.

'Well, there's nothing advertized anywhere so I've enrolled in an agency, and filled in tons of forms.' She sighed and raised her eyes to heaven.

'I shouldn't worry about a job too much,' said Ben, and grinned.

I told her it was Matt's birthday and offered to lend her some money.

'As long as it is a loan,' she said, and flashed me a grateful smile.

'I've booked us a restaurant in Chalfont. I thought a meal out would be nice. But I think we ought to give him something to open on the day.'

'Well, I've noticed he could do with a new watch,' said Ben, handing me a sticky spoon I'd missed.

Sighing in annoyance, I chucked it in the sink, where it landed with a clatter. Ben raised his eyebrows, and said it didn't matter how much I stomped around. I wasn't getting on a horse! I was stopped from making a sarcastic retort by Rory and Harry bursting into the kitchen with Finn close behind them.

'He's got Alex!' wailed Harry, rushing up to Ben, and, seizing his hand, he tried to pull him out of the kitchen.

'Wait! Slow down!' said Ben, picking up Harry. 'Now, start again. Where's Alex?'

'A man took him!' Harry said, his words coming out in a rush.

'What man?' Ben had gone very still. The colour drained out of his face.

'I think I might be able to fill you in,' said Finn, hovering by the door, eyes darting guiltily from me to Ben.

'What are you taking about?' Ben set Harry back on his feet.

'I just wanna say first, I didn't intend it to go this far. I needed the money, and he was offering quite a bit, just for giving some leaves to Mistral. He said it would only make the horse poorly. I swear I didn't mean to kill him!'

Finn's tone was almost pleading with Ben. He looked both scared and nervous. He had good reason to be. In two swift strides, Ben seized Finn by the throat.

'Please listen to me.' Finn's voice rose in panic.

Ben began to squeeze. Matt, obviously hearing raised voices, emerged from the study and, seeing his brother half throttling one of their grooms, demanded to know just what the hell was going on, even while taking Sam's hand and kissing it.

'I think we've just found the warped little mind which has been trying to put us out of business,' said Ben icily.

Matt looked at Finn, and, sounding almost disappointed, said, 'But why?'

'That's what I'm trying to tell you,' Finn croaked, trying to ease Ben's fingers from around his throat.

'Ben, let him go,' said Matt, letting Sam go himself. 'I think we'd better hear what he has to say.'

Ben, rather reluctantly, released Finn and stared menacingly at him, his fists clenching and unclenching by his side.

Finn coughed and, breathing heavily, rubbed his throat, leaning back on the door. Finally he mumbled, 'I was heavily in debt. I like a bet on the horses, and got myself into a bit of trouble. I was in the pub one night when this bloke sits down next to me and says, you work for Ben Carmichael, don't you? Yes, I said. Well, he says, how would you like to earn yourself some easy money? He said all I'd have to do is give something to one of the horses, just give it a bit of colic, like, nothing serious. Well, I told him to piss off, but when he told me how much he was gonna pay me, my first thought was that it would cover my debt, and get me out of the shit. I mean, nobody would get hurt – dead easy, I thought.

'At the time, I couldn't help thinking his face was vaguely familiar, then it came to me. He'd been in the local paper, about his wife dying in that accident, that woman that died here, at the Yard.'

Finn gazed at his feet, fidgeting nervously. Looking up at Ben, he blurted out, 'He scares me! He's really lost it! He's not right upstairs!' He pointed to his temple. Finn looked absolutely terrified, but I wasn't sure if that was because of this man he'd got himself mixed up with, or the look on Ben's face.

'Go on,' Ben demanded.

Finn cleared his throat, blinked, and continued shakily, 'He gave me some leaves in a bag, and told me to mix 'em up with something sweet. So I put sugar beet with 'em, and gave the lot to Mistral. I'm telling you, I swear I didn't know it would kill him! Just give him colic, like he said! Anyway, I met him in the pub to get my money, and asked him just what the hell was going on. I told him the horse had died. He laughed at me, and said he'd be needing me in the future. I told him to bollocks! But he just got really angry, and said he'd tell you what I'd done. He said I couldn't afford to be out of a job and besides, who'd hire me after that?'

'So you're telling us he blackmailed you into setting the stable block on fire, and letting Merrylegs out?' Matt, his lip curling in disgust, took a step towards Finn.

Finn nodded miserably. 'I didn't know what to do. After the fire, I was even deeper in the mire. He said he'd tell the police, because what I'd done was arson, and that carries a life sentence, and didn't I know just how awful prison was? I had to do what he said, don't you see?'

Finn slid down the door, shaking violently, and, drawing his knees up to his chin, buried his face in his arms.

'So what's made you tell us all this now?' Matt asked, glowering at him.

'Because this has gone too far!' screamed Finn, putting his hands over his head. 'I mean, I felt bad enough over the horses! Now he's taken one of the kids, and that's not what I'm about. That's going way too far for me. I just don't know what he'll do to him!'

'He hadn't better do *anything* to him!' Ben spat, leaping forward, and wrenched Finn to his feet. I honestly thought Ben was going to kill him. I had never seen Ben this angry before. It was a truly awesome sight. He frightened the life out of me.

Matt looked across at me and Sam, with our arms around Rory and Harry, and, seeing how frightened we were, it seemed to appal him. His face twisted in rage, and he seized Finn by his hair and yanked his head back, making him yelp in pain. In a voice that made my skin crawl he said, 'Where's Alex?'

'He's taken him to the canal!' he stammered, shooting terrified glances from Ben to Matt.

Swinging him round, Ben and Matt dragged him out of the house, shouting, 'You are going to show us exactly where that bastard has got him!' Taking an arm each, they rammed them behind his back, making him yelp again, and virtually ran him down the drive.

Rory and Harry, taking both me and Sam by surprise, wriggled out of our arms and belted after them, with me giving chase.

'Rory! Harry! Get back here,' Ben shouted, to which they took absolutely no notice, and sprinted towards the canal, with me closing in on them.

As I chased them along the canal bank I made one last desperate effort and lunged at them, knocking them to the ground, yelling at them for running off. Both boys were in tears, obviously fearing for their brother's safety, as indeed was I. They'd heard Finn just as clearly as we had.

'Looking for me?' said a voice, and a man stepped out of the bushes. Grinning evilly, he strolled over to the canal, holding a terrified Alex in front of him. Ben, Matt and Finn came to a slithering halt beside me, breathing heavily, with Sam bringing up the rear.

'Have you been telling tales?' Shaking his head at Finn, the man wagged a finger.

'Come on, Murphy, that has gone far enough! The boy hasn't done anything to you!' said Finn, his voice rising hysterically.

'I loved my wife, y'know,' the man called Murphy murmured, stroking Alex's hair. 'She was pregnant. Maybe we'd have had a son, just like this one. Do you know what it's like to lose a wife and child?' He surveyed Ben with a thoughtful expression.

'As it happens, yes, I do. I know what it's like to lose a wife,' replied Ben, not taking his eyes off Alex.

'And now you're going to know how it feels to lose a child. I want you to lose a child. I want you to suffer unimaginable pain, just like I have. We had plans. We were so excited, and then you destroyed them all!' he spat, glaring at Ben.

Matt, very tentatively, moved forward, trying to reason with him, only managing to get as far as reminding him that his wife had chosen to ride.

'Stay there! Don't you come near me!' he shouted, and, taking Alex by the scruff of his neck and one of his ankles, he whipped him upside down and held him over the canal. His head was inches from the water.

'You come near me and I'll swear I'll drop him!' he yelled.

Alex whimpered. Oh, God! He can't swim, I remembered in horror. I gazed at the the canal, the murky water clogged with reeds and an assortment of old rusty objects.

Alex began to cry, calling to me, calling his father. Giving an agonized moan, I appeared to spark something off. Rory, yelling his little head off, rushed at Murphy, barging into him, knocking the wind out of him. Murphy was knocked off balance and, almost in slow motion, fell into the canal, releasing his grip on Alex, who dropped head first into the water.

Ben raced to the edge of the canal. Ignoring several sharp objects, he plunged into the canal after Alex. Scrabbling in the filthy water, he surfaced, shaking water out of his eyes. He took a quick glance around him, and then dipped beneath the water again.

I stood on the bank for what seemed an age, my eyes skimming the surface for any signs of them. Finally, Ben emerged, holding Alex in his arms, and frantically paddled across to where I was agitatedly hopping from foot to foot, impatient to get to Alex.

Reaching down, I hauled Alex out of his father's arms and collapsed in a heap on the bank, covering him in little kisses, tearfully nuzzling him, wiping his dirty little face on my T-shirt. Alex, coughing and spluttering, clung to me and began to howl, noisily.

Ben clambered out of the water and flopped down on the bank, spitting out filthy water, and lay down on his back, panting.

Matt was still holding on to Rory and Harry, who would have jumped into the canal after their father. Yelling hysterically, they pointed to the canal. Following their rantings, I realized what had upset them. Murphy was lying half out of the water as though suspended by something, his eyes wide open, staring, shocked, frightened.

He had been skewered by something that looked like an old iron railing, a good two feet protruding out through the front of him. He was obviously dead.

I pushed Alex's head into my neck to hide that awful sight from him. Ben padded swiftly over to me, and gently stroked his son's back. Alex trembled and pressed into me harder than ever.

'It's all right, it's only Daddy,' I said softly.

Alex tentatively looked round, and, seeing it was Ben, flung himself at his father, very nearly depositing them both back in the canal.

Harry and Rory, shocked and shaken, stumbled across to me, and virtually fell into my lap, desperate for a cuddle. Harry, for once, was totally speechless.

Matt and Ben took one last fleeting glance at the canal and decided we'd better get back to the house and phone the police.

As we made our way home, Matt suddenly realized Finn was no longer with us. He'd disappeared, obviously not wanting to talk to the police. Matt watched Sam closely; she appeared to be in shock.

I made us all a cup of strong, hot tea, keeping a tight grip on Alex. I felt shaken, and not at all together. What with Matt, the wedding and reception, and all the planning beforehand, the incidents in the Yard had taken a bit of a back seat. They had rather abruptly been brought back into focus.

Two middle-aged men were soon climbing out of a plain car, and, opening the door, they introduced themselves as Detective Superintendent Bryant from CID and his colleague, Detective Sergeant Baker. They spent some time taking statements, and, with Matt showing them the way, they took a look at the body in the canal. The fire brigade and an ambulance arrived within ten minutes to take Murphy away.

Ben and Matt made no mention of Finn. He could sweat for a while, wondering if the police were coming for him. Finn might be a lot of things, but he wasn't in the same league as Murphy. On the strength of that, Ben would allow him to go free. He'd learnt his lesson.

By the time the policemen left, it was dark outside. The boys were so shocked, they seemed disorientated. I decided to call the doctor, and I thought he'd better take a look at Sam while he was about it.

While we waited for the doctor to arrive, I stuck Alex in the bath.

As I was putting the boys to bed, the doctor arrived. Giving them all a once-over, he decided to give them a mild sedative. It would do them good to have a deep sleep; and he said not to worry, as children were very resilient, and promptly dished out the same treatment to Sam.

The boys were subdued and quiet for some time, and were in no fit state to do anything or go anywhere. Alex had several nightmares, which wasn't surprising, seeing as it was he who'd been taken. Mercifully, Rory and Harry were spared that much.

Matt had a lousy birthday. With nobody in any fit state to go to the restaurant, I spent hours cooking him a lovely meal which nobody could get through their stiff upper lips.

Ben and Matt appeared to be deeply affected by what had happened. As for the boys and me, it took us a fair while to get over it, and Sam just seemed to have blocked it out.

Ben and I discussed it quite often. I couldn't quite get how much the tragedy had affected Murphy's reason. Ben, who never failed to amaze me, said he understood him: if anything happened to me, or our baby, he'd go just as crazy. I suppose, putting it that way, we're all capable of doing terrible things. All it takes is someone to press the right button.

I found myself extremely protective towards Alex, and if anyone new came near him I'd shove him behind me and start shooting suspicious scowls all over the place. Ben said if I could growl, I would have!

The boys were due to start back to school on the Monday, which happened to be the first morning since I'd known I was pregnant that I hadn't had morning sickness.

Gazing at my tummy in the bathroom mirror, I felt a rush of excitement and allowed myself a self-indulgent daydream, wondering if our baby would be a doctor, or a vet, or even a prime minister or a president. Mind you, to be a president, he'd probably have to be an actor first, I thought.

I shuddered. All those luvvies!

Then Ben came into the bathroom, caught my eyes in the mirror and smiled the wonderful smile I never tired of seeing. He swept me into his arms and I knew that all that was important was Ben and our family.

How could I have guessed that answering Ben's advertisement would change my life so drastically – or so beautifully?

Smiling up into Ben's eyes, I lifted my lips for his kiss. The boys would just have to wait for their breakfast for five more minutes!

THE EXCITING NEW NAME IN WOMEN'S FICTION!

PLEASE HELP ME TO HELP YOU!

Dear *Scarlet* Reader,

The end of July will see our first super Prize Draw, which means that **you could win 6 months' worth of free Scarlets!** Just return your completed questionnaire to us (see addresses at end of questionnaire) before 31 July 1997 and you will automatically be entered in the draw that takes place on that day. If you are lucky enough to be one of the first two names out of the hat we will send you four new *Scarlet* romances every month for six months, and for each of twenty runners up there will be a sassy *Scarlet* T-shirt.

So don't delay – return your form straight away!*

Sally Cooper

Editor-in-Chief, *Scarlet*

QUESTIONNAIRE

Please tick the appropriate boxes to indicate your answers

1 Where did you get this Scarlet title?
Bought in supermarket ☐
Bought at my local bookstore ☐ Bought at chain bookstore ☐
Bought at book exchange or used bookstore ☐
Borrowed from a friend ☐
Other (please indicate) _____

2 Did you enjoy reading it?
A lot ☐   A little ☐   Not at all ☐

3 What did you particularly like about this book?
Believable characters ☐   Easy to read ☐
Good value for money ☐   Enjoyable locations ☐
Interesting story ☐   Modern setting ☐
Other _____

4 What did you particularly dislike about this book?
_____

5 Would you buy another Scarlet book?
Yes ☐   No ☐

6 What other kinds of book do you enjoy reading?
Horror ☐   Puzzle books ☐   Historical fiction ☐
General fiction ☐   Crime/Detective ☐   Cookery ☐
Other (please indicate) _____

7 Which magazines do you enjoy reading?
1. _____
2. _____
3. _____

And now a little about you –
8 How old are you?
Under 25 ☐   25–34 ☐   35–44 ☐
45–54 ☐   55–64 ☐   over 65 ☐

cont.

9 What is your marital status?

Single ☐   Married/living with partner ☐

Widowed ☐   Separated/divorced ☐

10 What is your current occupation?

Employed full-time ☐   Employed part-time ☐

Student ☐   Housewife full-time ☐

Unemployed ☐   Retired ☐

11 Do you have children? If so, how many and how old are they?

_____

_____

12 What is your annual household income?

under $15,000	☐	or	£10,000	☐
$15–25,000	☐	or	£10–20,000	☐
$25–35,000	☐	or	£20–30,000	☐
$35–50,000	☐	or	£30–40,000	☐
over $50,000	☐	or	£40,000	☐

Miss/Mrs/Ms _____

Address _____

_____

_____

Thank you for completing this questionnaire. Now tear it out – put it in an envelope and send it to:

Sally Cooper, Editor-in-Chief

USA/Can. address
SCARLET c/o London Bridge
85 River Rock Drive
Suite 202
Buffalo
NY 14207
USA

UK address/No stamp required
SCARLET
FREEPOST LON 3335
LONDON W8 4BR
Please use block capitals for address

CAROU/5/97

Scarlet **titles coming next month:**

REVENGE IS SWEET Jill Sheldon
Chloe Walker is a soft touch for anyone in trouble. Thomas McGuirre is a man with no heart, set on revenge, no matter who gets in his way. So something (or someone!) has to give! But will it be Chloe . . . or Thomas?

GAME, SET AND MATCH Kathryn Bellamy
Melissa Farrell's career on the professional tennis circuit is just taking off. One day, with a lot of hard work and dedication, she may achieve her dream of winning Wimbledon. But Nick Lennox isn't prepared to wait for her. Unlike the attractive bad boy of tennis, Ace Delaney . . .

MARRIED TO SINCLAIR Danielle Shaw
Jenny has been engaged to Cameron for several years, but he calls it a day when he realizes that the family firm is far more important to her than he could ever be. Then Jenny meets Paul Hadley and realizes what love is all about. But Paul is married to the glamorous Gina, who will never let him go.

DARK CANVAS Julia Wild
Abbey has a steady, if dull, boyfriend and is at the height of her career. But then someone begins to threaten her, and Jake Westaway appoints himself her protector. But then he starts to *want* her . . . even though she's his best friend's woman!